PRIMAL HEAT

Books by Crystal Jordan

CARNAL DESIRES

ON THE PROWL

UNTAMED

PRIMAL HEAT

SEXY BEAST V
(with Kate Douglas and Vonna Harper)

SEXY BEAST 9
(with Vonna Harper and Lisa Renee Jones)

UNDER THE COVERS
(with Melissa MacNeal and P.J. Mellor)

Published by Kensington Publishing Corporation

PRIMAL HEAT

CRYSTAL JORDAN

APHRODISIA

KENSINGTON BOOKS
http://www.kensingtonbooks.com

APHRODISIA BOOKS are published by

Kensington Publishing Corp.
119 West 40th Street
New York, NY 10018

All Kensington Titles, Imprints, and Distributed Lines are available at special quantity discounts for bulk purchases for sales promotions, premiums, fund-raising, and educational or institutional use.

Special book excerpts or customized printings can also be created to fit specific needs. For details, write or phone the office of the Kensington special sales manager: Kensington Publishing Corp., 119 West 40th Street, New York, NY 10018, attn: Special Sales Department, Phone: 1-800-22-2647.

Aphrodisia and the A logo Reg. U.S. Pat & TM Off.

ISBN-13: 978-0-7582-3830-6
ISBN-10: 0-7582-3830-4

First Kensington Trade Paperback Printing: November 2010

10 9 8 7 6 5 4 3 2 1

Printed in the United States of America

Acknowledgments

This book will forever be labeled in my mind as "the burn out book." Making it through to the end was a task of herculean proportions. I would never have survived without the help of some very wonderful people, to whom this book is dedicated. First, of course, is my best friend, Michal. Never doubt that I appreciate everything you do for me. Even when I'm in deadline hell, I notice. Second, to Loribelle Hunt and Dayna Hart, who were standing by the phone waiting for me to call when a meltdown was imminent. Your fortitude in not putting me out of all our misery still astounds me. Third, to Rowan Larke and Robin L. Rotham, who held my hand and read far too many versions of these stories before we got to the final product. Fourth, to Emily Ryan-Davis and Jennifer Leeland, the most lightning-fast of beta readers in the history of beta reading. Last, but never least, to my editor and agent, without whom none of this would ever have come into being in the first place.

Thank you.

Contents

WICKED LORD

1

Brenna couldn't sleep.

She sat at her kitchen table, wrapped in a bathrobe and nursing a mug of decaf. Two in the morning was no time to pump caffeine into her system. It sure as hell wouldn't help. She wasn't an eighteen-year-old army private who could go days without sleep and not feel it. That time had come and gone over a decade and a half ago. When she was on duty tomorrow, she'd be hurting and wishing to God she'd found a way to get some shut-eye. A sigh slid from her, and she scrubbed a tired hand over her forehead.

This wasn't the first sleepless night she'd had recently, and they were becoming more and more frequent. The plus side was her house was spotless. The down side was . . . well, she was parked in her kitchen at o-dark-thirty blinking grit from her eyes. Again.

She focused on the only thing out of place in the pristine room. The little device sitting in the middle of her table. It was round, had a dome-shaped speaker on top, and could fit snugly in the palm of her hand. Reaching out, she pushed down on the dome and a high-pitched static with a buzzing, electronic squeal issued from the speaker. Wincing, she clicked it again and turned it off.

It was hard to believe that something so small could dull the massive psychic powers of an alien. Her commanding officer had had scientists working on the prototype for months, but now it was ready for use in their war against the Kith. She wasn't sure how it worked exactly, or even how they'd tested it to make sure it did work, but there were a lot of things she wasn't sure about anymore.

Which was what was keeping her up at night, if she was honest with herself. Not that she wanted to be. She'd be a lot better off if she could stuff her head back in the sand. Taking a sip of her coffee, she closed her eyes and slumped in her chair.

"Jesus," she groaned.

Pushing to her feet, she wandered into her living room, flipped the television on to the news, and plopped onto her couch. The headlines scrolled by, reports about the imminent alien invasion and what the military was doing to stop it. She shook her head and set her mug down on the coffee table.

It all came back to General Arthur and the Kith. An entire armada of alien warships had shown up almost a year ago, and they'd been orbiting Earth ever since, a constant menacing presence in the sky. They claimed to be from a planet called Suen. They claimed Earth was an abandoned colony settled by slaves of the weaker Kin race—weaker *humans*. They claimed they had no interest in Earth except to find their emperor's soul mate, his One, who was somewhere among the unwashed of humanity.

Right.

As if a fleet of warships traveled all the way across the universe for one human woman. Bren snorted and flipped her long braid over her shoulder. They could have at least come up with a story that didn't insult people's intelligence.

Leading the campaign of bullshit was Lord Farid Arjun. Her mind provided an image of the tall, blond, and gorgeous Kith diplomat. She shivered, a frisson of excitement, longing, and loathing went through her. The alien was her enemy, cold, condescending, and rude, but he could do things with his mind that were indecent, and since the first day he'd met her, he'd never stopped toying with her. She stomped down on that thought, embarrassed that she couldn't control her reaction to an alien with a smooth tongue gilded with lies.

No matter what diplomats like Arjun said, the world had devolved into mass hysteria when the Sueni arrived. Some people wanted to roll out the welcome wagon, but most were just afraid of a vastly more powerful race of people with technology and weaponry the likes of which had never been seen on Earth before. People were scared. Bren was one of those people. But more than scared, she was mad. Mad that anyone thought they had the right to show up after a couple of millennia and say, "Oh, we're back, slaves. Thanks for looking after things, now get back in your cage."

Hell, no. Earth wasn't going down without a fight, and she was determined to be on the front line. She'd been William Arthur's right hand for fifteen of the eighteen years she'd been in the service. She was behind him when he ordered a preemptive strike against the Sueni that had blown one of their ships out of the sky, and she was behind him when he worked to consolidate the military forces of Earth to create a global defense system.

But more and more often in the last few months, she'd questioned the orders Arthur had given. His new campaigns seemed to be less about protecting people than they were about gathering more power for himself.

She swallowed, clicked off the TV, and scrambled to her feet, all but running to her bedroom and slamming the door behind her to shut out the truth. Dread cramped her belly. She didn't want to think about this, didn't want to consider what it meant.

The ramifications were even more terrifying than the Sueni shuttles that came and went despite the warnings and missiles fired from Earth. Other than the one ship down, the Sueni hadn't lost a single person and had deflected further attacks. So far they'd done nothing violent. They hadn't even retaliated for the lost ship. It made her uneasy. The shuttles stayed no more than a few hours in one place before leaving again. They could be searching for something—some*one*—as they'd said, or they could be scouting out vulnerabilities for a violent, bloody endgame.

How much would Arthur's little white noise device, his new secret weapon, actually help them in driving away the Sueni? She didn't know. No one did. Yet. The one question that kept resurfacing in her mind was: when did it end? If they finally managed to get rid of the Sueni, what would be left of the world? Would Arthur hand military control back over to individual countries? If they tried to break away from him by force, who would win?

No one. That was the answer. Everything circled back to this being a no-win situation. Shrugging out of her robe, she flopped into bed and beat her pillow into a comfortable shape. If she could learn to nap through bombs going off outside her tent in a hellish desert, she could snooze through stress and doubts—doubts that might not be founded in anything other than sleep-deprived paranoia. She closed her eyes, shut down her mind, and *willed* herself into slumber.

But it wasn't dreams that found her. It was *him*. Again.

Heat screamed through her body, a sudden sexual awakening that was as much pleasure as pain. The shift was so abrupt, it was almost terrifying. Almost.

The moment sleep claimed her, he was over her, on her, in

her. Her body arched on the mattress as his cock filled her. And filled her. Her pussy throbbed, clenching tight. Her fists bunched in the sheets, her hips writhing as pleasure rocketed through her. She tried to jerk back, tried to escape the on-slaught of ecstasy, but there was no escaping her own mind. He came to her like this, in her dreams, flooding her thoughts with sensations so real she couldn't tell where the fantasy ended and reality began.

She wished it were just a dream, a fantasy, but she knew it wasn't. It was *him*. Farid. He was doing this to her. The Kith nobleman was using his mind to fuck her senseless. As much as she craved it, she hated it—*him*—hated the power he wielded, hated that the sensual alien had shredded her world when he'd landed on Earth.

Fire licked at her flesh, and she bit her lip hard enough to draw blood, fighting him, fighting herself. It was no use, she knew. She'd struggled every time he'd reached for her psychi-cally, and every time she'd failed. He sucked her into the mael-strom of carnality, drowned her in feelings she usually avoided at all costs. She hated the lack of control, the inevitable betrayal of her own body.

God help her, it felt so fucking amazing.

The sensation of being stretched beyond bearing was so vivid, she thought she would die. The last tethers between her and reality ripped loose as he began thrusting inside her. Then she was there, somewhere lost in a dream. The bed was still be-neath her, the soft sheets rough against her sensitized flesh, the thick, hot summer night breeze still brushed across her naked breasts, and yet he was with her, *in* her.

His green eyes sparked as he looked at her, a physical mani-festation of his power. The more excited he was, the faster the sparks would come, bursting like tiny fireworks in his irises. A distant part of her wondered if the sparks would stop when the white noise device was turned on, then she tamped down on the thought as fast as she could. The man was inside her head. He could read her thoughts.

He froze over her, as though he sensed that her mind had strayed to something besides what he was doing to her. She struggled to lock away the secrets she knew, scrambling for something to distract this enemy who was deep within her. Licking her lips, she watched his gaze zero in on her movements. His cock throbbed in her pussy, and she squeezed her inner muscles around him. He shuddered, groaned, and began thrusting again, caught in the tempest as much as she had been. She gasped when he ground his hips against her, forcing her thighs wide. A whimper escaped her when his big hand closed over her breast and he pinched her nipple hard between his fingers. Her body bowed under the lash of pleasured pain.

"Brenna," he breathed, and the word echoed in her mind. His need crackled through the connection between them, driving her desires higher. "Bren. My little *khalaa.*"

Her hands left the sheets, reaching up to bury in his hair. The silken strands sifted through her fingers and they both shivered. He leaned into her touch, his eyes closing as something beyond ecstasy flickered across his expression. Some part of this had to be pure dream. The man was never this open in real life.

Then he withdrew his long cock, only to slam deep inside her pussy, and nothing mattered but this moment. There were no secrets and no lies, no hiding. She didn't care what was genuine and what wasn't, only that he could give her what she needed. His heavy muscles played against her, the heat of his flesh branding her as their hips rolled against each other. The friction of his rougher flesh on her clit made her cry out, ecstasy reverberating through her. His strong hands slid under her, his fingers bit into her ass, and he lifted her into each hot, hard penetration.

"Oh, my *God*."

Sweat slipped down her temples to tickle in her hair. She shivered, sobbing for air as her nails dug into his flesh. A low growl rumbled in his chest, and the other side of his nature flashed in his eyes. The animal, the beast, the shape-shifter. Long fangs curved from his mouth and he hissed softly when she grinned at him and raked her nails down his back.

"Always pushing me, Bren." He shook his head.

She laughed up at him, mocking him and his control. If she had to be stripped of *her* control and if she couldn't win the fight against him *or* herself, she was dragging him down with her. Clenching her internal walls around his thick cock, she closed her eyes and smiled when he gave a low, helpless groan of pure need. His muscles bunched and released beneath her hands as he hammered into her, his thrusts picking up speed and force. The impact of his skin slapping against hers echoed in her bedroom, the sound shockingly carnal.

Her heart raced and her excitement built to a screaming fever pitch. She could feel an orgasm rising like a tide inside her, threatening, beckoning. God, she wanted it, threw herself toward it. If she couldn't have the self-discipline she always craved, she'd revel in the lack of it. It made her blood rush in her veins, her breath come faster, her muscles shake with pleasure and fear of how that pleasure overwhelmed her.

"Now." She wrapped her legs around his flanks, digging her heels in to lift herself higher into his thrusts. "Make me come."

"*Yesss.*" His groaned tangled with an almost feline hiss. His chest heaved in bellowing breaths, great shudders wracking his body. "I . . . can't hold on much longer."

"Don't. Come with—" She went over the edge before she could finish the sentence, the heat and need and ecstasy coalescing into one blinding explosion. Her sex pulsed around his cock, milking his hard length. He ground his pelvis against her clit and sent another wave of orgasm slamming into her, dragging her deeper. Her body arched and she screamed, the sound drowned out by the deafening leonine roar from him as he followed her into orgasm.

She clung to him, squeezing his hips between her thighs as he flooded her pussy with his hot fluids. His eyes widened, meeting hers, the green sparks coming so fast the entire iris seemed to glow.

He was so beautiful.

The smile that kicked up the corner of his mouth told her he'd heard her thought. She could only hope that was the only thought he'd heard. Ice flowed through her veins. If anyone *ever* found out about this, her career was over. If she found out he'd dug information from her while mind-fucking her, she'd never forgive herself. It might be worth it to see if sleeping with the white noise maker on could ward him off, but she had her doubts. The man had power that wouldn't quit, and she hated that she needed a machine to help her control the situation.

She swallowed, let her arms and legs fall away from him, and collapsed back to the mattress. His gaze shuttered, withdrawing as she had. His mouth opened and closed again. Sighing, he shook his head. At her or at himself, she didn't know. She worked hard to control her breathing, to slow her heartbeat down to normal levels, kicking herself as she always did for losing out to her baser needs.

He brushed tender fingers down her cheek and over her eyes, closing them. "Sleep now, *khalaa*."

A soft, replete sigh escaped her, and still she struggled against a command that went beyond words. He used his powers to fog her mind, to make the sweetness of dreams take her all the way under into real sleep, and she knew when she awakened he'd have evaporated like so much smoke on the sultry midnight breeze.

And she'd spend the day cursing herself for losing the battle of wills between them.

Again.

Farid clawed his way out of the dream, his skin aflame, his pulse still racing as his muscles shook with his recently spent orgasm.

Only he knew it was no dream, no phantasm. It had been a mental connection with his One. He rolled to the edge of his gelpad, tossed aside the soft *rishaami* bedclothes, and sat up, burying his face in his hands.

What was he doing? This was utter madness. He had no desire to bond with the woman or even tell her that she was his One. He'd seen long ago how such a bond could destroy people. No one would ever get close enough to him to be allowed that kind of power. It was never to be. Not for them. It was only when he slept, when the tight reins he kept on his control slipped, that his mind reached out for her.

"You did not sleep well, Lord Arjun?" The androgynous voice of the *Vishra* sounded through his chambers. The semi-sentient ship could read limited emotions, its technology inlaid with just enough psychic power to allow the Kith to link with it.

His hands fell away from his face. "No, I didn't."

A beat passed while the ship processed that information. "Would you like me to adjust the temperature or add a somnolence dose to the air?"

"Thank you, no. I'm going to rise and begin my work shift early." Trying to sleep now was an unappetizing prospect. He pushed to his feet, drawn to the wide windows across from his bed. Another warship like the *Vishra* drifted beside them in space, framed by stars. The ship looked like a great bird of prey, ready to dive on an unsuspecting planet at any moment and wreck havoc. A sharp beak at the front was the command deck and behind that graceful metallic curves formed the wings. Beautiful. And deadly.

The razer cannons on the wings could bring a planet to its knees. The fleet of ships could rule the galaxy. They'd had no intention to use the weapons, but when escorting an emperor across the universe, it was always best to be prepared. Not that that had saved those they'd lost along the way.

He shook his head to rid himself of his morose thoughts, his fatigue from too little sleep and too many worries, and his need for his One. It always came back to her for him. And he doubted she had the same trouble dismissing him from her thoughts. A low growl issued from his throat, and he spun on his heel, padded into his sanitation room, and went straight to the shower. A sigh slid out as he sent a mental command for the water to flow. It pelted him from multiple directions and he set his hands against the slick metal wall, bowed his head, and let the heated liquid slide over him, washing the scent of his own passion away.

The connection between his One and him was still open, and it narrowed as she transitioned into true dreams, but a final wave of her lust slammed into him, almost dragging him to his knees. His cock went hard in an instant, aching with need he'd just spent. Such passion under her cynical exterior. If he wasn't so attuned to her, he'd never have guessed it. The knowledge drove him wild, though, and the beast he always wrestled with for dominance purred in satisfaction as echoes of Bren's pleasure rippled through his body.

Anun save him. He groaned, and the sound resonated within the small, metal-walled room. The need for her nagged at him, his body demanding what he couldn't have. Closing his eyes, he slid his hand down his stomach until he grasped his cock. Another groan ripped from his throat. He pumped the length of his dick between his fingers, and the rhythm was fast, punishing.

He wanted her with him as she had been before and cursed his weakness. Testing the connection between them, he found she'd awakened. He drew away from the link between them so she wouldn't be forced to feel what he felt, though the beast within him struggled against the loss of contact.

Instead he conjured an image of her in his mind, allowing himself the true fantasy this time. Her long, rich brown hair spread over his bedclothes. Her toned body arched, her nipples tight with need. By Anun, she was beautiful. The hot water sluiced over his flesh, a liquid caress that only served to arouse him further. His breath sped and sweat slid down his face to mingle with the shower water. The sound of his heart pounding filled his ears as he pictured Bren's hands clutching at his shoulders, her legs wrapped around his waist as she demanded he take her, touch her, fuck her harder.

"*Yesss.*" The feline within made the word a hiss, and it echoed in the sanitation room. His cock throbbed, his hips slamming forward to plunge his shaft into the tight ring of his fingers. Too easily, he could imagine the slick sheath of her body. When the mental connection snapped into place, it was strong, and he knew her body as she did. Every curve, every smooth inch of skin.

His muscles locked as he came, the mere thought of her enough to shove him into orgasm. Come erupted from him in spurts, waves of heat flowing through him. He shuddered hard, stroked his cock until there was nothing left, and held tight to the fantasy of his One in *his* bed, where he knew she would never be.

He didn't want to *bond* with her, but given the opportunity to fuck her, he wouldn't hesitate. He craved her and he could never touch her, not truly, not with the way things stood between their people. Something painful wrenched deep inside him at that thought. So many tangled wants and needs, so many barriers and obstacles. He shook his head, slumping against the wall, as exhausted as if he hadn't slept at all.

Anun, he was tired of it. He wanted all of this madness to end.

"Shower off. Dryer on." The water stopped flowing and instead gusts of warm air shot from the same spigots that had spouted the water moments before. Even though the air was hot, he shivered as it hit the moisture on his skin, gooseflesh breaking down his arms and legs. Shoving his fingers into his short hair, he rumpled the wet strands and sent droplets flying.

A few minutes later, he was dressed, neat, and ready to start his workday. Walking toward the door, he stopped short when his gaze caught on a hologram flickering across one wall that he'd programmed his imager to display. It was the only part of his room that had any personal meaning. A hologram of his family, smiling and happy, mocked him silently. He had no family now. He was the last Arjun.

His gaze moved over his mother's face. She had laughter dancing in her eyes. His father radiated pride, one hand on Farid's shoulder, the other holding his mate's. In the center was his sister, beautiful and bright as a sunbeam. Cilji. She'd been so young then, and Farid himself had been barely of age. So long ago, so many wonderful memories that would never be more than that now. Gone. All gone. He'd lost them one by one, each death more heartrending than the next.

The image dissolved and a holofilm his mother had taken of his graduation from the academy began playing. He drew himself up, took a deep breath, and tugged at his sleeves to be certain they were in place. Turning away from what no longer was, he left his room.

It was rare he allowed himself to think of that time. He preferred the happier version of his family captured by the imagers. It must be this dilemma with Bren that had him tripping over the past, unable to get out of its way and let it rest.

But the past was what made him what he was, the loss of his family was what made the very idea of bonding with his One so abhorrent to him. He shuddered, Cilji's lifeless eyes flashing through his memory, her blood drying on his skin as the warmth left her slender body. He'd never understand the actions she or her One had taken. He just knew that he'd been left to pick up the pieces. He'd been left to answer the questions of others. And he was the one left wondering why.

The only answer he had was that he never, ever wanted to be in a position to make those same choices. He was of an age that he'd thought he could rest assured he didn't have a One, that he could marry a Kith of appropriate social standing and rebuild his line. He still intended to once they returned home. If they ever returned home. He ruthlessly subdued the feline's screech of protest at touching anyone besides its mate. The man had a duty to the Arjun name that the instinct-driven beast would never understand. Duty that had nothing to do with Bren or Ones or even desire. His body throbbed at the reminder of the desire Bren and he shared. If the dreams were so intense, it was dangerous to even allow himself to imagine truly touching her.

He sighed, rubbing the grit from his eyes.

"You look terrible."

Farid was chuckling before his hand left his face. The ship's second in command came striding down the hall, a wide grin on his face. "Haakesh. Diplomatic as ever, I see."

Haakesh gave a brief salute, the light overhead glinting off the short man's shiny pate. "It is amazing I've advanced this far in the fleet, is it not?"

"I think you have your One to thank for that. How is Mythri?" In truth, Haakesh was too likeable for anyone to ever take offense. His men loved him and would follow him anywhere. Add that to being a fearless soldier and it was no mystery why he'd achieved the rank he had. Whatever he lacked in finesse, his One more than managed to smooth over in her position in the diplomatic corps. To Farid's mind, the two of them were the perfect Kith pairing. His parents had been like that before they'd met their tragic end. One more reason to avoid Bren—even when things seemed perfect in a bond, they were always a single step from pain, disaster, and death.

Haakesh grinned wickedly, his white teeth flashing in contrast with his dark skin. "I left Mythri resting in our rooms. She'll be recovered sufficiently when her work shift starts."

Farid coughed into his fist to hide a smile, unable to withstand Haakesh's good cheer. "As her superior, I can only express the diplomatic corps' gratitude at your restraint."

The older man laughed, clapped Farid on the shoulder, and continued down the hallway and around a corner. The main shift was about to start. Farid's shift. When not guided by the sunlight on their home planet of Suen, they divided the day into three shifts. Mythri and Haakesh worked the second shift, which meant they could spend the other two together. Farid was glad for both of them that the emperor had seen fit to bring diplomats on this voyage.

Then again, it could be because Farid had suggested it to his younger cousin, and Kyber was an intelligent leader. Considering how poor their reception on Earth had been, Farid was even more grateful he'd convinced Kyber to allow his small coterie of diplomats.

Somehow, his attempts to explain the concept of a One, a bond between two minds in perfect sync, had gone awry. Humans were unwilling to believe that they would have come so far to find the emperor's One. It was only because he *was* the emperor that they were here. Not because the Kith wouldn't travel across space to find their One, but because only the emperor was powerful enough to sense his One from so great a distance. Even Farid hadn't managed to sense his until they'd arrived on the planet and he'd been face-to-face with her.

The Earthans' stubborn irrationality knew no bounds, and a wave of rage went through Farid as he remembered how their hysteria had cost Sueni lives. Thousands and thousands of Sueni lives. General Arthur had gathered the motley armies of Earth together and they'd launched nuclear missiles at the *Anshar*, the smallest ship in the Sueni armada. They'd choosen the spacecraft least able to defend itself, and the result had been devastating. Everyone on board had died. The loss of lives had reverberated along his senses, ripping him from a deep sleep. Their panic and pain had flooded his mind in a great wave. He swallowed, closing his eyes. It was a mistake the Sueni would never make again, and their razer cannons vaporized the almost daily warheads that launched into the sky, but it didn't bring back those who had died so needlessly.

Kyber had ordered his people not to fight back. He wanted his One and only his One. Once they found her, they would leave this rock hovering on the back end of space and never look back. Farid had been the one left to handle whatever fruitless negotiations were to be had with Earth. He knew he was merely dragging matters out until the emperor's One was found, but it didn't stop him from trying to do his job. If it rankled that Kyber had effectively tied his hands by allowing no retribution, he knew his frustration was nothing compared to those who had lost family and friends in the bombing.

Sighing, he shoved away the anger, the fatigue, and the relentless, completely unacceptable desire for Bren that nagged at him. He hurried his step to reach his office.

He had work to do.

Bren patted her hair to make sure it was in its usual tidy knot at the nape of her neck, resolutely pushing the erotic dream with Farid the night before from her mind. Again. There were some women who liked the titillation of sleeping with the enemy, but she didn't think much of those women. It didn't matter that the Kith could make a woman come with a mere glance, a simple thought.

Lord Farid was not welcome in her mind or in her dreams. He was a cold, heartless bastard. Condescending, smug, ruthless.

She clenched her jaw and shoved a loose bobby pin into place with more force than the action required. She winced when it scraped her scalp. Stomping on her wayward thoughts of the too attractive, too arrogant alien nobleman, she made her way through the security checkpoints in the Pentagon. The building was a far cry from the baking deserts and sweltering jungles she'd spent years in.

Dropping her purse on her desk, she glanced up to see Arthur motioning her into his office. He had a phone glued to his ear and a dozen stacks of paperwork on his desk. Dark circles made smudges under his eyes, and she doubted he'd been home the night before. She doubted his sleepless night had been as disturbing as hers.

She snapped to attention in front of his desk as he set the phone on its cradle. "Sir?"

"At ease, Sergeant Major."

She relaxed, tucking her hands behind her back, feet shoulder width apart. "What can I do for you, sir?"

Sitting back in his chair, he picked up a paperweight and tossed it from one hand to the other. "A new country will be joining our coalition. It's going to be a lot of work for you in the next few months. You know how difficult it can be to get a new member up to speed."

"Yes, sir." She'd been in the thick of it when they formed the worldwide coalition of militaries and had done more paperwork to make it all happen than she'd wanted to do in her entire life. She'd much rather be out in the field, but if this is how she could best serve her country, she'd do the best job that could be done. "Which country, sir?"

A triumphant, almost cruel expression crossed his face. "China."

That was not an answer she wanted to hear. The bottom dropped out of her stomach.

Oh, shit.

2

Bren licked her lips and tried to keep her voice even. "I thought China didn't want to join the coalition, sir."

Arthur's dark eyes cooled. "My efforts to convince them it's the best thing for their citizens were successful."

"Congratulations, sir." Another wave of dread went through her, numbness following in its wake. She wasn't sure what measures he'd taken to ensure their cooperation, but it would have to be extreme. China had made it very clear from the beginning they wanted to stand alone on this issue, that they wanted no part of an operation run solely at the discretion of the United States.

Who had Arthur threatened or killed to get what he wanted? She curled her fingers into tight fists, horrified she had to ask herself the question, and yet . . . not surprised by it at the same time. It *wasn't* paranoia that had kept her up at night, and that lame excuse crumbled in the face of the unrelenting truth before her. He wasn't the man she remembered, the man she'd respected, almost worshipped. Something had changed in the last few months. She wasn't sure if she was just seeing it *now*, and it had always been there, or if it was a new development.

He still looked the part of the perfect officer and gentleman. Soldier. Hero. The kind of man who ended up with commemorative statues after he died in battle. She stifled a snort at that— as if any of them did this for the glory.

But something about that caught her, made her pause.

She focused on his face and realized that that was the difference. Since the Kith had come and Arthur had had the chance to band together the militaries of Earth to fight them, it had gone from *saving* the world to *controlling* the world. Perhaps it was the glory or just the power, but it really didn't matter why, did it? Arthur, a man she would have sworn a year ago was a dedicated soldier to the core of his being, had lost whatever internal compass guided him. He'd crossed the line one too many times and never suffered any consequences for it. People were scared and they were desperate for the safety they had once known. The safety of ignorance.

All those people were willing to let Arthur do whatever he wanted in order to reclaim that security. They'd hand over their armies, their control, their independence, their money. Everything.

She could see in Arthur's eyes how much he liked that. It wasn't about safety for him anymore; it wasn't about protection or what was good for humanity. It was about *him* now. His power, his control, his ability to convince people they would never be safe without him in charge.

A chill rippled down her spine, and she swallowed hard, forcing her expression to impassivity. "You have a meeting with the president at ten, sir."

"Thank you, Preston." Arthur continued to stare at her for a long moment, and Bren refused to give in to the urge to fidget. "Dismissed."

She nodded and executed a quick about-face, marching out of his office and closing the door behind her. It wasn't until there was a thick wooden barrier between him and her that she let out the breath she'd been holding.

Perching in her office chair, she logged in to her computer and just stared at the screen. Her thoughts ricocheted in her mind, unable to settle. She kept coming back to the same conclusion she had the night before. Regardless of the Sueni fleet being here or gone, this was going to be a no-win situation for Earth. *Arthur*, the savior of humanity, was going to make it a no-win situation. People had died, and more people were going to, if Arthur remained in command.

So what was she going to do about it?

Her hands folded tightly in her lap, her nails digging into her skin. Whatever remained of her initial numbness evaporated. Panic and terror bolted through her, made her uniform dampen with sweat.

She could do nothing. It was in her best interest to keep following orders and just . . . living her life. Because the army *was* her life. This was who she was. It was all she'd ever wanted to be.

She'd run like hell from her foster family the day she'd graduated from high school, signed on with the army, and never looked back.

She'd been lucky and she knew it. Her foster father had satisfied himself with occasionally kicking the crap out of her and the other kids and neglecting them the rest of the time. And that had been one of the better homes she'd lived in after her parents died. She was just grateful to have never had to look herself in the mirror and see the empty, hollowed-out eyes of the walking ghosts some of those foster kids had become.

Bren had known then that she would do everything she could to make sure she was never anyone's victim ever again. She'd learn how to fight back, she'd learn how to never be weak, she'd learn how to protect people who couldn't protect themselves. And she had. The army had given her that. A sense of purpose, of duty, of belonging to something greater than herself.

But that was the problem, that was why she couldn't blindly follow Arthur now, because the army had given her a purpose, had made her country and its citizens more important than anything else. More than personal gain or power or prestige. She couldn't just stand back now and do nothing when the things she lived for were threatened.

She forced herself to cold, calm calculation. Now was not the time for panic. She had to do *something*. There was no question left in her mind about that. This was not optional. But what could she do? Who could she ask for help? Who could she trust? Conspiring against the most powerful man on the planet had gotten people far more influential than her killed. Who would be willing to step out of line to protect everyone *from* Arthur?

A flash of Farid's face entered her mind. She dismissed it, but then paused.

If Arthur was the enemy, then was the enemy of her enemy someone she could turn to? Farid hated Arthur, of that she had no doubt. He'd love some retribution for the preemptive strike against the Sueni armada. If she gave him the chance to exact his revenge, would it save the planet or make the situation worse?

There was only one way to find out, but she couldn't call him just to ask. No, this meeting would have to be private and it would have to be in person. She closed her eyes and sighed. Pulling her cell phone out of her purse, she opened up an encrypted email and composed a new message that would somehow interface with the Sueni ships. Her lips twisted. Apparently, they'd been able to dumb down their communication system to get the most advanced Earth technology to play well with them.

Lord Arj—

No, that wasn't right. She didn't want anyone who might intercept this to know what her real intentions were. Hell, she didn't even want the Kith nobleman to know what she wanted until she saw him. She wanted to look him in the eyes when she told him. She deleted what she'd typed and tried again.

Farid. No more teasing. Let's finish what we started in person. Meet me tonight at your original landing site. I need you.
—*Bren*

Her hand hovered over the key that would seal her fate forever. There would be no turning back. Her career—her *life*—would be over. Hell, if she were honest with herself, she should have reported fraternizing with the enemy in her dreams long ago, but there was no hiding this kind of breach. Arthur would find out eventually. She knew it. And then everyone would know she was a traitor. If her fingers trembled, she'd never admit it to anyone.

Clenching her teeth together, she pressed SEND.

Farid was more than ready to fall facedown on his gelpad. He had three hours before his next meeting and he didn't care what it took to make it happen, he was getting some sleep and *not* linking with Bren. "*Vishra*, please add the somnolence dose to the air in my room now."

The ship's response was immediate. "Of course, my lord."

"Thank you." He leaned back against the glass wall of the multiveyor while it moved backward and then slanted at a downward angle to take him to the floor with his quarters.

His work shift so far, like every work shift since they'd arrived, had been a lesson in the futile. Still, he refused to give up. This was what he lived for. The restrictions Kyber had placed on Farid's diplomacy made it all the more challenging. Given enough time, he *would* win, eventually. Whether he had that time before the emperor found his One was another story . . . and another challenge.

Lost in thoughts that had occupied every waking hour for months, he stepped out of the multiveyor and heard it swish closed and hum as it sped away.

A man came bursting through a door and slid to a stop before him. "Farid."

He blinked and looked up. "Kyber."

Of all the people aboard their ships, Farid was one of the few who could call his cousin by name. Even then, he usually did so only in private. It was a delicate balance between being family and being respectful of his ruler, no matter how much younger Kyber was than Farid.

"I think I've found her." A wide smile broke across the emperor's face.

Farid stared for a moment before that information processed. "Your One?"

"Yes. I know where she is now. I must go." Kyber glanced over Farid's shoulder. "*Vishra*, call the multiveyor for me."

The ship replied in that smooth, unflappable voice. "Of course, Your Majesty."

"Oh. Wait." Kyber turned back to his room and lifted a hand toward the open door. A pistol came whizzing through the air to slap into his palm. He slid it into a holster at his hip.

Farid couldn't stop a grin. "That's a handy trick."

"It only works when I'm upset or excited. I don't think anyone else has the power to do it." Kyber shrugged and forked his fingers through his long ebony hair.

"I don't," Farid replied. Not that he minded. More energy to try to harness was not something he desired.

Kyber's violet eyes glowed with latent power, paler lavender sparks flashing in his gaze as his anticipation rose. His mind latched on to the subject that Farid doubted was ever far from the surface. "Every time I connect with her, she's somewhere different. And she's always gone before I arrive to track her. But not this time."

Frowning, Farid gave his cousin's dilemma more thought than he might normally. "Perhaps her occupation requires her to travel a great deal."

"Perhaps." The emperor shook his head sharply, and his smile became blinding again as the multiveyor door slid open for him. "I'll find out when I get there. I'm sure I can get to her before she leaves."

It wasn't the first time his cousin had been sure, but Farid sent as much faith and support as he could muster along their familial link. Then he ran a tired hand over his face and turned to walk toward the corridor that led to his quarters. A noise down a small side hallway used for maintenance drew him up short. What *now?* He sighed and backed up a few steps, allowing his superior vision to peer into the darkness.

His mouth fell open at what he saw. Shaking his head, he tried to clear it. Tylara Belraj, uptight commander of the fleet and captain of the *Vishra*, had her arms pinned above her head and her pants shoved down around her boots as a man fucked her ruthlessly from behind.

Farid watched her slim, firm body arch in ecstasy. Her head rolled against her lover's shoulder, her eyes closed. Farid had never witnessed such an unguarded expression on her face. She looked . . . happy, joyful, lighter than he'd ever seen her. He would never have guessed that the woman was capable of such an emotion, let alone displaying it so openly.

Especially considering they were in an unsecured hallway that any civilian had access to. Releasing her hands, her lover shoved her hard against the metal wall, and his hips hammered forward to slap her smooth buttocks.

She opened her mouth and hissed, every ounce of her feral naturel alive on her face.

Farid stood there staring in stunned silence. He couldn't make himself look away as a gentleman should. The carnal display was arousing, reminding him forcibly of his own power-less, fruitless delight at reaching for his One.

And that was who this man was to Tylara. Her emotions, as tightly controlled as they were, couldn't contain that truth, and it ripped him into her maelstrom. He jerked back, trying to wrench himself free of his stupor.

Tylara's eyes flew open, their midnight irises almost white with the sparks boiling to the surface. "Farid."

Her lover's head whipped to the side and he snarled low in his throat. A predator possessive of his prize. His blue eyes flashed wildly, sweat ran in rivulets down his ebony skin, and waist-length braids swung around his face. A jolt shook Farid as he focused his senses on the man for the first time.

Johar Sajan. Brother to Cilji's perfidious, unstable One.

Shock made Farid sway on his feet. Tylara's One was a Sajan. He shook his head, clearing the fog of her lust from his mind as he turned and stumbled away.

"Farid, wait!"

He didn't listen, fleeing blindly down the hallways as he struggled to maintain the shields on his thoughts and emotions. What he felt was no one's business but his own.

His memories rose with horrifying clarity, brutalizing his mind. Cilji's face. His impetuous baby sister. Dead. Anun, no. Not that. Anything but that. Not those memories, not that fail-ure. *No.*

"Stop, Lord Farid!" Tylara's voice was that of the fleet com-mander, not one to ignore.

He pulled up, his gut churning with disquiet. Clenching his jaw, he waited for her to draw even with him. He could still scent the sex on her. He could also sense her upset, which was rare for the contained woman. Giving her a curt nod, he stared at a point just beyond her shoulder. "Tylara."

"Don't say anything, Farid. I don't want to hear it." She

shoved her fingers through her hair, working it into some semblance of its usual order.

"Johar Sajan." The words jerked out of him and his fingers fisted at his sides.

Huffing out a breath, she quit fussing with her hair. "I know his name."

"He's also your One."

She snarled at him, some of the beast ripping free of her tight restraint. "Stay out of my mind."

Finally meeting her gaze, he arched an eyebrow. "Your thoughts are chaotic, they're pushing out."

"You can block them." She crossed her arms over her chest and lifted her chin, managing to stare down at him though he was a full head taller than her.

"Fine."

She sighed. "It's not like with your sister, Farid. I'm in control."

Closing his eyes, he shook his head and an ironic smile tugged at his mouth. "If there's anything I know, it's that control and bonding with your One don't go hand in hand."

"I'm aware of that. I am in control enough not to force a bonding between us if he doesn't want it. Yes, I am far more powerful than he is and I *could* force it, but I'm not Cilji. He may be from the same family as Cilji's One, but they aren't the same men. I understand all of that." Agony flashed in her eyes. There was no deeper torment than this. "I also understand that he may decide it's not worth it to deal with someone as powerful as I am, that he may leave me for another woman, another bond. An easier bond."

"I'm sorry." He shook his hands out and tucked them into his pockets.

"So am I." A tremulous smile crossed her lips. "And, yet, I'm not. I could never regret finding my One, even if I know there may be no good ending that comes of it."

He shook his head. "I hope, for your sake, this turns out better than it did for my sister."

"No one will die, if that's what you mean." Her chin rose another notch.

"It is."

"Have some faith in me, Farid." She sniffed, her gaze cooling to that of the military commander she was. In that moment, she reminded him of Bren. His gut clenched at the thought. Too many emotions tangled within him today, and still he couldn't stop the instinctive craving he had for his One. Tylara's eyes narrowed on his face. "We've known each other long enough for that not to be an odd thing for me to expect from you. You've seen me work, seen me under pressure."

"Leave it be, Tylara."

She didn't. He stifled a groan and rubbed the back of his neck. This was not how he'd wanted this day to go. He should be deep in dreamless slumber. Instead, he was being lectured on faith by the highest-ranking officer in Suen's military. She poked a finger in his direction. "You want people to trust you and your control. You want to prove you're not like your sister, but no one else can ask for your trust? Is that truly fair? Or rational? Or reasonable?"

He clenched his teeth together to keep from saying things that would destroy years of friendly relations with the woman. He found his fangs had erupted from his gums to press against his lips. So much for his vaunted control. He wasn't doing very well with that today, was he? First, reaching for his One, and now, arguing with a friend. But she was right, wasn't she? He'd worked long and hard to prove he'd never end up like his sister—out of control in ways the Kith could never be and still expect to remain sane, to *survive* at all. That was what bonding with a One could do to a Kith, and only control and logic would keep him from his family's fate.

He met Tylara's gaze, hoping she couldn't see his turmoil.

"No, it's not reasonable, rational, or fair. I'm not like Cilji and neither are you. That doesn't make my concern for you and your safety illegitimate. Anun be with you."

With that, he turned on his heel and marched away. Thankfully, she didn't follow. He didn't know if he could handle much more today. Connecting with Bren always shook him, always let the beast inside him loose far longer than he normally allowed, always made him *react* when he should *think*.

No matter what political maneuvering he might be able to accomplish here, he had to consider self-preservation. He could only pray that the emperor claimed his One soon and they could leave this miserable planet behind. Only then would the temptation Bren presented be beyond his reach.

Ignoring the feline within's yowl of protest and pain at the mere thought of abandoning its mate forever, he turned for his quarters, once more in complete command of himself.

The personal communication imager in his pocket vibrated to indicate he had received a new message. He pulled out the handheld comm. and accessed the missive.

He had to read it twice before the words sank in. Bren wanted to meet with him. He shouldn't. He should stay as far away from her as possible. He should allow no contact outside of what was necessary in their professions when he went down to haggle with General Arthur.

His fingers were already moving over the imager, sending her a confirmation of their meeting. "*Vishra*, cancel the somnolence dose for me, reschedule the rest of my meetings for the day, and alert the cargo master that I'll be taking a shuttle down to the surface for a . . . rendezvous of a personal nature."

"Yes, my lord."

Night had fallen by the time Bren hiked up the side of a mountain in the middle of West Virginia, moving toward the same clearing she'd stood in when the Sueni had landed. She'd gone with Arthur when he'd been ordered to investigate. Less than a year had passed since then, but so much had changed. Technology, politics, religion, history. Everything.

Farid had been here that day, in his cat form. There'd been only ten of them in the landing party, half in human form, the rest in beast form. The humans had been all shapes, sizes, and colors, and they looked . . . like regular humans. Farid had moved forward, planting his feline self directly in front of her. He'd bowed his head but never took those icy eyes off her. She was caught by that gaze and the unearthly power she felt behind it.

Everything about him overwhelmed her. He was huge. And beautiful. Like nothing she'd ever seen before. Like nothing any human had ever seen before. They were dangerous and feline, colored like a snow tiger with dark stripes on pale fur. Only no cat could ever be that size. They had the bulk of a grizzly bear, but all the grace of a feline. She shook her head, pushing the memories away. It didn't matter what the Kith looked like or what had happened the day they arrived. What mattered was right here, right now, she needed the help of *one* Kith.

Farid.

Pausing beside a large tree, Bren let her gaze scan the area. Nothing moved, nothing was out of place. Only the moon lit the forest around her. She was about a quarter of a mile from the clearing, and she'd dumped her rental car outside the little town at the base of the mountain. The car was low end and she'd switched out the license plates on a similar model outside of D.C. Anything she could do to make herself harder to find, to keep Arthur from realizing what she was doing. She brushed a hand down her T-shirt. She felt naked without her uniform, but she couldn't afford to wear it. Uniforms were distinctive in civilian areas; they made a person stand out. That was the last thing she wanted right now. Dark jeans, a black shirt, and black hiking boots would have to do. She kept her hair back in its customary knot. That much wouldn't change.

Cold sweat broke out on her forehead and she closed her eyes for a moment. What the fuck was she doing? She wanted to vomit, and she swallowed the sour gorge that rose in her throat and coated her tongue.

Get a grip, Bren. Suck it up and do what you have to do.

Farid would expect a cold, methodical military woman—the same woman she'd presented herself as every time she'd seen him. Normally, it wasn't an act, but tonight it would be. She'd never been so rattled in her entire adult life. There were life-and-death, someone-was-shooting-at-her situations where she'd been calmer.

That was because then, there'd been no question who was right or wrong. She'd had a job to do and she would do it to the best of her ability. It might mean she had to kill someone. It might mean she had to die. It might even mean she'd lose a friend, a comrade in arms, but tonight wasn't about that. Tonight she was giving up her career by helping people who were officially at war with the military she served. Tonight she was betraying everything she'd ever believed in order to safeguard everything she'd ever sworn to protect.

Her country. Earth. Mankind.

More than that, tonight she had to *see* Farid again. She'd never dealt with him in person so soon after one of their psychic evening trysts. Her sex clenched in utter want while her heart pounded with trepidation. God, help her.

Slow, grueling minutes ticked by as she scouted the area to see if he'd come, all the while expecting an ambush of Kith soldiers, expecting Arthur to send men to kill her, expecting anything and everything.

"Bren." The deep rumble of his voice directly behind her

made her body jolt and her heart thud hard against her ribs. "You weren't followed?"

"No." She swallowed, glancing over her shoulder at him as his heat enveloped her. "You came alone?"

"Yes." His arm wrapped around her waist, whipping her around at dizzying speed until her back pressed to the rough bark of a tree.

"What are you—"

She didn't get a chance to finish the stupid question. His mouth closed over hers, his free hand bracketing the back of her neck to hold her in place for his kiss. It was the one thing he never did in her dreams. She'd been desperate, dying to know what his full lips would feel like as they played against hers. Would he be soft and gentle, building her needs with just the pleasure of his mouth on hers? Would he be rough, nipping and biting at her lips until she couldn't stand it anymore? She'd wanted to know even though she shouldn't.

If his kiss had been demanding, it would have been easy to fight him, to kick and hit and force him to let her go. She had the kind of training to make that happen. But his touch was reverent, worshipful. She hadn't expected it. He held her so tight, but his lips brushed hers in light strokes that had her straining to get closer, to deepen the contact.

A low growl shook his chest, shuddering through them both. He licked her lower lip, teasing her, probing for entrance.

Let me in. His voice reverberated in her mind. With that, the sizzling connection that bound her to him during the nights he shared her dreams snapped into place. She gasped, the dual physical and mental touch a shock. He took advantage, slipping his tongue into her mouth to tangle with hers. His fingers massaged the back of her neck, calluses rasping her skin as he let his hand drift down her shoulder and lower, until he cupped her breast in his palm. Her body jerked under the hot lash of pleasure, her nipple tightening to a painful point of need. His thumb stimulated the beaded crest through her shirt and bra, and she moaned into his mouth.

It was more than she could resist, no matter what kind of danger they might be in. She shoved her hands into his thick, silken hair. The texture was unlike anything she'd ever felt before. He groaned, thrusting his hips against the juncture of her thighs. She could feel the unyielding arc of his cock through their clothes, and she burned for him. Her pussy drenched with cream, her internal muscles clenching and loosening as her desire flamed out of control.

He jerked back, spinning her with that startling speed of his until they both faced the tree. She stumbled and caught the trunk in her hands, trying to maintain her balance. As if she could with him touching her.

His deft fingers popped the button on her jeans, slid down the zipper with a rasp of sound that made the hairs lift on her arms, and slipped into the vee he'd created. Her thighs shook as she fought to regain some sanity. He pressed his palm flat against her belly, holding her close while his cock rubbed her backside.

She clenched her jaw and tried to steady her breathing. She was here for a reason and getting laid wasn't it. A throb of want went through her, but she got a stranglehold on her self-restraint. "I . . . need to talk to you. I—I didn't come here for this. Not really."

"Of course you didn't. We're in the middle of a forest. Not the best place for an assignation. Nevertheless, I am going to take you, Bren. I've waited so long to get you alone, to touch you, to run my hands over your soft skin." His fingertips grazed the edge of her panties, sliding under the thin cotton. "The opportunity may never come again."

"But—"

He dipped into the curls between her thighs, and she knew he'd find her slick with juices. Heat burned her face, and she was angry with herself for never being able to stop how she reacted to him, angry at him for always tempting her into reaction.

A shiver went through her when he kissed the side of her neck, and his groan reverberated against her skin as he circled a finger around her clit before sinking into her wet core. "Do you know how good you feel to me, *khalaa*?"

"Y-yes." The mental bond was there whether she liked it or not. His desire trickled along that infinitesimal thread that joined them, and her pussy grew damper with every bead of his longing that reached her. Her own need sharpened, deepened, rose to match his.

He wasn't even inside her yet and she was already teetering on the very edge of orgasm.

His thigh slid between her knees, nudging her legs apart as he tilted her torso forward with his. His thumb toyed with her clit while he pumped two fingers inside her. Even as he worked her, his other hand eased her jeans and panties down around her thighs. Cool air brushed over her bared skin, and a shudder ran through her. His movements were slow, tormenting her. She had to bite her lip hard to keep from crying out in frustration. Her tension bloomed, and she was terrified to scream, to whimper, to make a single sound lest someone be listening, watching.

The backs of his knuckles rubbed her backside as he unfastened his pants. When the hot flesh of his erection met her skin, she moaned. Desperation wrenched deep within her. Yes. She wanted to be filled by him. The head of his dick slid over the lips of her pussy, not entering her. Need tore through her and she tilted her hips to open herself for his penetration, but her movements were hampered by her jeans shackling her legs.

He ran his tongue up the side of her neck and caught her earlobe between his teeth. His breath cooled the moisture on her flesh when he spoke. "Tell me to stop."

"I *can't*." The words ripped out of her, almost a sob. Her hips undulated helplessly. She wanted him too much to stop, her body's needs overruling her mind.

Lacing his fingers with hers, he pressed their hands against the tree and pinned her in place. A soft chuckle broke from him. "Good."

And then he arched his hips, piercing her with one hard thrust. She cried out, the stretch almost painful. After their late-night meetings, she hadn't expected it, but those times hadn't been real. Not like this. The carnality of it shocked her—his scent and feel overwhelmed her senses until everything narrowed to just him.

He froze behind her, still buried to the hilt inside her. Agony tore his voice to a ragged whisper, "I hurt you, *khalaa*."

Wriggling to get closer, to force his cock even deeper, she pressed herself into him. He was so big, he filled her so well. It was amazing. Mind-blowing. "Stop and I will do a lot more than hurt you."

He remained still, doing nothing to help her gain the satisfaction she craved. "Bren . . ."

"Don't make me beg." Because at this point, she would. Her body screamed with tension, fire and ice tingling over her skin. She gritted her teeth to keep from whimpering.

"I won't." He began moving again and she did whimper, so grateful that tears sprang to her eyes. She blinked them back, unwilling to let anything encourage him to stop again.

Sweat beaded on her forehead, sliding down her temples. The breeze wrapping around them chilled the moisture on her skin, but it was just one more stimulation, one more thing to make her moan. The thread of awareness that connected their minds filtered desire back and forth between them. Heat whipped through her, made her skin feel too tight, as though she would explode any moment. She closed her eyes, gasping for breath as he ground himself against her. "Oh, my God."

Her pussy flexed around his cock and she could feel her orgasm building, knew he could feel it too. He groaned, and his claws slid forward, digging deep into the tree bark. "Merciful Anun."

"Harder, *faster*. I'm so close." She didn't give a damn if anyone was nearby, and she knew that was stupid, that this was stupid, but it didn't stop her. He gave her what she wanted, his hips bucking hard as he slammed deep. Waves of ecstasy radiated out each time he entered her, her whole body focused on that one point that joined them.

His fangs grazed her throat, scoring her flesh. She threw her head back on his shoulder, gave him all the access he could want, and arched her hips to meet his hammering thrusts. Their skin slapped together, the sound loud in the quiet forest.

One of his hands dropped to fondle her breast, his claws scraping her as he slipped lower to flick over her clitoris. A thin cry burst from her, and she clamped her inner muscles around him, giving as good as she got. His groan was as helpless as she felt.

He worked her clit in time with his thrusts, arching her forward into his finger, and back into his cock. Then the point of his claw raked her sensitive flesh oh-so-lightly. But it was enough. She was so hot, so ready, it was enough to send her flying. Her mouth opened in a silent scream, her body locking tight. Her sex fisted around the length of his cock, pleasure cascading through her with each rhythmic pulse of her inner muscles.

He rammed his cock inside her, dragging out her orgasm as he sought his own. He hissed between his teeth, the sound not quite human. When he came deep inside her, his fluids filling her with heat, her sex clenched again, making them both groan. His mouth opened against her neck, licking and sucking at her sweat-dampened flesh as his voice filled her mind. *Yes,* khalaa. *Just like that. I have wanted this for so long.*

So had she, though she'd never confess it to him. She didn't even want to acknowledge it to herself. Her heart still pounded in her ears, her muscles beginning to cramp from the awkward, bent position. The cloud of lust began to clear from her mind, and reality came back in an awful rush. She closed her eyes as she scrambled to gather up the unraveling edges of her self-control. Jerking her hand out from under his, she scraped her palm against the rough tree.

God, she was pathetic. How hard up did she have to be to fuck a virtual stranger, an enemy, out in the open? Especially when she had come for reasons that were more than a little time sensitive. How long did she have before Arthur realized she'd defected? Tomorrow morning at the latest, and she doubted she'd be that lucky. She needed to know if she could count on Farid and his emperor for help.

Dancing her hips away, she felt Farid's cock slide from her body. A final shiver wracked her, pleasure ricocheting through her whether she wanted it to or not. And she did *not,* damn it. Why did the chemistry with *him* have to be so powerful, so right, so beyond anything she'd ever experienced before? She hated it so much. Almost as much as she craved it, him.

He sighed softly, righting his clothes as she did the same. Her movements were jerky, stiff as she lambasted herself for her stupidity. Mustering the flagging edges of her dignity and courage, she finally faced him. He wasn't looking at her. His eyes were closed, his head tilted as though he were listening for something. Foreboding rippled through her, the hairs standing up on the back of her neck.

"What's wrong?" she whispered as she pulled the gun out of the holster strapped to her ankle. Call it a reaction to him or just good old-fashioned gut instinct, but she knew something was out there. Could be a harmless hiker getting a voyeuristic thrill or it could be something much more dangerous. "I thought you were alone, Arjun."

Then she heard what his sensitive ears had picked up first. The sound of helicopter blades slicing through the air. It was moving far faster and far lower than a commercial helo would, which meant one thing. They were screwed. A spotlight hit the clearing she'd never reached, the glow filtering between the tree branches, as soldiers repelled out of the aircraft and hit the ground.

She turned to run, but Farid grabbed her, dragging them both to the ground. "Down!"

Machine gun fire rapped a staccato beat as bullets slapped into the ground beside them. A root from the tree they'd fucked against slammed into her belly, knocking the wind out of her. She gagged for air but scrambled forward to take cover.

"I thought you weren't followed!" He hissed, his fangs fully extended.

"Damn it!" Her heart pounded loud in her ears. She braced her back against the tree, held her weapon at the ready, and tried to steady her breathing so she could hear.

He snarled several words in his language that she was pretty sure were spleen-venting curses. The ground rocked beneath them as something large blew up, shooting flames and debris high above the canopy of trees.

"That would be my shuttle." His voice was clipped, cold.

She narrowed her eyes at him. "I didn't see or hear you land."

"I was here long before you were." If possible, his tone chilled even more, dipping into subarctic.

A distant rumble sounded as something farther away exploded. Oh, Jesus. Realization hit her in a sick rush. "And that's my car. Shit!"

He snarled again, his eyes boiling green sparks, but said nothing else. He scanned the trees, and she could feel the heat of his power pulse out in a wave. What he was looking for, she didn't know, but she took the opportunity to listen for approaching footsteps or movement. The machine gun fire had come at them from the north—the same direction as her car— his shuttle was south, but every second that passed meant they could be moving while Farid and she were pinned down. "Bren, where is your cell phone?"

"E.T. phone home?" She fished it out of her pocket and handed it to him. She could hear the whine of the helo coming back, spotlight on and ready to reveal their location.

"What?" He flipped open the slim phone and the screen lit.

"Nothing." She shook her head. "You'd have to be human to get it."

"I read their minds. They're using this to track you." He drew back his arm and launched her cell as far as he could.

She flinched as her one form of communication with anyone off this mountain shattered against a boulder. "Shit."

Grabbing her arm, Farid began to drag her toward the flame-engulfed shell of his ship. She kept her weapon at the ready, not looking directly into the fire so that it couldn't mess up her night vision. Getting that close to the fire would cast shadows and give even a moron a big clue about where they were. They wouldn't even need the spotlight on them. She whispered, "What are you doing?"

His fingers tightened around her wrist, though she'd made no attempt to escape, which just made her *want* to fight him. She gritted her teeth and refused to do something that would guarantee they got shot.

"I sense no people beyond my shuttle. I'm getting us out of here before we're killed. I hope you don't mind."

"Spare me the sarcasm, Arjun." She twisted her arm in his grip as they moved. "And let go of me. Now."

He did but cast her a cool glance as he moved behind her to watch her back. "My name is Farid."

"Whatever." Like it mattered what she called him. They needed to get out of this situation or her defecting wouldn't do shit to help anyone.

Farid had seen the opportunity to have her and he'd taken it. He was nothing if not ruthless. Even though he would never bond with her, he wanted her, wanted to know what fucking a woman made just for him would be like. She'd come to him, so now she was his. And he would have her for as long as he liked, as long as his people were on Earth. If an infinitesimal part of him hoped the emperor's One was never found and the Kith remained indefinitely, he silenced that inner voice quickly enough.

Though none of that mattered if he let them get killed this night. He kicked himself for having lost control and given in to the need to take his One without ensuring their safety. Guilt flooded him. He knew better, knew what could happen when he allowed even a moment's inattention.

Clenching his jaw, he slid his slim razer pistol from the holster at the small of his back and kept his senses wide open, noting every movement, every conscious being that littered the forest around them. There were the native animals to the area, prey and predators, but aside from that there were two-legged predators. Humans. Seven of them, all large, and moving the way only experienced warriors did.

Their aircraft continued to buzz low to the ground, a light cutting through the trees. The beast within him chafed at being hunted, wanted to return the favor, and shred them with his claws. But his One would be left alone, and he wasn't willing to do so. He had no doubt that she could take care of herself—she moved with the same air of experience as the warriors tracking them—but he had her by his side and he intended to keep her there. For now.

She paused, slipping behind a tree a moment before he would have warned her to take cover. He crouched beside her, one hand braced on the ground before him, his claws digging deep into the foreign soil. His heart pounded and he closed his eyes, allowed his other senses to come to the fore, and hid the sparks in his irises that made him easy prey. Using his razer would make the blue laser it emitted flash in the dark and alert others to their location. Better to handle the enemy silently. Bloodlust roared in his veins. The sound of a soldier's footsteps intensified, making them drumbeats against the ground. His scent drew closer, and Farid's muscles tensed, ready to spring and eliminate one of the threats.

He jolted when Bren's hand closed over his shoulder, not expecting his One to touch him. He froze, and the soldier passed them.

Bren's words were little more than breaths of air next to his ear. "Escape and evade. Do not engage."

A shudder passed through him as he struggled to control the conflicting urges ripping through him. His eyes opened and he glanced at her, sending words he knew he couldn't speak steadily out loud to her mind instead. *Tell me, has someone finally rebelled against your general and now they are hunting you by association, or have you finally come to your senses and now your general and his men are out to kill you?*

"How do you know they weren't after you?" He dug his claws deeper into the forest floor when her lips brushed his ear. "Your shuttle was blown, too."

He closed his eyes again, knowing the green sparks would be boiling fast and bright for anyone to see. *They could, I suppose, but why bomb your car if all they wanted was to keep me on the planet?*

"I-I want to depose Arthur." Her fingers flexed convulsively on his shoulder, biting into his flesh through his tunic. "I don't want anyone else to be hurt."

And you want Sueni help with that? His heart slammed against his ribs, and though his mind had already worked out that logical conclusion, everything he knew about this woman said she would never betray her beliefs. What had Arthur done to make her change her mind about him? The blood rushing so hot in his veins chilled at the possibilities, and he zeroed in his senses on his One to be certain that she was as unscathed as she'd appeared when he first approached her. He might not want to bond with her, but he would never allow anyone to harm her. For the moment, she was his, and he protected what was his.

Removing her hand from him, she put enough distance between them so they were no longer touching. "You don't want him in power any more than I do."

Less. Though he had his doubts about convincing Kyber to reverse his nonaggression policy on Earth. That was a fight for another time. Farid wasted no more time speaking, opened his eyes, and motioned her forward. They needed to get away from here if he wasn't going to be allowed to dismantle the men who dared to hunt his One. If they became a direct threat, he wouldn't hesitate. Any details he wanted about what Arthur had done would have to wait until they were safe.

Farid jerked out his handheld comm. device and keyed the imager to call for help from the *Vishra*. A shout sounded nearby and Farid looked up to see the soldier who had passed them had circled back around. He lifted a pistol, aimed it at Bren, and Farid saw in excruciating detail how his finger squeezed the trigger. The muzzle flashed. Farid's heart contracted, adrenaline exploding in his veins. He reacted without thought, with the lightning reflexes of his feline nature, launching his comm. into the exact path of the bullet. The imager burst into little more than metal debris. His other hand came around and he fired his razer at their attacker. The soldier screamed, dropped a small, round object to the ground, and convulsed as electricity sizzled through his body.

Time rushed ahead at light speed, and Farid's pulse raced to match. Bren blinked. "How the hell did you throw—"

Run! His senses vibrated with danger, shrieking at him that six more of the enemies sprinted at them from multiple directions.

Bren was already on her feet, her boots kicking up dirt as she obeyed. She shouted over her shoulder, "Did you kill him?"

This is a Class Three razer. At full charge, it can only cause unconsciousness. He'll be fine. Worry more about your own hide than his and move faster. Now! He watched her flip a rude hand gesture at him, but she obliged him by pouring on more speed. Another aircraft was coming—he could hear it whirring in the distance. More soldiers to come down ropes, more light to seek them out in the dark, and more enemies to hunt them. They dashed through the trees until they found themselves moving along a ridge that dropped into a wide, rushing river.

While Farid's superhuman speed could easily outdistance their pursuers, he wasn't going to leave his One's side. Sweat made his tunic stick to his back and dampened his hair. His muscles shook as his instincts screamed to run faster, to get away, and his lungs burned as he sucked in oxygen.

They broke into a wide clearing and were nearly halfway across when he knew they'd neither be able to escape nor evade confrontation with the humans. One came out of the trees in front of them, three more to the side. Trapped. Farid knew going back the way they'd come was futile, and the river boxed them in. The soldiers began to circle their prey. One of the aircraft reached them, circling overhead to shine a blinding beam down on them. Farid hissed, his feline eyes aching at the adjustment to fluctuating light.

Squinting against the glare, he focused his psychic power on the nearest soldier and shoved in the image that the man's arm was on fire.

"I'm on fire! Oh, my God. My fucking arm is on fire!" He

screamed, slapping at his shoulder frantically before diving on the ground to roll.

Spinning to level his weapon on the next soldier, he watched the man pull out the same kind of small, round object the other soldier had dropped. Bren gasped. "Oh. Shit."

He grabbed her arm and shoved her behind him, bracing for an explosion. It didn't come. Instead, a high-pitched squeal rent the air, and Farid felt as though something vital had suddenly numbed, a shocking blow that left his ears ringing. Something he'd always known was there was blunted, ineffective. A white-hot blade sliced through his mind. He staggered, his claws and fangs exploding forward. A deep roar issued from his throat, the feline taking hard, abrupt control of his body.

His vision tunneled to one focus, one purpose. He would kill now, the beast had been unleashed.

"Arjun!" Bren sprayed gunfire at the feet of the soldiers to send them scrambling back for the cover of the trees. She launched herself forward, plowed all her weight into Farid, and sent them both careening over the sheer drop into the river. Reflex made his muscles tense, his hand gripping his gun. Blind instinct made him reach for his One, and he wrapped his arms around her in the single heartbeat it took to fall.

Sanity returned with a cold slap as they hit the frigid water. The river dragged them under, whipped them around in dizzying circles before he could propel them to the surface. They broke through, sputtering and coughing up fluids. His hold tightened on both his weapon and his One for fear of losing either in the rushing current. His heart pounded so loudly in his ears, it almost drowned out the roar of the river.

White foaming water slapped him in the face with the force of a battering ram when they hit rapids. He tried to kick, to take the brunt of the glancing blows from protruding rocks. Agony made his body arch, made a chilling feline scream burst from him. Bren gagged when they went under again, screamed and clung to him, her grip as desperate as his was. The only truth he knew was that he could not allow her to die, too. Not his One. They dipped in the river's eddies, spun weightlessly, helplessly, jerked in any direction the water would taken them.

Endless miles sped by before the currents calmed, and his muscles shrieked, his body trembling. He swam with the stream, directing their mad flight through the water. Bren scissored her legs to help him, her expression one of grim determination. They braced each other to be able to stand upright and maintain their footing as they stumbled out of the sucking current. His wet clothing felt as if it weighed more than the *Vishra* as it threatened to drag him to his knees.

They staggered to the relative cover of a copse of trees, sobbing for breath, vomiting up water. He caught one hand on his knee to keep from slamming face-first into the forest floor and shoved his pistol into the holster at his back. Every inch of his body shuddered and cramped, pain taking on a new definition in his mind.

When he managed to look up again, it was to see Bren sagging against a tree with her eyes closed. She gasped raggedly. "Are you all right, Arjun?"

"Fine." Honing his senses in on her revealed scrapes and bruises but no serious injuries. Relief wound through him with an intensity that alarmed him. Shaking himself beastlike to fling as much of the water off him as possible, he pushed away the feeling and focused on something safer—the events in the clearing. His voice emerged a rough croak. "What was that device they used?"

"It was—" Her low whisper cracked and broke off. She cleared her throat, her expression closing to tell him nothing. "All I know is it was designed to target the wavelengths in the Kith mind and nullify psychic power."

"Madness," he breathed, horror cresting within him. "The

psychic power is what allows us to control the rampaging animal side of our nature."

"So I saw." She pushed herself upright, a low groan breaking from her. "Since you have your psychic mojo back, you can contact your ship and tell them to send a shuttle."

"I cannot." He rubbed a hand over the back of his neck. "It is too far for my powers to reach. I would be unable connect with them from here."

"You make it from your ship to Earth just fine when you connect with me." Her gaze called him a liar, though the word didn't escape her lips.

He looked away, unable to meet her brilliant blue eyes. "It is different with you."

"How?" Combing her fingers through her tangled hair, she squeezed out the water, worked it into a long, thick plait, and fastened it with a tie she pulled from her pocket. She flipped it over her shoulder and arched her eyebrows at him. "How is it different, Arjun? I'm not even Kith to . . . you know, boost your power source from the other end."

"You would not understand. It's complicated." Outside of that, he wouldn't tell her the truth. He never intended to initiate the One bond, so she had no need to know. "Suffice to say, we must wait until they realize I am no longer gone of my own accord."

The Sueni would search for him soon, but he was far from the site of his landing and out of range of any ability to contact his people. He sent psychic distress calls up and outward, pushing his power as far as it would go. Nothing happened. He shook his head and sighed. With the exception of Kyber, no Kith had the ability to reach so far with their mental power. And Kyber had been more than a little distracted of late, so Farid had no idea when the emperor might be open to contact. He snorted. At this point, he wasn't even sure where his cousin was. Back on the *Vishra*, still on Earth, possibly bonding with his One?

"Well, we can't stay here. They're going to search the river for us." Her lips twisted in an unpleasant imitation of a smile. "Of course, they'll be hoping the rapids took care of us and all they find is our dead bodies."

"Wonderful." His body screeched a protest when he began moving, but he gritted his teeth and pushed on. She was right. They couldn't stay here, no matter how much he might crave rest. He stayed behind her as she began hiking, forced his psychic and feral senses open, and remained alert for any danger.

3

Hours passed as they ghosted through the trees, dawn lightened the sky, and Farid's clothes went from uncomfortably clammy to merely damp. His muscles throbbed, and the slight stagger to Bren's stride told him she fared no better. The scent of water reached him long before the sound of a babbling brook. Thirst wrenched deep inside him, the hunger and fatigue he'd been pushing away suddenly demanding notice. "Let me see if the water is safe. Then we need to find food."

Bren nodded. He heard her stomach gurgle loudly and she pressed her palm to her belly. "I like that plan."

He noted the paleness of her face, the way stress pinched the skin around her mouth. She looked worn, battered. He wanted to take her in his arms and tell her he'd make everything right. He refused to let it shake him, this need to protect. It hadn't been this strong since his family was still alive, but that meant little. It was mere possessiveness. It would pass once he tired of her. No lover had ever kept his interest long, and while fucking his One had been excellent, the novelty would surely wear off. It had to. He dismissed the concern from his mind.

Sighing, he stared into the rushing water for long moments before he settled on his haunches and dipped his fingers into the cool liquid. Scanning it with his senses, he found no living organisms. Bringing it to his nose, he smelled it for impurities, flicked his tongue out for an experimental taste. It was different from the water on Suen, but he found nothing wrong with it. "I believe it stems from the same source as the river. It should be safe to drink."

"You're sure?" Her voice had more than a hint of doubt in it. "We should probably boil it first."

"You cannot bring yourself to trust me about whether or not the water is drinkable?" Irritation scraped over his nerves and he knew it shouldn't. She'd spent months considering him her vilest enemy, only dropping her guard when his dreams melded with hers. It wasn't as though he *wanted* her trust. Of course not. That would be irrational, and the rational side of him was what controlled the beast that always sought its mate. It was necessary to keep a tight grip on his animalistic nature, a constant struggle for his kind. He refused to fail, not the way Cilji had. Not the way his parents had.

"Fine, I'll drink the water." She knelt beside him, dipping her cupped palms into the brook. "If I end up sick and they overtake us because of it, I will find a way to get loose just to kick your ass. I didn't go AWOL for nothing. I'm getting Emperor Kyber to agree to help before this is all over."

He glanced at her. "I will do everything I can to help you convince him, Bren. I swear it."

She blinked, a smile that was both shy and sweet crossing her face. He hadn't even known she was capable of such an expression. "I . . . thank you. For coming, and for being willing to help."

He liked that smile, liked that her gaze shone with something besides disdain and distrust, and hated that he liked any of it. He shouldn't like her or want her to like him in return. He would use her for sex as she used him for his influence with the emperor. Nothing more. He arched an eyebrow, shoving any warmth he might feel for her to the deepest, darkest corner of his soul. "There, now, did you choke on those words before you got them out?"

A laugh bubbled out of her and she rolled her eyes at him, throwing her hands in the air. "You make it so hard to be civil with you."

"So do you." He shook his head when she stuck her tongue out at him. "Thus far, your entire planet has been an odd combination of fawningly welcoming and catastrophically vicious."

"We're a complicated bunch." She smirked. "You don't want to deal with us. Go away."

He snorted and scooped up another handful of water to drink. "Yes, that's going to solve your problems with Arthur now."

"We wouldn't have had these problems if you hadn't shown up." She sighed, and a wave of her powerless frustration billowed out from her like a cloud.

"I know." He nodded, feeling some of that dissatisfaction himself. After all these months of futile negotiating, he understood her position very well.

A flicker of surprise crossed her expression. "You . . . know?"

"Of course. I am not stupid or unaware of the consequences of our arrival on your planet and people." He leaned toward her, her delicate, feminine scent as heady to him as ever. He forced himself to consider the discussion at hand, not something that he'd had to do often as a diplomat. "You seem impervious to the damage you have caused to us though. Why is that, do you think? Is it truly that you think we brought it upon ourselves?"

"No. Yes. No." Her slender, dark brows contracted, the inner conflict roiling out to touch him. "I don't know."

"A definitive answer. I like those." He let a small smile tuck in one side of his mouth, wanting to soothe her, but not know-ing how, and knowing that he shouldn't care either way. What was so simple with other people in his profession was always complicated with his One. He didn't like it.

She huffed out a breath and pushed to her feet. "Quit poli-ticking me."

"Quit oversimplifying the situation to make it suit you," he retorted. He rose with her, towering over her. "There is no one who is entirely innocent here, but also no one who is entirely to blame. The nuances aren't mere inconveniences; they are vital to understanding the true meaning of the problem."

Which he'd been unsuccessful at discussing with any of the heads of state on Earth who would see him. America, espe-cially, was stubborn in its need to have a clear right or wrong, winner or loser, black or white. It bespoke a young culture, not yet matured to a full grasp of their own place in the order of things.

"You can do all the detailed navel-gazing you want, but don't miss the big picture . . . lives are at stake. Your people's, my people's. People have died and more are going to die unless we do something. You get to run off into space whenever Kyber finds his soul mate or whatever, but you leaving won't solve the problem. Not anymore. Arthur will still be in power after you're gone, and he's not going to give up that power without a fight. And again—the big picture—that means inno-cent people will die." She sighed, crossing her arms and draw-ing his gaze to her breasts. He could see the outline of her nipples through her shirt and his cock rose in eager response. She closed her eyes and shook her head. "I don't . . . think you brought this on yourselves. It's just that, as a soldier, it's never a good thing to think too long or too hard about the damage you do to the enemy. You have to have some emotional distance from that or it'll make you crazy. You don't survive in the military long if you can't make that separation between *us* and *them*."

"You've survived as a warrior a long time, haven't you?" He'd wager a great deal that she'd never had to struggle with this kind of gray area before, and he hated seeing the distress reflected in her expression.

"My entire adult life." She nodded, eyes the color of the bluest ocean on Suen moving over his face. She looked so lost, nothing like the hardened soldier he knew her to be. He reached for her, wanting to protect her from this pain, but she flinched away. "Don't. I can't stand it when you touch me. It makes me want things I won't do again. I'm not sure I can hold out if you put your hands on me."

It shook him that she confessed such a thing to him, made herself vulnerable, and gave him information he could use against her. The beast within him grappled for control, willing to take whatever she offered. His muscles tightened as he fought his conflicting urges. The man wanted to run as fast as he could from the sweetness of her vulnerability because he liked it too much, and the more he learned of her, the more he liked her. Not good. Not good at all.

The man won the struggle and he forced himself to step back out of arm's reach. He needed to get away from here, from her, before he gave into the feline's desire to convince her how often what they'd done the night before would happen again. And again.

"You lost your weapon in the river, yes?" He pulled the razer out its holster and tossed it to her.

She caught it but gave him a questioning glance. "Unfortunately."

"Keep my razer with you." He jerked his shirt over his head, folded it in precise quarters, and set it on the ground.

"Wh-what are you doing?" Her fingers tightened on the

gun, but her gaze locked on his bare chest, a throb of pure want passing from her to him and shredding his tenuous grasp on his self-discipline.

He unfastened his pants, shoving them down and stepping out of his boots at the same time as he pulled his legs free of his clothing. "Undressing."

"Why?" Her gaze dropped to his hard dick, her lips parting. A pulse of her desire hit all his senses at once. The scent of her wetness, the need trickling through the mental connection he hadn't been able to let go of entirely after they'd made love.

He was so close to dragging her to the ground whether she was willing to admit she wanted him or not that his hands shook. That kind of abandoning of self-restraint was his worst nightmare realized, was a step toward the kind of disaster that had claimed the entire Arjun line—everyone he had loved the most.

Rolling his shoulders forward, he stooped to let the beast within loose. A low buzz filled his ears, his psychic power melding and shifting with the feral instincts. White and black fur crisscrossed his arms in stripes. Dirt shoved under his claws as he hit the ground. His body twisted, his bones popped, and some of his muscles tightened while others loosened as he re-formed into a feline.

He hissed, shaking from head to tail as he settled into the new shape. Turning on his haunches, he launched himself into the waiting brush. He sent Bren a final thought to answer her question. *I am hunting. You wanted food, yes?*

An hour later, Bren checked the waterproof watch strapped to her wrist for the twelfth time. Her body still scraped, bruised, and aching from the wild river ride and hours of hiking, she sat alone beside a small fire. She'd used the driest wood she could find to keep the smoke to a minimum. No need to advertise their location. A headache throbbed at her temples, hunger gnawing at her gut. She'd found some berries to eat, but other than that she was going to have to wait for Farid to return. If he did. She closed her eyes. At this point, she wasn't sure what she'd do if he didn't come back. He'd been her only plan, and a half-baked one at that.

If Emperor Kyber wouldn't help her, she had no idea who else to turn to or how to get the whole world out of a pile of shit that was hip deep and only going to get messier from here. She didn't even know how they were going to get to the emperor's ship with Farid's shuttle gone. How long would it take for his people to come looking for him? Would Farid and she be able to evade Arthur's men long enough for them to hook up with the Sueni rescue party? So many complications, so many ways everything could and probably would go wrong.

She pulled in a deep breath, forcing herself to remain calm. This plan would work. It had to. People who didn't even know the danger they were in yet were counting on her.

God, she was tired. Her eyes were gritty, her body heavy and sluggish. A chill mountain breeze whipped through her clothes, and she stretched her hands toward the fire for warmth. Farid's razer lay across her lap, within easy reach. She needed sleep, but she couldn't let her guard down while Farid was gone. Hell, she wasn't even sure she could let her guard down while he was with her. A shiver ran down her skin, and she did her best to squelch it. She was too old to be this twitterpated over a guy—the better part of two decades dating military men should have cured her of any illusions she had left about them.

He'd seen the opportunity to fuck her and he'd taken it. She hadn't done a damn thing to resist him. The power of it still shook her, scared her, and pissed her off even more. At him and at herself. She shouldn't have wanted it so much, but they both clearly had, and their lack of focus had almost gotten them both killed. More than *their* lives were at stake here, so they couldn't afford to lose it again. This was one mission that could not fail. She wouldn't let her sacrifice of everything she'd ever worked for be in vain.

A twig snapped to her left, and she had his gun in her hand before the feline Farid broke through the trees. His black-and-white-striped fur made him stand out in stark contrast to the rich brown earth and deep green leaves of the forest around them. He didn't belong here. Alien.

Two rabbits hung from his mouth, blood dripping from his fangs. His gaze locked on her in that unsettling way only cats could manage. Her heart tripped and then raced. She felt trapped, hunted. Swallowing, she fought the urge to flee and slid his razer into her ankle holster. It was an awkward fit, but it stayed, and she felt better for having the weapon. Then she lifted her chin to stare back at him. The feral side of his nature shone from his eyes, and they gleamed like mirrors when the firelight hit them.

He approached her and dropped the rabbits at her feet. *Take care of these, if you would.*

The smooth, polite voice in her head was so at odds with the wildness she saw before her. She swallowed. "I wasn't sure you'd come back."

He tilted his head, a subtle tension running through his muscles. *I said I was hunting for your food. Would I not have to return to give it to you?*

His tone made her insides twinge with guilt. Clenching her teeth, she fisted her fingers in the legs of her jeans. His feelings were of no concern to her. "Why don't you go wash up in the stream? I'll get the food ready."

Fine. The betrayed timbre turned icy and clipped, and she knew he was not happy with her.

It shouldn't have bothered her. She shouldn't *want* to make the man happy, but she couldn't deny—at least to herself—that it disturbed her.

Considering he'd been her enemy only hours before, she had no real reason to trust him. Getting rid of Arthur was a benefit to him, and she wasn't going to fool herself by thinking that a little sex, mental or physical, would change that he and his emperor would keep her around only as long as she was useful in achieving their aim. They'd said they were here to get a woman, a very specific woman that they hadn't found yet. She could only pray that wasn't a lie and that she wasn't handing her planet over to a worse fate than Arthur had in mind for it. However, if they were lying, why hadn't they attacked yet? Or counterattacked after Arthur had brought one of the Sueni ships down?

Her headache gave an especially vicious throb, so she gave up on going over what she'd already been over a million times.

When she looked up, he was gone, splashing into the brook to wash the crimson stains away. She shook her head and dealt with the rabbits, refusing to admit how deep her relief was that he'd returned safely. He was just her ticket to getting help from Kyber.

It wasn't personal.

4
_____

"So, does every Kith have a One?" Bren's question shook Farid out of his hypnotic stupor. They sat staring at the rabbits roasting on a makeshift spit over the warm fire. He stretched his paws toward the small blaze, sheer feline lassitude sapping his will to move.

He rested his chin on his forelegs. *Why the sudden curiosity?*

"Just making conversation. Small talk." She shrugged. "You're the politician, isn't that what you do for a living?"

Prickly as always. He snorted. It was unfortunate for him that he liked her acerbic bluntness as much as he liked the unexpected flashes of sweetness and vulnerability. *No, not everyone has a One. They are seen as a great blessing from fate in my culture. Not only do you have someone whose mind is linked forever in perfect sync with yours, but children of such a couple are often more powerful than both parents. Something about the bond produces better offspring and more psychic power raises the prestige of a house.*

"Not everyone has one, but everybody wants one? Or *a* One, in this case." Plucking up a little twig, she twirled it between her fingers. She smiled and shook her head. "Fate is kind of a bitch in your culture. It's all about the haves and the have nots. Kith have cool powers, Kin don't. Some people have Ones, some don't. I like that in America, I get to choose my own fate. That way, if it all goes to pot, I have no one to be mad at but myself."

Speaking of Ones with his One was unsettling. Anticipation and uneasiness skittered through him. He pushed himself upright, shifted back into his human form, and moved to sit cross-legged on a smooth, flat rock by the fire. She watched him, but other than the barest shimmer of awareness passing through their link, she gave no indication that she even noticed his nudity.

He cleared his throat and avoided her comments about Ones altogether. "It's unsurprising that a woman raised in a democratic society where anyone can hope to attain the highest ranks of society—regardless of true ability to rule—would think that way, but my people believe fate gives us the power and ability we need for the social class we were born into.

"Children with the highest ability in each family become heir to that house. Each heir is taken to the royal vizier and tested, their destiny foretold. The most powerful boy or girl is then trained to ready them for the rigors of the throne, and their house becomes the royal house. Typically, the throne remains in the direct imperial line, but not always. Destiny can occasionally reshuffle the power structure of the Sueni houses, but the emperor is *always* the most powerful, and thus he rules all the houses."

He didn't say that sometimes a child would have the power, but not the restraint and fortitude to control their abilities. Cilji, as sweet and kind as she had been, and as much as he and his family had adored her, had been one who couldn't contain her power, neither her psychic abilities nor her animal nature. Her One had been as bad or worse. Yet another reason not to lose himself to that kind of bond. He sighed, hoping Tylara didn't suffer Cilji's fate with her own Sajan male. That family was well known for their passionate outbursts and unstable powers.

"With the whole power and testing thing, will it matter that the emperor's One is a human?" Bren tilted her head, and her braid slipped over her shoulder to dangle between her ripe breasts. "Or is that cancelled out by the One bond making better children?"

He shrugged, hypnotized by the movement of that thick plait instead of the dancing flames. "Only the viziers could tell."

Her voice went so soft, even his sensitive ears had to strain to hear her. "Did the viziers tell you you'd have a One?"

"No." It was the truth. The prophets had only said that he would lead the Arjun house, anything else was hidden from their sight. Unfortunate for him, on so many levels.

"So you might not have a One?" The almost hopeful tinge to her question made his belly knot and his gaze snap up to examine her face.

His hands clenched into fists, and he found he couldn't lie to her, but he also couldn't tell her the whole truth. "I know I do."

"Congratulations." She swallowed, her face wiping of all expression. "Since it's such a blessing in your culture."

"You don't think it would be for you?" Everything inside him froze as he waited for her answer. He knew it shouldn't matter, but it did.

"Having my mind no longer be *all mine* ever again? Being bound to someone forever?" Her eyes popped wide, something close to panic flashing in their ocean blue depths. "I can't think of anything more horrifying."

"I know exactly what you mean." They were probably the most honest words he'd ever said to anyone in his life.

Surprise flittered over her face before she looked at the fire again. She tossed the little twig she'd been playing with into the flames. "But . . . I thought you had a One?"

He stared at her, wondering if it would be easier to resist this pull she had on him now that he knew she was appalled by the very idea of the One bond. He hoped so. A smile quirked one side of his mouth. They were more alike than either of them would ever admit. Perhaps he owed her the truth about his motives, if he couldn't give her what most Sueni craved so much. At the very least, if she ever found out the truth, she would understand why he'd never bond with her.

"The One bond killed my family." He pushed his fingers through his hair. "Not long after I came of age."

"I'm sorry. My family died when I was a small child. I never really knew them." Her gaze met his, her voice soft. "Do all Ones go together, then?"

"No, a person can live after their One dies." He hadn't spoken of his family in years. Their loss was a wound that refused to heal, one he'd learned to live with, to ignore, but coming to Earth, meeting his One, had ripped it open and forced him to acknowledge it again, to admit how much it had shaped him and the choices he'd made in his life. How it had taught him to deny what others only dreamed of finding.

He closed his eyes for a moment. Discussing this was harder than he'd ever imagined. "My mother was a doctor who worked with those whose power was erratic. My father always thought it was too dangerous, but she was determined, and she was good at her work. The best. But . . . Father wasn't wrong. Her work was dangerous, and one day the danger caught up with her. A very high-powered Kith male, Eetash Sajan, lost control during a session and rampaged. Neither of them survived the encounter."

"Oh, my God." Her fingers splayed as though to reach for him. He felt a throb of her sympathy through the bond he'd narrowed to a mere filament.

It was almost his undoing, but now that he'd started he needed to finish, needed her to know all of it. She deserved at least that much.

He clenched his fists and plunged on with the twisted tale. "Father didn't last the week. He got his affairs in order, turned everything over to me, including guardianship of my younger sister, and then he slit his wrists in bed one night. The servants found him the next morning with a smile on his face."

"Jesus." He heard her swallow. "He knew he was going with her."

He stared into the fire, unable to look at her. "Yes."

He hoped that his father was right, that his parents were together now. They had loved each other dearly, and that love had sustained his family. He and Cilji had been lost without it. Its demise was what led his sister to her own end. Living without it was more than his father had been able to bear. Everything shattered and broken . . . by love. He closed his eyes. "That left just my sister Cilji and me in the Arjun house. She . . . was an incredibly gifted Kith. Powerful. Almost too powerful."

Bren leaned toward him, the end of her braid trailing perilously close to the fire. "More powerful than you?"

"Oh, definitely." He chuckled, a rare moment of lightness when he thought of his family. "She delighted in holding it over me, too."

"More powerful than the emperor?"

He hesitated. "Possibly."

"And that was a problem?" Her eyebrows arched.

"Socially? Not really." He brushed his hands down his naked thighs, shifting his weight on the hard stone. "My mother was Kyber's aunt, so we're close enough in relation to the throne that it wouldn't have been surprising."

She didn't seem surprised that he was the emperor's cousin, though the two of them bore little resemblance to one another. They both looked like their fathers. Bren's forehead wrinkled as she considered this new information. "Shouldn't Cilji have been the empress if she was the most powerful?"

"No. She wasn't in control enough." He shook his head. Therein lay the problem—the final seal to Cilji's fate, the reason Farid felt the need to *always* be in control. Not that that seemed to spare him where Bren was concerned.

"She was unstable? Mentally?" She tucked a stray wisp of hair behind her ear. "Or . . . like the people your mother worked with?"

"My mother's interest in her field started with Cilji's problems as a child. She'd improved a great deal, but when our parents died, she slipped beyond my abilities to help." He struggled to draw breath, pain streaking through him at his own helplessness. Laying this bare was like dosing the wound with acid. "I'd hoped when she found her One, it would help her regain control, balance her out. If he was in control, even if he had lesser powers, it could have anchored her. In fact, at the time, I thought it would be preferable if he had fewer powers."

"It wasn't?"

Each beat of his heart was a heavy thud, and his throat closed. He had to clear it twice before he could speak. "Her One was Eetash Sajan's twin brother." He swallowed. "No good has ever come of that family. Barely more than animals, some of them."

"It sounds like she and her One probably shouldn't have bonded." She drew in a deep breath that lifted her breasts.

Anun, but he'd rather have his hands on her soft curves than continue this story. "No, they shouldn't have. But it would take a great deal of control to stop it."

"And she had none."

"Very little." He closed his eyes, praying that someday he could think of this and not feel as though he were drowning. "But her One . . . blamed my mother for his twin's death, said the Arjun family was responsible."

"Oh, shit." Bren rose to her haunches, her whole body tensing.

"Yet, he wanted my sister. How can anyone not want their One?" His hands lifted, his fingers spreading. "He wasn't certain they should bond, though. She was an Arjun, and his grief made him even more unstable than he might have been normally. It was a toxic combination."

He looked away, still unable to believe how quickly his family had gone from whole and happy to shattered, broken, and on its knees. "Cilji bonded with him anyway. Against his will. She was vastly more powerful than he was, and she couldn't control it. She just . . . needed her One. It's what the Kith were made for. She loved him and thought bonding with him would change his mind about . . ."

"About blaming your family?"

"Anun, why?" He covered his eyes with his hand. "How could she do such a thing? It violates one of the oldest tenets of Sueni law." Twenty years later and he still couldn't fathom it. He'd loved his sister so much, but he would never understand what she'd done. Meeting Bren had only made what Cilji had done more abhorrent to Farid. "Sajan was . . . very angry about her bonding with him without his consent."

"Understandable." Bren gave in to whatever internal struggle she'd been having, rose, and walked over to his side of the fire to kneel beside him. She didn't touch him, and for that he was grateful. "Did he hurt her?"

"Not in the way you're thinking. He brought no physical harm to her." He swallowed but couldn't meet her eyes, couldn't bear to know if she condemned his sister or forgave her for her crimes. He still wasn't sure which he felt most. Nuances, as he'd told Bren, were the key to understanding. But love muddied all of it for him. "Cilji should never have bonded with him against his will, no matter how powerful she was. If she couldn't control herself with him, she should never have touched him, should have removed herself from the situation. I would have helped her in any way I could."

Bren's tone was neutral. "She didn't ask."

It wasn't a question, but he answered it anyway. "She was impetuous. Impulsive. Wonderful and funny and sweet."

"She was your baby sister." There was the slightest bit of wistfulness in her voice, reminding him that she had never known any family of her own. Which was preferable? To have had it and lost it like he had, or to have never known it at all? He couldn't say.

But a smile curved his lips when he thought of Cilji. She had been like a comet that had burned too brightly and was gone too soon. "She was, and I loved her dearly." His smile faded as the old guilt stabbed at his soul. "My parents expected me to protect her."

"You can't save someone from themselves." Bren's fingers brushed over his shoulder.

"No. No, you can't." He certainly hadn't been able to save his father. Or his sister. He wasn't even going to be able to save Tylara. Another one lost to the Sajans . . . to love . . . to the One bond. Everything came back to that, no matter how he might run it around and around in his head. No matter how much he might like and desire Bren, he could never find a way around the simple fact that he would lose his One someday as he had lost everyone else. And he knew he'd never survive it with his sanity intact. He would be as his father had been. Lost, bereft, empty. Nothing.

He heard Bren swallow, sensed her hesitation. "If Sajan didn't hurt her, how did Cilji die?"

"She killed herself." His voice went bleak, flat. "He was angry, he went back to the wild, erratic ways of his family and left her behind. He betrayed her with other women, many of them, trying to rip free of the bonds between them."

Her hand squeezed his arm. "It didn't work?"

"No, a bonding can never be undone. Only death will free you, if that's what you want." He leaned into her touch, some deep, unspeakable part of him craving the comfort she offered.

She stroked her fingers down his bicep, petting him. "So she killed herself to be free of him."

"Yes, but he couldn't live without her." His body reacted predictably to even her most innocent caress and he had to force himself to focus. "They were bonded whether he wanted it or not, no matter what psychic walls he might have built in his mind to defend himself again her."

"He committed suicide, too?"

His lust died as renewed rage fisted in his belly. "Yes, and he's lucky he did."

Her voice was as flat and cold as Farid's. "You were going to kill him."

"I wouldn't have made it the fast, painless exit he ensured for himself." He snarled, the beast unappeased about the loss of one of its own. "I wanted to *see* him eaten alive from the inside out the way she had been. Whatever she had done, she didn't deserve that."

"I'm sorry." Both of her hands cupped his cheeks, turning his face toward her. "Jesus, I'm so sorry, Arjun."

"Call me Farid." Anun, he needed her now. Snapping his hands around her waist, he pulled her into his lap and brushed his lips over hers.

She caught his shoulders as her legs straddled his, her jeans abrasive against his naked thighs. A dart of excitement shot from her to him, and he could smell how her body readied itself for him. "I don't think—"

Smothering her protest with his mouth, he kissed her again, hungry for her after that one small taste. His cock hardened at the feel of her soft curves pressed to him. He moved his lips over hers until she moaned, until her fingers dug into his shoulders, until she arched and writhed against him.

He craved the taste of her, the scent of her, the feel of her. It was an ecstasy that went beyond the physical. Touching her was as close to divinity as he'd ever been. He reveled in the carnality of it as much as he did connecting with her psychically. It was the one time she was open to him, and the one time he allowed himself to bury himself within her in every possible way. The feline purred as her hand stroked down his back, hissed against her lips as her nails raked back up his flesh. *"Yesss."*

His fingers balled in the back of her T-shirt, jerking it out of her pants. Slipping his hands over her supple skin, he flicked open her bra and ran his palms up and down the length of her spine. She threw her head back and he bit her slim throat. A gasp slid from her, and she rocked her hips against his. The rough friction of her pants on his cock made him snarl, but he arched himself into each of her movements. He tugged on the bottom of her shirt and she helped him take it and her bra off. He brushed a kiss over a dark bruise on her ribs, likely from a collision with a boulder in the river. She sighed, closed her eyes, and bit her lip. Then his hands were on her breasts, cupping them so he could suck the nipples one at a time.

Her breath tangled in her throat when he flicked his tongue over each taut peak in turn, and she sank her fingertips into his shoulders, clutching him closer. "Oh, oh, *oh*."

Sweat broke out across his forehead, sliding down his temples. He flicked open the fastening on her pants, gliding his hand inside the coarse denim, inside the soft panties, and inside the slick heat of her pussy. He groaned, delving in to stroke her blooming clit. She jolted, bucking her hips frantically. Her need careened into him through their link, breaking it further open than he'd ever allowed it before. He pulled his hand from her hot slit, and she shook her head in silent protest.

Bracketing her slim hips with his hands, he lifted her to set her on her feet. She swayed, looking dazed as she stared down at him. "Wh—"

Hooking his fingers into her belt loops, he pulled her pants down. Her underwear slid along with the jeans, and he had her back in his lap before she could blink, working the rest of her clothes off. Soon she was as naked as he was. It was the first time they'd been nude together outside of their shared dreams. He groaned, the reality more intense than he could ever have imagined. Lifting her, he set her astride him once more, only this time he faced her away from him. She pulled her braid off her shoulder so it wasn't pinned between them, tilting her head to give him access to her neck. He gently kissed a scrape on her shoulder, then licked a slow path from her nape to her ear, sucking the lobe into his mouth. She wriggled against him, and he groaned at all that soft, bare skin sliding over his.

She reached between her thighs and wrapped her fingers around his dick to tease both of them by rubbing the flared crest over her wet lips and clit. Gritting his teeth, he felt his fangs elongate, the beast more than willing to take whatever its mate offered and then some. The mate who would never truly belong to it. He grabbed her hand and both of them held his cock, guiding him to her heated channel. He filled her, her walls tight and so slick around him he had to hold on to his control with every ounce of his concentration to keep from coming the moment she'd taken all of him into her pussy.

Palming her breasts as she began to move on him, he rolled her nipples between his fingers and scraped the tight tips with his claws.

"Yes, *yes*. Oh, my God!" She leaned forward, closed her hands over his bent knees, and shoved her hips back into his upward strokes. Her nails dug into his flesh, her legs squeezing his thighs as she rode him. "Fuck me harder!"

He laughed, he couldn't help himself. Anun, he liked this woman so much.

Pulling her upright, he dragged his claws up her sides and made her shriek and giggle. He clamped his teeth on the back of her neck to hold her in place, giving her what she asked for and slamming into her sweet depths. She moaned, "Oh, God. You're—"

He rolled his fingers over her clit, and she gasped and tightened her sex around his cock. He released her nape and snarled, hammered himself inside of her, and drove them both to the brink of madness. His feral nature reveled in the unfettered race for orgasm. She slipped her fingers down his forearms until they both stroked her clit. Her backside spanked against his belly, and the impact of his flesh meeting hers with each thrust was erotic.

She glanced over her shoulder at him, her eyes hazy with passion. Her tongue flicked out to lick her lips, and he followed the motion, then mimicked it as he moved to slide his tongue over her soft, sweet lips. Sweat sealed their bodies together, and she twisted her torso to meet his mouth and his cock. He shuddered. Everything about her made him burn.

Her cries and moans filled his mouth, spurring him on to thrust harder, deeper. It was the headiest aphrodisiac he'd ever known, and he felt her pussy tighten on his cock every time he entered her. She broke away from his mouth to sob for breath, and he could feel through their link how close she was to orgasm.

Their desire raged along their connection, pushing each other higher, further. Their fingers meshed as they rubbed her clit faster and faster. Her head fell back against his shoulder, her body bowing as her excitement grew. "I'm going to—"

"Come for me, *khalaa.*"

She screamed, her sex clenching on his dick. She bucked and writhed like a wild thing, demanding everything he had. The beast answered the call of its mate. His control snapped, and he roared, his fangs erupting from his gums. He drove his cock into her, again and again, as she came apart in his arms. Her sex spasmed around him, and he crashed into his own orgasm full-force. His come jetted into her, and shudders wracked his body, dragging everything out of him until he could do nothing else but drop his forehead to her shoulder with a groan.

This wasn't what he'd intended when he'd told her why he could never bond with his One. He craved her too deeply. Her hands on his skin and her taste in his mouth could become an addiction if he allowed it. It was dangerous that her lust could drive their link further open than he'd ever intended.

The woman was a nightmare for his restraint.

5

The man was a nightmare for her restraint.

She jerked on her clothes as fast as she could, retreated to her side of the fire, and refused to meet his gaze or speak to him. He seemed just as content not to speak to her, and their connection had narrowed to a thread, for which she was grateful. Her desire for him was a weakness she couldn't afford. And she'd given him whatever he wanted twice now. Twice. What the hell was *wrong* with her? As she'd told him, this wasn't what she'd come to him for.

Still, the look on his face when he'd told her about his family had wrenched at something deep inside her. She couldn't have denied him anything at that point, and that scared her to death. His loneliness and pain had filtered through to her mind as surely as his pleasure did during sex. She knew those emotions, too, her own past as ugly as his. It was odd that she would have anything in common with an alien nobleman.

Shoving that disturbing thought away, she pulled out her pocketknife and sliced into the rabbit to test if it was done. It was. Tearing off a strip of meat, she blew on it and juggled it back and forth between her hands until it cooled enough to eat. She sighed when it hit her taste buds. God, it was good. Her stomach rumbled as it demanded more. She cut off another chunk, reaching over to give it to Farid. His callused fingers scraped her skin as he accepted the offering. She shivered and jerked back. Moving as quickly as she could, she divided the sizzling meat between them and inhaled it.

"Since I'm the politician and my job is idle small talk, perhaps I should start the conversation this time." His deep voice slid over her nerves like rough velvet. "I can feel that you're upset about what we did."

She flipped her braid over her shoulder. It would be better to rip the bandage off and get this over with. She met his gaze. "What happened just now . . . That will never happen again."

His nostrils flared as sudden anger coursed through their slender link. Those green eyes narrowed, and she saw a flash of fangs as his lips moved. "If that is truly your desire."

"It is." She nodded for emphasis, her chin firming.

A low hiss jerked from his throat and she watched his hold on his temper slip. "Liar."

She glared at him, his anger feeding hers, pushing it to irrational levels. Her heart rate elevated, and her breathing sped as she braced for a fight. "Fuck you."

"We seem to be circling our discussion." He gave her a cool smile that only pissed her off more.

Her sympathy for his sad past evaporated for the moment. She growled at him, her grip on her knife tightening as she seriously considered skinning his feline hide.

Smirking, he looked her over slowly, staring at her breasts. "That was a noise worthy of a Kith, little Kinswoman."

"I am not a Kith or a Kin." She slashed her hand through the air. "I'm human."

"Call yourself whatever you like, but long before you'd developed dialects of your own, you were Kin." He dipped one shoulder in a shrug. "You are, perhaps, best labeled as an Earthan Kin. Sueni Kin are much different, culturally, than you are. Biologically, however, you are the same."

"Thanks for the science lesson. Class is over, so why don't we finish the food and agree to disagree?" She made her tone overly reasonable, and he hissed at her. She got a perverse satisfaction out of the fact that she could ignite his temper as quickly as he could hers.

In seething silence, they finished their meal. Despite their skirmish, she couldn't help but enjoy the roasted rabbit. When the last bit of flavor burst over her tongue, she moaned low in her throat and pressed a hand to her belly. It had never felt so good to be full. She folded her knife, stowed it in her pocket, licked her lips, sat back, and glanced at Farid for the first time since they'd stopped arguing.

Heat reflected in his gaze, burning through her. He sprawled with feline grace over the flat rock they'd fucked on, his position emphasizing his naked beauty. His cock rose in a hard curve to just under his navel. *You made the same pleasured noise when I slid my cock in you, Bren.*

"Lord Arjun." Her tone was a low warning, just a bit breathier than she would have liked. She jerked to her feet and he rose with her, moving to her side of the fire.

His big hand bracketed her chin, forcing her to meet his gaze. Even that simple touch made her muscles shake, and desire battered against her control. He stared at her lips, his pale gaze taking on that intent look men got right before they kissed a woman. "Call me Farid."

"No." She swallowed back the sigh that wanted to bubble up, her focus locking on his erection. Heat shot through her, arrowing between her legs until she had to squeeze her thighs together.

"Call me Farid or I'll fill your mind with all your fantasies of me until you come." His thumb brushed over her lower lip.

"We both know I won't even have to touch you to make it happen."

He was right. God, he was right. Standing this close to his naked body, having him touch her, made her want to come on command. He was gorgeous—bigger and more devastating than in her dreams. She jerked her chin from his grasp but couldn't keep her gaze from traveling over his nude form, and fire whipped through her. The man had a body to die for. A few cuts and bruises from their adventures marred his physical perfection, but nothing could really detract from his gorgeousness. His dark blond hair was short, framing a sharp, angular face, a patrician nose, full, firm lips, and otherworldly emerald eyes that sparked pastel green fireworks. His shoulders were broad, heavy with muscle, tapering to well-defined pecs and rock-hard abs. A slim line of pale hair trailed from just below his navel to his thick, impressive cock. Her fingers twitched, itching to touch him, stroke him.

It was insane. What was she doing? Staring at him, practically inviting him to do whatever he wanted to her with her silence when she'd already decided *nothing* else would happen between them. A good offense was the best defense, so she narrowed her eyes at him. "Raping my mind is not the way to keep me from killing you."

He laughed at her, damn him. "What is that saying you Earthan Kin have? Ah, yes. 'You can't rape the willing.' I don't force you to fantasize about me; I would merely be bringing those fantasies to the fore of your thoughts."

"Slippery logic at best," she spat.

"Perhaps." His lips formed a thoughtful moue as though he considered something weighty. "Then perhaps I'll just kiss you. I could sense how much you liked it the first time, how you'd been wondering what it would feel like."

She snarled, angry at him for making her want him so much. It was always that way with him. He confused her, spun her around and around until she didn't know which way was up or what was right and what was wrong. Flames licked at her flesh, desire spiraling tighter and tighter inside her until she wanted to beg for some relief. She couldn't do this. She had a mission and it didn't include being a cold nobleman's fuck buddy, no matter how painfully heartbreaking his past. She hated that his past even mattered to her because she knew it shouldn't affect her at all. Her fists clenched at her sides and she glared at him. "I will kick your ass."

"Some things are worth a little pain." His gaze scorched her as it passed over her body. Her nipples tightened until they had to be sticking out against her shirt. She couldn't look. She didn't want to confirm how quickly he got to her.

His arm snapped out, wrapped around her waist, and yanked her forward until she tumbled against his broad chest. "Damn you, Arjun. I—"

He filled her mouth with his tongue, ending the conversation. This time he wasn't gentle, but demanding, commanding. It excited her far more than she could ever admit. He held her so tight she had difficulty breathing, and she didn't care. One hand slid down to cup her backside, lifting her into him as he ground his erection against her. She could feel the heat of his cock through her clothing and wanted nothing between her and it, wanted him inside her, moving hard and fast. His other hand moved to her breast, filling his broad palm with her softer curve. He pinched her nipple, twisting with delicate precision.

A cry caught in her throat, her arms twined around his waist, and she let her tongue slide against his. They nipped, sucked, and bit at each other, low groans spilling from them both. She glided her palms up the muscled planes of his back. Something else that contradicted the cool politician he showed the world. He should have been soft, but instead had steely strength, should have been weak, but instead was just short of feral in her embrace. His flesh was hot under her touch, and she knew he burned with the same heat that threatened to engulf her, made her pussy tighten and dampen.

Rough shudders went through him, and he plundered her mouth, his fangs scraping her lower lip. Her fingers clenched over his shoulders, clutching him closer. God, it inundated her, swept her under until there was nothing left but him. His taste, his scent, his touch on her skin. She wanted, she needed. Now. Right now.

The sweet ecstasy tempted her into losing control, losing everything but this moment in his arms. Her hands threaded through his hair, tugging on the strands as her passion peaked. She bit his lip hard, and he hissed low in his throat, the sound nothing short of animalistic. She pressed herself into his palm, and his thumb stroked in lazy circles around her nipple until she wanted to scream.

His deep voice flooded her mind, his mouth still playing over hers with an expertise that made her toes curl in her boots. *Give in to me, khalaa. Give me everything. I want all of you.*

The words jolted her out of the spell he'd woven around her. Panic arced through her system. Losing herself to the pleasure, to *anything*, wasn't acceptable. It was weak, and she'd sworn to herself long ago to *never* be weak. She couldn't do this. She couldn't *do* this. Not again. She had to get away from this frightening, consuming desperation. She had to escape him, escape herself. A harsh whimper burst from her throat and she brought her knee up hard, catching him in the balls.

A bestial groan of pain ripped from him, and she shoved him away. He hit the ground hard and she didn't wait to see if he was all right, she spun on her heel and ran. At this point, she didn't think of Arthur or Earth or anything bigger or nobler than herself. Nothing else mattered but getting away from her worst fear—letting someone close enough to truly need them. Farid could make her need that badly, and she couldn't have that. Not ever.

Nearly two decades of daily PT meant she could run a hell of a lot farther and faster than most women, and with her own lust riding her heels, she added speed even she didn't know she possessed.

Bren, wait! Farid's voice echoed in her mind, which only made her legs pump harder. Her muscles burned and sweat slid down her face, stinging her eyes.

A blur of color and terrifying speed came at her from the right, and she leaped sideways. Too late. Farid caught her around the waist and dragged her to the ground.

His palm slammed over her mouth, his green eyes fierce and sparking with power. *Be silent. I sense others. Danger is near.*

Her hands closed spasmodically around his upper arms, and she froze underneath him, working to level out her breathing. It was made more difficult by the fact that his long, hard, *naked* body was plastered to hers from chest to groin and he'd somehow ended up between her legs. Twin reactions sparked within her. The well-trained soldier waiting for a possible ambush, and the woman reacting to a man she craved touching her. Sweat beaded on her upper lip and gathered at her temples. Blazing passion and cold fear sent tingles rippling down her skin.

"They'll check the fire first. Let's get out of here." She pulled his hand away from her mouth and lifted her head to breathe the words in his ear. He shuddered, thrusting himself into the juncture of her thighs. Need screamed through her and she dug her nails into his biceps.

His gaze snapped up, looking at something she had to twist her head around to see. Power flashed in his eyes, a deep, terrifying hiss issuing from his mouth. Fangs bared, he jerked away and rolled to his feet in one smooth motion. She pushed herself upright less steadily, surreptitiously sliding his weapon out of her holster. A soldier in army camo stood with a submachine gun pointed at them. Her heart lurched. The kid couldn't be more than about twenty. Another of her worst nightmares realized, having to face and maybe kill one of her own.

"Drop your weapon, put your hands on your head, and get down on the ground," the boy barked. "Now!"

Farid flexed his clawed fingers and hissed. The soldier's weapon went right to him, and she knew if she left it to them, someone was going to die here. She'd rather that not happen. Her heart pounded, but she ignored it, reaching for that battle calm, that place where the adrenaline only enhanced her reactions.

She shifted her weight to drop to a crouch, sweeping one leg out to catch Farid behind the knees and knock him to the ground. Firing a quick shot with aim honed from long years of practice, she put a laser round in the soldier's bulletproof vest. He slammed back against a tree, shook as though he'd touched a live wire, slumped over, and lost his grip on his gun. He didn't stay down though. When he went for the weapon at his belt, she spoke. "Don't. I don't want to kill you, but I will if I have to."

"Fuck you, traitor." He grabbed his pistol and pulled the trigger. Bren dove left but knew she'd be too damn late to get out of the way.

Farid moved with that stunning speed of his, threw himself to the side, propelled her forward, and hissed when the bullet sliced into his arm. Blood sprayed over the ground and across green bushes, painting them in hideous rust red. Still, Farid *leaped* and had the kid by the throat, off his feet, and flattened against the tree in the time it took her to blink. The small, round disc of the white noisemaker fell from the soldier's grasp without turning on. The soldier gagged, clawing at Farid's iron grip. Farid shoved his face into the younger man's. The voice that emerged from his throat was more animal growl than human speech. "Speak to her that way again, and I will tear your limbs off one by one."

"Put him *down*, Arjun!" She barked out the words in the same tone of command she'd have used with a private fresh out of basic training, one she hoped would break through the feral beast to the logical man beneath. Her heart slammed against her ribs, her muscles shaking as her hand wavered from pointing the razer at the soldier to pointing it at the Kith. Fear coursed like ice through her veins, but she kept her voice firm. "*Now*, damn it!"

"Drop the weapon, Sergeant Major." Another soldier, older and obviously more experienced, slid from behind a nearby boulder. He clicked a white noise maker and tossed it to the forest floor near Farid. The Kith screamed, the sound of a big cat in pain. If anything, his grip on the young soldier tightened.

Bren focused on this new threat. The one with a gun pointed at her. Oh, God. She knew this man. "Zielinski."

His eyes were like shards of ice when he glared at her. "Always going out alone, Preston. Never a real team player. This time, it bit you in the ass."

Everything about this man was regulation army, from his high and tight haircut to his perfectly organized utility belt. Zielinski was probably the only soldier in the U.S. Army more anal than Bren. Until yesterday. If she had been Arthur's right hand, this man was his left. "Don't do this, Zielinski."

He snorted, his gun never wavering. "You're a traitor and an alien's whore, Preston. I'm not listening to a word you say. Now, drop your weapon and tell lover boy over there to let the kid go."

"What Arthur is doing is wrong. Think about it. Why haven't the Sueni attacked us if they're so dangerous? We shot down a ship full of their people and they didn't shoot back." She didn't know why it was so desperately important to convince this man, to not be the only one out on this limb, but she kept talking anyway. "How many humans have you been ordered to kill lately, Zielinski?" His gaze flickered just a bit, and she knew she was right. Her stomach clenched at how many had already died in this god-awful mess. "If Arthur was so set on *helping* people on Earth, then why would he need you to exterminate them?"

"Shut up. Shut up! I don't want to hear another fucking word out of you, traitor." He pointed his gun directly at her but spoke to Farid. "Drop my man, Lord Arjun, or I'll kill you both. Starting with Preston."

Farid's head whipped around, and the sound he made was pure animal, the deep, rumbling roar of a big cat. The blood drained out of Zielinski's face, and Bren reacted, aimed the razer at the white noise maker and fried the thing. Farid screamed again, and then there was silence. Everything froze, the people, the forest around them. Not a single bird chirped, no bugs buzzed nearby, even the wind seemed to stop as the starbursts in Farid's irises turned to solid green light. Bren felt a wave of white-hot power pulse outward, sending her stumbling back a few steps. Both the soldiers shrieked, grabbing their heads. She heard echoes of more human cries not far from where they stood. A chill ran down her skin as the soldiers slumped over. Farid dropped the boy to the ground, and neither human moved.

The Kith's chest heaved with every breath, sweat running in rivulets down his face and chest. She stared from him to the unconscious humans and back again. Her heart thudded in slow, unnatural beats in her chest. She didn't even know how he'd done what he'd done. She didn't even know *what* he'd done, but it had taken him less that a second to take out every single man who'd hunted them. "If you could . . . Why didn't you do that before?"

"I . . ." His hands shook, his clawed fingers flexed, and his throat worked for a moment before grating words emerged. "It's . . . difficult to cage it . . . once you let it out."

Their eyes met, and the explosion of tangled emotions and needs that broke through her were not all hers. Desire shuddered through her—his and hers. Heat followed in its wake, fisting her sex until she bit her lip to keep from crying out. She could see the evidence of his passion, too. His cock rose in a hard erection, precum dripping down the thick shaft, and she swayed toward him. Wanting.

Her nipples tightened to points, her pussy slicking with juices. Her body was more than ready, willing, to fuck him. How had he done this to her so fast? She could no longer push it to the back of her mind, couldn't ignore it. She pressed her fingers to her temples. "Stop. It. Now."

His gaze flashed with wild green sparks. His voice was ragged with hurt, the usual coldness wiped away. "For the love of Anun, woman, I've done *nothing* to you that you didn't want."

"All those nights—"

He cut her off. "Were *shared* dreams between two *willing* minds. I no more controlled them than you did. If you really think I could ever hurt you, why would you trust me to help you with Arthur? Why me? Why not one of the dozen other Kith you've met? Why not the emperor himself?"

"I . . ."

He hissed at her, fangs bared. He turned away, stalking in the direction of their campfire. She couldn't let him leave, not like this. The pain was too evident, too raw to ignore. It was even worse than when he'd told her about his family. This was a fresh wound, one she'd caused. A tormented man, an injured animal. It should have scared her, the angry beast, but it didn't. Whatever she might doubt about him, she knew he'd never hurt her, no matter which of his forms he was in—or even if he was somewhere in between as he seemed to be now. This side of him called to her in a way the cool, controlled lord never had.

That was what scared her. But it didn't matter. She couldn't let him go when he was hurting, when she'd been responsible for his pain.

She owed him that much. He'd saved her life.

He'd failed.

It twisted through him, a dark ugliness that threatened to drag him under. He could feel the control slipping through his fingers as the feeling ate at him. His cock ached with the desire Bren had awakened in him—even the echo of pain from her kick didn't quell his lust. At the same time, his flesh throbbed around the gunshot wound in an agonizing symphony that ricocheted through his brain. It did nothing to help him hold on to any kind of self-discipline. It also didn't keep the self-recrimination at bay.

He'd failed her, failed to sense the danger, failed to keep himself alert enough to notice they would soon be under attack. He'd let himself be distracted by the hunt for food, let the beast take over. Then beast and man had both been distracted by the old misery of his family's loss and the overwhelming connection with Bren.

It had nearly gotten her murdered. A split second slower and that bullet would have hit her square in the chest. The boy had aimed to kill. A snarl reverberated in his chest, the beast clawing for freedom, wanting to shred the one who'd threatened Bren. The only way to control the feline was to open the floodgates on his psychic power. Maintain the balance by loosing the reins on both.

It shuddered through him like electricity, sizzling and sparking. He held on with the tips of his claws, praying to Anun that his people would come looking soon. It might be another day before they did. He'd gone along with Bren's excuse of a sexual rendezvous, and no one was likely to want to interrupt him unless they were certain something had gone wrong.

Kith never reacted well to harnessing their appetites, especially those as powerful as Farid.

He shook away the thoughts, trying to focus and yet . . . not focus at the same time. He'd likely zero in on the only person still moving besides him. Bren. There was only one logical conclusion to what would happen if he *focused* on her. Bonding, with or without her consent. And he could never let his One that close. To let a One in was to love them, to love them was to lose them. He refused to lose another person he loved, so he would never love again. He had his friends, his distant relatives, and none of them owned a piece of his soul. There was no one he couldn't live without if he had to. Bren wouldn't own his soul, either. He could want her, but he couldn't keep her. He couldn't even *want* to keep her.

So he walked away.

"Arjun, wait!" He heard her footsteps pounding behind him and shot her a fulminating glance over his shoulder. He didn't stop until she ran to plant herself in front of him.

With more effort than he'd ever expended on it before, he retracted his claws, but he doubted he looked anything other than what he was—wild, half-feral. Everything he didn't want to be. Her ocean blue eyes locked on his cock, and he could smell her desire, her lush dampness. He groaned, his hands shaking with the need to touch her.

Her gaze slid up his body, and she froze and swallowed when she reached his arm. He glanced at it and saw how red streaked down his skin. "Jesus, that's a lot of blood. Let me look—"

"I don't care." And the vestiges of his control evaporated. He didn't want to think about how he'd failed to keep them from being set upon by enemies, how she'd nearly been slaughtered before his eyes. He wanted to forget, to be distracted.

The beast was in command now.

His fingers snapped around her wrist, dragging her toward him. He brought her hand up to his lips, swirling his tongue around her palm, biting the soft flesh beneath her thumb. His heart pounded, his breath rushing in pants as the taste of her filled his mouth. It wasn't enough, not nearly enough. He wanted more.

His free hand grabbed the hem of her shirt and wrenched it over her head. He was already at work on her bra when she let her shirt fall. The scraps of lace peeled away just as quickly, landing in a heap on the forest floor. He cupped her small, pert breasts in his palms, running his tongue over an extended fang as he stared at her bare flesh. "Do you want this or don't you?"

He circled her nipples with his fingers, chafed them until they hardened to tiny points, made her gasp in shock. "*Yes.*"

"Good, then don't kick me again." The way her lovely face flushed, her breathing sped, her heart hammered beneath her breast made lust explode with volcanic heat and force inside him. Beads of precum slipped down his cock, he needed her so much.

She shivered, arching herself into his touch, and he could feel any remaining resistance fleeing her mind. It aroused him even more to feel her passion flow toward him through their mental link. Her low moan kissed his ears. "Will those men wake up and find us like this?"

"No, they'll be out for some time. Stop talking." He backed her against a nearby boulder, forcing her torso to bow over the sun-warmed surface. He bent, sucking one nipple and then the other into his mouth until they were ripe and red. His tongue batted the sensitive crest, his fangs scraping her flesh. She wrapped her legs around his waist, rubbing herself against his erection.

A growl vibrated his vocal cords. Anun, he could sense how aroused she was, how hot and wet for him. He wanted inside her and thrust against her sex, stimulating them both until there was nothing left in him but the wildness. He burned for her.

Twining her fingers through his hair, she held him close and arched to push her breast deeper into his mouth.

He groaned and purred in the same breath, his fingertips skimming her ribs lightly, making goose bumps break over her skin. When he shoved her nipple hard against the roof of his mouth, she tugged on the strands of his hair. The sharp pain only fed his pleasure, knowing how much she craved him. She writhed against him. "Please!"

Yes. Yes, he wanted what she wanted. His cock working into her tight pussy once more. He kissed his way down her stomach, his fingers busy unfastening her pants. His teeth nipped at her belly button. "Lift your hips."

She braced her feet against the boulder, leveraging her pelvis up so he could slide her jeans and panties down in one smooth motion. Her boots and the rest of her clothing hit the ground and were kicked aside. His fingers slipped into the thatch of hair that covered her sex, a satisfied grunt rising from him at her slickness. He stroked her clit and her hips rose in quick snaps to meet his hand.

It wasn't enough. He wanted to be inside her, the feline craving that carnal connection. He pulled his fingers away and jerked her legs open, cupping her hips to hold her up. He settled between her legs, pressing her thighs flat to the rock. It was startling, that full-body contact. And so good. His lungs seized, his eyes closing as he savored the moment. Her sweet, female scent filled his nose and her soft, soft skin sliding against his made him clenched his teeth. She tilted her head back on the boulder, arching under him. He took the silent offering, his lips and fangs grazing her exposed throat. A backlash of pleasure whipped through the psychic link between them, making his dick throb as he felt her deepening passion, her wet readiness for him to take her.

Yes. Anun, yes, he needed to be inside her now.

The head of his cock rubbed against the damp, swollen lips of her pussy. She moaned, clamping her hands over his biceps. A feline roar ripped from his throat and he jerked back, pain exploding through him as she touched his wound. Spots swam before his eyes, cold sweat beading on his forehead. She yanked her hands away. "Oh, my God! I'm sorry!"

He closed his eyes, a shudder rippling through him as the agony receded again. Releasing a slow breath, he looked up to see her blue eyes wide with regret, but the tie between their minds still pulsed with her body's clamoring needs. He ignored the remaining pain and kissed her—inhaled her, really, plunged his tongue into her mouth, licked her, bit her lip. He tasted her blood, and it fed the animalistic pleasure rocketing through him. Her arms wrapped tight around his neck, and fire exploded in his gut. She wriggled between his hard length and the unyielding surface of the rock, working to lock her legs behind his waist. He purred at the friction of her skin against his.

His cock pressed for entrance inside her, and she pushed her heels into the backs of his thighs, open for his penetration. He snarled when he slammed into her. He loved the feel of her tight sheath around his hot flesh, squeezing him, milking him as he began to thrust.

"Fuck me hard." Her soft moans and cries drove him on, made him feel as though he were going to explode at any moment.

"*Khalaa.*" He purred, the beast staring down at his succulent prey as he rode her against the rough stone. With the last shred of his sanity, he held tight to the power building inside him, wanting to take more than just her body. Drowning himself in the essence of her, he took everything he could without sinking his mind into hers. The beast wanted to. Anun only knew how it wanted to. But he could never cross that line.

A hopeless groan pulled from his throat. He sank his cock into her hot depths again and again as they pushed themselves faster, became wilder. He could feel how close she was to orgasm and he thanked Anun for it. He wasn't sure how much longer he could hold on. The only sound between them was the sharp slap of his skin against her and the heavy pant of their breath as they struggled to drag in enough oxygen.

Her pussy fisted around his cock on his next swift stroke. His muscles flexed as he hammered into her, almost losing his tenuous grasp on the unraveling ends of his self-control. She squeezed her legs around him and he could feel how her orgasm built like an inferno inside her, feel the power of it, the heat, the sweetness. It fed his own craving, and his claws dug into her hips as he pulled her tighter to his pelvis, rocking deeper inside her. She sobbed on a breath. *"Please."*

He ground against her clit, sending fire streaking through his system. Her inner muscles squeezed hard, pulsing around the length of his dick. Her fingers slid into his hair, twisting tight as her pussy convulsed around him. He worked his cock in time with her contractions, dragging it out until he thought he'd die, but he didn't want it to end too soon; he wanted her—like this—forever. The beast purred at the barely coherent thought.

"So. Good," he groaned, his voice a bare rasp of his usually smooth, articulate tone.

He pounded into her, pulling away from the mental connection as he let the feline take over their physical coupling. The last fetters of his restraint ripped loose, and he drove himself toward orgasm. Throwing his head back, he roared and the sound echoed in the silent forest. He slammed deep and froze, a shudder running through his body as he came deep inside her. She gasped, her sex clenching around him one last time, making her moan and cling to him.

With a harsh groan, he sank down on her, lungs bellowing as he tried to catch his breath. His sweat-dampened forehead dropped to her shoulder and he shuddered, his hands flexing on her hips. She brushed her fingertips up and down his back, warm and satiated.

He struggled against the desire to purr and lay here forever letting her pet him. He loved her touch; it fed some deep longing within him that he preferred not to examine. He sighed and leveraged himself away from her. She unwound her legs from his waist and they both groaned when his cock slipped out of her. He lifted her higher on the boulder so that she was sitting on top of it. "Stay there."

Turning, he stooped to retrieve her clothes from where they lay in haphazard piles on the ground. He sighed again when he looked back and found that she'd taken the opportunity to straighten her disheveled braid. He wanted to see her hair down, wanted to bury his fingers in it, wanted her to let go of all that tight control of hers. It was *almost* gone when he fucked her, but he wanted it totally gone, wanted her as wild as she made him. Once he handed her garments back to her, she slid everything on except her bra and shirt. Both their chests were smeared with blood. His blood.

She didn't bother to cover herself, holding her shirt away from the crimson stains on her skin. "We need to clean up."

He shuddered when he thought of the frigid stream water on his overheated flesh. This part of their little escapade was going to be unpleasant. Still, they did need to cleanse themselves, so he tracked the scent and sound of running water to the stream and she scurried to keep up with him. They each hurried to bathe, their teeth chattering as the frigid liquid hit their flesh.

Bren slipped her clothing over her damp skin and rose to her feet, not meeting his gaze. Her thoughts had turned inward and he deliberately pulled away from any connection they had to give her privacy, but it pained him that she'd pulled back again, and the beast inside him clawed at the restraint he placed upon it. It wanted no part in any distance there was between it and its

One. The man always at odds with his feral nature, and frustration crawled through him at the constant inner struggle.

They followed the brook downstream toward their camp-site, but Bren drew to a halt when they came to another fallen warrior. Farid sensed the man was unconscious, so he made no protest when she approached the soldier warily and squatted next to him, her fingers pressing to his throat as she checked his vitals. She glanced over at Farid. "Any permanent damage to any of the guys you took out?"

"They are merely asleep." He shifted on his bare feet, wincing as a rock dug into his sole. "They will awaken in roughly eight hours."

She straightened, brushing at her pants. "More will come looking for them when they don't check in."

"Then we shouldn't linger, should we?" Shrugging the tight muscles in his shoulders, he hissed when it pulled at the wound in his arm.

"You threw yourself in front of a bullet for me. And then you reopened the wound fucking me." She strode across the riverbank toward him until he could feel the heat of her slim body. Looking him over, she shook her head. "Are you insane?"

He was startled into a laugh, the bark of sound cracking loudly in the quiet woods. He brushed at his bicep, careful not to touch the wound. "You have no idea how often I've asked myself that very same question of late."

"That's comforting." She rolled her eyes, but it didn't mask the concern in her gaze. He liked that, liked that his welfare mattered to her. He silenced the rational voice that told him any kind of caring between them was a mistake. She sighed. "All right, you're shot and you need medical treatment. It's at least twenty kliks to the nearest hospital, and you can be sure they've got people waiting for us in every nearby speck of civilization."

"Kliks?"

"Kilometers." She tilted her head, staring at his arm as though she might somehow sense the extent of damage to his body. Which her kind couldn't do, so he knew it was fruitless, but he enjoyed having her so near, wanted to pull her to him and continue his exploration of her pretty body.

Taking a step back to give himself more space, more resistance, he cleared his throat. His arm ached and his self-restraint hung by a thread. He forced his mind to *anything* else, anything stupid and inconsequential. "How does that in any way relate to the word—"

"Really?" She gave him a sour look. "We're going to have a grammar lesson right now?"

He huffed out a breath, annoyed. Only Cilji had ever been able to make him laugh and make him mad in the space of a few moments. "You're lucky that the bullet merely grazed me and that I can walk right now, so I'll talk about whatever I want to."

She blinked at him and her chin dipped in a quick nod. "Fair enough."

"I will not require the attentions of your doctors." He turned and began walking back to their camp, drawn by the scent of cooked rabbit and their fire. "I'll wait until we reach the emperor's ship. We have medical facilities there that far outstrip what I can find here."

He felt her exasperation radiate out of her, but he kept going. Her emotions would only feed his, and he was having a difficult enough time containing those without trying to shield himself from hers. Her footsteps sounded behind him as she jogged to keep up. "Look, Arjun—"

"We're wasting time arguing about it. The wound is painful but shallow and fairly superficial. I'll be fine until we get aboard ship." He glanced back at her, noting that she'd pilfered the soldier's smaller firearm before she'd followed him. "You're not going to change my mind, and seeking medical treatment here will only draw attention we don't want. My people will be here soon enough."

"Are you sure about that?" They reached the campsite and two more unconscious men awaited them. He knew there was another pair of them farther downstream, but he decided not to share that with Bren. He selfishly wanted her concern all for himself, and the men *were* just sleeping so they would be fine.

"Very sure." He bypassed the soldiers and retrieved his clothing, carrying them back to where Bren stood by the fire.

"Okay." She looked anywhere but at his nudity, which both amused and aggravated him because she was so determined to ignore how good they were together physically. "Let's get some supplies off these guys. They'll be picked up when they radio in. We're not that lucky. They'll have weapons, a med kit, and some MREs we can liberate." She glanced at him. "Just . . . don't eat the peanut butter in any of them."

"MRE?" His brows drew together, and he watched her roll one soldier over, pull a pack off his back, and begin rifling through it. "You're speaking a language that is *not* standard English."

"I'm speaking army." She grinned over her shoulder at him, left the bag on the ground, and quickly moved to the other man to search him for whatever items she considered useful. "The official translation for MRE is 'Meals, Ready-to-Eat.'"

"And the unofficial translation?" He stooped to pick up the pack, stuffed his clothing into it, and held it out for her to store the various weapons, packages, and metal Earthan gadgets she'd found.

"There are quite a few, like 'Meals, Rarely Edible,' 'Meals Rejected by Everyone,' and my personal favorite 'Meals Refusing to Exit.'" Her eyebrows arched as she arranged everything in the heavy-duty sack and closed its fastening. "Don't eat the peanut butter."

The things they expected their warriors to eat did not sound like the kind of fare that would keep them fit for duty long. Anun willing, he wouldn't have to eat any of it himself before Tylara, Haakesh, or Kyber sent a party to find him. "You'll tell me which container is the peanut butter."

"Yeah." She chuckled, shrugged into the pack, and bounced on her toes a few times to settle the sack into place. His gaze fell to her breasts as they jiggled. He wanted them bared and filling his palms, wanted to suck the nipples until they were deep red, until she screamed his name. He closed his eyes and tried to close his mind to the vivid image. When he looked at her again, she was staring back at him, her eyebrows raised. "I take it since I'm carrying your clothes, you're going feline on me rather than nudist hiking?"

I always knew you were a smart woman. The safest form for him to be in until he could wind his unraveling powers back in was one that couldn't bond with a Kin. His beast form. So he shifted, and all the while he clenched his jaw against the searing pain of damaged muscles wrenched into a new position. The bleeding restarted, streaking his fur with fresh crimson. He ignored it, forcing himself to stay the course. They weren't safe here and that was more important than his comfort.

"There's a ridge to the south of here that might have some caves to camp in tonight." She buckled a few straps into place on her pack and strapped on a belt with multiple weapons affixed to it. "It's going to be cold tonight if we have no fire *and* we're not running to keep our body temperature up like we did last night."

He nodded and didn't respond, focusing on the pain that jarred the wound with each step. Anything to keep his mind off of her slim body and how much he wanted to bury his cock inside it until they both came. He wouldn't fail to protect her again, to keep her from harm's way.

He couldn't lose her the way he'd lost everyone else. He

caught himself at the treacherous thought. He didn't have her; he couldn't lose her. But he couldn't deny that the very thought of her dying made him feel as though he been kicked in the chest. He couldn't deny that he wanted her more than he'd ever wanted any other woman in his life.

He'd always been drawn to her, but the hours in her presence had shown him *why* fate had made her his One. Stubborn and confounding, yes, but also brave, capable, smart, and honorable. She wouldn't be here with him if some inner compass hadn't guided her to it. Good to know that she could think for herself, though he knew in the military, that wasn't always considered an asset. She was, as Zielinski had said, *not really a team player*. Neither was he. Which was probably why he had never been interested in the Sueni military. He thought too much and talked even more. Excellent for a diplomat, terrible for an officer.

He glanced up at her, his gaze locking on the sway of her backside under the bulky pack. His mind strayed to things it shouldn't, like how soft the skin there had been when it rubbed against his groin as they'd fucked. The silence did nothing to distract him, and he jerked his gaze upward, watching her brush away a few wisps of hair that had escaped her braid.

How long is your hair when you have it completely unbound? Does it brush your backside?

She twisted at the waist to cast him an incredulous glance. "I don't see how that question is at all relevant, Lord Arjun."

How often must I ask you to call me Farid? He quickened his step, bounding forward until he was even with her. The movements jarred his shoulder, but he ignored it. *You use my surname and my title to put distance between us when we both know you do not desire distance,* khalaa.

"Fine. Farid. How about you answer some of my questions now?" She wiped sweat off her brow. "Why are you doing this? I know why I'm here. Why are you here?"

He blinked at her. *Isn't it obvious?*

"You really thought I was suddenly going to sleep with you?" Her tone said how much she doubted his sanity and his intellect if that were true.

No, of course not. He kept his voice light, but with enough bite to really sting. She didn't truly think she could best a diplomat at wordplay, did she? *I told you that when I first found you . . . before you suddenly slept with me.*

She laughed. "Okay, then, smart-ass."

He deliberately misunderstood her. *My ass is intelligent?*

She rolled her eyes before she jogged down an incline to a small ravine, her pack bouncing hard against her back. "All right, you didn't think I intended to fuck you, which I didn't *intend* to no matter what happened. So, then, answer my original question."

He made his way more carefully, trying not to jar his wound. *I came because it was obviously a ruse and I was curious to see what you really wanted.*

"You weren't worried it was a setup to get you captured or killed?" She fished out a canteen she'd stolen and took a deep draught of water.

No. He flexed his paws, stretching his sore muscles when he reached the bottom of the ravine. *You're too honorable a woman to do that.*

She snorted. "I would have had no problem frying your ass any way I knew how as little as a week ago."

I do not doubt your cunning, Bren. Or your tenacity. Or your ruthlessness. He didn't tell her that he admired those things about her. They matched qualities he himself had, but then, she was supposed to match him, wasn't she? He met her gaze. *But you're forgetting that I've been inside you—*

"Do we *have* to talk about that?" Her face flamed. She swallowed and looked aside. Pulling in a deep breath, she let it ease out. "We fucked. Okay. But you being anywhere near the inside of any part of my anatomy has nothing to do with . . . *any-thing*. Damn it."

The rumble that emerged from his feline throat was almost a chuckle. *As I was saying, I've been inside your mind. And, yes, I have. Because of our shared dreams, khalaa. So, I know how far you'd be willing to go to get what you want. You would not have betrayed my trust in answering your summons by killing me.*

She spun on a heel, marching away from him. When she spoke, it was on their previous topic, avoiding any hint that he might be right, that he might know something about her. The woman was so far beyond obstinate he wanted to shake her. That he cared so much what she thought of him was dangerous as well as stupid. Two things he tried to avoid.

"What do you care what I call you anyway, *Farid?* Half the time you don't even call me by my real name. What does *khalaa* even mean in your language? Is it an insult? Are you calling me something dirty?" The way her breathing hitched on the last word spoke volumes about exactly which definition of *dirty* she was using.

Neither slight nor sexual innuendo. He caught up with her easily, matching his stride to hers. Brushing his body against her leg every few steps only made her breathing more erratic. *The* khalaa *is a plant that grows on my world with small, bell-shaped flowers that are white on the outside and scarlet on the inside. What is unusual about it is that it thrives only in the harshest of environments—both arctic snow and burning desert—but nowhere else.*

"Oh." She brushed dirt off her shirtsleeve. "It sounds . . . pretty."

He bumped his head under her hand, and her fingers unconsciously stroked his fur. He purred a little at the soft contact. *Yes, it is. It reminds me of you for several reasons. Like the plant, you are a tiny patch of beauty in a wasteland, and you thrive in harsh conditions where others could not. You are also like the flowers, cool on the outside, with unexpected fire within.*

"I . . . didn't know." He heard her swallow, her step faltering. "I thought it had to be something bad."

I am not your enemy, Bren. Don't assume the worst of me. It stung that, despite all they'd been through together this day, she couldn't let go of her old prejudices enough to trust him.

"I'm sorry." Her mouth worked for a moment, that sweet vulnerability flashing in her ocean blue gaze. She stooped down until her eyes were level with his, her fingers curling into his fur. "I know you're not the enemy, Farid. The last twenty-four hours have had to be a nightmare for you."

He leaned into her touch and winked. *It hasn't been all bad.*

She snorted, closed her eyes, and leaned her forehead against his. "Hell, the last year has had to suck for you if all you wanted was the emperor's One." When she opened her eyes, they swam with tears that she quickly blinked away as though the show of weakness embarrassed her. "What I asked before about why you're here . . . I don't understand why you came to someone who helped murder innocent Kith. I was there in the room when Arthur gave that order, and I agreed with him."

You were doing what you thought was best and trying to protect your people. That's admirable. You were wrong, of course, but your intentions were good.

"Kyber's never going to agree to help me, is he?" Hopelessness flooded her expression.

He couldn't lie to her, but he couldn't deny that it was a distinct possibility. *I don't know, but I will do everything I can to convince him it's the right thing to do. Because it is.*

"Thank you. For everything." She looked away, breaking that fragile moment of peace between them. Letting him go, she stood and looped her fingers around the straps of her bag. She sighed and began hiking again, her face pensive.

He could have read her thoughts to find out what troubled

her now, but once he got inside her mind again, he doubted he'd be able to leave. Ever. It was best not to attempt it and to block her mind from his. He refused to think about how quickly she had shredded his control and reduced him to avoiding the connection that he'd once used to reach her from the ship.

It was a miserable tangle he'd landed in, and there was little he could do to extract himself. He refused to bond with her or open himself to loving anyone, but he didn't think he could force himself to back away, either.

Anun save him.

6

"I am *fine*." Farid's jaw jutted mulishly. He glared up at Bren from where he sat propped against the cave wall. They'd made camp for the night, eaten the foulness that was army rations, and then he'd squawked at her attempt to clean and bandage his wound. She resisted the urge to punch him. Barely.

So much for them getting along for more than a few minutes at a time. The only time they seemed to be in complete agreement was when they were having sex.

"You aren't fine, damn it." She ignored his protests, dropped the med kit she'd pilfered, and knelt beside him to get a closer look. She kept her touch gentle as she checked for excess heat and swelling that might indicate infection. He tried to shrug away and she glared at him. "It's going to be too dark for me to do this soon. You've been *shot*, Farid. I have training to help, so don't be an ass, and just let me see it."

"No." He caught her wrists and held her still, closed his eyes for a moment and swallowed. "There's only so much control I have, Brenna, and it's wearing thin. So while I would like nothing more than for you to continue stroking me with those soft little hands of yours, I think it may turn me into something far more bestial than you've seen yet and we'll spend the night rutting while my mind plunders yours. Unless that is your desire, I suggest you stop touching me."

"I asked you not to touch me before. You didn't listen." The thought of him rutting with her, of calling up that wild side of him, did little to discourage her body.

"I know. I wanted you then, I want you now, but I had my power tethered then. I let it loose protecting us, putting your men to sleep rather than killing them. You petting me does little to help me draw that power back in."

Her breath seized when he looked at her, the sparks in his gaze rolling faster the longer she touched him. Her pussy fisted on nothingness, her body so attuned to his. She swayed toward him, but jerked her hands away. "I . . . I don't . . ."

"Go to sleep, Sergeant Major Preston." He moved to stretch out on the floor, curled his arms under his head, and closed his eyes.

"Farid—" She stopped short and swallowed. "That bestial side of you doesn't scare me. I want you badly, claws, fangs, and all, and that isn't easy for me to admit."

"You think it's so simple for me?" His voice rumbled in the deepening darkness, at once soothing and arousing.

She shivered as chill wind whipped through the cave. The higher elevation was going to make for a cold, miserable night. But she was already consumed by her own misery. She did want him—all of him. The wild man, the aloof nobleman, he drew her in no matter which side of him was in control. She liked him, she desired him, and the longer she was with him, the more intense those feelings became. It was stupid, but she couldn't shut it down no matter how hard she tried. She hadn't been able to close him out when they'd only shared dreams, but now that she knew the pleasure of his touch, it was hopeless.

She sighed. There was no future between them. Hell, there

was no future for her, period. She'd accepted from the moment she sent him that message that she probably wouldn't make it out of this mission alive. All she could hope for was to convince Kyber to help her before Arthur caught up with her. It was too bad, really. She'd never met a man who got to her like Farid. What would it have been like to be free to explore that connection? She shook her head, dismissed the foolish notion, and answered his question. "I don't know what it is for you."

He took a deep breath and let it ease out. "It isn't simple."

"What is it?" Something inside her froze as she waited for the answer to the question, hoping for . . . she didn't know what.

"I don't know." His gaze met hers, the pale green irises sparking in the darkness. "Is it so difficult to believe that I am as lost in this as you are?"

"Yes." The answer was swift, honest.

"Surprise."

That startled her into laughter and she caught a flash of white teeth when he smiled.

"Let's get some rest." His eyes closed again, cutting off the brightest light that remained in the cave. All she had to guide her now were thin shards of moonlight.

She watched his chest rise and fall in slow, steady breaths for a moment. He always seemed so assured. As assured as she always wanted to appear. What had she expected him to say? That he felt something for her? That he wanted more than to fuck her? That he'd come to her because he was more than just curious about what she wanted? In the end, it didn't matter. He had a One out there somewhere who might want a chance to change his mind about bonding, and Bren was on a collision course with death. No one understood General Arthur better than she did, and she knew he would never stop until the traitor was dead. His betrayal of her faith in him was one more reason she was right never to be too trusting, too reliant, too weak.

It didn't seem she'd learned her lesson though. She'd shown more vulnerability to Farid than she had to any other man ever, including Arthur, and she had worshipped the man who had taken her under his wing as a skinny young enlisted soldier. So, what was she doing? And what was it about the alien nobleman that called to her so much? Was it that he *should* want her dead for playing a role in killing a ship full of Sueni, and yet he'd taken a bullet for her instead? Was it that he confused her, attracted her, argued with her, but still listened to her? He tried to understand her, even when he didn't agree with her. Had she ever known anyone like him before? She didn't think so.

She rose and stepped over Farid to slip deeper into the cave. The predator would insist he lay between her and the entrance so he could handle anything that might come in at them, and she wasn't up to arguing her relative ability to ward off an attack. Settling on the hard ground, she set one of her stolen pistols within easy reach, used the backpack she'd liberated as a lumpy pillow, closed her eyes, and tried to sleep.

It didn't work. She couldn't get her mind to shut down and the wind was starting to pick up, chilling her to the bone. She curled into herself tight, but it didn't help. The rock floor was cold, the wind was cold, and she was so cold her nipples had hardened to painful points.

She flopped over, knowing what she could do to get warm, and still hesitant to reach out and take it. He'd said his control hung by a thread, and she believed him. She might like making him wild, but was that really wise? Hell, was this whole operation really wise? She snorted. Another gust whistled through the cave, and she gave in.

Rolling to her hands and knees, she crawled over to where Farid lay sleeping. She picked up his arm and slid under it, pressing her back to his front. "God, I'm freezing. Your control is just going to have to hold."

He jolted awake, tightened his grip on her, and groaned. "Tormenting the enemy is not good conduct."

She wriggled to get away from a rock and came into full, hard contact with his swelling erection. They both froze, and he groaned again, the sound of a wounded animal.

"Farid." Her voice emerged a high, reedy sound of need. That he reacted so fast to her touch made her hormones scream in recognition. Her mind flashed back to that afternoon, his body pinning hers to the boulder, his cock filling her, his mouth on her nipples. Her sex went hot and wet in seconds, ready for more of his touch.

A rough chuckle rumbled from his chest, vibrating against her back. "*My* control? What about yours? I can sense what you're thinking and feeling right now, Bren."

"Then you know what I want." Him. She wanted him. If she wasn't going to survive this mission, then she was going to go out enjoying every second she had left. No more regrets.

"By Anun, yes." He rolled them both, pulled her on top of him, and cupped her cheeks in his palms. "Take your hair down. I want to see it."

She sat up, and he choked when it pushed her sex against his cock. A little grin tugged at her lips and she shoved her hips against him. She unfastened the elastic band around the end and slowly unwound the tight braid, shaking her head to loosen the strands until they brushed her hips. Tucking the tie in her pocket, she waited for his reaction.

He'd stilled under her, his gaze moving over her hair, her face, her body. His expression was almost . . . reverent. "By Anun, you're beautiful."

"It's just brown hair. A lot of it." She flushed, unaccustomed to that kind of perusal. Not from him or anyone else. Lustful, sure. But worshipful? Not so much.

"Come to me." He urged her closer, and the dark locks tumbled over her shoulders. He stroked his fingertips over the ends of her hair, twining the mass around his palm. He drew it forward and buried his nose in it, inhaling its fragrance. "Sweet and exotic, like flowers. It suits you, *khalaa*."

She chuckled and his eyes twinkled with merriment. "It's jasmine, actually. I have no idea what *khalaa* smells like."

"Not like this." He shrugged, letting her hair drift through his fingers. "But just as lovely. Like you."

"Thank you. That's very nice." To cover the fact that she was blushing again, she brushed her lips across his jaw, his chin, the tip of his nose, raining light kisses over his face before she settled on his mouth.

His hands cupped the back of her head, sliding into her hair. She shivered as his claws scraped her scalp lightly, but his lips soon distracted her. He licked his way into her mouth, twining his tongue with hers.

God, the man could kiss. He took his time with it, didn't rush or give it the cursory attention most men did on their way to fucking a woman. His pleasure in the simple art of the kiss was palpable. She liked that, liked that he would spend the time learning how she liked to be touched before he slammed his cock into her. Though she liked when he did that, too. Making him lose his cool was some of the most fun she'd ever had. Then again, he seemed to get just as much enjoyment from pushing her over the edge of her control, too.

His low groan was a beautiful sound, made her feel sexier and more powerful than she ever had in her life. The way he reacted to her, looked at her, touched her, was almost reverent, and yet more wary than a cornered wild animal. She didn't understand it, him. She wasn't sure she ever would, and that made her inexplicably sad.

Breaking away from the kiss, she sighed.

"Are you all right?" His thumb brushed across her cheekbone.

"Mmm-hmm." She forced a little grin to her lips. "Why wouldn't I be?"

The moonlight filtering into the cave cast shadows on his face, but she saw his blond brow arch. "I sensed your mood lowering. Something has upset you."

"Try to stay out of my head." She winced and tucked her hair behind her ears, sitting up again.

The man didn't miss a trick. Sometimes she liked that about him, and sometimes—like now—it pissed her off. His big hands moved to her waist, holding her in place. "I didn't read your thoughts, but I cannot help that people broadcast their emotions."

"People? Or just Kin?" She folded her arms, almost daring him to make this an issue of her lesser species status.

His eyes sparked at the challenge, a lazy grin exposing a long fang. "Kith do as well, though we learn to control it better."

"Yes, and isn't everything better about you?" She rolled her eyes and wriggled to get away from him.

"It's out of necessity, *khalaa*. Because of our extra abilities." He frowned, his grip tightening, which just annoyed her more. How had they gone from getting it on to arguing in under ten seconds? The man confused the shit out of her, pushing her buttons, pushing her boundaries. His hands slipped down to cup her hips. "It is not . . . not an insult to the Kin, it is just what Kith must do to cope with being one of our species."

"I know." She slid her hands up and down her arms, her anger evaporating as quickly as it had come. "I get it, I really do."

"What's your excuse?" His fingers squeezed her curves, a silent demand.

"Come again?" Uncertainty replaced the annoyance. How had this turned into something about *her*?

"For being so controlled." His eyebrows contracted in a deep frown. "For me, it's biological. You have no such reason."

Wariness slid through her, and her muscles tensed. "I have my reasons, they're just more historical than physiological."

"Tell me." His frown cleared, his voice turning soft, cajoling. She felt his honest desire to know, not to judge, trickle into her mind. How often had anyone cared to know, really *know*, how and why she was the way she was? Not often, and those that had asked had been met with the coldest shoulder she could give them. It was odd that the one man who asked that she *wanted* to understand her would be one so different from her that he might not be able to. Then again, maybe he could. A man with his sad past understood pain, suffering, loss, and fear. Those things were more universal than anyone would like to contemplate. Could she deny him the truth when he'd been so upfront with her?

She pulled in a deep breath. "My childhood was spent out of control, always dependent on someone else for everything, always waiting for something horrible to happen. I swore I wouldn't live like that, wouldn't be like that."

"I see." His palms slid in soothing circles on her back, his mind feeding her comfort and encouragement.

Just what she needed.

A wry smile tugged at her lips. "I told you my parents died when I was very young. I ... don't remember much about them at all. I lived with my aunt for a while, but she didn't really want to take care of a kid, and when she went to jail for one too many drunk-driving accidents, she turned me over to the foster care system. That's where they send orphans here, kids nobody wants." She wrapped her arms tight around herself, as if to ward off how helpless she'd been, how storm-tossed her life had become. It had the power to horrify her even to this day. "It went from bad to worse after that. Some kids get lucky in the system, get put in nice homes. I wasn't one of the lucky ones."

His concern, his outrage and anger on her behalf, broadcast through their mental conduit. "What did they do to you?"

"Mostly nothing. Just . . . ignored me, neglected me, collected a monthly check for my upkeep that never got spent on me. Some of them hurt me, kicked the crap out of me, used me as a punching bag when they'd had a bad day or too much to drink or both. One foster mother got pissed off about something I did and shaved all my hair off. It's why I keep it so long now—took forever to grow it back out." She ran her fingers through the tangled locks, remembering the humiliation of when she'd looked like a recovering chemo patient for months. Her throat closed tight and she had to swallow several times to be able to speak again. "It could have been a lot worse. I saw exactly how bad it could be in one of my first foster families. One of the older girls was pretty much a sex slave for our foster father. He was the town mayor—how warped is that? His wife knew about it and did nothing. No one did anything."

"I'm so sorry, *khalaa*. I wish—" He shook his head, cut himself off, all the while stroking her back, petting her, relaxing her into telling him more.

"I looked her up after I got out of basic training in the army. I didn't even know her that well. I was only there a few months before they moved me, but I had to know what happened to her." She closed her eyes, only to see that haunted, walking-dead expression the girl had worn. "She committed suicide a few years after I left. She was only fourteen. Sad, pathetic waste of life. She didn't even get a chance to live, and be strong, and stand on her own two feet. I doubt she ever knew what it was like *not* to be someone's victim." She sniffled, staring down at his chest until she was sure she wouldn't cry. "So, that's why I like to be in control, independent. It might not be as good an *excuse* as your physiological one, but it's all I've got."

He ran the back of his knuckles over her cheek. "You're a remarkable woman, Bren, to be so strong."

"Thanks." She huffed on a laugh, as flustered by the praise as she had been by the compliment to her looks. When she felt his pride in her come through their connection, a hot flush flooded her face. "Can we talk about something else now? Or, even better, do something besides *talk?*"

"We can do whatever pleases you." He flashed a little grin, a flicker of renewed desire reached her from him. "I'm at your disposal."

She felt his cock harden and prod between her thighs, and she let her hands drop to his pecs. His heart thumped under her palm, and the beat sped with each passing moment.

Heat centered low in her belly, gripping her tight. She leaned down and offered him her mouth. He took it, greedy for her, wanting her, even though she'd revealed how messed up she really was inside, his lust for her was undimmed. To say that pleased her was something of an understatement.

She smiled against his mouth, humming in delight when he licked her lips to show her he noticed. He noticed everything, reacted to her every moan and sigh when they had sex.

Planting her hands against the stone ground on either side of his shoulders, she made sure she didn't hurt him again by touching his wound. She pushed down on the floor, using it for leverage as she rubbed her sex against his to stimulate them both. She felt the flood of his passion enter her mind and liked it too much to care that she wasn't the only one in her head. Throwing her head back, she moaned. "I need—"

"Yes." He reared up and bit her exposed throat. "Me, too."

She tugged at his clothing, wanting him as unashamedly naked as he had been that afternoon, wanting him inside her again. "Help me."

"Yes." He arched his back, managing to work his shirt over his head while she stood to strip as fast as humanly possible. Being superhuman, he beat her to it and lay stretched on his pile of clothes, naked, hard, and waiting for her. His eyes gleamed with appreciation as his gaze roved over her body.

"Farid." She cupped her breasts, her nipples tightened, and heat arrowed between her thighs.

He shook his head. "You're so lovely. Don't cover yourself."

"I wasn't." She brushed her fingers across the soft undersides of her breasts, stroking in circles until she centered on the tips and teased herself while he watched. His big palm slid down the muscled planes of his belly, and he wrapped his fingers around his cock, pumping it hard.

Moisture flooded her sex, and she slipped one hand down to part her damp lips. He groaned, his eyes sparking. His gaze hardened with lust, the need sharpening on his face. "Come down here."

"I thought you'd never ask." She knelt beside him, still stroking herself, and smiling when he laughed at her. In all the times she'd seen him, he'd rarely laughed, and usually it was a derisive, condescending laugh meant to make the mere humans feel inferior or stupid. This side of him, the lighter, freer, more passionate side, was one she enjoyed. A lot.

He grabbed the hand between her thighs, pulling it to his mouth to lick and suck her wetness from each finger. She moaned and swayed toward him. Her free hand curled around his hard cock. He hissed and jerked, pushing his hips into her touch. She squeezed him tight, sliding her fingers up and down the long, hot shaft. The flared crest dripped beads of precum, and she rubbed his slick juices into his flesh. "I want to suck you, Farid."

His laugh was a rusty sound. "I don't know if I'll survive it, but I'm not going to refuse such an offer."

Tugging her hand away from him so she was free to move, she slid forward to press a kiss just beneath his collarbone. She lightly raked her nails up his sides, then circled one of his nipples with her fingertip. She heard him swallow, and she glanced up at him to see his fangs protruding from his gums and a muscle ticking in his jaw. She flicked her tongue over one flat nipple, blowing a stream of air over the dampness to make it bead. "You taste good, Farid. After every one of those dreams, I imagined what it would be like to touch you like this, to take you in my mouth."

He snarled, his claws scrambling against the stone floor beneath him. "Yes. Touch me. Taste me. Do whatever you want, just don't stop."

"Don't mind if I do." She winked at him before she kissed her way down his body, her hands stroking and massaging his hot flesh and hard muscles. Silk over steel.

By the time she reached his cock, his hands were fisted at his sides, his groans rumbling like thunder in his chest. When she took him in her mouth, he arched into her, his body bowing in a tight line. "Bren! *Khalaa!*"

She swirled her tongue around the head of his cock, catching the beads of moisture there. Sucking him between her lips, she worked her tongue down his hard shaft. He hissed, his muscles shaking. She wrapped her fingers around the wide base of his dick and used her other hand to cup his soft sacs. Her teeth scraped oh-so-gently against his skin and his fingers splayed against her head, sliding into her hair to hold her in place. His claws rasped against her scalp and goose bumps broke over her flesh. His low, helpless groan sent power rushing through her.

What made her moan was the intensity of the heat that gathered between her thighs. It was the same sensation as when he reached for her mentally, and she realized that was what he was doing now. She pleasured him physically and he pleasured her mentally, sensations shooting straight from her mind to her body.

Anun, that is so fucking wonderful. This time his groan echoed in her head as well as her ears.

She whimpered, her mouth still stretched around his cock. Her own hips worked in time with her lips as he plundered her mind. She could almost feel his cock fill her pussy as it filled her mouth. It was too much, her senses reeled from the duality.

Working his cock with her lips and tongue, she hummed around his shaft, and a low roar ripped from him. He fisted his hand in her hair, anchoring her there as he plunged his cock deep in her mouth. His pleasure crashed into her thoughts, overwhelming them until there was nothing left but the ecstasy cycling back and forth between them. Her sex fisted tight as his psychic power centered on her pussy, forcing her to experience that too full stretch of his cock pounding within her. It sent her over the edge, shoved her beyond anything she'd ever known before. She couldn't hold back from coming, her hips pumping, her moisture slipping in beads down the insides of her thighs. She sucked him deep with each wave of bliss that ripped through her.

He growled, pulling her mouth away from his cock. "No more, *khalaa*, or I won't last a moment when I get inside you."

"You were already inside me." She braced her hand on his muscular thigh, swaying hard as she shivered with the satisfaction still throbbing through her.

"So I was." His grin was slow and hot, possessive and greedy. "I want more. Ride me, Bren."

"Yes." She straddled his thighs, and he groaned when her sex moved against his. Positioning herself over his cock, she brushed the head against her slick sex. A muscle in his jaw ticked as he arched beneath her, pushing the first inch into her pussy. They both moaned at the hot penetration. She sank down, taking the rest of him more slowly.

His hands cupped her hips, and she shivered when she felt his claws scrape over her naked flesh. She loved seeing the evidence of his passion, his lack of control. The way starbursts exploded in his eyes faster and faster the more excited he became, the way his fangs and claws came out.

She stroked her fingers up his abs and pecs, feeling the flex and cord of the thick muscles there. She lifted and lowered herself on his dick, at first slowly, but faster and harder as the flames within her threatened to consume her. The thread between their minds stayed open, passion and exhilaration filtering between them, building with each pass. The mental connection enhanced the physical stimulation. The slap of their skin, the play of his muscles, the feel of riding high and wild with all that barely leashed power beneath her. The sweat that beaded on her skin, cooled by the chilly wind that whipped through the cave. Her nipples hardened to painful points, but she didn't care. It was one more feeling that shoved her closer to orgasm. She was so close, it shimmered just beyond her grasp.

He looped an arm around her neck, pulling her down so he could kiss her. Licking her lips, he made a slow, bone-melting show of it. He purred into her mouth, letting the rumble roll down his muscles until it pulsated through his lower belly.

She choked at the incredible sensation, digging her nails into his chest. "God, I can feel the vibrations *inside me*."

"That was, in fact, the point." He grinned and did it again.

A mindless whimper ripped from her as his purr reverberated against her clit. Her sex clenched tight, and her muscles shook as she held off coming then and there. "It's a damn fine point to make."

"I am known for my ability at convincing, arguing, speaking." His green gaze flashed with his amusement, his eyes heavy lidded with passion. "Making points."

"It's good to have talents." She sucked his lower lip deep into her mouth, scraping her teeth over his flesh as she pulled back and released him. "Tell me more."

He purred again, lower, deeper, and she moaned and undulated against him. She worked herself harder and harder on him, the stretch of his cock, the heat they generated together was incredible. Her pussy flexed every time she took him deep inside her, sending bursts of pleasure out from her core. Any second now, she would shatter. The ragged sound of his breathing, the building waves of power flooding through their link, told her he was there with her every moment.

He threaded his fingers through her hair, cupped the back of her head, and forced her mouth to his. *Come for me, Bren. Give me everything.*

She had no choice, she'd already come too far. A deep, rumbling purr broke from his throat, and she screamed against his lips, her body convulsing. Her sex fisted around his cock over and over until she thought she'd die. It was so good, so amazing.

Nothing that was so wrong had ever felt so right.

Farid.

He awakened with a jolt, clamping his arms tight around Bren to shield her. She lay sprawled across his chest, her legs straddling his hips. His senses opened wide and he felt . . . nothing nearby. The forest was quiet except for the small bits of Earthan wildlife. They were safe.

Kyber's impatient tones filled his head. *Are you nearly done rutting, cousin? I checked in with the* Vishra *yesterday to assure them I had found and bonded with my One—*

Truly? Congratulations. Farid was pleased for his cousin but was now doubly worried that they'd leave Earth in a horrific mess without a backward glance.

Wonder, joy, and awe radiated through the link with Kyber. *Her name is Jana Townsend. She is . . . everything I imagined and more. She is perfect.*

A stab of envy rocked through Farid at his cousin's easy

bonding, and he tightened his grip on his own One. *I'm glad for you both.*

Thank you. Kyber sighed and got back to his main point. *In any case, Tylara claimed that you—or someone else—disabled your shuttle so we couldn't track you, because it is not showing up on our ship's sensors. And it will be a few more hours before the site you landed on is within the line of sight of* Vishra's *imagers. Tylara worries more about the "someone else" touching your shuttle than you disabling it. Says you aren't stupid enough to do something like that. When I checked our connection last night, you were busy fucking someone, but Tylara is most insistent that I ask directly.*

Biting back a chuckle so he didn't awaken Bren, Farid answered the other man. *Thank Tylara for me. General Arthur's people blew up my ship. Kindly send someone along to this location to fetch me. I'll be bringing a guest with me.*

He debated warning Kyber about who she was. Better to let him think it was a random Kin lover he was taking along or wiser to tell him that he'd be having discussions he may not wish to have? Farid wasn't sure. He defaulted to honesty with his cousin. *It is Brenna Preston.*

The mental connection pulsed with wry humor. *You're a brave man.*

She wants you to help her depose Arthur. Farid ran a hand down her slim back, stroking the silky length of her hair.

Now he felt his cousin's wariness, rejection, denial. *I want as little involvement in human affairs as I can manage. I want to leave Earth as soon as possible.*

Hear her out. She has risked much to speak to you. Plus, Farid thought she was right. They did owe it to Earth to make sure they didn't leave the planet worse than when they'd found it. If Arthur was still in power when they left, he knew that would not be the case.

Still, resistance trickled through the narrowing link between

Farid and Kyber. The younger man's tone was grudging. *I will be returning to the ship with my One in three or four hours. Your human may have an audience with me then.*

Thank you, cousin.

A pulse of respect and affection came through the familial bond. *I do this for you, Farid. Not for her.*

Farid chuckled, slipping his hand down to cup Bren's backside, grateful his cousin couldn't see. She stirred against him and his body heated in eager response. Hearing the horrible things she'd survived as a child only enhanced how much he respected her, wanted her. *She won't care why, only that she gets what her people need.*

Kyber snorted. *I hope she has been worth the trouble it took to get her in your bed.*

More than worth it. Worth anything, but he kept that thought to himself. He could block the fact that she was his One from Kyber through a mental connection, shielding his mind, but when he saw them together and both psychic and animal powers focused on them, there would be no doubts left. Fortunately, Kyber was unlikely to say anything to Bren, but considering how long he'd sought his One, he was also unlikely to remain silent in private about Farid hiding the truth from his. As much as Farid craved Bren, the truth was something that still made him break out into cold sweat. Could he ever give himself so fully to such a bond and stay sane if he lost her? His father hadn't managed it, neither had his sister. Farid had watched the One bond destroy his entire family. Would Bren and he be any different? He had more than a few doubts on the matter.

I've given Tylara the coordinates I've pulled from your mind. Her people will send a shuttle. Expect them in an hour. Kyber withdrew, narrowing the connection to almost nothing.

Thank you, sire. Farid cut the link, sighing as he settled back against the hard stone ground. He'd insisted Bren sleep on him rather than on the rock, but he'd give much to have his soft gel-pad beneath him now.

An hour left to enjoy her, to have her with no complications between them. The world might be in chaos around them, but what they enjoyed together was unfettered by the anger and pain that would come later. If she found out the truth about why he'd pursued her, if she convinced Kyber to confront Arthur, everything would change. Dread fisted in his gut, and he wanted to hold on to this moment, this time, for as long as he could.

He tightened one arm around her, cupped her smooth ass in his palm, and set the other hand on the ground to push himself up into a sitting position. She sighed, cuddled into his chest once he'd settled back against the cave wall, and brushed her lips over his skin when she spoke. "Time to get up?"

He hummed in the back of his throat. "Kyber contacted me. The rescue shuttle will be here in an hour."

"An hour." She wriggled against him, stroking her palms up his ribs, and he felt her smile against his chest when his cock jerked in response. "This whole gentleman thing where I don't have to lay on the dirt and rocks is kind of nice."

His laugh was little more than an escape of air. "If I am touching you, it is difficult to notice anything else."

Such honesty was unwise, revealed too much, but the words fell from his lips regardless. The more he was with her, the more he wanted to be with her. Not just for sex, but for the pleasure of her company. He liked talking to her, listening to her unique, Earthan point of view.

"Mmm, that's kind of nice, too." She kissed his chest, flicking her tongue out to circle his nipple. He purred, using his grip on her buttock to lift her onto his cock. He hissed when her tight, wet sheath closed around him, and snarled when she bit his nipple.

"Kyber . . . said he was willing to meet with you. We should talk about what you should say to him." Farid congratulated himself on being able to put together two whole, coherent sentences. For a man who made his living on words, his tongue had twisted and his wits had scattered the moment she stroked those soft hands over his skin.

She fell back on her hands, bracing her palms against his thighs. "So talk. I'm listening. Kind of."

"When we're done. I can't think when you're offering yourself up like this." He pressed a hand to her back, arching her torso even farther. He dipped forward and sucked her nipple into his mouth. Letting her head fall back, she dug her nails into his legs. He shuddered, lifted his hips into the crux of her thighs, and buried himself deep in her sex.

The physical reality of her was so much better than even the fleeting psychic connections they'd had. Now, he had to hold back on the mental link lest he lose control and bond with her. The psychic and carnal connections at once might overload his senses. Sweat broke out on his forehead at the mere idea of binding her to him forever. Despite their differences, despite the fact that he refused to acknowledge what she was to him, his mind and beast had latched on to her. Neither instinct cared about logic or right and wrong. There were no gray areas for his powers, there was only what fate had given. Bren.

She belonged to him, matched him on every level, but he wouldn't take her. Not truly, not fully.

It would drive him mad.

The thought should have cooled his rising ardor, but it did not. It had already been too long for the impatient beast. Its baser instincts knew only the need to claim. Soon he might not be able to touch her at all, lest his instincts and powers flare beyond his ability to control. He'd never come so close to losing himself as he had each time he'd thrust inside her.

"This . . . feels . . . amazing." Her breathing hitched each time he entered her, her body bouncing down to meet his upward thrusts.

"Yes." His voice was little more than a growl, his vocal cords vibrating as he hissed. He tried to pick apart the details, savor them each in their turn. The scent of her arousal, her wet sex tight around his cock, the flush that highlighted her cheeks, the sparkle of desire that flashed in her heavy lidded eyes.

He lifted his hands to cup her small breasts, his thumbs chafing the nipples until they darkened to a deep rose color. A smile curved his lips as he watched her body respond to him. Her pussy clenched around his dick each time he flicked a claw over her tight little nipples, dragging groans from them both.

She pushed her breasts into his hands. "God, Farid."

"I know exactly what you mean."

Her laugh was a rich, throaty sound that made his cock ache. He craved her so much. He held her hips down and rotated his pelvis against her clit, making her sob and wrap her arms tight around his waist, her hands rising to clutch his back.

He plunged inside her, and it felt so incredible he almost came. His lack of restraint should have stunned him, but with her he could do nothing except react. Her little gasps and cries, the slickness of her sex as it hugged his cock, the way her nails bit into his back, told him all he needed to know. She wanted him as desperately as he wanted her. Nothing else mattered. Not species or control or destiny. Just this, just her.

For the moment, she was everything.

Eternity, right here in his arms.

He ground himself against her, wanting to be as deep inside her as possible, wanting to claim all of her for himself, but hold part of himself back, that last, final part that he could never, *would never* give her. He cupped her ass, pulling her tight to him. His fingers slid inward to tease the pucker of her anus. He probed the tight recess, entering her a little at a time, pressing his finger in and retreating, again and again until she took his finger easily. He rubbed the head of his cock through the layer of flesh that separated her two channels.

"Farid!"

The sharp need in her voice only drove him on, made his movements faster, rougher. Her nails raked down his back, and the pleasure-pain made him shudder.

Her mouth closed over his shoulder, sucking on his skin before she bit down. Hard.

The feline within him snarled at the feral display, reveling in the ecstasy as much as the man did. Everything about her matched him, her passion always rising to meet his, whether the beast or the psychic was in command, she was there, throwing herself into their coupling. It never failed to arouse him.

"Please, Farid. I need more."

And he knew he'd give her whatever she wanted, needed, craved.

He sank his finger deep into her ass, plunging hard with both his hand and his cock. He fought the widening of their mental link, his control slipping through his fingers as she screamed and fisted around him. Her ecstasy exploded through his mind, pulling him through the connection toward her. The feel of her sex clenching around his dick made it difficult to think, to breathe.

He came hard, and he gave his body over to the sensation, to the carnal rapture that could never be matched by any other lover. But he ripped his mind free of hers, wincing at her soft cry of pain. It was dangerous that she could even feel the loss of him. She shouldn't even notice unless he'd specifically wanted her to.

She was far too attuned to him, considering they weren't bonded.

Or not attuned to him enough, considering how much the beast wanted to bond with her, considering how much the man loved her.

It was the most devastating revelation of his life.

7

They hadn't had time to have that talk Farid wanted. They'd been well into a second round of fucking by the time he'd alerted Bren to the fact that the shuttle was minutes from touching down outside their little cave, and they'd had to scramble to get dressed. She tried to ignore the fact that they reeked of sex. Likely the beast and psychic powers the Kith had would have told them what had been going on for the last day anyway.

It rocked her that it *had* only been a day. So much had changed so quickly, including how she viewed Farid . . . and the Sueni people by extension. The truth was that she'd wanted to use them as a means to an end. The Sueni would benefit if Arthur was gone, and she wanted Arthur gone for the benefit of Earthans.

Now she looked at them as just . . . people. Not overbearing, superhuman enemies. It was difficult for someone trained to dehumanize her adversaries in order to stay sane. For the most part, she had no regrets about what she'd done in her life. She'd killed people, yes, but she'd known they were people who were just as intent on killing her. She didn't even remember their faces anymore. The Sueni had been no different, until now, until this.

Knowing Farid had changed everything. *Liking* Farid had changed everything. She'd seen, so very clearly, how much icy control he had to have in order to keep his animal side in check. As much as she liked to chip away at that cool reserve, she understood if it was *all* gone, he'd be a serious danger to himself and others. But he went too far the other way, so uptight that he didn't allow himself to enjoy living. She wished she could be there when he found that inner balance he needed. The too tempting man would be irresistible.

The floor of the shuttle shuddered under her feet as they took off. She swallowed, all the blood draining out of her face as it hit home that she was about to leave the planet. What she had to do when she left it was more terrifying than she cared to think at this point. She *had* to convince Kyber to help. She could not—*would* not—fail. Farid reached over and slipped his hand into hers, as always sensing her moods, and giving her exactly what she needed, even if she wasn't sure herself. She squeezed his fingers, feeling something tight ease within her chest at his comforting touch.

Forcing her morose thoughts from her mind, she focused on staring out the window to her left. The ground below rushed away with enough speed to make her stomach feel as though it were floating. There came a place where the blue sky turned strange shades of white, the little ship shook and jolted hard, and she realized they'd left Earth's atmosphere. She pulled in a deep breath just to prove she could in the emptiness of space, and soon the sky was inky black with millions of stars cartwheeling before her. After a few tense moments where she squeezed the hell out of Farid's hand, everything stilled to a perfect, silent calm.

"It's . . . breathtaking." And it was. The most beautiful star-studded night she'd ever seen. Only it wasn't night, it was outer space. She shook her head. Of all the things she'd thought she'd do in her life, all the places she'd thought she'd go, this hadn't been anywhere near the list.

Farid brushed his thumb over her knuckles but remained silent. He hadn't spoken much since they'd come aboard, and not at all to her. A niggle of worry fluttered through her, but she tamped down on it. He had as many concerns on his mind as she did, and his expression as he stared down at his boots was troubled.

She brought his hand to her lips and kissed his palm. They were the only people in the back of the shuttle, and the pilots had other things to do besides watch her, so this might be the last time she was alone with Farid. If she didn't live through this, if Kyber was the evil, oversexed monster Earthans thought he was, or if Arthur managed to kill her, then she was glad she'd experienced this last day of freedom with Farid.

He gave her a small, distracted smile and tugged his hand from hers, tilting his head toward the window. "Look."

Turning in her seat, she saw the Sueni fleet looming huge and vivid before her. Until now, she'd only ever seen it in satellite images and video feeds. Her stomach flipped. It was much more imposing and terrifying from here. She actually thought she was going to convince the man who ruled all of these ships—and an entire planet full of beings with superior physical and mental powers—that he should do what she told him to and get involved in what might become a very ugly war? She closed her eyes to shut out the sight of a massive spacecraft zooming closer with every passing moment.

The shuttle jolted when they docked with the ship, the locks on the door hissing as pressure released. Bren busied herself with unfastening the shoulder restraints on her seat while Farid did the same. Checking to make sure her hair was in its neat braid as she rose from her seat, she brushed at her dirty clothes.

Not exactly the impression she wanted to make, but beggars didn't get to be choosers, and she was definitely here as a supplicant.

Farid jerked her out of her musings when he touched her elbow to direct her attention to someone who had boarded the shuttle. He dropped his hand quickly, as though the contact burned him. She glanced at him, but his gaze was remote, telling her nothing, and the fact that he seemed to have withdrawn completely the closer they came to the Sueni ships was a kick to the solar plexus for Bren. His voice was that cool, distant tone he'd used when they first met—the one she'd hated so much. "May I introduce you to Admiral Lady Tylara Belraj, commander of the Imperial Fleet, and second in command to the emperor on this expedition?"

Tylara Belraj. Of course, Bren had heard her name before, usually spoken in the hushed, reverent whispers used for movie stars. She was a compact, angular woman, with midnight eyes and short ebony hair. There wasn't a strand of gray, but Bren got the impression that the admiral was quite a bit older than she looked. Perhaps Kith didn't age the way Kin did. Tiny white sparks flickered in her gaze, but other than that, she showed no expression.

Bren gave her a crisp nod, one military woman to another. Tylara returned the gesture. "It is good to finally meet you, Sergeant Major. I've heard a great deal about you."

"None of it good, I'm sure." Bren didn't bother to hide a small smile.

Tylara's eyebrow arched. "A worthy adversary is rarely spoken highly of—it is a sign of respect that we dislike you so much, is it not?"

The woman's tone was so deadpan, Bren wasn't sure if she was teasing or serious. These Kith were a whole different beast, literally.

"She is joking, Bren." Farid's words were the ones she needed to hear, but he stepped away from her.

The admiral's slim, dark brow rose a bit higher. "I wasn't aware that I had a sense of humor, my lord."

Bren forced a chuckle, not looking at Farid.

"Don't encourage her, Sergeant Major." Farid sighed, moving to put even more distance between them. His words about her using his title to push him away came roaring back to her. Hearing her rank had never been such a knife to the heart. Locking down on the anger and confusion that battered her, she straightened to rigid attention and gave him the kind of impassive stare she would have the day they'd met. It seemed apparent he wanted them to go back to that, so she obliged him, no matter how it pained her.

If Tylara took note of their frosty exchange, she showed no sign of it on her face. Instead, her nostrils flared and she sniffed the air. Bren fought a flush. God, was the sex wafting off them in waves? A ferocious frown pulled at Tylara's mouth, and her dark eyes flashed dangerously. "You are injured, my lord."

He gave a short nod. "A flesh wound, nothing more. I'll see the medics in a moment."

The admiral's hands curled into fists. "It is fortunate you were injured, Farid, because I have half a mind to throw your stubborn hide into lockdown for the night."

"Under what charge, your ladyship?" His eyebrow lifted lazily and not a single ounce of worry filled his expression.

"Reckless endangerment," she shot back. "You should have told us who you were meeting for your assignation if it would have posed a greater risk to your life than the average Kin."

He tilted his head as though considering the many ways he could argue that logic. Always the negotiating diplomat. "I only endangered myself, Tylara."

"You are under my protection, Lord Arjun." Her nostrils

flared with annoyance. "When you take risks like that and endanger yourself—"

"It makes you look bad?" He smirked.

Her face went completely blank and her chin raised a notch. "You know that has nothing to do with it."

"You're right. That was unworthy of me. I apologize." He bowed at the waist but offered her a sly wink. "Of course you care deeply about my well-being."

Her jaw clenched and she shoved a hand through her short hair. She growled something that had to be a curse word. "How do the Earthans say it? You're a *pain in the ass.*"

Bren snorted.

"Didn't I just tell you *not* to encourage her?" Farid shot Bren a nasty look, sliding his hands into his pockets.

She lifted her hands and shrugged. "You're apparently encouraging her all by yourself. You don't need my help."

Tylara leapt on that one. "No, he needed *our* help and he didn't alert us to the fact that he was potentially putting himself in danger by meeting *you*. He should never have been shot. They should never have had the opportunity."

All amusement fled Bren as guilt hit her square in the chest. She swallowed and made no reply. What could she say? Meeting with her *had* put Farid in harm's way. It *was* Bren's fault he'd been hurt. Something else to tangle her up. She liked him, was grateful to him, but hated that he'd pokered up the moment they were with his people again. It made her stomach queasy, but she steeled herself against it. She had a job to do and her personal feelings about anyone didn't matter anymore. Convincing Kyber to undo the damage his arrival had done to their world was the important thing.

"You can go see the medics now, my lord." Tylara's gaze swept Bren from head to toe. "I'll see that Sergeant Major Preston is shown to her quarters so she might . . . refresh herself."

Quarters? Likely a holding cell until the emperor deigned to speak to her. Her heart twisted at the thought of Farid leaving her alone. Until this moment, she hadn't realized how implicitly she had come to rely on him. It had all happened so fast, too fast for her to see it coming. She *depended* on him, trusted him, without reservation or hesitation, the one thing she'd promised herself as a teen that she'd never do. Fool. Even as an inexperienced girl, she'd known better. There was no excuse for her now.

She focused on the wall behind the admiral's shoulder. "Goodbye, Lord Arjun. Thank you for all your . . . help. I apologize for your arm and hope you're feeling better soon." She met Tylara's eyes for a fleeting moment. "I'm ready when you are, ma'am."

"No." Farid's hand settled on the small of Bren's back, the gesture at once possessive and protective, a tiny spark of the Farid she had gotten to know. "I'll take her, and then I'll have the scratch tended to."

Through her clothes, Bren could feel an undercurrent of his power, almost a whisper through her mind as he spoke telepathically to Tylara. Bren couldn't quite make out the words, but she knew they were there. Odd. Was it because he was touching her or because of the more intimate aspects of their interactions lately? She'd like to ask Farid when they were alone again but had no idea if such a thing would be allowed—by him or by the admiral.

It wasn't as though she'd be free to roam around anyway. Why would they trust a traitor to her own recognizance on their ship? She wouldn't in their place.

Her chin lifted and she didn't look at either of them. It didn't matter what they did with her, so long as Arthur was stopped. She'd accepted the moment she sent the message to Farid that this mission would claim her life, one way or another. It already had. She could never go back to the military or her old life now, whether she was right and Arthur was stopped or not. The army wasn't that forgiving of stepping outside of protocol. Her career was over.

Only this mission remained.

Farid's fingers flexed on her back, urging her forward. "This way, please."

She fell into step beside him and he dropped his hand the moment they were out of Tylara's sight. He didn't speak to her, didn't look at her. They wound down long, tubular corridors with round overhead lights that engaged when they passed and through doors that parted long before they drew near. He pulled her into a tiny, round glass room. "What's this?"

A smooth voice that was neither male nor female, but . . . almost both, sounded from overhead. "It is a multiveyor, Sergeant Major. It allows me to convey my passengers in multiple directions."

"And you're the ship?" Bren's eyebrows arched, swaying a bit when the glass room began sliding at a rapid downward diagonal. Well, the talking spaceship made it official. She'd fallen into a strange science fiction movie, complete with hunky alien invaders. She shook the foolish thought away.

"I am the *Vishra*, yes. Flagship of the Imperial Fleet." The door to the room slid open again, spilling them out into a hall that looked exactly like the one they'd just left. Farid towed Bren out and around another corner before they reached a door.

"Open," Farid ordered and the door obeyed, sliding aside for them to enter. "Kyber has found and bonded with his One. He'll return to the *Vishra* shortly and he'll meet with you when he gets here. His estimate would put it at another hour or two."

"He can't hurry?" She searched his gaze, hoping he understood her urgency, but was met with a calm, blank mask. "This is important. I wasn't kidding when I told you lives hang in the balance. Who knows what the general will do next? The plans he has for China could turn bloody."

"I know. I am sorry." He shrugged a broad shoulder. "He has waited years to bond with his One. *You* have only hours to wait to get what you want."

She pulled in a deep breath. "I'm trying not to be impatient, I really am, but—"

"I'm afraid you have no choice but to wait." He jerked his gaze away from hers as though he couldn't even bring himself to look at her. His hands flexed at his sides. "Is the room acceptable, Sergeant Major?"

God, how stiff did he sound? Was this really the man who'd touched and kissed and sucked every inch of her body, bent her over a boulder and fucked her hard? Something deep inside her crumbled and she had to clench her jaw to keep from crying out.

Sweeping the room with her gaze as he'd asked, some distant part of her was surprised by how spacious it was. But a cage was a cage, wasn't it? Utter terror squeezed her soul at being locked in, trapped, helpless. A million horrifying childhood memories flooded her mind. She'd promised herself she would never be helpless again, never be weak. She'd failed at everything, all of it. How would she live with herself if she failed to convince the emperor? She honestly didn't know.

"The room is fine." Swallowing, she stared out the wide window that stretched along the wall across from the door. "You can go now, Lord Arjun. I assume you'll have the *Vishra* lock me in when you leave. Don't let me keep you."

She heard him take a step and swayed on her feet so badly she had to lock her knees to stay upright. She heard the door swish shut. Dread twisted dark and ugly within her, and her heartbeat roared in her ears, drowning out the sound of him sealing her in.

Her breath caught in shock when his hand clamped over her shoulder and spun her around. His mouth slammed over hers, his tongue thrusting between her lips. Torment filled the voice that sounded in her head. *I sense your fear,* khalaa. *You are not a prisoner here. You are safe. I would die before I would see you hurt.*

Yes, she'd learned that when he'd thrown himself in front of a bullet for her, but right now, it wasn't enough. She sobbed into his mouth, hating herself for needing him so much, but taking what he offered. Twining her arms around his neck, she shoved her hands in his hair and held him tight.

His palms cupped her ass, lifting her until she could wrap her legs around his flanks. His cock rubbed against her clit with each step as he began walking. Where he was carrying her, she didn't know and didn't care. She bit and sucked at his lips, desperate for him. Molten heat flowed in her veins, tingles skipping over her flesh. One of his steely arms banded around her, holding her in place while the claws on his other hand pierced her braid, unraveling her hair.

Her back smacked into a door frame, and it hit right between her shoulder blades. It hurt, but she ignored it, flaming out of control as he thrust against her sex through their clothing. A moan bubbled out, lava flooding through her, heating her pussy until she twisted in his embrace. She ripped her mouth free of his, arching helplessly. He bit her throat, his fangs scraping her skin.

A desperate cry broke from her, the sound high and thin and so needy it should have shamed her. It didn't. She just needed, welcomed the heat and sensation, the lustful craving. It was too damn good to regret. Later, she would kick herself for this. For now, she threw herself into the maelstrom and reveled.

Farid shoved away from her, dropping her to her feet. She fell back against the door frame, moaning a ragged protest, bereft without his touch. His gaze sparked wildly, his chest heaving. He looked at something behind her, and she peeked over her shoulder to see the door attached to the frame sliding aside.

"Take off your clothes, Bren. Now."

Flicking a glance around the small room, she jerked her shirt off. The room was round and made of matte silver metal. Something that looked remarkably like a perfectly cylindrical toilet stood on a raised platform on one side of the circle and a taller cylinder that might be a sink stood next to it. Directly opposite those was a series of thin tubes sticking out of the walls and ceiling over a drainage hole. "Shower?"

"Yes." His fingers snapped around her wrist, dragging her inside. "Over a day of running around in the wilderness means we need to bathe. And I need to fuck you."

The words were harsh, crude, but they still turned her on, made her sex clench and they raced to strip. His shirt tore as he wrenched it over his head. Watching his body come into view made heat burst within her. She didn't even try to disguise it. He would know anyway. He always knew. Joy and pain twisted her heart, but she pushed them both aside and cleared her throat. "How do you turn the water on?"

He shot a distracted glance at the spigot and it began spewing water. The small room quickly heated and filled with steam. She tugged off her boots, socks, ankle holster and gun, and set them aside. Then she popped the tab on her jeans and unzipped them, shoving them down. Her bra followed suit, and she set them all on the floor away from the spray of water.

Farid's heat enfolded her from behind. She turned to him and his gaze heated as it took in her nudity. She returned the favor and let her gaze slide down his body, his hard cock, the head slick with precum. She wanted to touch him, but the way he'd flashed hot and cold made her uncertain. She backed toward the shower, shivering when a wave of mist hit her bare back. Tilting her head back, she let the water sluice through her hair. "I want you."

"I know." He watched her escape, his grin widening. The predator was in his eyes as he stalked her across the room, matching her step for step. Her heart pounding loud in her ears, she backed up until she hit the wall and waited for him to come to her. He didn't disappoint. One big hand planted on the wall over her shoulder, the other at her waist. The water slicked his hair to his scalp, dripping from his chin and nose as he stared down at her.

He showed her the hand near her shoulder, now covered with a milky substance that was a liquid somewhere between the consistency of oil and lotion. It didn't seem to have any smell. She tilted her head. "Soap?"

Nodding, he slid the slick oil down her arm. "It's used to wash your body and hair, so that's as close a translation in your language as you're going to get, yes." His voice was calm, his tone cool and logical. "I'm going to take you hard, Bren. I'll build it up slowly until I make you wild, make you scream and claw my back."

His words sent a shiver coursing through her and she tried to hold on to her desperate need, the way the muscles in her thighs shook and her breathing sped to little pants. She glanced back and saw the groove he'd pulled the bathing oil from. She reached over her shoulder and dabbed her fingers into the cream. Grinning, she circled her fingertips over the flat, brown disc of his nipple. It beaded under her touch and her grin turned into a wide smile. She loved that he reacted to her every time.

Her heart thudded hard when she realized this might be the last time she touched him, kissed him, fucked him. She swallowed a lump in her throat, blinking to hide the tears that burned her eyes. Tucking away how much that hurt to even think about, she focused on him, this time, this moment. If it was all she had left, she was going to wring every single sensation out of it she could. Starting now. She skimmed her hand down the ridges of his abs, exploring every inch of him as she washed him.

He purred, returning the favor. This time they could go slowly, as he'd said, with no fear that they'd be caught with their pants down and end up dead or captured. No part of them was spared as they massaged the bathing oil in and let it rinse away under the hot spray of water. They kissed and sucked, fondled and played. It was bliss. She loved it, the way they teased each other to the edge of madness.

Languid heat wound through her, and she moaned when he parted the folds of her sex and dipped into the wetness there. She arched her hips forward, pressing into the sensual caress. Slipping into her hot channel, he pumped his fingers into her until she bit her lip to keep from screaming. His thumb rubbed over her clit and she damn near came. Her sex closed tight around his thrusting digits, and he chuckled, the sound echoing in the room and in her mind. The link between them was narrower than it had ever been before, and she knew he fought to close it and could not. It pained her that he wanted to, yet even that tiny filament let their pleasure flow back and forth. It was as natural as breathing now, and she'd lost the will to fight that the connection even existed. It enhanced her desire, her fulfillment, as she knew it did his. How could she reject something that felt so incredible? She couldn't. She didn't even want to. She just wanted this time with him to stretch on as long as possible. She wished he felt the same but knew he did not.

He flicked his nail over her clit, making her muscles jolt. "Farid!"

"I seem to have lost your attention, *khalaa*. Perhaps I should work a bit harder." He brought his other hand up to cup her backside, slipped between the cheeks, and used the oil to ease his passage as he slid a finger into her anus.

Her lungs seized, her mouth falling open at the incredible sensation. His hands worked her ass, her pussy, and her clit at the same time. She swallowed, heat trickling through her as her anticipation built and sharpened. Her muscles quaked and sweat mixed with the water to slide down her skin.

A second digit probed her ass and she moaned, moving to take him deeper, to enjoy the hot stretch as he scissored his fingers to widen her anus. He kissed her shoulder. "I'm going to fuck you here. Hard, as I promised."

"Yes, *yes!*" Excitement exploded through her and she rolled her hips, working herself on his hands. He rubbed the pad of his thumb over her clit until she sobbed for breath. He added a third finger to her ass, and she didn't even try to stop the scream this time. "*Farid!*"

"Bren," he growled. His fangs were fully extended, flashing each time his chest rose in a harsh pant.

She kissed him, flicking her tongue over his fangs, nipping at his upper lip. He shuddered, slamming his fingers deep inside her. The hot water cascaded over them, caressed them, sealed their bodies together. She moaned into his mouth, allowing herself an abandon she'd never have considered with anyone else. Just Farid. Only Farid. His wildness, his lack of control, the way she felt it shimmering from his mind to hers made restraint impossible. She let go of control and held on to him instead. Sliding her fingers in his thick, wet hair, she sucked his full lower lip into her mouth.

She cried out in protest when he slid his fingers from her body. "Please!"

Yes. Scream for me, Bren. Beg me for more. His voice floated through her mind, softer than the steam that embraced them. He bracketed her waist, lifting her against the wall. She

snapped her legs around his waist, opening herself to his penetration. Cupping her thighs, he hitched her higher and pressed
the head of his cock to her anus.

He eased his grip on her legs, letting her own weight impale
her on his dick. Even with the oil, the stretch was painful. He
was so big, so hard. The pain just added to the pleasure, twisted
in to something darker, hotter.

Tightening her grip on his hair, she moaned when he was
fully seated inside of her. Her back bowed against the wet wall,
warm water slipping down her skin. She shivered, sobbed,
overwhelmed by everything she felt and might never feel again.

He nudged his cock in her ass, and her senses rioted. Her
heart pounded so loudly in her ears that it drowned out every
other sound. He rolled his pelvis against her, making her vaginal walls spasm in automatic response. "Oh, my *God.*"

"*Bren.*" He choked, shuddering in her arms. She felt his
claws press into her flesh where he supported her thighs. She
shivered, digging her heels into the tight globes of his buttocks.
Still, he didn't thrust deep and hard the way her body craved,
just maintained that gentle rotating that drove her mad. He slid
his tongue up the side of her throat, his voice a tortured rasp of
air, full of self-loathing. "Anun, I can never get enough of you.
No matter how much I want to, I can never get enough."

"Never get enough," she gasped. "Farid, please. *Move.*"

He opened his mouth on her neck and scored her flesh with
his fangs. But he gave her what she asked for. His cock withdrew and plunged deep. He built his rhythm in slow incre-
ments, made her dig her nails into his scalp and move her hands
down to rake his back as need screamed through her.

Reaching up, she hung on to the spigot and used it for leverage to rock herself into his thrusts. He chuckled and picked up
the pace to a speed and force that made her sob. Her sex fisted
each time he entered her ass, and she dragged his masculine
scent in with each gasping breath. Every sensation piled on top

of the last, and she didn't know how much more she could take before she came. She threw her head back against the wall, shoved herself toward him, and moved with him as he worked his cock inside her. The water flowed over her face, making her close her eyes and just *feel*. His hands, his scent, his dick filling her ass again and again, his taste when he brushed a kiss over her mouth.

It only made it better that she could feel how much he enjoyed fucking her this way, that he was with her every second, that he loved how she loved this. As much as he wanted to hold back, he couldn't keep that from her, couldn't close her out.

Look at me, Bren. His irises sparked incandescent green when she did as he demanded. *I want to watch you come.*

He reached between them, flicking a single claw over her clit with a delicacy that sent her tumbling over the edge. Her muscles locked around him, her sex clenching on nothingness while her anus tightened on his thrusting cock. It stung that he still moved in her, it took her beyond any definition she had of pleasure and pain, and it sent her into another wave of orgasm. She shattered, her screams reverberating in the metal room.

His deep roar echoed her cries, his big body tensing in a tight arc as he slammed his cock into her one last time and jetted his cum into her ass. A long groan pulled from him as his muscles shook, his hips still pumping. He buried his face in the crook of her neck, chest heaving as he gulped in ragged breaths. "Oh, yes. Bren. My Bren."

No. She wasn't his and he wasn't hers. They never would be. He had a One out there somewhere, and so she would lose him, one way or another. A pang hit her chest and she closed her eyes. God, it hurt to think of losing him, of leaving him, of him leaving her. There was no good solution to their relationship. If that was even the word to use. They were ... *friends*, though she hesitated before applying such an innocuous label to something as volatile as they had. They fought, they laughed, they fucked. It wasn't about species, biology, or even chemistry. It was him. Farid. Hot and cold, kind and protective, hard and rough. She hated to think of a time without him. A bitter smile curved her lips. Her own future was so up in the air, she might not live long enough to deal with a future without him.

She loved him.

God, why did admitting that to herself burn so fucking badly? It was like a wound she didn't think could ever heal.

She loved him, and even if she survived all that was coming, even if Kyber helped her, even if Arthur was stopped, she *still* couldn't have Farid. His place was with his people, and her place was with hers, helping in whatever way she could. She couldn't leave, and he couldn't stay.

And even then, it wasn't that simple. Not for his kind. She loved him, but he'd never said a word about permanency. Why would he? He was just passing the time with her until he gave in and found that thing that all Kith seemed to be looking for, the thing that had brought them to Earth in the first place.

A One.

A shudder racked her body when he withdrew from her ass. "I've lost your attention again, *khalaa*. Tell me what you were thinking of."

The truth spilled from her lips. "You. Just you."

"I like that." His tone was smug, and she pinched him, which just made him chuckle.

She smiled in response and collapsed against him, utterly spent. The water cut off a few moments later, leaving nothing but the sound of their too rapid breathing. She sighed and unwound her legs from his waist, but he didn't set her down. He shifted her in his embrace and lifted her against his chest. She rested her head on his shoulder, curled her arms around his neck, and closed her eyes. "Mmm . . . that was fun."

His chuckle was a low vibration against her cheek. "I'm delighted you thought so. We'll have to do it again soon."

Something about that tugged at the back of her mind, some warning about planning for the future, but she was too tired to care, too content to take notice. Right here, right now was where she wanted to be most. The steady beat of his heart under her ear lulled her, and she let go of everything else, drifting as he carried her out of the bathroom and into the bedroom. "Whatever you say."

"Ah, bliss." He rested his chin on top of her head. "I've finally found what makes you pliant and agreeable."

She giggled, but the sound was soft and sleepy even to her own ears. She'd never felt so warm, so comfortable, so safe. If this feeling never went away, she wouldn't regret it. A tiny part of her knew he wouldn't be there when she woke up, that this moment of renewed closeness they were having would disappear as it had when they'd reached the Kith ship. She shut that thought out. It was stupid, but she needed the fantasy for just a little while longer. Reality would only bring suffering and death. Hers and others. Farid laid her down on something supple that molded to her body, but she was too tired to open her eyes to see what it was.

His lips brushed her forehead, making her smile. "Sleep now, my O—"

She was out before he finished the sentence.

Farid was almost grateful to escape to his office after being poked and prodded by the medics. He considered going back to his quarters but didn't want to face his bed alone. He'd much rather join Bren in her room, but testing the link with her revealed she was deep in dreams. If he went to her, he'd end up taking her, and he knew she needed sleep.

He sighed and sank into his desk chair, rubbing his fully healed shoulder. He hadn't realized how much the wound nagged at him until it was gone. He stretched the kinks out of his arms and prepared to catch up on the work he'd left behind and bury himself in the quagmire of Suen-Earth politics. It was a mess, but at least one he understood, one he had some hope of bringing some order to someday, especially if Kyber could be convinced to join Bren's cause.

The situation between Bren and Farid was one he didn't know how to handle. He shouldn't have touched her again but hadn't been able to keep himself from reaching for her when he saw her standing there, alone and scared, and pretending she was in control. She would have convinced anyone but him—he knew her too well now, loved her too deeply to leave her when she needed him. It was hopeless. He felt as if the weight of an entire warship rested on his chest, choking the breath from him. Love meant no control, and no control meant dancing on the edge of disaster and praying not to fall. Foolish. *Hopeless.* He closed his eyes, shook his head, and forced himself back to the task at hand.

Tapping his fingers lightly over the hologram his imager automatically projected to hover over his desk, Farid set to work. Pictures and words flashed before him, too fast for him to decipher where one left off and the next began, but they stored in his mind to be processed by his psychic power. He opened a connection to this portal of the *Vishra*, sinking in to the information. News reports from all over Earth, information on their Internet, hundreds of languages, thousands of documents, millions of words. They streamed into the open conduit of his mind.

"Lord Arjun."

He jolted free of the connection with the ship, the abruptness of the loss a painful wrenching in his mind. He swayed in his seat, pressing his palms flat against the desktop to keep himself upright. He blinked hard, focusing on the man before him.

Johar Sajan stood in the doorway dressed in his Imperial Guardian uniform. He inclined his head slightly, his braids falling around his shoulders. "I apologize for disturbing you."

"Come in, please." Wariness slid through Farid, but he motioned for Johar to sit in a chair opposite his desk. "What may I help you with?"

"Nothing, my lord." The Guardian sat, his fingers gripping the arms of the chair. "I've instructed the *Vishra* to have your human meet us here when the medics are done attending to her minor injuries from your forest escapades."

"Why do you need to speak to both of us?"

"I don't, my lord." The man's gaze roved about the room, a hum of energy around him that he couldn't contain. "The emperor demands your presence, and my captain has tasked me with escorting you down to the planet."

"I see. We'll . . . wait here for Bren then." To give himself something to do, Farid pushed away from his desk and stood, walking over to a reproducer unit in his wall and calling for two canisters of *paayal*. The fiery drink should mellow them, since this was likely to be an awkward experience for both men.

"It shouldn't be long." Johar accepted the canister and crossed his long legs at the ankles.

Farid resumed his seat and took a deep drink, wincing as the acidic bite of flavor hit his taste buds. His belly cramped as he tried not to stare at the man who looked so much like Cilji's One. A man who, despite his youth, had changed Farid's view of the world forever. He swallowed and groped for the first topic he could think of. "How is everything with Tylara?"

The Guardian's expression flattened. "It's . . . complicated."

"Ah." Farid shifted in his seat, at a loss for words for one of the few moments in his life. A reluctant smile tugged at his lips as he recalled Bren's assertion that small talk was his profession. He wasn't doing well today.

Johar took a deep swallow of his *payaal*. "I've heard Preston is here to ask the emperor to have Arthur removed from power."

"Word gets around fast." Farid saluted the other man with

his canister, though his nerves jangled even more at moving the conversation from Johar's One to Farid's.

"I hope she succeeds in convincing him."

He blinked, startled by the sudden vehemence in the man's voice. "Oh?"

"My father was the first officer on the *Anshar*—it's why I volunteered for this expedition rather than remain with the Imperial Guardians tasked with protecting the Empress Dowager." Johar's smile was a chilling thing to see. "I would like nothing more than to repay the Earthan general in kind for his barbarism. And they call my family animals."

Farid ran his finger around the rim of his canister. "I am sorry for your loss, Sajan."

The words should have been mere reflex, but he found that they were true. Johar, like Farid, was now the last of his line. He could sympathize with what that would do to a man. For the first time, he looked at Johar and saw . . . a person. Like Bren and her change from seeing the Sueni as her enemies to seeing them as people like her, Farid now looked at Johar the same way. They were nothing alike, he and this man, and yet they had everything in common. It was unsettling.

"And I for yours, all those years ago." Johar's gaze was open, his words frank. "I was . . . angry for a long time over the loss of my brothers. The twins were too young to have died."

"As was my sister. She was wrong to do what she did." He could understand holding on to such anger. He had done the same. He drained the last of his *payaal*. "I'm sorry for that, too."

Johar shook his head, the intensity of his feelings making his fangs emerge. "And I'm sorry for what happened to your mother. She was a good woman, and she was only trying to help."

"We could keep apologizing all day."

The Guardian gave a bark of laughter and a wide smile, his

emotions far closer to the surface than Farid's—but that was the way of the Sajans—it didn't make *this* Sajan the monster Farid had painted in his mind. Perhaps it was knowing Bren, having her transition to a friend and a lover, that made Farid see so clearly. If he could not blame Bren for being one of Arthur's people, he could not blame Johar for being one of the Sajans. Neither of them was guilty by association, just as Farid was not to blame for what Cilji had done. He could see on Johar's face that he didn't hold Farid responsible, and for that he was far more grateful than he would ever have guessed. Something inside him loosened, crumbled. Somehow, when he wasn't looking, the burn of anger had finally guttered out of Farid's soul. He knew he had Bren to thank for the change within him. His One.

Anun, but he loved the woman. She deserved far better than the half-lies he'd told her so far. He owed her the truth, even if he wasn't certain he could let go of control enough to bond with her. It still terrified him, the thought of losing those he had the deepest bonds with again. He wasn't sure he could ever overcome that.

The Guardian leaned forward to set his empty canister on Farid's desk, then braced his forearms on his knees. "My One likes you, respects you. She is your friend. I have no desire to make that friendship difficult for her."

"Nor would I wish to come between a friend and her One." Farid nodded to the other man. He doubted the two of them would ever be friends—their personalities were too divergent—but he saw no reason for them to hold on to hostilities over events that neither of them had had any say in. It was a relief to be able to set something so painful where it finally belonged. In the past.

"If you were the only thing coming between my One and me, we'd be doing much better. She thinks I'll leave her for someone easier to deal with, thinks I can't handle her power because Sajans are half-feral." An annoyed hiss issued from the Guardian. "Maybe she's right—my people have always been wild—but that's a problem for another time."

Bren's scent called to Farid from down the hall, and he could hear her voice as she spoke to . . . Tylara. He arched an eyebrow at Johar. "It looks like your troubles are coming to visit you."

"Yes, I can smell them." The enormous Guardian climbed to his feet with Farid when the two women entered the room.

"Admiral Belraj." Johar bowed to Tylara. The two were both in their uniforms, wore high boots and black pants with a single gray stripe down the side, razers strapped to their hips, and tunics wrapped around their chests diagonally to button at the right shoulder, and still the contrast between them was marked. Tylara was a study in self-discipline, with short black hair, her eyes barely sparking despite her great power, her blue tunic perfectly creased with rows of silver embroidered symbols up the sleeves. Johar's braids swung riotously, his eyes flashing, his tunic a brilliant scarlet with a single gold star over his heart. Completely opposite, yet Farid could see how they would complement each other. If they wanted to. He hoped they worked things out.

Tylara's gaze narrowed as she looked at him, and Farid felt a pulse of the anger and frustration that wedged between the two. "Guardian Sajan."

Bren's eyebrows arched so high Farid would have been unsurprised if they reached her hairline. He sent her a private thought. *Yes, of the same Sajan family as my sister's One. An older brother. Johar Sajan.*

"I'll leave you all to your work. I just came to deliver Bren. I've informed her that the emperor requested her presence." Tylara inclined her head, her cool gaze never leaving her One. She turned smartly and marched out the door.

Johar snarled and stomped after her, nodding to Bren as he passed. "I will meet you both in the shuttle hangar bay."

Brows contracting, Bren looked to Farid. "What was that all about?"

"She's his One. They haven't bonded yet, and apparently their courtship isn't going well." As if Farid's courtship—if that's what he called what he'd been doing—was going any better. At least Tylara and Johar had the openness of honesty between them. When things were settled with the emperor, Farid needed to have a private conversation with his One that was long past due. He wasn't looking forward to it.

Bren winced. "That sucks."

"Yes, it really does."

8

Bren stood before a full-sized hologram of the emperor and his One. The floor of the shuttle shook under her feet as they sped through the atmosphere on Earth, rocketing toward the surface.

The imperial couple sat on a larger, plusher version of the little ship that held her, Farid, Johar, and a pilot in the scarlet uniform of an Imperial Guardian. She sized them up for a moment as Farid made formal introductions. Jana Townsend was the new empress's name. The girl couldn't have been more than twenty-one or twenty-two, but then, Kyber looked young himself. Much younger than Farid. Then again, she'd seen hardened soldiers at that age, killing machines. Age didn't mean much, experience did.

Though Jana wore a serious expression, her eyes reflected a deep happiness, a contentment that was enviable. Her hand rested securely in Kyber's grip, and they leaned toward each other, their shoulders brushing, even as they sat and faced her.

Bren wondered what that kind of bond would be like. She couldn't imagine anything more intense than the brief connections she'd had with Farid. Twin emotions ripped through her at the thought. First, a throb of utter longing, a craving for something deeper, something stronger and more lasting with the man she loved. Second was the knowledge that nothing she had with him would be as deep or as strong as the bond with his One would be. The mere thought of anyone having more of him than she did made her insides twist with dark, ugly jealousy.

She could see why Farid might fear that kind of connection, considering what had happened to his parents and his sister. He'd seen exactly how bad such a bond could be, all the worst possible outcomes, as it destroyed his family one by one. Sympathy went through her, but she didn't allow herself to look at him. He'd probably take it for pity, and that was the last thing she could feel for someone strong enough to live through all of this and still hold on and keep going.

Kyber flicked his fingers and a woman's face filled the panel. She looked like Jana, older and softer, but definitely a relative. The view expanded and beside the woman stood a man about the same age. A husband? A relative?

Bren's stomach jolted as Arthur appeared on the other side of the woman. Her eyes, gray like Jana's, filled with tears. "We just want our daughter back. Whatever the emperor wants, we'll do it. She's . . . she's our baby, our little girl."

Arthur's hand closed over the woman's shoulder. "The United States and our global coalition is going to do everything in its power to get Ms. Townsend back. We have reason to believe that she's been kidnapped and brainwashed by the Kith emperor's unnatural psychic power. She thinks she wants to be there. I'm afraid rescuing her will take a show of force we haven't demonstrated before, but we will. We will not stand for this travesty; we will not stand by and see our people stolen and made into slaves again." His brown eyes met the camera and seemed to look straight at Bren. "We want the woman back."

Her. He wanted her. He didn't give a damn about Jana. Other people had gone to the Kith ships and Arthur hadn't cared. He'd washed his hands of those who left the planet willingly, called them traitors to their country and their species. People like Bren.

The panel wavered as Kyber and his One came back into focus. Kyber's ebony brow rose. "You see why I sent for you."

Her stomach flipped, horrible realization rippling through her. "Whether they realize it or not, the Townsends are now General Arthur's prisoners. Bargaining chips. He knows they matter to your One." She swallowed, lifting her chin. "You want to trade me for them."

"I can't say I didn't consider it. For my One, there is very little I wouldn't give." A besotted smile curved his lips when he looked at Jana. He shook his head and sighed. "However, I can't do that."

"Oh? Why not?" Numbness spread through Bren's limbs, a sense of unreality enveloping her. There was no way to fight her way out of this one, nowhere to run or hide. This ship bore her wherever the emperor had decided she would go. For all she knew, they were dropping her off on Arthur's doorstep.

Johar spoke up from the front of the shuttle, his voice matter-of-fact. "Because you're his cousin's One. When Lord Farid bonds with you, you will be a Sueni citizen, and as much the emperor's responsibility as anyone born on Suen."

She swayed on her feet, one too many blows to her composure to absorb what the Guardian was saying. She looked over at the blond nobleman, her lover. "Farid?"

There wasn't an ounce of blood left in his face. His hand lifted toward her but dropped when she flinched. "I didn't want you to find out this way."

A bitter little laugh ripped from her throat, tears welling in her eyes. She blinked them away, embarrassed they had formed at all. "No, why don't you tell me the truth, Farid? You didn't want me to find out *at all*."

"Not at first, no." His voice was a low rasp of pain. "I'm sorry."

Well, that answered any lingering questions she might have about his feelings for her. Her throat closed, and no words came forth. There was nothing she could say to that. Agony unlike any she'd ever known before wrenched inside her. "I understand."

"It's not you . . . I do . . ." For once the diplomat seemed to be at a loss for words.

"This is neither the time nor the place for this conversation." If there ever was a time or place. She turned back to the projection of the emperor, desperately trying to lock down the emotions that threatened to drag her into a dark, horrible abyss. "If you're not going to trade me, then you want to use what I know about Arthur to get the Townsends back."

His lavender eyes sparked appreciatively. "Yes, exactly. And in exchange, I'll agree to help you remove General Arthur from power."

Jana's hand closed over his shoulder, and she leaned closer to the panel on her end of the transmission. Her long auburn hair fell forward and anxiety flooded her face. "You'll get my parents back, right? And everything will be okay?"

"I'll do everything I can, but we'll have to move fast." Bren straightened to attention, relieved that at least one part of her life was going according to plan. She only hoped they were able to find the girl's family. "Arthur knows I defected, and the longer I'm away, the longer he has to mitigate the usefulness of whatever information I have."

"Fast is good with me." One corner of the empress's mouth kicked up. "That's why we called you before you even got here, just to hammer out the details." Her eyes cut to Kyber, who gave her a disgruntled look. She petted his arm, her smile every bit as besotted as his had been, and he relaxed into her, grinning back. "I just can't leave the planet until we have them back."

Johar piped up again. "We'll be touching down in fifteen minutes, Your Majesty."

"Good. We'll see you when you get here." The emperor flicked his fingers again and the transmission ended.

"*Khalaa* . . ." Farid's deep voice trailed away, his features still bloodless.

She just stared at him. "You know what amazes me? The emperor would cross the universe to claim his One, and you won't cross a room for yours."

A muscle ticked in his jaw. "You know I have good reason to doubt how *wonderful* the One bond can be."

Glancing at the cockpit, she saw both of the Guardians studiously ignoring the conversation unfolding in the back of the shuttle. She pitched her voice low. "I know why you fear the One bond, why you fear love. I get that, I really do, but I also know what it's like to face your worst fears. What do you think I've been doing for days? I left the army, the only place I've ever belonged, the only home I've ever known, to come to you. I gave up everything and I *depended* on you to help me, to keep me safe. I never wanted to depend on anyone ever, not totally, but I did. I believed in you, trusted you . . . loved you."

Salty moisture stung her eyes again and she snapped around to stare out one of the small windows as the shuttle raced closer to land. A small choking noise rose from Farid, but she didn't look back at him. She couldn't.

Was there anything worse than to be in love alone? She'd never felt more helpless in her entire life.

And yet, pathetic fool that she was, she didn't regret it. A single tear slipped down her cheek and she swiped it away. She had a job left to do, even if the rest of her life was in shambles. At least the first part of her mission was complete.

She wasn't a total failure.

Farid drew a deep breath. "Bren, please. I lo—"

A huge boom rocked the shuttle, and she tumbled forward. She tried to brace herself with her hands, but she was moving too fast to stop. The last thing she saw out the window was red fire and black smoke streaking the blue sky. Her head slammed into the wall and the world went dark.

Bright sunshine warmed her cheek, blinding her as she opened her eyes. She moaned, grabbing her throbbing head as she sat up. Her ears rang, and when she looked at her hand, it was wet with her blood.

She blinked hard and swayed but forced herself to climb to her feet. Her movements were ginger, her hands braced against the wall of the shuttle as every muscle screamed in battered protest.

It took her a moment to realize she'd braced herself against the floor and she was standing on the window she'd once looked out. The shuttle was on its side, the door sagging halfway open to let the sunlight in. They'd been shot from the sky and had crash-landed.

And now she was alone.

Crawling across the chairs bolted into the floor, she worked her way toward the door. The staccato report of machine gun fire sounded outside the shuttle, and she froze, clinging to the broken door. White noise flooded the field they were in, and American and Sueni fighters buzzed through the air, firing at each other.

On the ground, men and women in army fatigues battled a handful of men and women in Imperial Guardian uniforms. Blue lasers burst from the razers the Guardians held, sizzling as they hit the humans. The stripes on an enormous feline blurred as it sped past her to drag a soldier to the ground. Three men lay scattered around the ship, dead, their eyes staring blankly at the cloudless sky.

Despite the chaos of battle, the bursts of gunfire, the roar of the Kith, the hammering of Bren's heart, she could still tell the Sueni forces were badly outnumbered and outgunned.

There was no sign of Farid. No Johar or Kyber or Jana. No one Bren knew.

Stumbling out of the remains of the shuttle, she winced when she hit the ground. Her knee throbbed from the crash and her head felt like a jackhammer was going off inside of it. Scooping up a pistol from one of the dead soldiers, she checked the clip to see how many bullets she had left. Almost full.

She pushed on, needing to find Farid, to make sure he was okay. Sweat slipped down her face to sting her eyes as she pressed her back to the ship, sliding along to peek around the far side. What she saw made her heart seize. Farid and Johar pinned down against the side of another shuttle, surrounded but still fighting back. Johar had lost his shirt, and he looked even more animalistic with his chest bare, his roar cutting through the sound of gunfire.

More men were coming, so she scuttled backward, dropped to her belly, and army-crawled toward the cover of two big army Hummers. Her elbows and knees screamed in protest, but she propelled herself along in spite of the pain. Rounding the front end, she was halfway to her feet when the cold steel of a gun muzzle pressed against her temple. "Preston."

"Zielinski." Her heart thumped hard, and she struggled to keep her voice even. "I see you enjoyed your little nap."

"Shut up, Preston." He motioned her to her feet and stared at her for a moment. "Come with me."

She moved in front of him, holding her gun out to the side, but he didn't demand she drop it. Confusion swamped her as he directed her to the open door at the rear of the Hummer. "What the fuck is going on?"

"There." He jerked his chin toward a slim woman curled up and moaning on the floor of the vehicle. She rocked herself in a fetal position, and her red hair glimmered like a copper penny.

"Jana," Bren breathed, reaching out a hand to cup the girl's shoulder. Cutting her gaze to Zielinski, Bren glared. "What did you do to her?"

"I didn't touch her, I swear to God. But I . . . You don't want to know what Arthur intends to do to her. I . . . I didn't radio in to tell anyone I found her." His eyes went wide, the same disbelief flashing across his face that he was doing what he was doing that Bren had felt when she'd contacted Farid.

Realization dawned, and she nodded, sliding a hand around Jana's arm and pulling her out of the Hummer. "Come on, honey, we need to go now."

"She's just a kid. An American. I didn't sign on to hurt our own people. It's not right. She hasn't even done anything wrong." Zielinski kept talking, justifying himself, while Jana swayed to her feet and looked dazed and confused.

Bren glanced at Zielinski. "Come with us."

He shook his head. "I'd be more use to you here. Unlike you, no one knows about me, about this."

"Then get out of here before they see you. I'll be in touch." She watched him nod, watched his gaze firm as he set his feet to the same terrifying path she had, and turned to walk away. "Thanks, Zielinski."

He glanced back before he disappeared behind another burned-out shuttle. "Don't thank me for doing the right thing."

Bren pulled a whimpering, flinching Jana around the Hummer and into the protection from gunfire between the two army vehicles. Bren's mind raced, and suddenly she knew her place in this whole mess. It wasn't just getting the Sueni on her side. She'd helped Arthur put together the coalition, so she had contacts in every single one of those countries. If she could convince Zielinski to defect—hell, if she herself could defect—

she could get others to join in. She had always been too up-front, too blunt to consider a career in Army Intelligence, but Farid could talk anyone into anything. Kyber had promised the Sueni would help, and with Bren's contacts and intimate knowledge of the coalition, they could make this work. They might not beat Arthur today, but they would beat him. A fierce smile curved her lips. They would *win*.

All she had to do now was survive this battle.

So, she'd better get on that. Her smile wiped away as though it had never been. Razers and machine guns spat fire at each other, and she could still see Johar and Farid fighting back to back against Earthan soldiers.

"Stay here, Jana." Bren let go of the girl to shimmy forward and peek around the front of the Hummer they crouched against. Things were clear for the moment. Everyone was occupied with their own fights. She looked back to motion Jana forward.

And the day went from bad to total clusterfuck when she saw the girl had moved to stagger around the back of the vehicle. She was going to get herself killed standing out in the open that way.

A soldier in camos came tearing around the Hummer, bringing his weapon to bear on the young woman. Bren shoved to her feet, lifted her pistol, put two bullets in the soldier's chest, and caught Jana around the waist to slam her to the ground.

"Kyber." The girl shook and sobbed, the first words she'd spoken since Bren arrived. "They have him. They . . . They're hurting him." Jana's whisper broke and she choked, retching. "I can feel it. They said they only wanted *me*, but they're *hurting him*."

Bren wrapped an arm around Jana, keeping her head down. "It's all right, honey. We'll get you out of here and then we'll find him."

Her narrow back heaved as she vomited on the grass. "My p-parents."

"And your parents, too." Bren pushed them both to their hands and knees. "Let's go."

When she looked up, she saw five more soldiers coming at them with submachine guns. Her blood froze in her veins. Shoving Jana back down, Bren covered the girl's body with her own, closed her eyes, braced for the impact of bullets, and prayed she survived long enough to finish what she'd started with Zielinski. She clenched her jaw.

A heart-stopping roar sounded overhead, and a shadow covered them. She looked up to see Johar braced above her. His fangs were bared and he fired his razer at the soldiers surrounding them. Three went down with gurgling screams. Bren brought her pistol around, and took out the last two, but not before a bullet slapped into the Kith's chest and he tumbled back to land in a heap on top of them.

Jana screamed, writhing as though she were in agony. Bren shook her. "Are you all right?"

"*Kyber.*" The girl twisted until she was face up, the fires of hell in her eyes. "I-I can feel every punch, every kick."

Her arms wrapped around her ribs and the air whooshed out of her as though someone had slammed their boot into her.

Johar groaned, the sound of a wounded animal. Bren left the girl on the ground. There was nothing she could do for the psychic pain, but she set her weapon aside, ripped her shirt over her head, wadded it up, covered the bullet hole, and leaned all her weight onto it to try to staunch the bleeding. He hissed between clenched fangs, his claws digging into the ground beneath him. "Lost my mesh armor in the crash. Was pinned by it. Had to take it off. Tylara will kill me."

She shook her head at his ramblings, pressing hard on the wound. Only some of it made sense. "Hang in there, Johar."

A big hand closed over her shoulder and she scrambled for the gun she'd dropped. "It's me, *khalaa*."

Relief ripped through her, so deep it shook her to her core. She couldn't speak, could do nothing but nod and keep her hands over Johar's wound, his dark red blood oozing between her fingers. Farid was alive. Thank God. Thank *God*.

Farid dropped to his haunches beside her, motioning three Kith Guardians forward. "You two, take the empress and get to one of the shuttles. Get her out of here. The rest of us will handle Sajan."

One of the Guardians spoke. "But the emperor—"

Farid shook his head, his voice a calm command, if roughened by the beast as the white noise suppressed his psychic powers. "His scent is fading. They've taken him beyond our reach. Save the empress, get back to the *Vishra*, and Admiral Belraj will organize a rescue. Go now."

"Do . . . as he says." Johar swallowed, sucking in a harsh breath. "The captain's dead. I'm . . . the ranking Guardian. Obey Lord Arjun."

"Yes, sir." Two Kith peeled away, one scooping up the heaving Jana, the other ready with his razer rifle to handle any threats that came their way.

"*Khalaa*, keep pressure on the wound while we get his arms and legs." Farid's hand squeezed Bren's shoulder, his touch a comfort even in the midst of mayhem.

She dipped her chin in a short nod. "Ready when you are."

The men moved to lift Johar, and she went with them, doing everything she could to stop the blood from flowing but to not hamper their progress. Every moment that passed, Johar's face lost color. His blue eyes locked on her face. His lips moved but no words came out.

"Hang in there, Sajan. We'll get you back to Tylara in no time." She tried to give him a reassuring smile but doubted it would have the desired effect. Gunfire and grenade explosions sounded in the distance, and her heart thudded in her chest. Icy tingles raced up her limbs as adrenaline and fear coursed through her. She pushed both aside. All she had to do was keep moving. Just put one foot in front of the other. Keep going. Don't stop.

Then there was a shuttle in front of them, and they were on board. They set Johar down and left Bren to tend him as they got the ship airborne. She braced her foot on the metal wall, struggling to hold them in place as the shuttle banked hard and rocketed into the sky.

The Kith's breath slowed to a rattling whisper, and Bren turned toward the cockpit. "Farid, is there a first aid kit on board?"

Farid slid out of his seat, stumbling as the ship hit turbulence. He slammed hard to his knees but had himself up in moments. Slapping his palm against a panel, it slid open and a dozen containers tumbled out onto the floor. He picked through the mess, ripped out a package, and came up with a slim metal tube. He shoved it into Bren's hand. "Press it to his neck."

She did as he commanded, felt it vibrate in her hand as it did whatever it was supposed to. Johar gasped and shuddered. "Tell my One . . . I love . . ."

"You can tell her yourself, Sajan." Farid's tone was rough, fierce. He clamped his hand on the wounded man's shoulder. "I'm not going to let a man who saved my One die. Don't even think about it."

Johar met his gaze, and his voice was a mere whisper in Bren's mind. *My brothers . . .*

"Have paid for what they did, as my family has paid." Farid's knuckles whitened as he squeezed tight. "I've finally realized that we are not them, and we have our own lives to lead. We are not guilty of their crimes, and we can make different choices than they did, no matter how similar we might be to them. We are not locked into their same fate."

Nodding once, Johar blinked and turned his head away to stare out the small window as they left Earth for deep, black space.

Bren swallowed, unsure what the exchange meant. If it meant anything at all. But Farid had called her his One. Utter longing had spread through her at those words, a wish that they would be true.

"My lord, I'm receiving a transmission," the pilot called from the cockpit. "The empress's shuttle never took off. She . . . she gave herself over to the Earthan forces in exchange for the emperor's freedom."

The breath left Bren's lungs in a rush. "They said all they wanted was her, and she could feel them torturing Kyber."

"Arthur will never honor that deal." Farid ran a blood-crusted hand down his face.

"You have no idea what he'll do to her if he knows they can feel each other's pain." She closed her eyes for a moment, a parade of horrors the young couple would go through marching through her mind.

"Anun save them." He sighed, but angry sparks had begun to boil in his eyes. "And pray to your God that we reclaim them both soon, else Anun won't be able to save this world. Tylara will rip it apart to get to the emperor."

Johar rolled his head, meeting Bren's gaze. "Why would Arthur do this? What could he possibly gain by starting a war? We've done *nothing* to any of you."

"It's not about the Sueni anymore. That's what I've been trying to tell you. That's why I'm *here*." Bren shifted on her battered knees, wincing but refusing to move lest she lose the pressure on Johar's chest. "General Arthur wants power. He wasn't always this way, but you gave him a taste of ultimate, unmitigated, unchecked power, and now that he has it, he wants to keep it."

Farid finished her thought. "So starting a war with us will

keep people scared, make them think they still need him, and keep him in power."

"Forever, yes." She nodded. "Or for as long as he's still alive. And then the next military dictator can step into his place, likely with a whole lot of bloodshed and death."

"We won't let that happen." Farid's low rumble reassured her on a deeper level than she understood, and she felt his mind brush hers, lending her a warm comfort. "The Sueni are now deeply invested in Earthan politics."

Which was why she'd come to Farid in the first place. Even if he never gave her what she needed as a woman, he'd ensured she got what she needed as a soldier, as a person, to be able to look herself in the eyes. She wasn't broken like her foster sister had been, she'd done her job, protected people as she'd always promised herself she would. And she would keep on protecting them, using people who believed as she did, like Zielinski. This was all she had lived for, once.

Now, she could only hope it would be enough, if Farid never changed his mind about wanting to bond with his One.

With *her*.

He'd almost lost her.

A week had gone by since they'd escaped the carnage of that Earthan battlefield, and the thought still staggered him, nearly drove him to his knees. He'd almost lost her. If not for Johar, he would have. The scene had unfolded before him, Bren protecting the empress, shielding her from harm while men surrounded them. He'd known he couldn't reach Bren in time, that she would be gone forever. Like the rest of his family.

Would it have mattered that he hadn't bonded with her yet? The loss would be even more devastating than his parents, his sister, *because* Bren was his One. As it should be. He'd finally answered his own question. He'd rather have her for whatever time fate granted him than to live without her.

If she'd have him.

Farid swayed on his feet, staring through a glass window into the *Vishra*'s medical ward. How long had he stood there thinking? He didn't know. The horror of all he had witnessed replayed in his mind over and over again. Bren's brush with death, Johar's blood spilling across the green grass, the empress's psychic link torturing her as Kyber was tortured.

Anun, where was his cousin now? Farid didn't know, and he swallowed the sick feeling that lodged in his throat. He blinked hard and forced himself to focus. On the other side of the glass was Tylara, hovering over a sleeping Johar, her hand tucked in his, her gaze locked on his face. He'd survived the bullet wound to his chest, barely. It would be quite some time before he was back to normal, but he would make a full recovery.

Taking a deep breath of the astringent air that typified this kind of ward, Farid let it ease out again. Johar's returning health was the *only* good news. The empress lay in a room not far from where Farid stood now. To the human eye, she looked fine fully dressed, but upon examination from Kith medics, they'd found her body bruised, and she reeked of sex and Arthur. She was holding together remarkably well, considering. Perhaps too well. Farid shook his head, pummeled by more worries than he knew how to handle.

The emperor hadn't been found in the week since he'd gone missing, and Kyber hadn't reached out psychically. Likely the result of constant exposure to Arthur's white noise machines. There was no way of knowing if he was alive. The Imperial Guardians were ready to mount an offensive, the feeling of rage building in the fleet pounded at Farid's temples.

They stood on the brink of war, and only the fact that the emperor was on the planet's surface had kept Tylara from allowing the ships to open fire.

Farid had worked himself into exhaustion for days, scrambling to find a way to save his cousin, his emperor. Under

Bren's direction, Farid had begun exploiting fissures in Arthur's coalition. Some countries were more open to negotiation than others, and he resorted to threats and dark promises where he had to. Before Bren and he were done, Arthur would have no one to turn to, no one to command.

The thought of Bren stabbed at Farid's heart. Anun, but he missed her. Missed her smile, her laugh, the flow of her thoughts and feelings through their link. Other than acting in her new capacity as an official Earthan advisor to the Sueni military, Bren hadn't so much as looked at him. The connection between them narrowed by the day, and soon he wondered if it would be there at all. He could read her mind as he did most Kin, but he couldn't bring himself to force the contact.

Until now.

Turning on his heel, he left the medical ward and wound his way through the ship's corridors to Bren's quarters. One way or another, they needed to figure out how things would be between them. Trepidation twisted in his gut, and he snorted. In his life, he had never imagined such dread at facing one slender Kinswoman. But the woman in question owned his soul, and that made all the difference.

He needed her, craved her, and he could no longer pretend otherwise. He didn't even want to. He was hers, all hers. He had hurt her by keeping the truth from her, and his heart was hers to do with as she wished. If she rejected him, he had earned it, but he would no longer hide behind excuses and lies. No matter how many horrible examples he'd seen of One bonds shattering lives—his parents, his sister, his cousin if he was ever found—Farid still wanted his chance with Bren. Life was too short and love was too precious not to take the risk.

The door to her quarters opened for him, and he saw her sitting in a chair, her bare feet propped on the window as she stared out at the fleet of battleships. "Hello, Farid."

"*Khalaa.*" He closed the door behind him but moved no far-ther into the room.

The gown she wore clasped at one shoulder and left the other arm bare. It was odd seeing her in the kind of *rishaami* garment worn by Sueni women. To him, she was everything that was good about Earth, that was nothing like Suen. She rolled her head on the back of the chair and shot him a glance. The blue sheen on the green fabric complemented her eyes, and her dark hair hung in thick waves down to her waist. The sight of her kicked him in the chest the way it had for the last week. Thanks to Anun that she was alive, even if she was never his.

"What can I do for you?" She cradled a canister between her palms, and from the smell of it, it was *paayal*.

"Bond with me." The words jerked out of him, but he didn't regret them, he couldn't. It wasn't what he'd intended to say when he came here, wasn't what he'd expected, but everything about her had always been more than what he expected.

She froze with the canister halfway to her mouth. Then she shook herself a bit, took a sip, and set the drink aside. "I don't think that's what you really want, is it?"

Anun, that stung. He flinched at having his deepest longings thrown back in his face, but he knew he deserved it for having kept the truth from her for so long, for being too cowardly to face his fears. "Perhaps it's you who doesn't want it."

"I told you I love you." Pain reflected in her eyes at those words—because she'd said anything to him or because he hadn't responded in kind? He wasn't sure. The bond that would once have told him was almost gone, and the beast inside him writhed in agony at the lack.

"Love and bonding . . . those are different things." She'd once told him such a bond was the most horrifying thing she could imagine, and a part of him wondered if a woman as fiercely independent as she was could ever accept such a total sacrifice of self. He craved it like the sweetest, most potent drug. Growing to know her had only made the addiction stronger, sent its roots deep into his soul until he knew he'd never be free of her, even if he lost her now, he'd never be who he'd been before he knew her. But with knowing her came the understanding that she might never need him the way he needed her.

Her eyebrow arched, but otherwise she remained still, barely breathing. "Are they so very different?"

"Yes." He moved toward her, wishing he could touch her, but knowing he should not. "One is to give your heart and soul to someone, the other is to give your life, your mind, your memories. Love is beautiful, but it can die if you don't nurture it. Bonding can never die, even if love does. It will eat you from the inside out if you don't keep the love alive."

She tilted her head back to hold his gaze as he stepped within arm's reach. "You'd be locked to someone forever that you learned to feel nothing for."

"Or learned to hate." As his sister and her Sajan had, but Bren and he were different, and they could make their own destiny, as she would say.

"Yeah, that's going to take some getting used to." She shrugged her bare shoulder, the soft *rishaami* shifting with the movement.

His gaze followed the lines of the garment down to where it cupped the swell of her breast. His body clamored, the beast clawing for freedom, reminding him how long it had been since he'd been inside her sweet, hot body. He swallowed, jerking his gaze away to meet her eyes.

A knowing smile tilted her lips. "I feel it, too. The craving."

Craving, yes. A need so deep it consumed him, ruled him. He closed his eyes. "You're not afraid that we'll end up like Kyber and Jana? Like my parents? My sister?"

"I'm terrified that we'll end up that way. God, seeing what happened to Jana, watching the girl be tortured by psychic proxy?" She sucked in a deep breath. "I'd be a fool not to be scared. But you told me some things are worth the pain. *You're* one of those things for me.

"So, yeah, bad things could happen, Farid. Bad things can always happen. You've seen them happen firsthand and so have I." She sighed and he heard her gown rustle as she stood. She moved toward him and he backed away, knowing if he touched her, he would be lost, and he knew they both needed to finish the conversation they'd started. When the backs of his knees hit the edge of her gelpad, he sat and stared up at her lovely, precious face. There was some small flicker of light, of hope in her eyes that was so different than the contained expression she showed the world. "You know how I grew up, Farid, how I've lived my life, what I've seen and done. Bad things happen even to good people. You think I don't know that?"

"No. Yes." He shook his head. "Anun, I don't know."

"We have to hold on to the best life offers us." She cupped his jaw in her palms, and he leaned into her soft touch with a purr. "We have to savor the good times to shore up our defenses against the bad times."

"How can you be so . . . hopeful . . . for such a steadfast cynic?" He'd been inside the woman's mind, loved her, and still didn't understand her. She'd told him she loved him, that she knew how to make the hard choices. Lesser species or not, the woman was far stronger than he was. She deserved better, and it wasn't the first time he'd thought so. But it was the first time he'd looked inside himself and demanded that he *be* better, be what she needed. Not for the moment, for whatever current crisis they faced, but forever.

He wanted to keep her, and he would do whatever it took to convince her. Even if it meant facing his deepest fears of loss, even if it meant giving up control, because he knew, no matter what, that Bren would never accept him controlling her. She wanted all of him, just as he wanted all of her.

"It's not easy, but I manage. I expect bad things to happen. Every day, all the time, but that doesn't mean I don't recognize the gifts I've been given or that I don't appreciate every single one of them. Like you." She bent forward and kissed him. His hands bracketed her hips, and the feel of her warm curves through her clothes made his cock go rigid. Just that light touch had his tenuous grasp on his restraint ripping away. He jerked his mouth from hers, thrusting her away from him in a desperate bid for sanity and she rocked back on her heels to maintain her balance. That flash of hope he'd seen in her gaze sputtered out, and she dropped her hands, pain and confusion filling her expression. "I'm sorry. You said you wanted . . . I thought you came here because . . . I don't know. I guess you don't even really want the easy sex anymore, let alone the bond."

"Easy sex? When has the sex between us ever been *easy*?" He caught her arm, dragged her back until she tumbled onto his lap. "I want to touch you again, but that's not why I'm here. I have to say it before you make me so crazy I can't put a coherent thought together." He curled a knuckle under her chin and forced her to look at him. "I love you. I need you. I trust you. I want to bond with you and never, ever be alone again for as long as we both live—however long or short that is. I want to be the person who never leaves you. I want to be the person you can always depend on, who never abuses your trust. I just want you."

"I do trust you. I never would have come to you if I didn't. I know I can rely on you, depend on you. I always will. You respect me even when you don't agree with me, and I've never known anyone who could compare to you. I *love* you." Tears welled up in her eyes, and it killed him that his warrior woman would cry. Still he felt the unfurling of the link between them as it widened, as her emotions bled into his. "I knew that you'd go to your One someday, and all along some part of me knew that you were . . . mine."

He closed his eyes as he felt all the tangled, wonderful things that filled her heart. Respect, friendship, desire, joy . . . love that would sustain him all the days of his life, even if that life lasted far longer than hers. She would always be the strongest, best part of him. "I am yours. I always will be."

She shifted on his lap, straddling his thighs. Her lips brushed over his, gentle and hesitant. "I love you so much, Farid."

"Show me how much." He kissed her, took her mouth with a greed that he couldn't stop. He let his own feelings flow back to her, his relief that she could forgive his doubts in himself, in their bonding, his wonder that he'd found her, his endless passion for her, his feral craving, his deep love. The sweetness of it cycled back and forth, building, sharpening, but he knew it was only a tiny fraction of what was yet to come, and for the first time in his adult life, he welcomed that. He slid his hand down the back of her gown, the heat of her body warming the fabric. He broke away from her mouth, kissing her jaw, her ear, sliding his tongue down her throat. "Every moment without you has been a torment."

"I want you, Farid." She moaned, rubbing herself against him, her breasts brushing his chest, her sex hot through their clothing. "I want every part of you inside me, bonding with me. I want you to make that noise that's not quite human and not quite animal. I love that. I love pushing you past your limits."

"You're the only one who can." And his mouth claimed hers, his tongue thrusting between her lips. She answered his wildness with her own, raking her nails up his back as she jerked his shirt from his pants. His hands were in her hair, pulling her head back to expose her throat. "Tell me how you want me, Bren. Tell me you crave me. Tell me you need nothing else right now but my touch."

"I do." She sobbed when he nipped at her neck, writhing against him.

"Say it."

Her voice was a barely coherent rush of breath as she twisted in his arms. "I love you, want you, crave you, need you. Right now. Please."

The rough sound he made was the one she'd described, and he let the animal instinct guide the psychic power. He loosed the fetters on the feline, setting it free to claim its mate as it had wanted to all along. It had taken the man so much longer to catch up, but both sides of his nature were united in a single purpose now.

Bren. One. Mate. Everything.

He growled when she worked her gown up her hips, unfastened the shoulder clasp, and pulled it over her head. He palmed her bare breasts, chafing the tips with the pads of his thumbs. He sucked her nipples into his mouth one at a time, nipping and biting them as he had her throat. He'd take her a piece at a time tonight. Every inch of her would be his.

"Yours, yes. Every inch of me." Her back bowed and she pressed herself into his mouth and hands. He hadn't even realized he'd sent her the thought, but he let the link widen further with every passing moment. It was good, right, perfect. She tugged at his shirt until he simply ripped it in half, his claws shredding it, and he threw it away. He wanted nothing between them. Her fingertips circled his nipples. They hardened for her and he groaned. She giggled, the sound light and young. Carefree. "And all of you is *mine*."

Her nails flicked hard over his nipples, making him jolt and hiss. She giggled again, pushing him back until he braced his hands on the gelpad. Then she swirled her tongue around the beaded areola, sucking hard. His cock throbbed in his pants, his hips bucking. Anun, if she kept that up, he wouldn't make it inside her before he came. And he wanted her with him, every step of the way.

He let himself fall back on the gelpad, wrapped his hands

around her knees, and slid her forward until her sex hovered over his mouth. The scent of her wetness was intoxicating. He couldn't wait to taste her, slide his tongue over her slick, swollen lips, and feel her come against his mouth.

"Farid . . ."

"Every inch of you, *khalaa*." He kissed her there, and she screamed. He clamped his hands over her thighs, dug his claws into her flesh, and held her down. He felt her shock at the contact, it thrummed through the conduit between them. But after the shock came the stunned pleasure that made her hips arch, made her moan and sob. He loved it, loved that he could do this to her, loved that she gave him everything. He licked her sex, her passionate response to him increasing her wetness until it flooded his tongue. He sucked on her pussy lips, lapping at her sweet cream. He bit at her hard clit, and she begged in incoherent thoughts and words. Begged him never to stop, begged him to let her come. He stabbed his tongue into her tight channel and purred against her overheated flesh.

A series of high, thin cries broke from her mouth, and her pussy spasmed around his tongue. He worked her hard, then suckled her clit and purred again, deeper and longer. She sobbed, shaking with another wave of orgasm that broke through his mind as it broke through her body. Jerking feebly, she tried to escape. He gave her clit one last lick before he let her up.

Collapsing beside him, she shuddered. He rolled to his side and reached for her; she threw herself into his embrace, wrapping her arms around his neck to hold him near. He closed his eyes, his chest rumbling with a purr. His cock was desperately hard, but he savored this quiet moment with her, this eye in the storm of their bonding.

She looped her leg around his thigh, opening herself to his thrust. He reached between them and wrenched open his pants, freeing his cock. Her lips brushed his neck, and then she bit him. Hard.

He roared, the feline provoked, and he slammed himself inside her. She cried out but arched herself closer instead of pulling away. She wanted this, the feral side of him. All of him, he'd promised. So, he gave it to her.

Claws and fangs bared, he stared into her eyes as he worked his cock in her tight sheath. He let the animalistic possession flow through their link, the side of him he'd always worried would scare her to her very independent soul, but he saw only acceptance on her face, felt only love come through to him.

He drove his dick into her, building the speed and force of his thrusts as he expanded their connection. Soon her thoughts and hopes and desires tangled with his, until he didn't know whose was whose, which was which. Their minds danced together, melding, yet separate. His hips pistoned hard, their skin slapping together with each deep penetration. A carnal symphony that pleasured the feline as much as the psychic. Her sex clenched around him, and she clung to him, depending on him to guide her, to lead this dance, and bring them both through it.

He had never loved her more.

The heat of his power gathered inside him, building to a fever pitch. It was almost painful to keep it locked within him. His heart pounded so loudly, it drowned out every other sound. Slipping his hand between them, he rolled his thumb over her clit. Her pussy contracted every time he stretched her with his cock, and soon he gave up thinking and reacted on pure feral instinct. His palm cupped her ass, pulled her tight to the base of his dick. He ground against her clit, sensing which rhythm, which angle, which touch pleased her most. Sweat dampened their skin, sealing them together.

She gasped, her hand clutching his arm. "Farid, please! I'm going to come."

"Yes!" He rammed himself deep one last time, shoving them both over the edge. Her pussy clamped around him tight, making him groan between gritted fangs. The heat inside him erupted with volcanic fury, burning away anything that wasn't her, that wasn't *this*. His cum pumped into her body, and he let his psychic energy pour into her mind. No barriers, no limits.

Starbursts flashed before his eyes, and he closed them tight, his mind spinning as it meshed with hers. It was beyond his control, and he let it slip through his fingers. The beast was satisfied, a purr sliding free. He held on to her, gathering her to his chest, where his heart hammered. She was there with him, clinging to him. His power hit her full-force; she screamed and came again. He opened his eyes to look at her beautiful, precious face, saw that his power reflected back at him, that green sparks flashed in her ocean blue gaze. The pleasure was twice as intense, the fulfillment beyond reckoning at finally being one with a woman crafted just for him. His memories and emotions tripped over hers, but it was so good, so perfect. He believed. She belonged.

All of her, all of him. Them. One.

Carnal Empress

1

He was naked and on his knees.

Kyber. Her One.

Chained in the middle of a small, cold room, his arms were stretched out to the sides, wrists in heavy manacles. A thick collar wrapped tight around his neck and attached to the ceiling. He sagged against the bonds, his long ebony hair falling forward to cover his face.

He didn't even look up when the door opened, gave no indication that he'd even noticed.

Jana's heart stuttered, her palms moistening on the handle of the gun she held. Was he more damaged than their intelligence had led them to believe? There was no way a Kith, especially the Kith *emperor*, wouldn't detect someone's approach. A low hum vibrated through the air in this entire military compound. White noise, with an extra added squeal that dampened the Kith's psychic ability. Still, Kyber's animal side should have sensed her, smelled her. He didn't so much as twitch.

She swallowed, giving herself a moment just to *look* at him.

It had been so long—months—since she had seen him, touched him. Dark, ugly bruises and fresher crimson lash marks mottled his once flawless skin, needle tracks from whatever they were drugging him with scored the insides of his arms.

But he was alive. That was all that mattered. He was alive and whole and could heal from whatever they'd done to him. Relief made tears well in her eyes, but she blinked them back. Holstering her weapon, she moved to kneel before him.

She lifted her hand, and his head snapped up, startling her. He lunged for her, wrenching at his shackles. His fingers were tipped in deadly talons, long fangs curving from his mouth. Her breath seized in her lungs as his violet eyes locked on her face, alert . . . and glittering with hate. Hate for her. Hate she'd more than earned.

Rage tightened his bruised features, and his eyes narrowed to dangerous slits, pale lavender sparks roiling in his irises, but not as fast as they would have if the white noise weren't pumping through every inch of this hellhole. The chains rattled as he struggled against them again. He hissed at her, more beast than man gazing out of those eyes at her.

Heart pounding in her ears loud enough to drown out all other sounds, she scrambled back. She closed her eyes for a moment, shutting out the ugly truth written on his face. He despised her. Her One despised her. Sucking in a deep breath, she forced herself to calm. She'd known it was coming, known she deserved it, and it was hard pretending that everything was going to be all right, but she had to. She always had to.

She met his gaze, unflinching before the disgust reflected back at her. "I'm going to get you out of here and back to your ship. We'll deal with everything else after that."

He snarled, the feline sound a subvocal rumble in his throat. It raised the hairs on her arms, and unease crept up her spine. Despite the fact that he was chained, she felt like the helpless prey to his ruthless predator.

Pushing herself to her feet, she tried to ignore that the tight space stank of blood, urine, and fear. She pressed her finger to the little Sueni communication device nestled in her ear that allowed her to speak to the team of Imperial Guardians on this mission. "Emperor located. Rendezvous in ten minutes."

A small click answered her, an acknowledgement of information received.

Time to get to work. Their window of opportunity was fast closing, and they might never get the chance again. She loosened the straps on a small backpack and dropped it on the floor to dig through. Setting aside a U.S. Army uniform for Kyber to wear as a disguise, she pulled out the equipment she needed.

"Turn your face away and close your eyes." She wrapped her hand around the chain that attached to his neck. The collar would have strangled him if he'd tried to shift forms. Her insides chilled at the thought.

He glared at her, distrust evident in his gaze. She arched her eyebrow at him, shrugged, and lit the tiny laser cutter. The flash of light and intense heat made him flinch and jerk away, finally obeying her. The flicker of animal wariness, of caged beast, that shone in his eyes before he closed them made her belly clench with guilt. She shook her head and got back to the task at hand. No bigger than a ballpoint pen, the cutter made quick work of his manacles.

He was on her in moments, one hand fisting in her shirt and the other wrapping around her throat to slam her against a wall. His speed was breathtaking, making him little more than a blur that left her gasping. Her fingers snapped around his wrist, trying to free herself from his grip. It was a futile effort. The sparks in his eyes were wild, terrifying. Her heart tripped before it raced.

"This is some kind of trick. A new game Arthur is playing with my mind." The voice was guttural, broken, barely human. Nothing like the urbane, skilled lover she had once known.

"Has it been fun rutting with him all these months? Does he make you moan, Jana?"

Shock and horror flooded her system, a dark wave of the memories than never stopped haunting her exploding through her mind. *No.* She couldn't think of that. Not now. She stomped the ugliness down as fast as she could.

She choked a bit when Kyber's fingers flexed, wrenching her back to the present. "I . . . I haven't been with Arthur for months, Kyber. It was only that first few days. I've been on your ship, working to . . . find a way to save you."

"*Lies.*" But the self-doubt on his face, the uncertainty of what was true and what was false made her chest squeeze with more guilt. She moved one hand to cup his cheek, but he caught her wrist, pinning it to the wall beside her head.

Her jaw clenched and she stared up at him. "This isn't a trick, Kyber. I'm here and I will get you back to your people."

"My *people*." He looked stunned but shook his head, a lock of inky hair whipping into his eyes. "My people would never have let my O—the *empress* come with them."

She snorted, twisting against his hold. "They couldn't stop me. I'm the empress. You weren't there to countermand me, so they're bound to obey me. All they could do was come with me to protect me. And you."

The doubt wavered a bit, and he licked at a cut on his lower lip. "I smell no Kith."

"Hard to infiltrate a human compound when the sparkling eye thing gives you away. Plus, the white noise dulls the Kith abilities and makes them a liability." Hell, the humming electronic squeal of it made a headache begin to throb at the base of *her* skull, so she didn't even want to know what it did to a Kith. She kept her voice even, her tone firm and sure. "Bren thought it best to only bring Sueni *Kin* Guardians with us."

His nostrils flared, as though trying to catch some hint of Suen on the air. He looked a bit dazed. "Bren. Farid's One."

"Yes."

"They bonded after I was taken." His head gave a tiny shake as though trying to clear it. Watching him struggle made tears well in her eyes, but she blinked them away and gritted her teeth.

"Yes, your cousin bonded with his One. Life went on without you." Her voice came out harsher than she intended, but it was either that or break down, and she couldn't do that. Not here, not now. Not ever. She jerked her chin in the direction of her gear. "We don't have time for this. Get dressed so we can go. Or stay here and see what Arthur does next."

He shoved away from her with a sharp hiss. The back of her head *thunked* against the wall, but she ignored the sting. Instead, she watched him hunker down and grab the garments she'd brought, sliding them on with quick efficiency.

Even as battered as he was, she couldn't tear her gaze away from him. He was a little leaner than he had been, but his muscles still rippled under his skin and he moved with the deadly grace of a feline. He was a beautiful man, as beautiful as he had been the day he'd made her *his*.

She shook herself, palmed her weapon, and pulled the extra out of her ankle holster. When he turned back to her, she handed him her backup pistol. His fingers trembled a bit as he took it, and she flinched when he trained the gun on her. "I'm getting you out of here and back to the *Vishra*. Point that thing somewhere else."

He jerked the muzzle toward the door, indicating she walk out first. "You'll forgive me if I don't think giving you my back as a target is wise. You've already betrayed me . . . more than once."

Her stomach cramped at hearing the words fall from his lips, but she refused to crumble under the hurt, the self-loathing. "I wasn't lying when I said I was only with Arthur for a few days."

"We'll see, won't we?" He motioned her out with the gun again, his eyes narrowed and cold.

Pivoting on her heel, she pushed her way through the door, leading with her weapon as Bren had taught her. Adrenaline surged, and she welcomed it, channeled it, let it sharpen her senses. Scents intensified until she could smell the jasmine of Bren's shampoo, hear the thump of footsteps down the hall.

The other woman stood guard at the door, her back braced against the wall across from them, her weapon at the ready.

"Farid let you come without him?" Kyber's voice was a low growl.

"Of course." She cut a pointed glance to Jana. "*He* knows he should leave military operations to military personnel."

Jana just arched an eyebrow. "Save the chit-chat for later. Let's go."

Bren's gaze twinkled with laughter, but she nodded and motioned for them to follow her down the corridor. They stepped over a pair of soldiers that had been knocked out and tied up. All was quiet as they wound their way through the bowels of this isolated military compound. Bren and Farid's intelligence had shown this was the best time to try to rescue Kyber, just after the dawn shift started, and hours before anyone checked in again. Everything was going according to plan. So far. Jana wouldn't draw an easy breath until they were back on board the Sueni flagship, orbiting far above Earth.

Bren held up her hand and they halted, breath baited as they waited to see what was out there. This wasn't good. Unease slid through Jana. They were supposed to be joined by Imperial Guardians at this juncture. There wasn't a soul in sight. Bren pivoted on her heel, pointed to her eyes, and then to the corner ahead of them, silently telling them to stay where they were while she scouted ahead. Jana dipped her chin in a short nod.

She closed her eyes and worked to steady her breathing, listening for Bren's return, listening for footsteps that would indicate someone else approached. Jana had known that she was the weakest link on this mission, that she shouldn't come, but her every waking moment since Kyber was taken had been about freeing him. She couldn't stand by and do nothing. She *had* to be here for this.

Her eyes popped wide at the sound of boots ringing on the linoleum floor *behind* them. Damn. She shifted her grip on her weapon. Someone was coming. More than one someone, and she'd guess from the heavy footfalls they were big and male. Double damn.

Lifting her hand, she cued her ear comm. She made her words no more than a breath of air. "We have company here, Br—"

Kyber didn't wait for her to finish her sentence. Dragging her into a short side corridor, he crowded her into the darkest corner. She wrapped her arms around his waist, pointing her pistol in the direction of the passing soldiers. If the men so much as slowed their step, they'd be in for a nasty surprise.

Every second that ticked by ratcheted her tension up, making her muscles go rigid. And they weren't the only thing. Kyber's rising erection dug into her hip. Her breath tangled in her throat, her eyes flared wide, and she snapped her gaze up to meet his. Volcanic heat exploded in her belly, shocking her with its force. He was plastered to her from breast to groin, and she could feel every inch of his hard muscles, his hot cock. Her nipples tightened, her pussy dampening, fisting on nothing. After all she'd been through, she'd never imagined wanting sex again, but . . . she wanted. With Kyber. Now.

He glowered down at her, the lavender sparks in his irises

roiling fast. His voice was a quiet hiss. "It is a biological reaction, nothing more. Don't think it changes anything."

Shaking her head, she swallowed. She knew it meant nothing, but it took every ounce of her willpower to keep from rubbing herself against him like a cat in heat. Her sex was slick with juices, and she craved the feel of him thrusting hard and deep within her. Tingles raced over her flesh, her eyelids drooping to half-mast as sensations she'd forgotten she could experience ricocheted through her. There'd been a time when her minutest physical reaction elicited a highly pleasurable response from him. He'd stroked, kissed, and explored every millimeter of her body.

But that was before Arthur.

Cold punched through her, killing the heat building within. The reminder of that man made her stomach turn. Pressing her back tighter to the wall, she tried to escape Kyber's touch. Fruitless, but she tried.

It was Kyber's instinct to find her and bond with her that had brought them to this ugly, awful place. He'd come from Suen for her, gone down to Earth's surface for her, which left him vulnerable enough to be taken captive by the leader of Earth's military forces. General William Arthur. God help her, his name alone had the power to make her want to vomit.

Arthur said she'd been kidnapped and he'd make the Sueni pay until she was returned to her family and home. She'd have done anything to save her One and offered herself in exchange. Her mind was intertwined with Kyber's, and she could feel the way he was being cruelly tortured.

Arthur used that to his advantage, forcing her to sleep with him as the price to return Kyber. Even though she knew it would distress her One—and his mental command told her not to do it, that he could escape without her sacrificing herself—

she did what she'd thought she had to do to help him. She'd been unable to bear the thought of him in pain; she'd experienced every blow with him.

What she hadn't expected was that the link between her and her One would be severed in that moment of betrayal, and her mind would be once again her own. Once her purpose was served, and it was obvious fucking her, *hurting her* no longer tormented Kyber, Arthur had shipped her back to her parents as a media show of how dedicated he was to protecting Earthans. Who would have believed her if she'd told the truth about him? Everyone thought she'd been brainwashed by the Kith.

It wasn't until Farid and Bren's fast-growing intelligence ring had found Jana and brought her to the *Vishra* that she'd learned how big a fool she'd been. Arthur hadn't let Kyber go. She was just another tool in the general's war games. Bile rose, coated the inside of her mouth, and she swallowed the bitter self-reproach. She stuffed the horrible emotions deep, deep down in the darkest crevice of her soul. Just as she'd been doing for years. Since her brother died. She had plenty of experience in convincing everyone that everything was just fine. This was no different.

That Kyber thought she'd stayed with Arthur for *months*, that she'd *enjoyed* what he'd done to her in bed made her ill, made her angry. She hadn't slept through the night since Arthur, hadn't been able to escape the nightmares. Enjoy it? It was everything she could do not to wretch when she let herself think of it. Hell, *let* herself? Those memories didn't stop. Not ever. She'd like to *let* herself think of something else for once, and familiar despair bubbled up inside her.

She clenched her jaw and quashed all those feelings, too. She rolled her head against the wall and focused on the task at hand. Her grip tightened on her gun, her hand steadying.

"The pattern of their step says they hunt something. Us, no

doubt." Kyber's tone was detached, almost disinterested as he shared that fact with her.

He peeled himself away from her to position himself at the mouth of the hallway, preparing to spring at his approaching prey. Jana swallowed and crouched behind him, praying harder than she'd ever prayed before that they'd all get out of this alive.

The muzzle of a machine gun came into view. Kyber froze until the rest of the man was within arm's reach. Stepping forward, he slammed his fist into the man's throat, who gurgled and choked, twitched and went silent. Dead. Kyber swung his body around and used it for cover as the second man opened fire. The sounds exploded in the silence, jolting Jana forward. She lifted her weapon and pulled the trigger, catching the second man in the leg. He screamed and went down in a spray of blood. Kyber swung his pistol around and put two bullets in the soldier's head.

Then it was over. Kyber gently lowered the first guard to the ground. Jana's hands trembled, her palms slippery with sweat. "I've never shot anyone before."

The comm. in her ear fuzzed for a moment before Bren's voice came through. "We're taking fire on the ground floor, southeast corridor."

Jana tried to slow her heaving lungs, adrenaline ripping through her system. The light *rat-tat* noise in the distance finally reached her ears. Gunfire. She transferred her weapon to one hand and cued her comm. "Same here. We just took care of two guards and we weren't discreet. We'll come to you."

"Roger." The comm. clicked and Bren was gone.

Kyber wavered on his feet and Jana grabbed his bicep to keep him steady. Her heart thumped hard and she checked him over for bleeding. Had he been shot? She hadn't seen anything. Oh, God. She tugged on his arm. "Are you all right?"

He shook his head. "The squealing noise . . . and the drugs

they gave me . . . they slow everything down, fog my senses. Nothing is as it should be."

"We just need to get you away from the noise, and the medics can handle the drugs when we get you back to the ship." She said it as much to reassure herself as him, but they'd come too far to fail now. "Can you walk or should I tell them to come get us?"

He snorted and straightened, arching one regal brow. "If it means getting out of here, I can *run*."

That sounded like the Kyber she knew. A wide grin flashed across her face and she shifted her grip on his arm, shoved her fingers into his silky black mane and yanked him down for a hard, quick kiss. If she was going to die, she wanted the taste of her One on her mouth to be the last thing she experienced. "Just in case."

For a moment, he looked dumbfounded, and a flash of old desire streaked across his face. Before he could figure out how to respond, she dropped his arm and skipped back. Checking her weapon, she nodded to him and turned to lead the way down the hallway. She'd spent more hours than she could count memorizing the layout of this facility. She could probably navigate it in her sleep. Of course, the schematics didn't include guards with guns. She ignored the way her belly clenched at the memory of the shocked look on the soldier's face as he'd landed, howling, in a pool of his own blood. She'd do whatever it took to get her One free. She'd already done much worse than shoot a man in the leg. She'd failed that time, and it was far from the first time she'd failed someone she loved. She had to succeed this time. She *had* to.

Maybe then the night terrors could stop, and she could finally lay the past to rest.

The heat from Kyber's body enveloped her from behind as she paused at a corner and peeked around to see if anyone awaited them.

"There is no one. Let's go." His voice was terse, angry, and she knew he was pissed that she'd made him want her with a simple kiss. That was how it was supposed to be with your One, but he didn't want to be her One anymore, did he? He'd cut the connection between their minds.

She'd had a little over twenty-four hours to share his thoughts, emotions, memories, but the connection had been so deep, so instantaneous, that she hadn't known where he ended and she began.

Now the only person in her head was *her*. Alone, echoing, and empty after the intensity of being One with him. She had no one to blame but herself, she reminded herself with ruthless force. She'd been a fool, made the classic, stupid mistake, and played right into General Arthur's hand.

And it cost her everything.

She hadn't even managed to save the man she loved from torture and imprisonment. But she wasn't that girl anymore. She'd sold herself, her love, and her freedom short in the past, and now she needed to right the wrongs her naiveté had caused.

She had to make everything all right again, so she didn't have to work so damn hard to pretend it was. The horrible, strangling pressure that built inside her like a volcano might ease for once. It would be too devastating to bear if it ever erupted. So, she couldn't let it. Not ever. She had to keep it all under wraps.

They ghosted down hallways and up two flights of stairs to get to the ground level. Every time they reached a door, she used the tiny handheld Sueni imager Farid had trained her to operate to override the locks and security systems. The problem with trusting technology too much, he'd said, was that someone with better technology could annihilate your defenses. Jana was just glad her hands didn't shake too badly while she was using the contraption. She tried to suppress the reaction from too much adrenaline surging within her veins but knew her success was limited.

A tiny spurt of triumph flashed through her when they finally met up with two Imperial Guardians on the other side of the last door. Of course, that also meant the exchange of bullets she'd heard two floors down now boomed like cannon fire. She tried not to wince as the roar bombarded her ears. Now she knew why they hadn't run into any more soldiers. Bren had kept them occupied up here.

The Guardians gave Kyber brief salutes and he nodded in return. "You're both new."

"Yes, sire." One stepped forward. "I'm Natheem, and this is Dhalesh. The Guardians needed replenishing after the battle . . . when you were taken. We transferred from the fleet."

Dhalesh glanced at her. "Bren says reinforcements will be on their way, so we need to extract the emperor *now*." An incredulous smile flickered over his face for a moment. "She says this mission has turned into a 'SNAFU and a complete clusterfuck.'"

Yep, that sounded like the army-speak Bren used when things got tense. Jana nodded and stifled a grin. "Well, let's unclusterfuck it, shall we?"

"Yes, Your Majesty." He spun and led the way, the second Guardian taking the rear of their little party. They moved at a fast clip, and Jana looked back to make sure Kyber was keeping up. He was. He didn't so much as spare her a glance but held his handgun at the ready and his long fangs protruded from his mouth. Perspiration rolled down his face, so she knew he wasn't holding up as well as he pretended.

Her heart hammered and she tried to focus on everything at once. Every shadow was a threat, and the white noise scraped at her nerves. The bursts of machine gun fire grew louder and louder as they raced toward the rest of the rescue party . . . and the exit.

Jana's little group turned the last corner and all hell broke loose. The Earthan soldiers were now sandwiched between them and Bren. But, *fuck*, there were a lot of them. For an insane split second, Jana considered standing there and letting them end the twisted misery inside her, but Natheem shoved her, propelling both of them toward the far side of the corridor's mouth. She lifted her weapon and fired blindly as she dove for cover. A man screamed, went down, and Jana's shoulder hit the wall as she crouched behind the corner. Kyber knelt while Dhalesh stood above him so they could both return fire down the hall. Jana just hoped like hell they didn't hit Bren's group on the other side.

The door to freedom stood wide open, twisted and warped by some kind of explosion. So close, and yet so very far away. "Shit."

Fear curdled in her belly, making it heave as the stench of blood and smoke flooded her nostrils. The screams and whimpers, the swearing, the crack of bullets. Sweat stung her eyes along with tears as she gasped in little sobs of breath. It overwhelmed her, made her hands shake, but she didn't stop, didn't pause. She ran through the bullets in her clip and fished an extra out of her backpack, jamming it into place, and kept firing. They picked the humans off one by one, but it was obvious that both sides were going to run out of ammunition before anyone had an upper hand.

The sound of gunfire petered to a halt. The humans must have decided Jana's side of the hall was most vulnerable because what remained of the soldiers launched themselves toward her. The blood froze in her veins when her weapon gave the distinctive click that said it was out of bullets. The sound was echoed by Natheem's machine gun. He growled and shoved her back behind the corner as the first human reached them.

"Stupid piece of Earthan—" He slammed the butt of the weapon against a man's face, toppling him to the ground with blood gushing from his nose and mouth.

Jana jerked to her feet to escape the dark crimson spray only to be confronted with a soldier of her own. He swung his fist at her and she reacted on pure instinct, on the training she'd demanded Bren hammer into her for months. Blocking his punch, she brought the heel of her hand up to connect with his nose. The sickening crunch of cartilage sounded too loud to her ears, but she didn't have time to think about it before the next man was on her. She shifted her weight, slamming her boot into his groin. A shriek whistled from his throat as he dropped to his knees. She kicked the side of his head and he went down, too.

A third man launched himself at her, dragging her to the ground. Her screech was cut short when they hit the linoleum hard. Her breath wheezed out of her lungs, and she choked for breath, panic setting in. She looked to Natheem, but he dealt with two soldiers of his own.

A hard fist connected with her ribs and she groaned, her boots squeaking on the tile as she scrambled to get out from under the human. Her nails raked down his face, stabbing for his eyes. He yowled and jerked away but didn't ease his weight enough for her escape.

She hit him but couldn't get enough leverage to make much of an impact. He slapped her hard and the coppery taste of blood filled her mouth. Terror exploded through her. A man on top of her, holding her down, hurting her. It was too much like Arthur, a realization of the waking nightmare her life had become, and suddenly she couldn't draw breath. A scream tangled in her throat and she froze. He drew his hand back and she saw the dull gleam of a long knife. She knew it was over. Closing her eyes, she felt a wave of resignation roll through her.

The man's weight jerked away from her suddenly, and her eyes flared open to see Kyber's claws slicing through the soldier's stomach. Crimson sprayed everywhere, the heat of it soaking through Jana's clothes. A deep roar ripped from the huge Kith as he shook his flailing prey and then threw the soldier's lifeless body against the wall.

Scrambling to her feet, she wiped the back of her hand over her bloodied lip. "Thanks."

He hissed at her, baring his fangs, and whipped around to leave her there. She swayed, taking in the carnage around her. Somehow she'd ended up halfway down the hall toward the exit, and Bren and her group of Sueni Kin were helping take down the remaining humans. Jana slipped in a puddle of blood and had to catch herself against a wall to remain upright. Some distant part of her mind realized what she was feeling was shock, but she just staggered for the exit and the pure, clean air that would be outside.

Her two Guardians fell into step beside her, Dhalesh swinging his handgun like a club on a last standing human as they passed. The Sueni grunted and tossed the empty weapon aside. "Empress, next time anyone says we should sneak in somewhere and therefore have to leave our razers behind, say no."

She sputtered on a giggle, stunned that she could laugh at all. She caught sight of Kyber's large form passing through the doorway ahead of her. He stopped, threw his head back, and stared at the brightening dawn sky.

Glancing back, Kyber arched an eyebrow at the three of them. "Guardians have gotten disrespectful in the last few months."

"I like them this way." Defensiveness crept into her tone at the criticism of men who'd put their lives on the line for this mission. "They did a good job."

Both Kin looked startled and grinned but said nothing more. Then she was outside, and nothing had ever looked more beautiful than the pink, orange, and yellow that streaked the horizon. She dragged in a deep breath but didn't get a chance to release it before Bren came barreling out the door behind her.

The older woman keyed a small handheld comm. "Admiral Belraj, I think it's time for the cavalry to make an entrance. Army reinforcements should be here . . . about thirty seconds ago." As if to emphasize her point, a bullet slapped into the side of the cinderblock building and sprayed debris at them. Two camouflage-painted Hummers exploded through the compound's gate, huge guns mounted to the back.

The Sueni group reacted en masse, ducking and zigzagging across the wide lawn. None of them could return fire, so it was time to run like hell.

Kyber took a position just behind her, following Dhalesh and Natheem. Her legs burned as she sprinted to keep up. Every muscle in her body screeched in protest, but she pumped her arms and legs and refused to let herself stop, even when machine gun fire made dirt and rocks explode into the air beside her feet. Sweat slid in rivulets down her face, sticking her stolen uniform to her back. Her lungs were on fire, starved of oxygen as she fled their pursuers.

The air vibrated with the sound of approaching aircraft, moving too fast to be anything from Earth. Jana grinned and watched a shuttle settle on the grass near them, while two fighter wings fired razer cannons on the soldiers behind them. The transceiver in Bren's hand chirped and the gravel voice of Johar Sajan, captain of the Imperial Guardians, came through. "My One is as prepared as always."

Bren barked out a laugh as she pelted up the ramp onto the shuttle. Her voice was breathless when she spoke into her comm. "If I swung that way, I would seriously make out with your One when I got back up there."

"As long as I got to watch." Johar sounded so nonchalant, Jana blinked for a moment before what he'd said processed. Her lips twitched as she threw herself into a seat. Kyber landed next to her and the shuttle was off the ground before the ramp was finished closing.

"No." Tylara's amusement rippled through as she interjected into the comm.'s channel.

Bren dove for a chair as the ship banked hard and rocketed skyward. "Aw, but honey."

Bracing her feet against the floor and her hands on the ceiling, Jana tried to keep herself from tumbling into Kyber's lap. He arched his eyebrow at her and buckled himself into his seat. "Apparently, those who choose the military life are insane, regardless of species or culture."

"You caught that, too, huh?" Jana managed to get her straps in place before the ship shuddered and passed through the planet's atmosphere.

"Pretty much, Majesties." The older woman slumped back with a deep sigh. "Mission accomplished with minimal injuries and no lives lost." Her sea blue eyes flashed sadness for a moment before she closed them. "Sueni lives, anyway."

Not for the first time, Jana wondered how Bren had managed to admit that everything about the way the military had handled the Sueni arrival was wrong and then defied everyone and everything she knew to help the Sueni defeat Arthur. Just because it was the right thing to do. It took guts Jana didn't think she'd ever possess.

She folded her still-shaking hands, exhaustion sweeping through her in a rush. The last year had been such an emotional rollercoaster for her. She'd been twenty-one when the Sueni showed up on Earth, and she was as terrified as everyone else by what their arrival meant. When the war broke out, she'd believed the press that said the Kith had come to take over the planet, to conquer and make humans their slaves again. Especially when Emperor Kyber showed up in the small town her parents lived in to examine all the young women for one to fulfill his notorious Kith sexual appetites.

He'd chosen her, claimed her as his One . . . and a whole new world opened to her, but someone like her—a Kin woman—couldn't possibly be destined to be an empress of a powerful race of people. She was a flight attendant who hadn't even gone to college. No one special. Just an average American girl with nice parents in a nice town. She'd had a pretty *nice* life. She wasn't a world leader, would never truly match Kyber, but she'd loved him the moment she'd met him. It had been like a fairy tale—too good to be true.

She'd dreamed of him for years before he arrived. Maybe that was why when he had arrived, when her eyes had met his, everything had clicked into place for her. There'd been no hesitancy, no fear, no shyness. He was hers, this powerful alien emperor. He'd always been hers.

And she was his.

It was simple, uncomplicated. For the first time in her life, everything was *exactly* as perfect as she always pretended. She had known no one would ever fit her like he would. He was her soul mate, would love her forever. What wouldn't she give for something like that? Who wouldn't hold on to that with all that they had?

She'd been a virgin the first time he'd touched her. No man had ever lived up to the one in her fantasies. Their kisses didn't elicit a tenth of the response as the man in her dreams, so she couldn't even fathom going further than a simple kiss with them.

And then her dreams were real. Touching Kyber was like touching a live wire. Explosive. Passionate. Wonderful. He was everything she'd ever imagined and more. The ecstasy of it had left her barely coherent, her thoughts and memories and life tripping over his in her mind. But he had been with her, and she'd known she'd never been safer in her life. Even their shared dreams hadn't prepared her for how good it would be with him. His touch, his kiss, his desires, his barely contained animalism.

God, she'd loved it. Inexperienced or not, she'd known what she had was precious. Something she would fight for, sacrifice for.

She'd never have guessed she'd do both.

But it only reinforced what she'd learned so long ago when her brother was killed—that was just how life went. There was no such thing as fairy tales, no matter how handsome the prince who came along, no matter how bright your smile or how hard you pretended, the other glass slipper would always drop.

And shatter.

2

It took hours for Kyber to get himself free of the medics, his military and political advisors, his cousin, Tylara, his Imperial Guardians. When they finally left him in peace, he lay back on the soft pillows piled on the gelpad in the medical ward. "*Vishra*, lock the door and allow no one else in."

The ship answered in its well-modulated, androgynous voice. "Yes, Your Majesty."

A series of clicks sounded inside the door as the locks engaged. He sighed and closed his eyes, swallowing. Relief flooded him, but it was also tinged with wary uncertainty, and a sense of unreality expanded inside him, numbed him. After so long, could it be true?

He was free of pain, clean, on his own ship, among his own people, and had full use of his powers now that the agonizing static ringing had left his ears. A low growl rumbled in his chest at the thought. So many months without the psychic power to leash his feral nature meant the beast had a deeper grip on his body than he'd ever allowed before. He wasn't certain if he could completely cage it ever again. He wasn't even sure if he wanted to.

He, like the animal, wanted nothing more than to rip his enemies to shreds.

But that was wrong. He was the emperor—he was supposed to be in control at all times. Instead, this expedition had been one disastrous failure after another, and he'd learned when his father was murdered that if an emperor failed, it cost lives. *Kyber's* failure had cost lives.

Windows lined one side of the room, the many ships of his armada spreading out around the *Vishra*. The vast blackness of space, the flicker of millions of white stars, did little to soothe the seething rage and pain inside him.

Nothing was right, nothing was as it should be.

At the center of all that darkness twisting and knotting inside him were two people. Jana and Arthur.

Jana had gone to Arthur because she hadn't trusted Kyber, hadn't listened to him when he'd told her that he could free himself, that she should relay his psychic messages on his location to his Guardians and keep herself safe. Instead, she had sacrificed herself for him.

Not that. Anun, please, anything but that.

His stomach pitched and rolled, and he wanted to flee the reminder as badly as he'd wanted to flee Arthur's clutches. There was no agony greater for a man than knowing his woman betrayed him with another. With his mind linked to hers, the memories were etched into his thoughts like acid. His greatest enemy's hands on his One, fucking his One, the man who would use every means available to torture Kyber. The same horror he'd felt then gripped him now, the searing agony he'd have done anything to escape, including try to tear himself free of the psychic One bond.

Even away from Arthur's constant torment, his gleeful reports of how Jana had grown to like what he did to her and vivid descriptions of Jana's body—things only Kyber should know—there were some pains Kyber would never get away from, some wounds the medics couldn't heal.

Exhaustion crashed over him in an overwhelming wave. He hadn't slept in more than fits and starts since he'd been taken. The constant noise, the nudity, the freezing cold, the beatings, druggings, and restraints made real rest impossible. Which was Arthur's aim. Kyber's world had come down to *surviving* each moment, each heartbeat. A snarl wrenched from his throat, his fangs pressing against his lips as hate burned in his soul and spread until not a single particle of Kyber wasn't consumed by it.

The man might be free, but the beast's lust for vengeance wasn't satisfied. His mind latched on to that, spinning his thoughts out of the rational man's control. Darkness tunneled his vision, and he shook his head to try and clear it. He needed to chill the rage to cold calculation, needed to plan for what to do next. He was the one who was supposed to have the answers, but answers evaded him now.

Whether he wanted it or not, his body dragged him toward unconsciousness. His fingers bunched in the bedclothes beneath him as he fought it, his words slurring as the last question he had slipped from his lips. He wasn't even sure he wanted to know the truth. "*Vishra*, how long after I was taken did the empress come aboard?"

There was a short pause before the ship answered. "There are several variables that could affect the answer, but by the simplest calculation, it was approximately seventy-nine hours, six minutes, and twenty-three seconds, Your Majesty."

"Three days. Not months." His chest tightened, some fierce emotion cutting off his breath, but his exhaustion would no longer be denied.

The ship's response was the last thing he heard before the oblivion of slumber claimed him. "Yes, sire."

Some part of his mind remained alert, refused to relax, to trust that this wasn't some drug-induced hallucination that he would wake up from, that he wouldn't still be writhing on the floor in agony when he opened his eyes. It wouldn't be the first time Arthur had done such a thing to him.

He didn't know what was right, what was *real* anymore, but sleep pulled him in directions he couldn't control, deep into dreams of the last time he had made love to his One. What stunned him was that he could *feel* Jana on the other end of the fantasy. As much as he'd tried to shred the ties that bound him to her, the thinnest thread still connected them. So minute, he doubted she could even sense it, but it was there. Now that his psychic powers had returned, he had no doubts that they were still linked. Anun help him.

But in the dream, he was smiling, so happy, so content. Kyber doubted the muscles in his face remembered how to relax into such an expression anymore. He couldn't remember the last time he'd smiled. It might have been that day, that moment.

They were aboard his personal shuttle, sumptuously appointed with couches, a wide bed, and every amenity an emperor could desire when skimming through space. Most of the time, Kyber never used any of those things. He just enjoyed the few moments of privacy and independence flying himself alone in his own ship afforded him.

He tapped his fingers over an imager, finishing a communication to the commanders in his fleet. Jana wandered up behind him and wrapped her arms around his neck. She was naked and smelled of warm woman, hot sex, and Kyber. A smile curved his mouth when he stood and turned in her embrace to kiss her.

She hummed against his lips, leaning into his body. "Take me back to bed."

"Yes." He danced them in slow circles to the rear of the shuttle before he pushed her backward onto the bed, watching the way her lovely breasts bounced when she landed.

"I could have gotten down here myself." She propped herself on her elbows.

He winked, already tugging at his shirt. "Yes, but it's my turn to be on top."

She laughed, then frowned when she poked her fingers into the gelpad beneath her. "You know, I've been meaning to ask you, what's this made of?"

"The gelpad?" He flung his shirt over his shoulder. "I have no idea. Some kind of gel."

She snorted and rolled her eyes but bit her lip as she watched him strip. Her gaze heated, and the desire he saw there made him groan.

"Have you any idea how long I have dreamed of this moment? Of having you in my bed?" He shed his garments as fast as possible, fumbling with buttons until he could finally wrench the last of his clothing off.

"And here I am." A quiet smile bowed her lips, her gray eyes serious. Too serious. He loved it when she laughed best, it loosened something deep inside him.

"Yes, here you are." He grabbed her legs to pull her toward him.

She pressed her thighs open in invitation. He ran his tongue over his teeth, staring at the wetness gathered on her vaginal lips, his fingers tightening on her ankles. Fire blazed within him, her every reaction calling to him through the wide connection they shared. His chest tightened with wonder at having finally found her. He had waited so long. "I want to lap up all your sweet cream, Jana, and fuck you with my tongue until you come for me."

A hot blush pinkened her cheeks, her eyes closing, her innocence a delight to him. As delightful as knowing that he was the only man who had ever touched her. She was the most precious gift fate had ever given him. He loved her with a pure, deep passion that made his chest ache.

Even her shyness couldn't disguise how his words made her wetness increase, and her scent made his cock throb with a fierceness he couldn't contain. If he sank himself inside her now, he wouldn't last long enough to make her come. It was embarrassing how simply being near her, sliding his hands over her, shredded his vaunted imperial control to nothing.

He moved to the end of the bed, sprawling catlike, and propping his head in his hand. He didn't touch her. He didn't think he could stand it if he did. Instead, he opened his thoughts to her, seeking that link that bound his heart and mind and soul to hers.

She writhed on the bed covers. Her eyes flew open, latching on to his face. He offered her a smile that he knew bared his fangs. He wanted her and the beast was even more insatiable. She licked her lips, the surprise and uncertainty fading from her gaze as he sank his consciousness into hers. She would feel how much he loved the mental contact with her, how it met needs even the ecstasy of physical contact could not.

Her fantasies overlaid his, their thoughts and desires tangling together. Her breathing sped, her nipples beading before his gaze. Her creamy flesh flushed, the pulse pounding visibly at her throat.

She slid her foot up his calf. His body jolted and he caught her ankle, gently setting her leg away from him. "No touching, my empress."

"But I want to touch." Her gaze zeroed in on his painfully rigid cock, and she licked her lips. A shudder rippled through him and he wrestled with the beast within that wanted to spring, pounce, and claim every inch of her as his own. He tamed it easily and focused on her.

Her knees pressed to the gelpad as her hips began to undulate. The musky scent of her arousal intoxicated him. A purr rumbled in his chest, spilling from his lips. "Lovely. If you want to touch, Jana, then touch yourself. Show me what you'd like."

"You can sense what I'd like. You're in my head." She bit her lower lip, her white teeth sinking into her plump pink flesh. Anun, he loved how she reacted so beautifully to every stimulus.

He slid his hand down his stomach until he could grasp his dick. He felt the swelling of her excitement through their connection. "Yes, I can tell you like this."

A soft moan bubbled out of her as he began stroking his erection. His cravings fed hers, and soon she gave in to the temptation to let her fingers slip between her thighs. He could feel how her flesh felt under her own fingers, just as he let her feel how his hand felt moving over his hard sex.

"Oh, my God. This is . . ." Her voice trailed off into a soft whimper, her hips bucking to meet the thrust of her slim digits inside of her soaking channel.

Working his cock hard, he rolled his thumb over the head. He twisted his hand, stroking the shaft through his tight fist. She moaned each time he pumped himself. He watched her gaze lose focus as the pleasure took her. Her mouth fell open and low cries ripped from her. He let his need slam into her mind, his ecstasy at connecting with her, his joy at finally having her. It was enough to make her come against her hand.

He choked, his own orgasm slamming into him. The muscles in his belly locked, a hiss ripping from him. His fluids spilled over his stroking fingers and onto the bedclothes.

"I still want you inside me, Kyber." Her gray eyes reflected her unsated greed when they met his. "Please."

He crawled up until he could settle against her curves, loving how they fit his angles perfectly. She was made for him. His cock hardened with renewed need. He groaned and sank down on his elbows to kiss her. Her legs snapped around his waist and she lifted herself into him. Giving in to the intense yearning, he eased his cock deep inside her. Her narrow walls clamped around him and he had to grit his teeth against the lust that gripped him. He licked his way into her mouth, thrusting his tongue with the same rhythm as his cock moved within her.

She moaned against his lips, any remaining shyness fleeing under the onslaught of their mutual desire. They raced for orgasm together, each feeding the other's most carnal hungers. Her pussy flexed around his cock, her passage so tight he thought it would drive him to utter madness. She bit his lip hard, screamed, and raked her nails down his back as she came apart in his arms. She called to the wildness in him the way nothing else did. He broke his mouth away from hers, threw his head back, fangs bared, and roared as he pumped his cum deep within her.

"Kyber!" Her channel pulsed around his cock, echoing the satisfaction that throbbed through their bond, driving them both to greater heights than they'd ever imagined. "Kyber, I love you. I love you so much."

"Jana. My Jana. My One. I love you, too." He sank down on her, more content than he'd ever been in his life. This was everything he'd ever wanted. And he had his whole life to enjoy it. With her.

Kyber's eyes flared wide, ripped from a dream that had become a nightmare, and for a moment he had no idea where he was. Confusion and terror exploded through him. He wasn't in his cell, wasn't in his shuttle, or in his own bed. He jerked automatically against the chains that bound him, only to find he wasn't shackled. Instead, he flipped and landed hard on the metal floor on his hands and knees. He groaned as pain shafted up his legs and stabbed into his brain. Anun, but he knew pain now. It was as familiar to him as breathing. Days that bled into endless nights of unending, unstoppable agony.

"Sire, are you all right? Should I unlock the door and allow medics to come in?" The *Vishra's* voice was as close to panic as it could ever be, and everything came back to him in a swift rush.

Jana. His rescue. His return to the ship.

His erotic dream shared by his One—just like they'd done before he found her.

He shook his head and dragged himself to his feet, swaying when he straightened too fast. He slumped against the bed and cleared his throat. "I am fine, *Vishra*. Thank you."

Boosting himself back onto the gelpad, he dropped his head into his hands. The dream mocked him. He'd thought he had forever with that sweet, pure bond. Instead, it had died in mere hours. Even the connection he had now with Jana, the sharing of the dream, was a pathetic shadow to the openness they had known. He tamped down on that link, shoring up his defenses against it.

"What shift is it, *Vishra*?"

The liquid voice flowed over him. "The third work shift just began, Your Majesty."

He used to work the first shift and most of the second, but no one would expect to meet with him for hours. Closing his eyes, he let gratitude sweep over him. He wasn't ready to deal with being the calm, composed emperor just yet.

"If you would like to arise, the empress had a set of your clothing placed in the clothing cleanser in the sanitation room."

Kyber winced at the mention of the empress. Jana. He didn't know what to feel with her, either, didn't know what to do. They weren't who they had been, *he* wasn't who he had been. Months of nothing but feral rage to survive on had made him someone he'd never dreamed of being. Someone he'd never wanted to be. He didn't even know who or what he was now.

Padding into the sanitation room, he stretched his arms above his head and loosened the kinks in his muscles. It felt amazing to be able to move free of restraints, something he'd never take for granted again. He slid on the clothes Jana had left and wandered the halls and stairways of his ship. He avoided the imperial office suite, and habit took him in the direction of his quarters.

The door to his rooms stood open. He froze, wariness bringing his senses to full alertness. Jana was in there; he could smell the sweetness of her skin. The beast came to full alert, and he couldn't stop his body from reacting to her scent. His cock rose to chafe against his fly.

She bent over a small table against one wall, her profile to him. If she knew he was there, she gave no indication of it. He focused on her, not allowing himself to look at the bed where they'd never had a chance to lay together. He stilled a derisive snort. Anun knew, in the year it had taken to find her, when their shared dreams had grown more frequent and more erotic, his fantasies had never restricted their love play to the bed. There wasn't a surface in this room that he hadn't imagined they'd use. Against the wall, on the floor, in every chair, even bent over that same table. So many hopes shattered, but the carnal reminder made his dick harden to the point of rigid pain, and he gritted his teeth, cursing his body for betraying him. Her signature and his were overlaid in the room now. It sent a ripple of some emotion he didn't care to name down his spine.

His hands shook as he watched her, and he tried to get a grip on the lust streaking through him. Her body was leaner, more muscular. Likely the result of training to hunt, to fight as he'd seen her do. She tucked a strand of hair behind her ear. She'd cut it short. The waist-length auburn strands now barely skimmed her jaw. It made her look harder, less innocent. Or maybe it was the cynicism in her eyes that had never been there before.

"Did the *Vishra* tell you the truth about how long I've been here?" She turned to face him, her gray gaze placid. There was no hint that the dream they'd shared had affected her at all. He didn't like that, but he pushed the thought away.

He nodded, folded his arms, and propped his shoulder against the doorjamb. "Yes, but coming into this room tells me even more. Your scent and psychic signature inundate everything."

"Well, that's good, I guess." The bright smile she gave him didn't quite reach her eyes. Her smoky gaze flickered for a moment, but he couldn't decipher the emotion there. He'd once been able to read her like a book, her wants and needs as apparent to him as his own.

"I guess," he echoed her but couldn't believe she'd describe anything about this as *good*. This wasn't good, they weren't good. Something inside him broke at the awkwardness between them. They had never been awkward before, and bitter pain expanded within him. "How could you do it, Jana?"

She didn't pretend to misunderstand him, but she looked anywhere except him. "I would have done anything to save you."

"Except listen to me." Striding forward until he'd forced her against the wall beside the table, he kept his gaze locked with hers. Her expression didn't change, her thoughts beyond his reach. Bracketing his hand around the underside of her jaw, he spoke in that rusty voice that sounded nothing like his own. "I know you heard me tell you not to do it."

202 / *Crystal Jordan*

"He said he just wanted me returned to my family." Her eyes widened when Kyber touched her, the first real indication of the Jana he'd once known. "He said he'd let you go."

"So you trusted him and not me?" His One hadn't trusted him to find a way out of the mess he'd been in, and look where they'd ended up. Who had failed whom the most? Was it something intrinsically wrong with him that had made his One unable to believe in him? He didn't know, he didn't know anything anymore, and that scared him, made him angry—with himself, with her, with destiny, with the whole universe and every soul in it. He was *supposed* to know.

His throat worked when he swallowed. Whatever opportunity he'd had to communicate his whereabouts the day he'd been kidnapped had died when he cut the connection with her. The One bond was the deepest and most fundamental part of the Kith psychic gift. It had held out against the white noise machine Arthur had used on him. For a time.

"I would have done anything to save you and our bond, Kyber." That forced smile curled her lips again, so brittle he thought it would crack. "I *did* do anything, didn't I?"

"You didn't save me *or* our bond." It was so slender and blocked it was hardly worth calling a bond anymore, let alone a One bond. Then again, their bond had never been as perfect as he'd imagined, he reminded himself with ruthless force. He'd lived with a perfect union before, seen how it worked with his parents. Always together, always open and trusting, always in perfect harmony.

"I did what I thought was right. And you're safe now." Her calm infuriated him. He was the one who should be in control here.

He wanted to shake her, want to make her respond and *feel* a tiny portion of the pain and horror that ripped through him.

His grip tightened on her jaw. "You thought it was right to fuck another man, Jana? You honestly thought that would save me?"

Those gray eyes narrowed, and her hiss was worthy of any Kith. "I honestly didn't think you were going to save yourself in chains, Kyber. What was giving a description of the inside of a cell or transport van going to do to help the Guardians find you?"

"Yes, because my sense of sight is the only thing I have. What about distinct smells, my heightened hearing?" His fangs erupted from his gums, the beast's fury pumping through his system. "You trusted a stranger over your One."

"That stranger held the key to your freedom. And we knew each other for *one day*, Kyber. You were almost as much a stranger as he was." She jerked her chin out of his grasp, but he crowded her between the wall and the table. She wasn't going anywhere. "What do you want me to say, Kyber? I was wrong. I'm sorry. Does that change a single thing? No, it doesn't. But I'm going to hold things together and make it through this just like I did when you weren't around."

"Of course, because I'm the one who needs saving. What use do you have for me?" His One bond was a failure, this expedition was a failure, *he* was a failure. He'd never have what his parents had. Not then, not now, not ever. And that made him angrier, made guilt twist through him that his One had given so much so uselessly to free him from a trap *the emperor* should have avoided.

"I'm going to be fine." Desperation edged her tone, and he wondered how often she told herself that. How many times would it take to convince herself it was true? She met his gaze boldly. "What use you find for yourself is up to you, but I don't need you. I don't need anyone. We were happy before we were together and we'll be happy after we're apart."

"After we're apart." His voice was pure animal's snarl.

"Hoping that I die sometime soon or just planning to leave? Do you think the One bond is that easy to escape? We're stuck with each other, Jana. The only thing that makes it go away is death."

Her jaw jutted stubbornly. "I don't like to argue with people, Kyber. This is pointless. Nothing will change by hashing out what we both already know. There's no need to discuss this. Let's just get on with our lives."

Anun help him, her stubbornness aroused him, made the beast purr with the challenge. He glared down at her, his heart pounding as her scent, her nearness, made his body scream for relief. "So everything we've been through doesn't matter to you, is that it?"

"If it didn't matter, I wouldn't have come along to drag you out of that hellhole, would I?" Her head leaned back against the wall. "But bringing it up doesn't help it get better."

"Denying its importance doesn't help it get better either." He snorted. "If anything could ever help it get better."

"God, you're maddening. I said I don't want to talk about this, and you can't make me." She arched an eyebrow, her look as haughty as any empress could ever hope for.

He hissed, the beast going wild. He should want to control it, should try to rein it in, but he didn't. The woman's obstinacy made him insane. He sank his free hand into her shorn hair, pulled her head back even farther, and exposed her throat. Running one finger down the collar of her shirt, he pushed the fabric aside. She didn't protest, didn't struggle.

Close door. He sent the mental command to the ship and the door to his chamber obeyed.

"As you desire, Empress. We won't talk." His nostrils flared to catch the scent of her dampness, her desire. It was heady, shredding what little remained of his control. "We seem to be able to connect in dreams again, in sex, so I'm going to fuck you and I won't be gentle."

"Good." She spoke as bluntly as he did, her gaze never wavering. There was none of that shyness in the woman before him, none of the girl he had known. If he had ever known her.

He leaned forward and bit her neck. Hard.

She jolted against him, a low cry breaking from her lips. Tiny beads of her longing bled through their hair-thin connection, and it served only to fan the flames of his lust. The beast didn't care about the past, the future, or any of the uncertainties of the man. His body demanded surcease that only hers could grant.

Fisting his hand in her shirt, he ripped open the front of it. Her underclothes received the same rough treatment until her breasts were in his hands. He didn't bother retracting his fangs as he sucked and bit at her tight little nipples. The scent of her wetness increased and his cock throbbed in response. He wanted inside her. Now. It had been so long.

"Kyber!" Her hands twisted into his hair, pulling hard. The pain only increased the pleasure, made him burn for more, for *her*.

He wrenched open the fastenings on both of their pants, shredded her panties with one hand, withdrew his talons, and shoved his fingers into her sex. She was slick with cream and more than ready to take him. He shuddered, the beast within him clawing for freedom to reclaim its mate, to fuck her until there was nothing left but sweet oblivion.

Yes. The beast was harder to control now, the months of torture had reduced him to little more than an animal, and he embraced the feline more than he ever had before. At this moment, he didn't even care if that thought was wrong. He dropped to his knees before her, jerked her pants and shoes off, and tossed them aside along with her destroyed underwear.

He had to taste her again, to feel her come against his mouth. He wanted to *own* her pleasure, wanted her to beg him to come, wanted her to know that no one else could give her what he could, no matter what might drive them apart.

He purred when he licked her clit. She screamed, her hands jerking on his hair as she wriggled to escape. Her ecstasy flooded through their link, and he dug the claws on one hand into her hip, holding her in place. He kept the claws retracted on the other hand, pumping his fingers deep into her hot slit. Her cream slid over his taste buds, and the instinct that had driven him to find her in the first place clamored with a recognition he didn't want to acknowledge.

One. His One.

A growl rose in his throat, and her slim body writhed in response. She lifted one thigh over his shoulder, opening herself wide to him. Her fingers stroked through his hair, her palms cupping the back of his head to urge him closer. His cock jerked at her gentle touch, craving that softness as he'd craved nothing else before. Sweat broke out across his forehead at the many conflicting needs that darted through him. He flicked his tongue over her clit, the tight little bundle of nerves hardening. Adding a second and then third finger to her wet pussy, he stretched her, let her juices drench his hand as her lips grew even more swollen and slick for him.

"God, I'm so close," she breathed. The muscles in her thighs tensed, and she dug her heel into his back. She arched against the wall, moving with the rhythm his fingers and tongue set for her.

He slowed down, batted her clit lightly, and buried his digits deep inside her but stopped moving. He sent a thought to her. *You won't come until I tell you to, until you beg me for it.*

A low, helpless moan broke from her. He felt her resistance

thrum along their link, a spurt of rebellion, of anger, and a memory she quelled before he could see it. "I won't!"

"You will," he growled. He hated that she hid from him—it only spurred him on. He swiveled his fingers inside her, curling them until he rubbed over the spot he knew would make her squeal.

The effect was electric, a scream sounding above him as she jerked and danced between his body and the wall. "P-please, Kyber. Let me come. Please, please, *please*."

No. He grinned against her sex, letting a cool breath blow over her hot, wet pussy. *He* wanted to be in control as he hadn't been of anything in months. If he couldn't control the beast, he could control this. He needed it, and she would give it to him.

She choked on a sob when he pulled away to shove his pants down his thighs. A hot rush of her anger whipped through their connection, but he dragged her down to his level and put her on her hands and knees facing away from him. The beast liked her in this position, purred as he mounted her from behind. He was beyond wild, driven only by the need to fuck, to brand her with his scent, his essence.

He plunged into her pussy, seating himself to the hilt. Another sob tore from her, but her back bowed and she slammed her hips back into his, taking him as deep as she could. The feel of her tight, sleek channel wrapping around his cock made his jaw lock, made him hiss through gritted teeth. His belly slapped against her ass as he drove them both hard and fast, gripping her waist between his hands. He was relentless, didn't want to think, to feel with anything but his body. This was fucking, not lovemaking. It would never be perfect like it had been before, never be *fine* as she insisted. Ever.

She was not his One, not truly, not anymore.

The beast snarled at the reminder, thrusting deeper inside her. Punishing them both for him craving her so much he couldn't breathe. His muscles burned from the hard use, his lungs heaving as he panted for breath. Her sex clamped around his cock, so hot and wet and welcoming he thought he'd die of the pleasure after so long of knowing only pain.

"Kyber!" He could hear her nails scrabble against the metal floor as she rocked herself into him. He felt the grip and release of her inner muscles around his thrusting cock. She held off her orgasm, not coming until he allowed it, just as he'd ordered.

A rush so hot and sweet it terrified him rocketed through his body, his mind. The carnal scent of sex, of her, of him, of them mingled in the room. He ground out the words that would send them both flying. "Come for me. Now."

Her long, thin scream echoed in the chamber as she obeyed him and let go of control. Her pussy flexed around his cock, her internal muscles milking him hard. It had been so long since he'd felt her completion ripple through their bodies and their link at once, calling to him like a siren's erotic song. Even if he'd wanted to, he couldn't have stopped himself from coming with her.

Orgasm ripped through him and he released all the pent-up frustration, rage, need, and longing into her. He jetted into her wet slit, filling her with his cum. Shudders wracked his body, over and over, until he slumped against her. Spent.

A deeper peace than he'd known in months flooded him and he closed his eyes to savor it. It wouldn't last. Nothing this untamed ever did. It shouldn't. He needed to get a handle on the beast inside him, lock it away as he had before, and leave only the psychic behind, the rational ruler. Hadn't his childhood taught him that lesson?

None of that answered the question of what to do now. About Arthur and Earth. About Jana and the One bond. All of it tangled together in his mind, the animal instincts and reactions muddying any logic Kyber might put to it. What should he do? What was the right thing? Who was he if he couldn't contain the animal? Who would trust an emperor who was more beast than man?

His One hadn't trusted him. Maybe being in his mind had shown her something he couldn't admit. Maybe she was the only one who could understand—if they could reach each other again, if they could *know* each other.

3

The days ground by into more than a week, and all they did was fight and fuck. Kyber wanted to delve into what had happened with them, with Arthur, and Jana was just as determined not to. It didn't help. Soon she doubted they would be able to stand being in the same room together . . . except for the times they couldn't control the animalistic craving that cycled between them, betraying them both. Together even when they were apart, it was their curse, their burden.

Jana lay in the huge bed they didn't really share, the gelpad cupping her like a lover as she stared up through the skylight at an endless panorama of stars. She missed him. She had missed him while he'd been gone, missed him when they were apart now. That was the most damnable part of the entire thing. Even as their infinitesimal connection remained withered and almost dead, as it seethed with all the things she couldn't acknowledge lest they break her, she hated every single moment without him. Yet she was desperate to keep Kyber out, to never let him into her mind again, to keep him from seeing she wasn't as together as she pretended. She'd had her chance with him, her moment of perfection, and it was over.

Everything they'd had, everything they'd ever been to each other was ruined.

Even the sex, as hot as it was, was a mockery of what they'd once shared. It was empty, broken, like they were.

Like she was. She stomped down on that thought, denying it. She was fine. She could forget all the bad things, put them all behind her, if she just kept going. If she just outran the memories that hounded her.

Closing her eyes against tears she wouldn't let fall, she swallowed and dragged in a deep lungful of air. She shouldn't allow herself to think about it. It wouldn't help. She knew that by now. It didn't change anything. She threw aside the silken *rishaami* bedcovers and jerked to her feet. Time to get up, get dressed, and get on with her day.

Restless energy vibrated through her, and she couldn't get her mind to settle as she walked toward her office. Since Kyber's return, she'd found herself at loose ends. She no longer needed to plan or train for his rescue, and the Sueni no longer needed her to make decisions that were once made by the emperor. It had been overwhelming at first, so many advisors, so much to learn, but she'd dedicated every waking moment to it, driven to right all her wrongs, to make certain no one else suffered for her mistakes.

But the emperor was here now, and he was determined to do it all himself, to be the perfect ruler, sliding back into place as though he'd never been gone. A bitter smile curved her lips. It sounded like something she would do.

But the difference between Kyber and her was that Kyber expected himself to be perfect and allowed no room for human fallibility, for failure. She put on the mask of perfection, but she knew she never was. It was a sham, a lie she told the world. It had started when her older brother died, and her parents needed so desperately for her to be healthy and happy. They'd lost Craig, and they'd clung to Jana. Their only child, their baby. She'd learned to be what they needed her to be, just as she'd done for the Sueni when Kyber was gone. A harsh laugh bubbled out of her, echoing down a long corridor.

Circular lights brightened overhead as she walked, gleaming off the metal ship that wasn't *quite* the color of any metal on Earth. It was silver, but not. Darker, richer. Her steps were a dull thud against the floor, and the deeper into the spacecraft she went, the higher the level, the more people she passed. She forced the smile onto her face that she'd used as a flight attendant. Odd that her experience there—and her experience with her parents—would come in handy as an empress, but she hid her tension behind a pleasant facade.

"Your Majesty," they called her. They issued slight bows, stepping aside to give her the right-of-way. It felt so wrong, so false. This wasn't her life. The unreality expanded inside her until she thought she'd scream, so she made a sharp right turn where she should have gone left to her office.

"*Vishra?*"

The ship's mellifluous voice responded, "Yes, Your Majesty?"

"Please send a message to Lady Brenna Arjun and ask if she's available to meet me for a sparring lesson. Do *not* make it an order."

"As you wish, Your Majesty." A glass panel to her left flickered to acknowledge the command, and there might have been a hint of disapproval in the ship's calm tone.

Jana had learned the first week she was here that if she wanted to enter a doorway, it opened for her, regardless of whether the people on the other side had locked it. Being the empress overrode all but emergency lockdowns and made every word that came out of her mouth a royal edict.

She'd accidentally walked in on Farid and Brenna as well as Tylara and Johar on different occasions doing things that were downright indecent. Then again, Kyber had done all that and more to Jana in the week and a half he'd been back, expanding her definition of physical pleasure by the day. A shiver ran down her spine, utter want throbbing within her sex. She gritted her teeth and shoved the longing aside. The ecstasy of Kyber's touch was empty without that perfect bond between them.

Shaking her head, she slammed her way into the large sparring room she used. She pulled on a set of exercise clothing from a storage container hidden behind a wall panel. A harder version of the gelpads that lay on Sueni beds covered the wide floor and she moved to it to stretch her tense muscles.

The ship's imagers could provide a hologram to instruct her on sparring, but nothing replaced pitting her mind and body against another person. She needed to burn off the frustration and strain, to bury the self-loathing and doubt. To make the ugliness go away so it could be okay again the way she needed it to be. Kyber's sense of failure filtered through their link, and it made her feel horrible, guilty.

She was the one who'd failed. It was her job to make it all right for people. Her parents, the Sueni, Kyber. She had done that, and she still couldn't make the memories stop. Why couldn't she forget? Why couldn't she put the memories aside the way she always had when things went badly? She did her best, but there were days like today when the darkness filled her until looking at herself in the mirror made her sick to her stomach. All she ever saw was Arthur. His hands biting into her skin, ripping at her clothes, pinning her down. She hadn't even fought back, let him do whatever he wanted to her, needing her One to be free so badly she'd believed the general's lies.

Her stomach heaved and she bent to brace her hands on her

knees. Swallowing the rising gorge, she choked and scrubbed her palm over her eyes. The door to the room swished open and she forced herself to straighten.

She smiled but couldn't meet the older woman's gaze. "Bren, I'm glad you could squeeze me in."

"Of course. It's no problem." Bren was already dressed in a loose exercise outfit.

"There's no 'of course.' Thank you." There were very few humans on board, and only Bren had ever treated Jana like she was the same as everyone else, had never once bowed to the empress while giving her the surreptitious glances that said they knew what she'd done with Arthur. It was something she valued more than she could ever say.

"You're welcome." Bren swung her arms, linking her fingers together to bend and stretch. "How are things with Kyber?"

The laugh Jana managed sounded more like a sob, so she cleared her throat and pinned her gaze to the floor. "Everything's fine. Why wouldn't it be? We're so happy he's back."

She startled when the other woman touched her arm, finally meeting her gaze. "It's okay if everything isn't all right, Jana. No one expects what happened to just disappear. People make mistakes."

"No, Bren, they don't. Not like I did." Jana twisted out of the gentle hold, blinking back tears at even that slight show of kindness. She could not lose it, she *would not*. "We both know you would never make the same choices I made."

"No, I've made other mistakes that cost lives." Bren's gaze hardened with tough sympathy. "I was involved in the preemptive strike that killed thousands of innocent Sueni people. You think I don't feel guilty now? You think it doesn't haunt me? We *all* do things we wish we could take back."

Jana swallowed and nodded, stepping back. "Thank you."

"Don't thank me for the truth." She sighed and moved to the middle of the mat. "It isn't kindness, it just is."

"Yeah, so I hope you're feeling energetic today." Desperate for a change of subject, Jana grinned and knew it was more a baring of teeth. "I need a sparring lesson bad."

Bren huffed a little laugh and danced on her toes. "No, you want a sparring partner to help you blow off steam because you're having a shit day and want to beat the crap out of someone."

"Kin can't read minds." Jana rolled her eyes and lunged for the other woman.

Bren feinted left and brought her arm around to backhand Jana across the face. "It doesn't take a psychic to tell that one. Been there and done that. More than once."

The hit sent Jana stumbling back a few steps and left her ears ringing, but she dropped down to sweep her leg out to knock the other woman off her feet. Bren went down hard, grunting as she hit the ground. Both women rolled away, leaping to their feet to circle each other. Jana shook her head to get the buzzing out of her ears, balancing on the balls of her feet.

Her heart pounded, adrenaline sharpening her senses. God, it felt good to be able to channel the bottled up *feelings* somewhere. She let it rip through her, welcomed the rush. The emotions tripped over each other, tangled and twisted. Her focus snapped on Bren, who watched her like a hawk, waiting for an opening. Jana's patience snapped. She wanted a fight, was spoiling for it, and charged in with a sharp uppercut.

Bren blocked the swing, driving her fingers under Jana's ribs. "Get your head in the game, girl."

She choked, spinning away from the hit to minimize the impact. Snapping her fingers around Bren's wrist, she slammed the butt of her other hand against the older woman's diaphragm. "My head is fine, thanks."

Flushing bright red, Bren gagged on a breath, but a muscle in her jaw twitched as she gritted her teeth. Her foot shot out to make hard impact with Jana's thigh. The leg crumpled out from under her, and Jana rolled into a somersault to keep from going face-first into the mat.

Sweat ran down her face and she swiped it away from her eyes. Her muscles burned from the exertion, her leg already throbbing from a forming bruise. Hauling herself up off the floor, Jana panted for breath. Anger sizzled through her at the mistakes she knew she was making. More failure. She squelched the thought, the feeling, locking it away. Pretend the darkness, the suffering, the grief wasn't there, and don't let it own her. It was how she'd been living for so long. She crushed that thought, too, shook out her hands, and faced Bren, ready for anything.

A feral smile curved Bren's lips, the expression more suited to a Kith than a human woman, but she pulled it off. Terrifyingly so. Jana narrowed her gaze, settled into a half-crouch, and powered herself forward to catch the smaller woman around the waist and drag her to the ground. They wrestled for the top position, elbows and knees flying as they thrust sharp jabs into each other's bodies. The only sound in the room was their harsh breathing and the crack of flesh hitting flesh.

Jana flipped Bren onto her back, drawing her fist back for a hard strike. Bren brought her feet up, planted them on Jana's stomach and sent her tumbling into a wall. She wheezed on impact, easy prey, but Bren stayed where she was, sprawled across the mat. "Okay, Empress, you're going to have to take that shit out on the imagers. I've got plans with Farid tonight that don't include me being so sore I can't move."

A chuckle rippled out of Jana. She dropped her head back, sweat sliding down her temples. "At least not for a starting point, huh?"

"Exactly." Bren rolled her head on the mat, offering up a wink. "If all goes well, we'll both be limping tomorrow."

Settling more comfortably against the wall, Jana drew up her knee and draped her forearm over it. She ached from the inside out, but not from the fight. Closing her eyes, she sighed. "If you've been here and done this, who do you usually spar with at times like that?"

"Tylara." The older woman groaned, and Jana opened her eyes to watch her sit up. "She needs someone who's willing to kick her ass, and as an admiral and fleet commander, she scares most of the other people too much to give her good sport."

Jana flicked her fingers. "Ah, not a good career move to beat the leader of your military's ass. Even if she wants it."

"Exactly." Flopping over onto her hands and knees, Bren crawled to her feet.

"She's lucky you don't suffer those little qualms."

A wicked smile curved her lips and she dusted off her knees. "Damn straight."

A snort sounded from the door and Tylara's voice entered the fray. "Don't make me laugh, little Kinswoman. You *try* to kick my ass, which others are too terrified to do, you don't actually *succeed*."

"Oh, reeeeally?" Bren stretched her arms over her head, giving a long, bored yawn. "Is that why you were scraping yourself off the floor last time, running to cry to Johar about how the big, bad Earthan gave you a booboo?"

Tylara smirked, her dark eyes sparkling with both power and amusement. She ran a hand over her short hair, the cut perfect for her angular features. "You're assuming I don't like that sort of thing. Perhaps I go to Johar to get a *booboo* when you aren't up to scratch."

Jana cracked up at the byplay between the two older women. The laughter felt like it struggled past the huge weight resting on her chest, a weight she never escaped. If she ignored it, it would *have* to go away. It only had power if she let it. She clenched her jaw, stood, and brushed off her hands. "Oh, them's fightin' words right there."

Bren grinned while Tylara just looked confused, as if she had no idea what Jana had just said. The three of them gathered at the door, Bren still working the kinks out of her muscles. Both women were shorter than Jana. Bren could *almost* look her straight in the eyes, but Tylara barely reached her chin. Her delicate size was an illusion, though. Of the three of them, Tylara was easily the strongest and the fastest.

"Your Majesty?" A deep, masculine voice echoed down the hall. All three women poked their head out the door to see Johar's approach. "The emperor would like to see you, Your Majesty."

A long beat passed before Jana realized he was talking to *her*. It still surprised her when they addressed her as the empress. This life was so far removed from anything she'd ever known, anything she'd ever expected her life to be. Bren and Tylara both gave her expectant looks, though the Kith woman's face flushed a bit when her One drew near.

"He'd *like* to see me?" Jana arched an eyebrow. "That almost sounded like a request."

The Guardian wisely kept his mouth shut, but his eyes twinkled with good humor.

Her lips twitched. "You drew the short straw in coming to get me, huh?"

"Yes, Your Majesty." Folding his arms behind him, he rocked back on his heels. The scarlet tunic of his uniform stretched tight across his broad chest. He tilted his head in the direction he'd come. "Shall we?"

"Sure, why not?" She forked her fingers through her sweat-dampened hair. It would be nice to be allowed a shower before her next round with Kyber, but she doubted Johar would agree that stopping off in her chamber would be a good idea. Likely Kyber had sent Johar to fetch her personally instead of asking the ship to give her the request to ensure that she obeyed the summons. She sniffed. The man knew her too well. But then, he'd once shared all her thoughts and memories, hadn't he? She glanced at the other women. "I'll see you guys later."

Both of them nodded in return, and Jana fell into step beside Johar. "Any idea what Kyber wants?"

He tucked his hands into his pockets and slanted her an inscrutable glance. "I couldn't speculate."

A chuckle rippled from her. "Of course you couldn't. Or wouldn't."

His deep blue eyes flickered with baby blue sparks, and his tone went dry. "You are wise beyond your years, Your Majesty."

"How many times do I have to ask you to call me Jana?" She didn't feel very majestic with her hair plastered to her skull and her leg aching from the kick Bren had delivered.

He shrugged. "You may ask as many times as you wish, Your Majesty, but you are still my empress."

And what could Jana say to that? She and Kyber were still bound, so she *was* the empress. She sighed and shook her head, following his lead around a few corners and down a short flight of steps to a multiveyor. The glass door slid around in the clear tube to admit them. Stepping onto the metal platform, she closed her eyes for a moment. The tube overlooked a huge cargo bay, and the rapid drop never failed to make her stomach float. She usually preferred to take the stairs.

It took her a moment to realize the multiveyor had passed the floor with Kyber's office on it. Unless she missed her guess, they were going to the royal chamber. Excitement twisted with dread, her typical reaction to seeing Kyber. And, unless she missed her guess, Johar was along to babysit her on a trip to get laid. A hot flush raced up her cheeks and she stared out the windowed walls. "So, how're things going with Tylara?"

"Well." Johar's easy tone was a little too smooth, and a subtle tightening in his muscles told her he wasn't comfortable with the switch in topic.

A tiny spurt of malicious glee went through her. It wasn't nice, but for once it wasn't just her who felt off-kilter. It was well known that Tylara refused to bond with her One because he came from a family renowned for its unstable psychic power. He was a little more animalistic than some other Kith, but Jana had never been uncomfortable in his company before. She assumed whatever was wrong with him was something a Kin couldn't sense. A stab of guilt went through her for stooping low enough to take a shot at his love life. Hers wasn't exactly ideal.

His face was a calm mask when she met his gaze again. "Here we are."

She knew. That awareness vibrated through her whenever she drew near her One. The door slid open, spilling them out not far from her chamber. "I can take it from here."

"Very good, Your Majesty." Johar stepped back into the multiveyor, leaving her to her fate.

Dragging in a deep breath as she walked down the hall to their quarters, she squared her shoulders, stepped inside, and straightened to almost military attention. Her chin lifted and she focused on the far wall. "You sent for me?"

She could feel his cool regard from where he sat on the gel-pad, his gaze sliding over her body. As usual, he wore a simple gray tunic and black pants, nothing that indicated his rank. The clothes fit his muscular form to perfection. She swallowed, unable to keep her body from responding. Heat rippled through her, arrowing between her legs.

I can feel your desire. His telepathic voice held amusement.

"You can hardly be surprised, Kyber." She snorted, clenching her fists where they were hidden behind her back to keep from reaching for him. She craved him so much, but letting go too much might let him in too deep. She couldn't risk it.

"Come to me."

Her eyebrows arched, and she let her tone turn chilly. "You just send for me for sex?"

"We can do that, too, but I *wanted* to share a meal and a conversation with you where we didn't fight." She watched him rise to his feet from the corner of her eye.

"I'm not hungry." She turned away from him and toward the sanitation room. The door opened for her automatically. She wasn't going to stand there and wait for the inevitable passion to erupt between them if they argued; she was getting her shower.

A pulse of his frustration hit her through their link, but he didn't reply. What could he say? They both knew it was just an excuse to shut him out again. She stepped inside the sanitation room and reached for the tab to unfasten her top. "Close and lock door."

A soft swish and click indicated it had obeyed her, and she continued to strip on her way to the clothing cleanser. Wadding the sweat-drenched outfit in a ball, she stuffed it in one of the glass bins on the machine. "Clean."

It gave a low whir in response, and she turned toward the shower. A single step down into a circular area with a drain in the middle was the only real indicator that this was a shower. "Water on."

Multiple spigots in the wall shot out scalding water that pelted her from every direction. She sighed as it sluiced down her skin, washing the sticky-sweaty feeling away.

The door hissed as it opened behind her. Shit. She'd forgotten that the imperial power to override locks worked for Kyber, too. She froze, every muscle in her body tightening while she watched him step into the room. Naked. His violet eyes were heavy lidded, but nothing could disguise the sparks of lust . . . and anger . . . that danced in his gaze. He strode into the shower as though he owned it, which he did. The water ran in steamy rivulets down his big body, over the hard pecs and tight ridges of his abs. His cock stood in a firm arc against his flat belly and her body reacted to the blatant display of desire.

"Don't walk away from me, Jana. If we have nothing else, we have this. We *want* this. Come here."

Closing her eyes, she tried to resist the pull he had over her. Even without seeing his muscled body, she could feel the flow of his craving through their tiny link. It made her heart pound, fed her own hunger. Her sex heated, the lips going slick. She swayed toward him, her nipples hardening as her breathing sped to soft pants. "I'm taking a shower."

"I'll wash you. Come here."

Her feet carried her forward without any real direction from her brain. It was madness to think she'd ever be able to resist him, and the months apart had only sharpened her body's yearning. She was so damn weak, no matter how hard she tried to lock it tight, to keep him out, there was always a teeny thread that let him in. Self-loathing swamped her, but she shoved it away. Kyber would want to *talk* about it, and she just couldn't do it. As he'd said, they had nothing but the sex. It was bitterly ironic that sex was what had gotten her into this mess in the first place.

Reaching for the dispenser of liquid cleanser, she worked it into a lather and began washing herself. A shudder of longing she couldn't stop went through her when Kyber's hands joined hers and moved over her bare curves.

A dark frown drew his eyebrows together when he took in the distinct footprint that was beginning to show on her leg. His voice was gruff with concern. "What happened here? Who dared to injure you?"

She shrugged, sliding her fingers into his long, silky hair. "I was sparring with Bren when you sent Johar along to fetch me."

"Ah, yes. My warrior empress." A faint smile curved his

lips. He knelt, stroked a palm over the back of her thigh, and swept the lightest of kisses over her bruised flesh.

It was moments like this that made her want to sob. He should hate her for what she did, for how she'd unwittingly helped Arthur turn Kyber into a near-beast, how she had helped an enemy destroy them both. She would understand him having ugly feelings toward her, but it was times when he gentled the feline enough to be almost *loving* with her, the way he had been the first time he touched her, that made her feel like she was going to crawl out of her skin with the need to escape.

"This is from my rescue." He brushed his lips over an older bruise on her other leg, and her belly cramped.

She shook her head. "No, that's from Arthur."

"W-what?" He jolted slightly, staring up at her. "The ship said . . . that was months ago."

Her toes curled against the floor. "I know. I have the medics heal it, but it just keeps coming back. Same bruise, same place where Arthur hit me."

His first hit. One of many. The images were burned into her memory, always there, playing on a nonstop loop in her head, no matter how hard she tried to squelch it. The medics said it was psychosomatic, but knowing that did little to help her. Kyber looked confused, opening his mouth to speak, but the last thing she wanted was to talk about *that* while naked and in Kyber's arms.

God, she would give anything to forget, to distract herself from the constant bombardment. Tightening her fingers in Kyber's hair, she pulled his head up to kiss her. He suckled her bottom lip, then let his tongue glide into her mouth. A moan spilled from her as fire flickered to life in her belly, spreading quickly until her body sizzled and ached with need. He pulled her down until she was on her knees with him and hauled her flush against him, her curves melding with his harder planes.

Bending her back over his arm, he sucked her nipples into his mouth one at a time, then plucked and rolled the tight tips between his fingers. Goose bumps broke down her limbs, and she clutched him closer, gliding her hands over his wet flesh and solid muscles.

The water poured over them, each droplet sliding down her skin a liquid caress. Her pussy flexed on nothingness, and she wanted to be filled until she couldn't take any more. He licked a hot path from her breast to her throat, biting down on the sensitive tendon that connected her neck to her shoulder. She jolted, sobbing for breath. He caught the sound in his mouth, pulling her tight to him as his lips met hers. His rougher flesh stimulated her nipples, and one palm cupped her ass, rubbing her against his thick cock while the other hand bracketed the back of her neck, holding her there for the slow, scorching kiss. She loved kissing him, the sweetness of it, but she craved the beast he tried to lock inside the perfect emperor. She bit his lip hard enough to draw blood, and he snarled, the feline coming to the fore. He gave her what she needed without her having to ask, stripping away her control, which scared her as much as it titillated her.

His mouth slanted over hers, the possession apparent. The kiss went wild, each of them sucking and nipping at the other. His fangs scraped her lips, and she tasted the coppery tang of blood. Whether it was his or hers, she didn't know. Her fingers twisted in his hair, while the nails on her other hand raked down his back. Volcanic heat erupted within her. He groaned, his claws digging into her waist, and he pulled away to spin her on the slick floor.

She gasped as he forced her forward onto her hands and knees. The head of his cock slid over her clit, the lips of her pussy, and she cried out with the desperate need that flashed through her. "Oh, *God*. I want you inside me, Kyber. Now. Please, now."

A deep, feline growl sounded behind her and his claws splayed against her back. His dick slid into her pussy one slow inch at a time, filling her just as she'd wanted to be filled. God, he was big. It felt amazing. He retracted his talons, stroking down her skin. Dipping his fingers into the moisture between her thighs, he trailed his hand up to sink his thumb into her tight anus.

"Kyber!" Her nails scratched against the wet floor as she rocked herself into his hand, his cock. The water streamed her short hair into her eyes, and she blinked hard, shoving herself into his touch. He pumped his finger into her ass, rubbing his cock through the thin wall that separated the two. Heat rocketed through her, slamming into her so hard that she sobbed for breath. Yes. Any moment now she was going to—

"No." His voice was a harsh rumble, half-animal, half-man. "Don't you dare come on my cock."

A long, whimpering cry broke from her throat as she tried to hold off her orgasm.

"You'll beg for it. You don't get to control this, Jana. You don't get to deny it or run away from it the way you do everything else." He growled, jerking out of her pussy. She moaned a ragged protest, her thoughts scattering into frantic, beseeching incoherency. He removed his digit from her tight anus and replaced it with his dick. The stretch stung, made her dip lower and arch her back to take him deeper. He gave her no time to adjust to the invasion before he began thrusting in her ass. Her arms collapsed out from under her, her inner muscles flexing as fire streaked through her. He stroked a hand over her buttock, drawing it back to smack her. The sound echoed loudly in the metal room, and she screamed. He purred. "You'll beg me to come, Jana."

Arthur had made her beg, too. Not for pleasure like Kyber, but for an end to the pain. Now, the pain never ended, even during the pleasure. Deep down, in those dark places in her soul she tried to hide from just as he'd accused, she knew she deserved it, but somehow with Kyber, the agony wasn't a horror, it was what she needed to survive the ecstasy. She couldn't stand it, but she wanted it so badly, wanted *him* so badly.

He curled his taloned fingers over her shoulders, pressing her deeper into her prone position as he powered into her. She lay there, her body rocking with his hard thrusts, her cheek pressed to the hot, wet floor, and her knuckles stuffed in her mouth to keep from screaming for more. The water stroked her sensitized flesh and waves of need built inside her, cresting higher and higher until she knew she'd be consumed by it. Orgasm shimmered just beyond her grasp; she could feel it, and she wanted it. She reached her free hand between her thighs, rubbing her fingers over her clit. He swatted her ass again. "No. Stop that."

"P-please," she sobbed, a tear slipping down her cheek to blend with the warm shower water. "Please, Kyber. Make me come."

Moving her hand farther back, she cupped the heavy sacs between his legs, squeezing her internal muscles tight around his cock. He roared, the feline breaking free. Hammering into her ass, he pushed them both to the edge of their endurance and shoved them over. "Now, Jana. Scream for me."

She gave him what he demanded, her shriek reverberating off the walls. Orgasm thrummed through her, made her muscles clench. She pushed her fingers into her pussy, stroking herself as he slammed his cock into her ass. Her sex pulsed against her hand. Tingles broke over her skin, and shudders ran through her. Every time he entered her anus, another spasm fisted her sex, and they both groaned.

Shoving his dick deep one last time, he ground his pelvis against her ass. His fluids flooded her and an aftershock of orgasm tightened her channel around her thrusting digits. Through their link, she could sense how much he liked the feel of her ass around him, how he didn't want it to end, how he hated that she could call forth the beast in him faster than anything else. How she could strip him of his control as fast as he stripped her of hers. He hissed and continued thrusting into her until his cock softened.

She collapsed to the floor when he finally pulled out of her, and she slammed down on the connection between them. She couldn't do this anymore. He would break through, he would *know* her. Every time he hammered away at her control, he got that much closer to the darkness. She was alone, always alone, always the one trying to hold it all together. Low sobs tore from her throat, as empty and bereft as she'd ever been in her life. He reached out a hand as though to comfort her and she flinched away. "Don't touch me. I can't stand it."

"Water off." The shower cut off at his command. He rolled away from her, dragging himself to his feet. His tone was frustrated and angry. "I have a meeting with Farid, but when I return, we *will* talk about this, Jana. You can't run forever, you can't pretend it didn't happen."

"Go away." Her breathing hitched as she worked on slowing her tears. She forced herself to sit up but couldn't find the energy to pick herself up off the floor.

A thick ebony eyebrow arched as he stared down at her. "Even if I go away, you'll never escape it."

"Go to hell." The words ripped from her throat, all the ugliness inside her slamming against the dams she'd built, frothing over on to the one person who'd never let it rest. Unless she made him hate her as much as she hated herself. "I hate everything that's happened to me since you came into my life. I was happy before I met you. Maybe I slept with Arthur to get rid of you. You're nothing but a monster."

Every inch of color fled his face. "You don't mean that."

"Yes. I. *Do.*" Another tear slid down her face, and she stomped on the biggest red button she knew he had. "You were supposed to *protect* me, Emperor Kyber. Your One. Instead, you got yourself captured and turned your wife into a whore."

The sound that came from his mouth was that of a wounded animal, but she also saw the rage behind those violet eyes, the feral nature he tried so desperately to hide from others. "You chose to make a whore of yourself, but if you liked it with Arthur so much, I'm sure we can make arrangements to have you dropped off on his doorstep."

She swayed hard, grateful that she still knelt on the wet metal. "Get out!"

He hissed at her, his hurt and fury and self-loathing ripping through their bond, shredding what little remained of her control. Snarling, he spun on his heel and left her there, snapping that fragile, beautiful link and leaving her gasping at the agony of loss. Again. Always.

It hadn't hurt this badly since the first time, when she lay naked beneath Arthur's heaving body. Her stomach turned. She squelched the thought, the memory, the horrifying nightmare, the way she'd been doing for months now. Constantly battling to stay sane. It was her own fault. She'd taken a bad situation and made it worse. She was a traitor and a whore.

Closing her eyes, she bowed her head and let the exhaustion and utter despair sweep over her. She'd been fighting it for so long. She was so tired. She just wanted it to be over. She didn't want to have to hate herself forever, she didn't want to have to see that betrayed, agonized look in Kyber's eyes ever again.

Worse were the memories she could never escape. She'd thought finding pleasure at Kyber's touch would help ease their power over her, but she was wrong. They plagued her night and day, and no matter how she tried, she couldn't be rid of them. They were as vivid now as when they had happened. Every sensation. Arthur's breath on her face, his hands on her skin, his penis pushing into her unprepared body, tearing her, hurting her. And he'd enjoyed that, the pain. He'd laughed at her when she'd cried, when she'd begged. For Kyber, for herself.

Her stomach revolted, sent her scrambling, crawling, and slipping across the cold, slick floor to the commode. Sobbing so hard she choked, she vomited, her muscles locking as the spasms ripped through her. The sound of her retching was loud and grotesque in the metal room, echoing to mock her.

"Oh, God." If Kyber's touch couldn't erase the memories, nothing could. Some final, fragile wall crumbled inside her. He was right, she couldn't hide from it forever. She couldn't pretend anymore. It was hopeless. It would never get better, she would never be whole again.

She couldn't live like this.

Anun, help him. Kyber had fucked his One hard, careless of her comfort, her needs. He'd fucked her like the monster she'd called him. He hated it. He would give anything to make it stop, to be in command of himself and wipe out the animalistic urges that dragged him to Jana. Without the white noise to dull his psychic gifts, the longer he was near her, the more difficult it was to maintain the distance he wanted over his emotions, to crush the ties that bound them. They could never trust each other again. All she saw was the monster, the one thing he'd feared the most about himself.

It made him sick to his stomach.

The multiveyor at the end of the hall slid open and he drew a deep, steadying breath when he saw who stood inside. Farid. He'd hoped to have a moment to regroup after leaving Jana before he had to deal with anyone. He nodded, unable to meet the older man's incisive green gaze. The multiveyor's door had scarcely closed when his cousin rounded on him. "What are you doing, Kyber?"

Kyber would have taken offense, wanted to, in fact, but he was too tired and drained to care that the question was presumptuous of one of his subjects. Besides, if his cousin couldn't be frank, who could?

A few months ago, he would have said Jana. She was his One, his equal in every way. Now? He didn't know. She obviously wanted nothing to do with him, and any attempts he'd made to breach the walls between them had been met with chilly indifference. He scrubbed his hand over his face and gave the only answer he had to his cousin. "I have no idea."

"You'd best get one, cousin, before it's too late." Farid didn't tell the multiveyor to move, so they stayed where they were. He propped his hands on his hips, the expression on his face dour.

Kyber sighed. "I know."

"Do you?" Farid's voice was deceptively mild, but his eyes were narrowed and assessing.

"Yes." Kyber thrust his hands through his hair, knotting his fingers in the long strands. "I may be younger than you, Farid, but my abilities are far stronger. I can sense the impatience of the fleet growing. I *know* that my time is running out."

He was a man at war with himself. Conflicted on all fronts. What to do with Jana, what to do with Earth, what to do with his people. The last week of indecision couldn't continue. He needed to make a final choice, set his feet to one path and stay the course.

Farid set his hand on Kyber's shoulder. His voice was quiet, understanding. "Can you forgive yourself?"

Kyber could pretend ignorance, could demand what he'd done to warrant absolution, but he knew. If it weren't for his arrival, his single-minded quest to find his One, Arthur would never have had a chance to gain all the power he had. He'd still have commanded the most powerful army on the planet, but not consolidated all the major armies on Earth, not have had the chance to become a dictator. It wasn't to that point yet, but it was coming and Kyber knew it. Farid's One would never have defected without that possibility being an utter certainty.

And it was all Kyber's fault.

He was the catalyst that had brought all of these pieces and players into place. His quest, his expedition, his overwhelming focus on finding Jana while ignoring the politics of Earth and how the Sueni arrival affected the planet made him as culpable as anyone else in this awful game.

Ignoring Earth's politics had cost every person on board the *Anshar* their life. It had put his One in a situation where she felt the need to sacrifice herself for him. Guilt slammed into him, sucking him into an endless void. This wasn't the first time someone he'd loved had sacrificed themselves for him. Would the pain of it never end? Did he deserve for it to end? Each life that had been lost was a mark on his soul.

He opened his eyes and told the one, simple truth he had. "No, I can't forgive myself."

Farid nodded. "We can't leave until it's right again."

A wry smile pulled at Kyber lips. "Are you saying that because you believe it is so or because of who your One is?"

"Both, Your Majesty."

"I've made a mess of everything." He dragged a palm across his eyes and sighed.

"Making mistakes is part of living, cousin." The hand on his shoulders squeezed tight, and sympathy came through the familial link between them.

He huffed out a breath. "When have I ever been allowed a mistake? I'm the emperor."

Farid dropped his hand and sighed. "Even emperors aren't perfect. They have to learn and grow like everyone else. Having a destiny isn't the same as living with that destiny."

"And if I can't be trusted with that destiny? If all I am is a broken, bestial remnant of my former self?" Kyber swiped his hand through his hair again, staring out the windows of the multiveyor at the Sueni working in a hangar bay below. People who relied on him to make the right choice. Everyone was counting on him.

"The beast is as much a part of us as the psychic, Kyber. The feral instincts ground the mental powers the way the mental powers cage the beast. Sometimes I think your mother did you a disservice after your father died, expecting you to never make a mistake again." His cousin joined him to look down at the hangar. The multiveyor rocked slightly as it started to move, called by someone else on board.

"She and Father were so perfect together, always in accord. They were nothing like Jana and me." The worst part was that Kyber *liked* arguing with her as much as he liked touching her. The beast enjoyed the challenge. If it was only Arthur they argued about, it would be one thing, but they debated everything. They were never in perfect agreement, there was never any harmony. It was wrong to like it so much.

Farid snorted. "You were young when your father died, cousin. You never knew them as adults, never saw how your father loved to needle your mother into losing her composure. I know after he died she never let herself lose that composure, never let you lose yours, but that wasn't how it was when the emperor lived. They were a complementary set; they weren't always aligned."

Kyber didn't remember anything like that, but perhaps Farid was right. He hadn't known them, not really. Just as he hadn't known Jana. He sighed and set all that aside. "That doesn't help me handle the situation with Arthur and Earth."

He could take his people and leave here, never to return. But he could not. Arthur needed to die . . . for the people he'd killed, for what he'd done to Kyber, for what he'd done to Jana, for what he'd deliberately done to their bonding. The time for standing aside and hoping action wasn't necessary had come and gone long ago.

A humorless smile curved his lips. It was an excellent thing when the man's justice went hand in hand with the beast's vengeance.

The multiveyor moved sideways and up a few floors, and the two men turned to greet whoever entered. Tylara, Tylara's second in command, Haakesh, and Haakesh's One, Mythri. Possibly the most powerful group of Kith in the entire Sueni fleet. Kyber fought a groan, struggling to lock his thoughts and emotions away. The last thing he wanted was his highest-ranking personnel reading his mind. The grin on his lips widened. His mind wasn't a good place to be just now.

However, it gave him the perfect opportunity to start down the path he'd chosen. Each person bowed their head respectfully as they stepped inside. The multiveyor's door slid closed and he addressed the ship, "*Vishra*, take us to my office."

"Yes, Your Majesty," the ship's liquid voice replied.

His gaze swept the group. "I know you've all been waiting for some word from me on how we're to proceed from here."

"It's only been a handful of days since your return, Your Majesty. Everyone would understand if you needed more time to acclimate yourself to your life again." The sympathy and quiet strength in Mythri's gaze made him glad she was in his diplomatic corps. They'd need that strength before this was over.

"Thank you, but it's time to get back to work." The multiveyor slid to a stop, and he led them into his office suite. He propped himself against his desk and waited for them to arrange themselves on the various chairs and couches that scattered around the room. "You all have duties to attend to, so I won't keep you long."

Tylara leaned forward in her seat. "This is more important right now, sire."

"Thank you." He took a breath, testing the emotions of those around him. Anticipation rose in the room, though their faces reflected only mild interest. The power he was born with was what made him emperor. Time to start acting like it. "I'll need all of your help for this. We're going to remove Arthur from power, which I'm sure doesn't shock you, and I know Farid and Bren have been trading technology with different countries for their cooperation in providing information on Arthur's activities and, before my rescue, my whereabouts."

"None of the technology could be used against us," Farid interjected. "No weapons."

"Of course not." Kyber nodded. "What I propose is that we step up that campaign and continue it even after the bulk of the fleet has returned to Suen. One ship will remain here."

He felt their surprise but no resistance to what he was saying. An excellent sign. "It's not enough to simply end Arthur's influence here. The power structure of this planet has been thrown out of balance because of our arrival. I propose we become a new trade partner and that we serve as unbiased mediators, if needed."

A sigh of relief came from Farid. "My One and I would like to be with that ship. We'll help reestablish peace here and make sure future Sueni-Earthan relations are based on mutual prosperity rather than animosity."

Mythri reached for Haakesh's hand, and they shared a look of complete understanding. She met Kyber's gaze. "We'll stay, too. Haakesh can command the ship left behind. There are Sueni who have married the Earthan Kin they brought on board. They might wish to remain here as well."

"Or they may wish to go with us. The Earthan partners in those pairings will, of course, have Sueni citizenship." Kyber tapped his fingers against his thigh. "We can put a call for volunteers in the fleet and see where we stand."

He looked to Tylara, his military commander. She was quiet for a long moment. "I would suggest that the *Vishra's* sister ship, the *Jagata*, be the one to stay. It is the one most able to defend itself, should anything happen. I also believe that as we journey home, we should establish communication imager relays so that we're not cut off from Earth entirely."

"Agreed." Kyber slid his hands in his pockets and sensed their approval in his plan, their relief to have a mission to accomplish. A sigh eased out of his throat. One problem solved, but so many other questions still to answer.

Mythri's eyebrows arched. "What does the empress think of your plan, sire?"

"She doesn't know about it." The empress thought he was a monster. He forced a wide smile as he stood to indicate the meeting was over. "I'm afraid this is an idea that's only just become concrete enough to mention. As Her Majesty is recovering from a sparring lesson with Lady Arjun, I haven't had time to speak to her about it."

Tylara snorted. "Hardly a *lesson* at this point, sire. Your One is a quick study. Bren has to work to stay ahead."

Rising from his seat, Farid turned for the door. His eyes twinkled. "It's good for my One to have a challenge from someone she knows isn't holding back on her."

"She has the Kin Guardians for that, too." Tylara brushed at the sleeves of her dark blue uniform as she followed Farid. She glanced at Kyber. "The empress did quite well while you were away, Your Majesty. Not just with learning to fight. She's made an excellent impression on all my staff. Johar says the Guardians quite like her as well."

The Royal Guardians would protect and serve the imperial family whether they were likeable or not, but hearing Tylara compliment *anyone* was unusual.

"I agree. Farid and I have been training her with the diplomatic corps, and I've been most impressed with how quick a study she is." Mythri's smile was kind and sincere.

"I have no objection to your new plan, sire. I think it's excellent." Worry flashed over Haakesh's normally good-humored expression, and his One tucked her hand in the crook of his arm. He spoke plainly, as was his nature. Kyber had always liked that about him, until now. "However, I think I speak for everyone when I say that we respect your One very much, but it has been noted that she's withdrawn from her duties and her interactions with the public since your return. She seems unhappy, and we're concerned that the reunion of the imperial couple has not been as amicable as we might hope. There are, of course, extenuating circumstances, but I've heard rumblings in the fleet that the reason we didn't leave as soon as you returned is because you may decide to leave the empress on Earth, thus defeating the purpose of our expedition. I'm sure our new mission will curtail that rumor, but . . ." He drew a breath and let it out, covering his One's hand with his. "I hope, for your sake and Empress Jana's, that you can find some peace between you."

"I'll take all of that into consideration." What else could Kyber say? He *had* threatened to dump Jana back on Earth and leave her at Arthur's mercy. Not that he could ever have followed through with the thought. Even at the height of his rage, he couldn't imagine doing such a thing to anyone. He wasn't that cruel.

He sighed. Jana. Anun, their bond was a tangled mess he'd never undo. Listening to his people sing her praises stung. While he wasn't here, she had become the woman he'd always known she was capable of being. A leader, respected and obeyed by beings vastly more powerful than she was. It was unsettling to know that she was more perfect for an emperor now than she ever had been, but he was less a ruler than he had ever been. And she wanted to be rid of him. He snarled, the beast awakening with a vengeance, dragging him to his basest instincts. Every time he thought he had a handle on it, it slammed into him when he least expected it. The memories, the horror, the agony. Of what Arthur had done to him, of what Jana had done with Arthur.

He froze, hissing as every sense went on alert. His claws and fangs slid forward as the power within him reacted to an attack that wasn't forthcoming. The group still standing in his doorway turned back to stare at him in confusion, and Kyber shook his head. Some painful awareness awakened within him. Something pressed against his skin, as if pins were digging into his flesh. It niggled at the back of his mind, like a memory he couldn't recall or a word that hovered on the tip of his tongue. He rolled his shoulders, pushing the sensation away.

But it wouldn't be denied. Soon the niggle became a tug and the tug became an urgent yank that sent pain shooting through his skull. He groaned, bending forward and catching his hands on his knees. He might have kept right on going all the way to the floor if Farid hadn't moved forward to grab his shoulder and hold him upright. Somewhere in the distance, he heard Farid's voice shouting. People erupted into the corridor outside his office, diving into action. Answering Farid's call? Kyber didn't know, that hot blade slicing through his mind obliterated anything else.

And then he understood.

It was the connection with his One, ripping wide open, shoving past the barriers he'd erected to confine it, block it.

He saw through Jana's eyes as she picked up his razer from the table by the wall, felt her resolve, realized without a shadow of a doubt what she was going to do.

"*Noooo.*" The sound that wrenched from his throat was that of a wounded animal, tripping over a low sob.

Jerking free of Farid's grip, Kyber shoved his way out the door and spun for the stairway that would lead him down to the level with his chambers. He couldn't wait for the multi-veyor. His arms and legs pumped as he sprinted faster than he ever had in his life, pouring on every ounce of his superhuman speed, leaping down the stairs, desperation whipping through him.

Jana, no. Don't do this. I forbid it. The tone was his most royal edict, words that should be obeyed without question.

He felt her derisive snort through their connection, sensed that she was shoring up her own defenses against his mental commands.

He was losing her.

His lungs burned with strain, sweat sliding down his face to burn his eyes. He reached the right level and shot out into the hallway. Every muscle in his body screamed with the imperative to reach her, to stop her, to save her.

Please, Jana. But he knew she no longer listened.

Rounding the last corner, he made the door fly open with a single thought and raced through, his hand already outstretched to rip the gun from her hand. The gun she'd pressed against her temple.

She'd already pulled the trigger, and the weapon discharged as it flew through the air, blowing a hole in the sanitation room door.

"No!" She leapt for the razer and missed, hitting the floor hard on her knees as a helpless, hopeless sob ripped from her. She was still naked and damp from their shower. Tears sheened her beautiful grey eyes as she stared up at him.

Relief wound through him as the weapon landed safely in his palm. He closed his eyes for a moment and swallowed, struggling to catch his breath, to understand that he had gotten there in time. He'd never been more terrified in his life, not even when Arthur's men had captured him.

"Give me the gun back, Kyber."

"*No.*" Horror fisted inside him, and he stumbled back a step, clutching his razer tight.

"Please, Kyber. You want this. I want this. Hell, every Sueni you dragged with you wants this. Just give me the gun and walk away. That's all you have to do. Just walk away." Tears slid down her cheeks. "P-please, Kyber. *Please.*"

He shook his head so hard, his hair whipped into his eyes. "No one else wants this, Jana."

"Yes, they do." Her laugh was a harsh, painful sound. "You think it's easy to hold my head up? You think it's fun knowing that everyone who walks by me *knows* I whored myself out? That everyone thinks I was an idiot?"

"They don't think that." The words were especially bitter after the conversation he'd had in his office. "You obviously have no idea what they're thinking."

"It doesn't matter. None of it matters." Her eyes focused on the razer in his hands, a longing in her gaze so keen it sliced through him. Her voice was a low sob of air. "Our connection was so perfect, so pure. I hate myself for what I did to us. We're broken. *I* broke us. I can't live with myself anymore, Kyber. I can't." She swallowed, her fingers trembling as she lifted them toward him. "Give me the gun back."

He gathered the power within him, focusing on the metal of the weapon, and made it shatter into a thousand unrecognizable pieces. He dropped them to the floor. "You will not kill yourself using *my* weapon. You will not kill yourself *at all.*"

A low cry of pain spilled from her as the razer turned to little more than metallic dust. "I did everything I said I would do. I saved you from Arthur, brought you back to your people, now just let me finish it." Her palms pressed together in supplication. "I just want it to be *over*. It'll all be okay for everyone then."

"It will never be finished between us, Jana." The words, the truth, jerked out of him while his body still trembled with shock. He'd almost lost her. His One. "It'll never be okay without you."

"I'll beg. That's what you want, isn't it? I'll beg, Kyber." She buried her face in her hands and sobbed. Her every emotion spilled out. Her pain, her desperation, her deep, terrifying loneliness. She was open to him as she hadn't been since before Arthur.

He groped his way along the connection between them as he stepped toward her cautiously and laid a hand on her bent head. She shuddered and he felt how she tried to writhe away from the automatic reaction to her One's touch. He refused to allow himself satisfaction that she couldn't escape it any more than he could. Instead he followed the dark streaks of pain that flowed through her mind. It was unnatural, this anguish.

When he ran up against a wall in her thoughts, it took him a moment to understand what he was looking at. This wasn't a barrier erected by her. It was shoved there . . . by *him*.

What she'd said about the bruise that never healed, that always returned, rushed back to haunt him. Horror exploded inside him as he realized exactly what he had done. In the moment of her betrayal, in his deepest moment of agony, he'd forced a block into her mind. And there it still rooted deep in her subconscious like a festering sliver, forcing her to relive what Arthur had done to her all day, every day. Literally. Her mind would have made every moment of it real. How his fists had struck her, how he'd hurt and humiliated her, how his fingers had wrapped around her throat to choke her and make her fight him, how he had loved the power her fear gave him.

Bile rose in Kyber's throat as those violations poured through him, as he lived them with her. How had she survived like this? How had she held on? How had she kept from going insane all these months? He didn't know. He only knew it took a strength he wasn't certain he possessed himself. And he, her

One, the person she was most defenseless against, had done this to her. Made her endure it over and over and over again.

Guilt so great it threatened to consume him crashed into him, rocking him back on his heels. His knees buckled and he crashed to the floor before her. "What have I done?"

Only her tears answered him. He closed his eyes, rested his forehead on her damp hair, and focused his power on the mental barricade he'd made. Grasping the ugly splinter, he tugged gently. It held firm. She shuddered, each of her sobs flaying him open like a blade. The beast within flailed helplessly at its mate's pain. He ripped the sliver out with a sharp pull. Her hoarse scream echoed off the walls in their room and she collapsed against him, the darkness trapped within her flooding both their minds. He gritted his teeth, cradled her close, and rode out the storm, absorbing as much of her torment as he could.

"I'm sorry, Jana. I'm so sorry." He rocked her, stroking his fingers through her short, silky hair. He'd never felt so unworthy to hold her. How could she have borne his touch the last week? She humbled him, just by being who she was. His One. He shook his head. No. He didn't deserve to call himself that anymore. However inadvertent his actions had been, his betrayal was far greater than hers could ever have been. He kissed the back of her head, felt her stir against him, her mind finally grasping what had happened, what he had done to her, why she'd been unable to put the past behind her. If nothing else, at least now she could heal. He was glad for that but braced himself for the kind of vitriol he'd spewed at her.

"It was . . . it was because of *you*?" Through their bond, he felt the swift rush of her relief at the end of the misery, the shaky realization that it wasn't something fundamentally wrong with her that had made her slowly lose touch with sanity.

He swallowed, wishing more than anything that he could change how all of this had gone. Starting with the moment he'd reached this planet. He'd made so many mistakes, had cost so many people so much. Easing her out of his embrace, he looked her in the eye when he confessed what he had done. "Yes, I . . . I forced you to relive it." He shook his head, his hair sliding over his shoulders. "I'm so sorry . . . I didn't know."

A wan smile crossed her pale features, but the storm clouds had cleared from her silver eyes. "You were being tortured at the time."

"That's hardly an excuse for torturing *you* for months." He shook his head, dropping his hands from her shoulders so he no longer touched her. The beast mewled at the loss of contact with its mate. His stomach lurched as he thought of the rough treatment he'd given her whenever he'd had any kind of contact with her since his return, how he'd made her beg before he'd allow her pleasure. He swallowed the gorge in his throat, and moved to rise, sickened by his own actions.

Panic flared through their link, and her fingers bunched in his tunic. She swayed toward him. Her eyes were so wide, they threatened to eclipse her face. "Don't . . . leave me alone like this. Please."

"I won't." He covered her hands with his, disengaged her fingers from his shirt, and lifted her palms to his mouth to kiss them. "I won't. Unless you'd prefer someone else stay with you. I can send for them."

"*No.*" The anxiety spiked again, vehemence lacing her tone. Naked vulnerability shone on her face. "I don't want anyone else."

Closing his eyes, he let the sweet relief explode through him. He felt as if he'd been spared a trip to the executioner. "I'll stay as long as you need."

"Good," she whispered. She tugged her hands from his and leaned in until she could wrap her arms around him and press her cheek to his chest. "Hold me."

Yes. He needed that, too. More than the sex, more than even

getting her to talk to him, he'd craved that closeness. It was why he'd searched for her so long, why he'd left everything behind to find her. He was completely unworthy to touch her, but if she wanted his arms around her, he would give her what she wanted. His palms slipped up and down her naked back, her skin cool and smooth under his palm.

They stayed there for a long, long time. He sent her pulses of comfort through their link, letting a low purr rumble in his chest to relax her. His eyes drifted closed and he sighed. It had been so long since he'd felt . . . calm. Quiet. Peaceful. He smiled, remembering Haakesh's words.

Jana's hands stroked his back in slow circles. His purr deepened, the feline loving her petting as much as the man did. She shivered, burrowing deeper into him. "Mmm. I'm cold."

Pulling back a bit to brush a hand down her hair, he offered a little grin. "Well, you are naked and on a metal floor."

"I know where I am." The dreaminess evaporated from her voice, and she wrinkled her nose.

"Right, then. I missed my invitation to change the situation. My humblest apologies." He kept his tone light and teasing and was rewarded by her sweet giggle. He gathered her into his arms, carrying her to their bed. Laying her on the gelpad, he pulled the bedclothes up to cover her nudity. "Let me get a chair."

"No." Her fingers closed spasmodically over his wrist. "Stay with me."

"All right." He offered her a reassuring smile before he bent to remove his boots and then settled onto the gelpad beside her.

She rolled into his arms, and he caught her close. The beast reveled in the feminine scent of her skin, wanting to renew the bond between them, to allow no barriers ever again. The man knew that she'd been through so much, that wasn't the best thing for her. She would need time, space. To think, to consider, to *reconsider* everything they were to each other and how they would move forward from here. If she even wanted to move forward. At this point, it might not even be possible to move forward. Some things that were broken could never be fixed. Their connection might be one of those things. He couldn't be sure, and that terrified him, kicked him in the stomach, and he suppressed a groan. Leaning away from her, he stroked her hair away from her face. She stared up at him with those serious gray eyes, and he tried to smile at her but couldn't manage it.

She was so beautiful. Emotion cinched tight around his heart. How would he ever live without her if the harsh reality of morning brought the decision that she'd rather not stay with a man who'd hurt her? What if she was determined to remain on Earth when this was all over? Once Arthur was gone, there would be no threat to her. If she wanted to stay, he wouldn't stop her, and emperor or not, he knew he'd never deserve her again. If he ever had in the first place. He'd been so arrogant, so presumptuous. She was his One; therefore, she was his and only his, just as he was hers. Every other experience paled in comparison to connecting with her. When they'd bonded, he'd known she agreed with him, that they were in perfect unison.

Now, he didn't know anything for certain. Not with her. Would she want to keep him? Should he keep her? Wouldn't she be better off without him, leaving in the past all that being his One had put her through? He'd survived all that Arthur had to offer, the beatings, the blood, the numbing of his psychic gifts, but it was sheer torment to even consider surviving the loss of his One. She was strong enough to heal, to dismantle the walls she'd built to isolate herself from all she'd been forced to feel, to be whole without him, and he would be broken and alone all the days of his life. But he was the emperor. Shouldn't he do everything in his power to make sure those under his protection had what they needed?

He couldn't imagine a time when she might truly need or trust him again, not after what he'd done to her. Unlike him, at least her intentions in this mess had been good. She'd tried to help him and received only pain for her efforts. He shook his head, swallowing. *His One,* and he'd used his powers to harm her.

There was no excuse for him, and no hope for *them.* Not anymore. He couldn't even blame Arthur for that. He'd done the damage himself.

He truly was a monster.

4

It was the tickle that woke her. Something soft and silky curled around her ankle. Jana's eyes popped open, and she blinked several times.

Kyber. In cat form. Lying across the end of the bed.

He wrapped and unwrapped his tail around her ankle, his pale gaze locked on her, and she froze like prey before a dangerous predator. Swallowing, she leaned up on her elbows and he zeroed in on her breasts when the slick *rishaami* bedcovers slithered down her torso. She resisted the urge to yank them back up and hide herself. He'd seen everything she had to offer. Hell, there wasn't an inch of her he hadn't kissed, bitten, sucked, or stroked.

Still, something had shifted the night before, and they'd entered a new phase of their relationship. She just didn't know what that phase was or where it put either of them. She didn't know how to act around him anymore. Biting her lip, she glanced away and focused on where the fur on his silken tail brushed her skin. Gooseflesh rippled up her legs and she shivered.

Are you all right?

She forced a smile. "Of course I'm—"

Don't. You don't have to pretend with me, Jana. I saw the truth, I know what happened.

She took a deep, calming breath and gave him the truth—a truth she hadn't allowed herself to admit since her brother died. "No, I'm not all right. Everything is not *all right.* But I hope I will be."

Are you angry? Do you . . . hate me for putting you through what I did?

The questions weren't as simple as they seemed at first. She made herself be brutally honest, to not hide from the bad things inside her. Was she angry? How could she not be? He'd used his powers against her to create a situation where she was forced to endure sexual degradations every day for months. God, yes, she was angry. And hurt. And betrayed.

Did she *hate* him?

Her eyes squeezed closed and she sighed. She wanted to hate him. God, she wanted to. It would be so easy. Too easy. It would solve nothing and would only hurt them both.

That was what it came down to, wasn't it? Who'd hurt who and when. Who'd been more hurt. Who'd been hurt the longest, the deepest. They could hold on to those things and point fingers and cast blame. They could be angry and bitter and distrustful. They could continue to hurt each other in some twisted game of one-upmanship.

Or they could act like adults and get over themselves.

She'd hurt him. He'd hurt her. Okay. It sucked. A lot. But that was where they were at. Their bonding was never going to be what it was in the beginning, no matter how much they might want it to be. No matter how much *she* might want it to be, but she wasn't that girl anymore, the one he'd found, the one he'd bonded with. And he wasn't that man. They were different. Everything that had happened in the intervening months had changed them both forever. And maybe it had changed them too much, made them not the right people for each other anymore.

As much as she'd give to have prevented all of the pain and suffering they'd been through, to have had everything be okay, she didn't want to be that old Jana again. She was a hell of a lot stronger than she'd been a year ago. She'd been broken and she'd survived. Barely, and not because she'd wanted to, but she'd survived. She had a long way to go before she was back on her feet, but not having to endure Arthur's torment every day and knowing that it wasn't some sick, masochistic tendency that had left her unable to put it aside would be a big step forward. What had happened would always mark her life, but now she could begin to heal.

A shaky breath eased out of her and she met Kyber's gaze again. He hadn't moved from where he lay at the end of the bed, but while she'd been entrenched in her own thoughts, he'd shifted back into his human form. He regarded her steadily, just waiting for her. The bond between them had narrowed enough that he couldn't have read her thoughts, but he'd allowed her to process her feelings without interrupting or interfering.

"Yes, I'm angry." She nodded hard to emphasize her point. "At you, at Arthur, at life, at everything. But I don't hate you."

His mouth worked for a moment before he spoke, and she could see his eyes dampen. "Thank you . . . for not hating me."

She snorted. "It feels weird to say you're welcome, but . . . you're welcome."

Pulling in a deep breath, he blinked away the tears and met her gaze head-on. "I'll do what I can to reinforce the barrier between us so you don't have to *feel* our connection, but . . . the block I put in place and removed last night isn't the only wall in your mind, Jana. The others aren't of my creation."

"There are barriers besides just narrowing our bond?" Her

eyebrows drew together, uncertain what he was getting at. "And I can make a psychic block in my own mind?"

"Everyone can. It's what allows us to push things away, to gain emotional distance from what upsets us." He forked his fingers through his hair, his expression pensive. "Think of it this way, the bond between us is like a tunnel. It's still there, and it can be widened and narrowed, but we've each built a wall on our side to protect ourselves from each other. Even then, there are emotions and thoughts that seep through the walls. A One bond is the most powerful psychic connection for my people—destroying it is impossible, but that doesn't mean we ever have to connect more than we do now."

That made sense . . . kind of. She could feel a disconnect between their minds, but she'd assumed it was because he was trying to cut their connection. An ugly thought occurred to her, and she hesitated before she gave it voice. "*Can* we connect more than we do now? Is it possible to remove those walls?"

"I . . . do not know." His hands lifted helplessly. "My powers allow me to 'see' these things, but even I can't destroy the blocks you've made for yourself. It isn't simply the wall against me, it's the walls against everything. The defenses you shored up to stay sane these last months have also walled you into one corner of your mind."

"Yeah, I have a lot of shit to deal with." Dark humor swept through her at that simple truth.

He gave her a crooked smile but didn't say anything.

She let what he'd said process, trying to see where all of this left them. "So, if we . . . if we can't break down the walls between us, then our bond isn't really a One bond."

"No." He sighed. "Our bond at this point is probably no more powerful than those between couples who are not Ones."

Maybe that was for the best for both of them. She compressed her lips to keep from crying, forced herself to meet his gaze and make the offer that might give him the chance to heal, too, with or without her. "I did manage to hear some of what you were thinking last night, and you might be right about me staying on Earth when you leave."

He choked a bit. His fingers curled around the same ankle his tail had, his violet eyes devoid of any sparks at all. "I understand. You'll . . . need to stay here until it's safe for you to go down to the planet."

"Right. It all comes back to Arthur, doesn't it?" Tears welled in her eyes and she stared up at the skylight for a moment, blinking rapidly. He hadn't even tried to convince her to stay with him. It was one thing for him to feel guilty for what he'd done, but another thing to love her again. Regardless of what he had done, she was still a woman who cheated on him with his worst enemy. A man who had spent months torturing him. Could Kyber ever love or trust a woman like that? She doubted it.

"Yes, it does come back to Arthur." Kyber's breath whooshed out of his lungs and his fingers tightened on her ankle. "He murdered thousands of innocent Sueni people. He shattered my life, and you're the only one I know who understands exactly what that means."

She did know. God, did she ever. She swallowed hard, wanting his arms around her so badly she ached. "Come here."

He rolled to his hands and knees, crawling up the bed until he lay next to her. Wriggling closer, she wrapped her arm around his lean waist and rested her cheek on his chest. His heart beat frantically under her ear, a fine tension running through his muscles. She closed her eyes and stroked her hand up and down his chest in soothing circles.

"I'm sorry I said those horrible things to you." She blinked back the tears that welled in her eyes. "I don't think you're a monster, and I don't think what Arthur did is your fault."

"Thank you for that, too." Turning his head, he kissed her forehead. His fingertips trailed up and down her naked back. It was delicious to have his hands on her again. Not demanding, not greedy, angry, or taking, just enjoying the feel of her. She'd missed that, missed the quiet moments with him as much as she'd missed the implicit trust that had coupled the intensity.

They'd never have that back again, and the time she had left with him was fast fading. Everything was still mixed up and confused in her head, but it had hurt to hear him think that he shouldn't keep her, that they were too damaged to have any hope of a future. She wasn't even sure he was wrong. If it might not even be possible to reopen their One bond, then how was she any more useful to him than any other woman? She wasn't even Kith. She had no special powers or gifts that might help him rule Suen. It might even be better for him to find someone who was powerful in her own right, who could give him an easier bond that wasn't weighed down by the tragedy they shared.

It might even be better for *her* to walk away from this mess forever. Painful, yes, but maybe better in the long run to cut her losses. She just didn't know what to think anymore. Until she straightened things out for herself, she was content to hold him and be held by him. His heartbeat steadied under her cheek, the tension melting away as he cuddled her closer. She curled her thigh over his, closing her eyes to savor this new place with him. It wasn't where they'd started, it wasn't where they'd been, but it wasn't bad. It was nice. It felt good.

It was enough. It would have to be. It might be all she had to remember him by.

"Lower the temperature a bit." Arthur's calm, chilling voice held a note of steely command. "We wouldn't want him to get too comfortable."

Shudders wracked Kyber's body from the bite of the already

frigid air on his naked skin. Little clouds puffed from his nose and mouth every time he exhaled. He knew it was a dream, a nightmare, a memory, yet he couldn't rip himself from it.

It was worse when Arthur was there. It was always worse. There were beatings every day, needles filled with drugs that burned his veins, the constant cold that froze him to the bone, and the squeal of white noise hammering his eardrums. But when Arthur came, it was worse.

A feral part of Kyber knew the older man wanted to establish himself as the dominant beast, liked that he could be there himself to keep Kyber helpless and on his knees. Arthur's pleasure at Kyber's pain made him snarl, his fangs elongating. He lunged at the man, the heavy chains ripping into his flesh.

"Eager this morning, aren't we? Your wife was eager this morning, too, when I fucked her." Arthur's chuckle echoed in the room, echoed through Kyber's mind. He struggled against the nightmare, but it was no use. Locked tight in its grip, he could only play it out to its inevitable end.

Arthur plucked a heavy baton from one of the guard's belts, stepping into the small room to circle his prey. Terror made Kyber's heart hammer against his ribs. His chest heaved with each breath, cold sweat running down his chilled skin. Arthur ran the tip of the heavy stick over the back of Kyber's shoulders, ratcheting up his anticipation, his dread, of the agony to come.

He gritted his teeth, wrestling with his fear, embracing the hate that darkened his soul. He met the man's gaze, saw the cold, calculating insanity in the dark eyes that stared back at him. "Enjoy it now, bastard. I'm going to kill you someday. I'll win, in the end."

Then it began.

The first hit crashed into the back of his head hard enough to leave his ears ringing. The next caught him at the small of his back, forcing his body to arch in reflex. Arthur laid into

Kyber's back, leaving a latticework of streaking fire in his wake. Kyber couldn't keep back the groan of agony when the heavy wood slammed into his kidneys. He'd be pissing blood for a week, and his body twisted away from the source of his misery. The baton came down on his thigh, and he screamed, the sound not human, but pure feline fury. Arthur shoved the point of the stick into Kyber's belly, laughing when he gagged.

The pain crested as the strikes came too fast for him to tell where one ended and the next began. Nothing was spared, his arms, legs, ass, back, and face all took hits. His lips split and blood gushed from his nose. His eyes began to swell shut, limiting his vision to tiny slits of light. His muscles burned as he fought against his bindings, wild as a caged animal, lashing out with his fangs and feet and claws. Arthur continued to laugh at the futile efforts. He whipped the baton around, jamming it into Kyber's balls.

His stomach heaved, and he vomited up blood. The copper taste filled his mouth, the chains rattling as he jerked against their hold, his mind no longer in control of the spasms that ripped through his limbs.

Through the convulsions he saw Arthur coming toward him with a long wand that would send electricity shooting through Kyber's body.

"Kyber!" The door to his office whooshed open, and he was on his feet, fangs and claws bared, a roar wrenched from his throat as he spun to confront the intruder.

Jana skidded to a stop in front of his desk, her gray eyes wide. "You had the nightmare again."

Yes, and they were coming with more and more frequency. He didn't say anything, didn't trust his voice to respond. Beads of sweat slipped down his face, reaction shaking through his muscles. His instincts sent him conflicting information. Kill the threat, claim the mate. Her scent beckoned to him, sweetly intoxicating. His cock hardened to the point of pain in mere moments and he dropped back into his chair, nudged himself closer to his desk, and hoped it made his condition less obvious. He tried to shove away both the ugly memories and the feverish desire.

He was slowly going mad. He hadn't touched her in almost three weeks, determined to allow her time to heal, to come to terms with all that had happened without any physical demands from him.

He knew it was the right thing to do, knew he had no right to lay a hand on her ever again, but that didn't stop the cravings of his body, the clawing need that frayed his control.

The feral side of his nature was not enjoying being leashed again, but he needed to find some kind of internal balance. Logic and emotion, beast and psychic, they were both part of him, as Farid had said.

Kyber's hands fisted where they rested on his desktop and he bit back a groan when she drew closer. The traditional *rishaami* gown she wore clasped at one shoulder and left one arm bare. The gown made her look every inch the Sueni empress.

The door swished open again, and her new assistant stepped into his office. Kyber had insisted on her taking the young Kin as her personal secretary. Partially because she would need the help now that his advisors and assistants were again working for him instead of her, and partially as a safety precaution. The young Kin had had extensive warrior training and was considering a career as a Guardian. And Kyber also wanted to make sure she *always* had someone with her. A shudder ran through him at the thought of how close he'd come to losing her. Another moment, a single heartbeat later, and he would have been far too late.

The last few weeks had been frantically busy for her, he knew. He'd taken the fetters off his staff, stopped trying to prove he could do everything himself, and now she had more work than she knew what to do with. He wanted to show her that he trusted her to be his empress. She was needed, she was useful, she had a place here if she wanted it.

If she wanted him.

If they could break down the walls between them. He'd tried, thrown himself against his own wall, but had made no more than small cracks and chinks in the barrier. It was more than just the hurt they'd caused each other. It was Arthur, it was the guilt, it was . . . everything. Could she ever trust that he wasn't a monster who would hurt her again? He didn't know. Even if they were *both* willing, he wasn't sure they could connect again. Not fully.

He could only pray to Anun that she would be willing someday, would choose not to remain on Earth, would give them the chance, the *time* to see if they could rebuild what had broken. But he felt the moments slipping between his fingers. As soon as the Arjuns' Earthan sources confirmed a location for Arthur long enough to attack, the fleet needed to leave. They had to get back to Suen. They'd been gone too long as it was.

Jana braced her hands on his desk and leaned forward, recapturing his attention. She glanced at her assistant. "Would you give us a moment, please?"

"Of course, Your Majesty." He bowed to them both and withdrew, closing the door behind him. Kyber sent a mental direction to the ship to lock the door.

She wandered over to the wide windows that lined the wall behind his desk. "Just now, you were thinking about how you need to get back to Suen."

"Yes." He'd widened the cord between them as much as he could, but with the barriers at each end, only the occasional thoughts flowed back and forth between them. Unless, of course, they felt something strongly, like a vivid nightmare. He pushed down the horror that curdled in his gut. He rubbed the back of his neck, his hair tangling in his fingers. "First, we need to remove General Arthur from power. Bren and Farid are looking for opportunities to get close to him."

"I know." Her gray gaze flicked to him, but they were calm pools of silver that matched her clothing. They told him nothing, gave him no hope that he'd ever truly reach her. "Removing him from power is a nice way of saying you're going to kill him."

He offered a nod. "Yes. One way or another, he will die for what he's done. To my species and to yours. People on Earth have suffered because of him, too."

"Yes, they have." Her shoulder dipped in a brief shrug. She bit her lip and her fingers slipped up and down her bare arm. He forced himself to look away. He wanted to kiss every inch of that creamy skin, wanted to strip the silver *rishaami* away until all of her was as bare as the one smooth arm.

Her full lips compressed and she stared hard out the window. "You'll leave as soon as Arthur's taken care of?"

"Of course." Why would he tarry longer? He'd only come here for her. A pulse of her upset strummed along their connection, but he didn't know what caused it.

"I see." Her head bowed, her forehead resting against the thick glass. "Your people must miss you. It's your mother who's serving as regent while you're here, right?"

"Yes, Empress Dowager Dhyaana." His eyebrows drew together at the odd question, but better an innocuous conversation than horrible tension. Aside from the nightmares, the last few weeks had been far better than any since they'd first bonded. It was good to just have her here, to look at her and savor her presence.

Jana turned to prop her shoulder against the window and crossed her arms. "She was okay with you leaving everything behind and having to rule?"

"Not much upsets my mother. She's like Farid that way."

He chuckled, a flash of his mother's serious face going through his mind. "Though ruling Suen is something she's used to. She was regent from the time I was twelve until I came of age. She's ruled the planet longer than I have and done a fine job of it. I had no qualms leaving her in charge."

She tilted her head, and her red hair swung against her cheek. "Farid's father killed himself after his One died. Were your parents Ones or just married?"

It was odd to speak to anyone who didn't know the entire history of each member of his family. Sueni children learned about them and could probably recite more facts and figures about him than he could remember about himself. He tapped a finger on the sleek metal surface of his desk. "It's not unheard of for Ones to be unable to face life without each other, but my mother is possibly the strongest person I've ever known. She lost her One, dealt with a traumatized child and a rebellion, and held everything together."

"Never flinched, huh?" She hugged herself tight, her voice subdued, bleak. "She sounds perfect—just the kind of woman who should be an empress."

He didn't understand the bleakness, but he'd talk about whatever she wanted to talk about. "Not perfect, but an amazing woman. She loved my father very much. I remember how they were together before he was killed. She was very different after that, sadder, more sober, but she never backed down, and that saved our people, our planet."

Perhaps his cousin was right that it was his father's needling that made his mother loosen her control, made her laugh. He'd been so young when it all ended.

"She must miss you." Jana sighed, staring out the window again, this time toward the planet below them. Did she want to return so badly, then? His gut clenched tight with dread. Her voice went soft. "I can't imagine going so long without seeing my parents."

"I miss her." He tried to smile and failed. His mother had been his touchstone for most of his life, given him a model of control to emulate, especially after they'd lost his father. Something else to feel guilty about, his father's death. He'd thought he'd outgrown it, but the cycle continued. He shook his head, groping for something else to think about. "Mother's only demand was that I bring home a bride and preferably a grandchild or two."

"Or *two*?" Jana glanced at him for the briefest moment, her eyebrows arching. "She expected your One to be a baby-making machine?"

He shrugged. "If I had found you as soon as I arrived, and if I'd managed to get you pregnant right away, we could have had a child by now."

"Yes. We could have." Regret welled in her eyes and she returned her focus to Earth, refusing to look at him. He could see her face in the window's reflection.

Swallowing, he shifted in his seat, uncertain what to say. With the exception of his mother, there had been very few women he'd tried to connect with in his life. He'd never needed to. Without the easy bond he and Jana had once shared, he didn't know how to get her to *want* to stay with him. How to break through and reach her was a question he couldn't answer. "According to the royal vizier, *if* I survive long enough to father children, I'm supposed to have two."

"Your mother might be disappointed with only two." Jana laughed softly. Her chin tucked to her chest, her eyes closing. "And did the vizier promise that those children would be with your One?"

Every drop of blood drained from his face at the firm confirmation that she planned to leave him. He pressed his hands flat to the top of his desk to keep from toppling over with the pain of it. "No, he promised me nothing except that I would be emperor."

But there would be no children, no life, no future, no hope without her. There would be only his duty, his throne, his cold, empty existence.

"Are these children supposed to be powerful Kith like you?" Conflicting emotions filtered through their link, hurt and longing and dread.

His claws slid forward to scrape against the metal desk, the sound sending a chill down his spine. He cleared his throat, forced the words out. "Yes, one would rule Suen and the other would succeed the royal vizier."

She pulled in a deep breath and the emotions stopped flowing between them. Her tone was one of mild curiosity. "So, two boys, then?"

"No, a boy and a girl." He watched her closely for reaction. Her sharp withdrawal from their small connection pained him, one more demonstration of how hopeless it was for them. He could read her mind but refused to stoop so low. She deserved better than that from him. She deserved better than he'd given her for most of their time as a bonded pair. He sighed. "I'm not sure which would be the ruler and which would be the prophet. It's not uncommon for a woman to be empress in her own right."

She finally met his gaze again, and her expression reflected genuine interest. "So, it's the eldest child rather than the eldest male who inherits the throne?"

He shook his head. "Not the eldest child, per se. It's not even guaranteed to remain in my direct line—it can go to a child in another powerful family, usually related closely to the royal family—but more often than not it does run in the direct imperial line. The throne goes to the most powerful child in each generation. It's all decreed by destiny, fate." He rocked his hand back and forth through the air, trying to put into words what was so obvious, so entrenched, in his society. "Though, sometimes the destiny isn't always clear, even to the most powerful vizier."

"That's just . . . *nothing* like what I'm used to."

"Our cultures are very different." He appreciated that about her, her differences from him, her unique perspective. If she went to Suen with him, she'd never be the kind of empress his mother had been, but she didn't need to be. He just wanted her to be herself, and to be with him.

"What happened to your dad?" She rolled her shoulders. "I felt a bit of upset when you thought of him."

Kyber swallowed, unprepared for the abrupt topic change, for the kick to his heart and conscience that came whenever he thought of the last time he'd seen his father. "He died."

"I caught that part." She arched her eyebrows. "How? I remember . . . vaguely . . . from when we first bonded that it wasn't a natural death."

Bracing himself for the wave of guilt that crashed over him, he met her gaze. "There was a rebellion in the empire when I was a child. Ten, perhaps eleven. There'd been rumblings of one for years. There always are."

"People wanted out and you wouldn't let them?" Her gaze narrowed and she propped her hands on her hips.

He snorted. "No, you have to work very hard to get into the Imperial Alliance, but you can leave any time. It's a federation of planets, not a dictatorship. This rebellion started as a protest against ill-treatment of Kin on one of the border worlds. Father was trying to sort it out peacefully but had little success. The behavior of the Kith on that planet was abhorrent. In the end, Father offered asylum to the Kin there and ended up bringing a motion to the Imperial Senate to revoke the planet's membership." He pinned his gaze to the desk before him, the events of that time lasered into his mind as clearly as if they had happened yesterday. He had the sick feeling that his time of imprisonment with Arthur would be much the same. "The ruling

Kith of that world did not take the news well. Thus the rebellion."

She dropped her hands from her hips, her fingers brushing against her dress. "Did the senate kick out the planet?"

"The vote went through after my father's death." A small, sour smile formed on his lips. "It was the first proclamation my mother made as regent."

"How did they kill him?" She pushed away from the window and stepped toward him, her soft boots making her steps a whisper against the floor.

He let his head fall back against the chair, sighing. "You had to ask."

"Of course. This is a big deal to you." She settled her hip against the edge of his desk, her scent enveloping him and making the beast writhe with the need to touch. "I remember that much from the short time I was in your head."

"Yes, you did see everything for a moment, didn't you?" And he wanted her to see it all again, to know all of him, to let him know all of her. How would he survive being bonded to her from across the universe? It would be a thousand times worse than when he'd merely sensed her from Suen.

"A very short moment. I don't remember much since we were busy with . . . other things." She didn't define what other things she was talking about. Bonding. Sex. Hours upon hours of endless sex. Then her parents' frantic pleas for her return, then his capture, then Arthur and the end of their bond. So swift a conclusion to something so bright with promise. Their love had scarcely had a chance to live before it died. Uncertainty flashed in her eyes, a return of the bleakness. "Unless you don't want me to know. I would understand."

"It's not that," he hastened to reply. "It's not a pleasant memory."

"Tell me." Her fingertips brushed over the back of his hand, the first physical contact he'd had with her since the day she'd

tried to commit suicide. The reminder sent contradictory feelings racing through him, icy fear for what had almost happened
then, and white-hot lust for the deeper contact he craved now.

He dragged in a deep breath. "One day, I sneaked out on my
aileron—a single-person vessel like our fighter wings, but without the weapons. I was soaring above Suen's highest mountain
range, playing, having a bit of fun for once. I just wanted to
have a moment where I wasn't the prince, the heir apparent to
the throne."

"That's understandable." She folded her fingers around his
hand. "Even when they don't mean to, our parents can put a lot
of pressure on us to be what they think we should be."

"Yes, but pressure doesn't make up for what happened. My
father came after me himself, worried about the threats he'd
been getting from the rebels." He cleared his throat, forced
himself to finish telling the tale. "They killed the Guardians
with him first. Father . . . They . . . fired at him, disabled his
aileron. He knew he was going down, so he crashed his ship
into them rather than give them the chance to come for me."
Sweat slid down his face, and his voice was hoarse. "I can still
hear him screaming through the comm. Feel through our connection that agonizing last moment of heat and violence from
the explosion, the scent of his flesh burning. And my mother's
grief, her realization of what happened."

His stomach heaved and he stared blindly in front of him,
not seeing the furnishings of his office, but the flaming ball of
melting metal hitting a snowy mountainside.

Jana's hand tightened on his, her grip almost painful, pulling
him back to the present. "Why were they after you?"

"Because I was meant to rule. The viziers prophesied it." He
swallowed the bile, the self-blame. "I was young enough to be . . .
malleable. Be taught the order of things with Kith and Kin,
who should be master and who should be slave. If they couldn't
capture me, they'd kill us both and end the imperial line."

"Jesus," she breathed. Her nails dug into his palm, tears welling in her eyes.

He jerked his gaze away from her, unable to bear the sympathy. His words were a harsh rasp. "He sacrificed himself for me. My own father, gone. Because of me, because of my destiny, because I snuck out and was irresponsible."

Her free hand cupped his face, slid into his hair, urging him to look at her. "You would do the same for your own child. What parent wouldn't?"

"They could have had more children. He and my mother could have been happy." How could he ever honor such a sacrifice? His father's for *dying* for him, and his mother's for *living* for him when it would have been so much easier to follow her One to the grave. Every mistake he made was an insult to them, to all they had done for him. He checked that thought, stopping it. Giving himself no leeway for human mistakes wouldn't help him not make them anymore. Something else his cousin was right about. Something else he needed to learn. The realization didn't stop the guilt.

She stroked her fingers over his jaw. "We are so alike, you and I. We both have an overdeveloped sense of responsibility. You expect yourself to be perfect because your father died, I expected myself to never show anyone when things weren't perfect because my brother died."

As she had with him, he'd sensed this was a sore point for her, a raw wound, and he desperately wanted to talk about something, *anything* but his parents. "Tell me."

"I just . . . tried to be this perfect person for them, so they didn't have to worry about me. But I always knew it was a lie, and it taught me to cover up everything bad. I always knew inside that I failed to be what they needed, whether they saw it or not." Her eyes were sad, the gray of a storm-tossed sea. Her voice dropped to a whisper, "Like I failed you."

He was on his feet, her arms in his hands, towering over her before she had time to blink. He shook her. "You did not fail me. You saved me. If anything, *I* failed *you*. Failed you as a man, as a protector, as a One."

"We both failed then, because I didn't save you." She shook her head, her lips set in a stubborn line. "Bren and Farid and Johar and Tylara found you and made the plan that saved you. I was dead weight."

That kind of talk made alarm roar through him. "Jana, you can't—"

"I want to live, Kyber. Don't worry. It's not that." But her gaze was still shadowed with old pains. "It's just . . . I'm in touch with reality, okay? Let's not make me into something I'm not."

"And what are you?"

"I'm just me." That bare shoulder twitched in a shrug. "No one special."

"No one special?" He shook his head, incredulity sliding through him. "Jana, have you heard nothing I've said? You were *destined* to be an empress. You were always special."

She sniffed. "That's got nothing to do with me. That's just who *you* are. I didn't do anything to make that happen."

"Neither did I. I was born to be the emperor, Jana. I did nothing to earn it. It was my destiny. My father *died* because it was my destiny." He moved his hand to her face, brushing the pad of his thumb over her cheek. "And you were destined to be my empress. You were always going to be special to me."

But not special enough to keep.

Jana kept the thought to herself, unable to put voice to the pain that had grown within her for days. She could finally admit that things weren't okay with her, and it was an amazing relief. Kyber hadn't turned away from her. He was fine with her being . . . who she was. She'd liked being useful again, having duties that were her own and not just hand-me-downs from him. It gave her a sense of purpose. She liked that. She'd missed it.

She'd also been frustrated as hell.

Kyber stroked his fingers over her face, and her body heated. He hadn't had sex with her since she'd tried to kill herself. At first, she'd worried that it meant he didn't want her anymore, that her actions had sickened him and turned him away from her forever. However, he'd left the connection open enough that she could tell how desperate he was to touch her. He just . . . stopped himself, held back, caged the need. It was because of the guilt, because he worried about losing control of the beast, because he worried about hurting her.

He ate with her, talked with her, spent time with her, but he didn't sleep with her. He hadn't once brought up the subject of her remaining with him. Now that he'd pointed it out, she *felt* the impenetrable barricades that kept their connection from breaking wide open. The link between them was no longer pinched, and he wasn't closing her out, but it also wasn't what it had been when they first bonded. They had, essentially, called a ceasefire and retreated to their own sides.

On the one hand, it was good to have some quiet peace. It had been a long time since she'd had anything even close to tranquility in her life. She was the only one in her head, and it gave her time to think, to reflect, to begin to heal. The memories of Arthur were where they belonged—in the past, something that had happened months ago. She had some emotional distance now, they weren't a constant parade through her mind. She'd broken down some of those others walls that Kyber had mentioned, shoring up others that would give her a buffer from the worst of what she'd been through. Not denying it had happened, but not centering her every waking moment around it either.

The time had also given her a chance to work out exactly

where she wanted to go from here, exactly *what* she wanted for herself. Kyber. Forever. Even with the walls blocking their bond, it was better to be together than to be apart. They'd never get that first, perfect connection back, but they could have something just as good if they tried. They'd grown apart, but they could grow back together, she was sure of it. Given enough time. If she stayed here, they'd never have the chance to see how good it could be again.

And she was about to crawl out of her skin needing him. Now seemed as good a time as any to start finding common ground. Even in their worst moments, they'd had chemistry that could put a nuclear bomb to shame.

His eyes sparked down at her, his thumb sweeping over her lower lip. She could feel the heat of his desire, see it in his violet gaze, and he vibrated with the tension of keeping it in check. The hint of a fang showed when he swallowed. "Jana, I . . ."

She leaned into him, turning her head to bite the base of his thumb. "Kyber, I want you."

He groaned. "Jana . . ."

Sobering, she met his gaze steadily. "I need to know, Kyber. I want . . . I want your hands on me when I don't *have* to remember his hands on me. Please."

He closed his eyes. A wave of his emotions broke through to her: shame, self-reproach, and longing. She knew she'd won when he looked at her again. "You don't ever have to beg me for anything. I'll give you whatever you want, whenever you want it. I would do anything for you."

Her fingers slid down his arm, her nails scraping his flesh. Her voice was fierce, demanding. "Then give me what I want. You. Your hands on my skin. Let me remember what it was like before Arthur, when the only people in our bed were the two of *us*."

"We're not in a bed." His mouth snapped closed and he winced at the asinine statement, while she grinned at him. It felt nice to have the upper hand for once. She knew what she wanted and she pushed that toward him through their connection. He shuddered. "You don't have to do anything you don't want to. We can stop any time you say."

"I want you to lay me over your desk and fuck me hard. No holding back."

His breath caught, then eased out on a low groan. "You should be treated gently."

"Sometimes. But sometimes I like it a little rough, sometimes I want the beast in my bed as much as I want the man." She flicked her tongue against his palm, watching the amethyst fireworks burst faster in his irises. "You know I enjoyed everything we did after you returned. There was enough of a connection left for you to be certain, even if my screams of 'yes, yes, Kyber; please, Kyber, just like that' weren't enough of an indicator."

A flush highlighted his sharp cheekbones, and she felt his thick cock press against her lower belly. Lust pulsed through their link, heating her from the inside out. Her pussy dampened, her nipples hardening to tight peaks. She licked her lips and his gaze followed the movement. She did it again, slowly and with relish. He shuddered, the flush darkening his bronze skin.

She pulled back until her buttocks hit the edge of his desk. The metal felt cool through her *rishaami* gown. Lifting her hand, she unfastened the clasp at her shoulder. He swallowed, his fingers twitching as though he would do it himself. She knew he wanted to. The gown slithered to the floor and she kicked it aside. It left her in nothing but a pair of soft, knee-high boots. He groaned when her naked form came into view, and power pumped through her. She loved that he always reacted to her. Even when he hadn't wanted to.

Slanting him a wicked grin, she scooted up onto the desk and crossed her legs. "Help me with my boots, would you?"

His lids dropped to half-mast, the sparks rolling to a full boil in his eyes. "You're a sadist, my empress."

"You find looking at me painful, Kyber?" She brushed her palms over the tops of her thighs, then dipped her fingers between her legs. The first touch on her clit made her moan, but she'd rather it was his hands on her slick, overheating flesh. She held his gaze. "You don't have to watch if you don't want to."

His chuckle was a rusty sound. "Do you honestly think I could walk away?"

"Sure." She lifted her shoulders in a brief shrug, and his gaze zeroed in on the way her movements made her breasts sway. Uncrossing her legs, she let him see how soaked her pussy had become for him, and she thrust her fingers deep into her passage. "I think you can do anything you want to do."

"Not anything." He plucked her hand up and brought it to his mouth, sucking the juices from each finger one by one. His hot, wet tongue moving over her skin made tingles break down her limbs. "I can't stop wanting you. I'll want you forever."

"Then keep me forever. Don't leave me on Earth." The words spilled from her before she could stop them, and the very air around them froze as they both stilled.

His pupils contracted to pinpoints, his throat working. She felt his shock roll through their bond. She swallowed, the bottom dropping out of her stomach. Opening her mouth, she scrambled to find the words to take back what she'd said. He groaned, speared the fingers of his free hand into her hair, and used his grip on her hand to haul her closer. His lips met hers, his tongue sliding in to stroke hers. *Yes. Stay with me. We can find a way to work everything out between us. Together. Never, ever be parted from me again.*

Together. Yes. That was exactly what she wanted, too. Somehow, they could make this work. It would take time to find each other again, to trust each other with a full connection, to break down the walls they'd built, to forgive themselves and to love each other, but the possibility was there. They had to try.

She whimpered into his mouth, wrapped her arms and legs around him, and clung tight. He ran his hands down her bare back and kissed her softly. Long, slow, drugging kisses that made her writhe with need. Her nipples rubbed against his tunic, aching points that emphasized her desire. Her empty sex flexed, wanting to be filled by him.

Gooseflesh rippled in the wake of his fingers as they moved over her skin. Her nipples throbbed, and a familiar rush of sweet lust raced through her. More moisture flooded her core as she pressed herself into him subtly. His broad palm slipped lower to cup her backside, his hand hot against her cooler flesh. She shivered, biting down on his lip to stop a low sob of longing. God, she wanted him. Now. Always.

"Yes," he groaned, breaking the kiss to lick a hot path down her neck. "Now. Always."

She laughed, tilting her head back to give him as much access to her throat as he wanted. His teeth grazed her neck, his fangs scoring her flesh lightly as he bit down. Her entire body jolted, her hips jerking as she began to arch in wanton abandon. Flames licked at her pussy, made her cry out as sharp hunger ripped through her.

He growled his approval against her skin, the feline loving how wild she was. A smile curved her lips, and she fumbled with the tunic fastenings at his shoulder. He pulled back just far enough to be able to rip his shirt over his head and fling it to the floor. His ebony hair tumbled down to the middle of his back, and she wound her fingers through the silky strands. It was a shiny blue-black color, like a sleek raven's wing. "You're a very beautiful man, Kyber."

Embarrassment made the flush of lust running under his skin deepen. He jerked open the fly on his pants. His chest heaved as he panted for breath, flashing his fangs with each inhalation. "Thank you, but you are the one who is lovely."

"I mean it. All of you is beautiful. Inside and out." Sliding her fingers down the muscled ridges of his abs, she circled his bellybutton before reaching the unyielding arc of his cock. His skin felt like it was on fire, and his dick twitched when she touched it. His desperate need pulsed through even their weak connection—how he wanted to take her hard and fast, make her scream in pleasure and come while he buried himself deep inside her pussy. She moaned, the carnal images bombarding her mind. "God, Kyber. Now. Right now. Hard and fast and *now.*"

"Lean back," he breathed. She did as he asked, braced her hands behind her, and arched herself in silent offering, so eager for him she felt how her wetness slipped down to dampen her inner thighs. His irises flashed with sparks of power, his gaze moving over her body. His palms covered her breasts, his thumbs chafing her nipples. "Lovely."

One hand trailed between her breasts, over her ribs, and into her creaming sex. She set her boot heels against the desk, lifting herself into his touch. Heat streaked through her with every subtle flick of his talented fingers. He twisted her nipple, pinching it while he sank the thumb on his other hand deep into her pussy. She gasped, closing her eyes to relish the sensations rocketing through her body. She laid flat against the desk, the cold metal making her body bow in shock.

His groan echoed in the room and in her mind. *Look at me, Jana. I want your eyes on me.*

A shiver passed through her, her gaze focusing on the hard lust that tightened the flesh over his cheekbones. He hissed, the beast rippling just below the surface. Their need slipped through the link, mingling, rising. Sweat gathered on her flesh as she burned for him. He shoved one long digit deep inside her, then another and another, until she moaned. He moved his hand to the other breast, giving that nipple the same treatment. He rolled the tight tip between his fingertips and she cried out. "I love your hands on my skin, Kyber."

Bending forward, he sucked her nipple deep into his mouth, his fangs sharp against her sensitive flesh. She twisted her fingers in his hair to hold him close. He feasted on her, still driving his fingers into her sex. *Do you know how good your tight little nipples taste, Jana? The way your pussy clenches around my fingers brings out the feral in me.*

She choked, her inner muscles flexing for him just as he'd said. They both groaned, and she forced herself to keep her eyes open and locked on him. He glanced up from where his mouth and teeth and tongue played over her breast, his eyes sparking. She worked herself on his thrusting fingers, desperate, greedy for more. "I want you inside me. Don't make me wait."

I won't. I swear it. His voice was a throaty purr in her mind. He released her breast, blowing a stream of cool air over the beaded crest. She sucked in a breath, her hips twisting against the desk.

He withdrew his fingers from her pussy, and she sobbed at the lack of contact. He murmured a wordless, soothing croon as his fingers wrapped around her ankles, bringing her boot-clad feet up to rest against his shoulders. Then her hips were in his hands and he was lifting her into the heavy thrust of his cock.

"Kyber!" He was big, and the way he held her legs made the angle so tight she could barely breathe. If she hadn't been so wet it might have hurt. As it was, she moaned every time he penetrated her.

She brought her hands up to cup her breasts, plucking at her nipples. His gaze gleamed as he watched her toy with herself. Her knees bent over his broad shoulders as he leaned forward to shove his cock deeper. He grinned down at her, his fangs showing, his excitement feeding hers. Turning his head, he ran his tongue around the top of her boot, where the leather met her flesh. *I love you in just these, Jana. The sight arouses me.*

She laughed, her heart thumping at this lighter side to their lovemaking. It felt good. "Fuck me harder."

"As my empress desires." His white teeth flashed as his smile widened. He did as she demanded, hammering into her pussy. She moved one hand down to play with her clit, flicking her fingers in time with his hard plunges. Her sex clamped around his cock, and she could feel her orgasm shimmering, sending waves of building pleasure through her.

Panting breaths pulled from her throat, and the muscles in her legs strained as she tried to push closer, to move faster, to increase the sensual friction. Her head thrashed on the desk, and she moaned. He answered her unspoken demands, his claws biting into her hips as he lifted her deeper into his thrusts. She could feel the hard point of all ten talons, but the sting just whipped into the vortex of sensation that threatened to consume her. And he was there with her, a muscle ticking in his jaw, the beast shining through his eyes as much as the man. He was wild for her, feral and possessive. His hunger poured through their connection, making her scream as she slammed into her orgasm.

He threw back his head and roared, his fangs extended, the big cat taking over. His chest heaved with each breath, sweat sliding down the flexing muscles of his chest. Her inner walls fisted around his cock every time he sank into her. There was the slightest pinch on the link between them, a narrowing when orgasm urged them to fling it wide open. Together, but not yet ready to trust all the way. The barriers between their minds held firm. Still, he fucked her hard, just as she'd asked him to, grinding himself against her as he sought his own release. Aftershocks of orgasm went through her, left her sobbing and shuddering, shivers racing over her skin. He hissed, slammed into her twice more, and pumped his cum into her pussy.

Her body arched as ecstasy lashed through her. "So good, Kyber. It's so good."

"Yes." He let her legs fall to the desk, slumped over her, and dropped his head between her breasts. His hair tickled her skin, made her squirm. He turned to kiss the swell of one breast. "I'll never get enough."

"Don't get enough." She stroked her fingers through those silky strands, and he purred. She smiled, closing her eyes as she worked to catch her breath, to slow her heart. A sigh slid from her throat, and she breathed out the deepest longing of her soul. "Don't ever, ever get enough."

5

Jana sat curled on Kyber's lap. He had his feet propped on his desk and his hands stroked up and down her bare back. They were naked and still sweat-dampened from their last round of lovemaking. She grinned and cuddled closer, breathing in the warm scent of him. "Are they going to wonder why we missed the rest of our meetings today?"

His torso rumbled in a chuckle, and he kissed the top of her head. "No, my empress, they aren't going to wonder. They'll know exactly what we've been doing in here."

"Oh." She sighed, unable to muster the will to be embarrassed. Her fingers drew patterns on his chest, swirling over his pecs and down his abs. When she brushed his nipple, his cock jabbed into her hip. "You're insatiable."

"When it comes to you, yes. I freely admit it." His claws splayed across her lower back, and she shivered.

"Good." Satisfied pleasure bloomed in her chest, the feeling so sweet, so unusual for her, that she blinked back sudden tears. She cleared her throat, shifted on his lap, and reached between them to stroke his dick. He arched into her touch, a hiss tripping over a purr. She grinned, then moaned when his fingers slipped between her thighs.

He hummed. "Mmm, wet. I'm not the only insatiable one."

"Oooh, yes." She slid her legs open, fire licking at her core. Biting her lip, she squeezed his cock tighter and pumped him harder.

"That's my duty, I think." He licked her lips, sucking the bottom one into his mouth and scraping it with his teeth.

She moaned, melting into his kiss. He had the most amazing mouth, his taste sliding over her tongue. He palmed her breast and her nipple tightened for him. She squirmed, her sex drenching with juices, and his talons flicked over her nipple. Rolling her thumb over the flared crest of his cock, she dragged her fingernails lightly up the long, hard shaft.

He hissed into her mouth and dropped his feet to the floor. The chair swiveled until his elbow smacked into the desk. He snarled but didn't stop, grabbing her hips and moving her until she straddled his thighs. She clutched his shoulders for balance. He settled her over his cock and forced her down onto the full length of it. The stretch made her grit her teeth, but she was already too far gone to mind about the sting. Throwing her head back, she arched against him and her nails sank into his flexing muscles. He lifted and lowered her on his dick, working her hard, driving them both toward orgasm.

The feel of him inside her was beyond incredible, made fire and lust and a longing so deep she couldn't contain its rage within her. Their connection had opened to a wide cord, and needs and images seeped through the cracks in the psychic walls they'd built to flow back and forth between their minds. She could tell how much he liked having her take him deep, how her scent called to the feral side of him, how her wetness made his jaw lock as he fought coming right away. It turned her on even more, made her burn hotter for him, made her pant for breath.

Sweat sealed the front of their bodies together and their skin slipped and slid as they moved against each other. His rougher flesh stimulated her sensitive nipples, piling more sensations on her already overloaded system. Contractions built in her belly, and she cried out, riding him fast and wild.

He pushed her down to the base of his cock, lifted his hips into her, and exploded inside her. It was enough to send her flying. Her sex milked his length, shivers racing over her skin. He groaned, his head falling back against the chair, his eyes rolling back.

The cord had restricted again as orgasm hit them, each of them pulling back behind the barricades, unable to make that final psychic connection. The pall of Arthur still hung over them, the commitment to give their bond another chance too new to rely on just yet. If they opened themselves wide to each other, were fully vulnerable again, would it end in disaster as it had the first time? She didn't know, and that scared her. Could she survive that kind of pain again? If she had all of Kyber and he turned away from her again, she doubted she could stand it. A shiver went down her spine.

An imager flickered to life and projected a hologram above his desk, flashing the date, time, and a reminder of another appointment they were going to miss. The numbers sparked something in her mind and realization slid through her. "Shit!"

When she pulled herself up and off his cock, he groaned and reached for her. "Where are you going?"

"Nowhere." She swatted his hands away, scooped her gown off the floor, pulled it on, and finger-combed her hair so she looked more presentable. "I don't look like I've been sexing you up for hours, do I?"

He blinked and shook his head, his mouth gaping.

Snatching his pants off the corner of the desk where they'd fallen, she threw them at him and hit him in the face. "Put these on, would you?"

"I'd rather you took all of yours off again," he grumbled but obliged her by standing to slide them on. Then he flopped back down, every inch the disgruntled feline, the denied emperor, as he draped a knee over the arm of his chair, and laced his fingers over his flat belly. "Can you tell me why you're calling a halt to our lovemaking? I thought we were having a rather enjoyable reunion."

"Well, you're about to meet my parents. Sort of. I thought you'd like to have your pants on." Jana pulled in a deep, steadying breath. She set her palms on the desk. Keying the imager on the smooth glass surface, she received a prompt for orders. "Please connect to my parents."

"Of course, Your Majesty," *Vishra* replied. The imager flickered for a moment as the direction processed, then a hologram of the Sueni imperial star began to spin as the call was made.

"It is really so urgent that you contact them *now*?" Kyber's voice faded for a moment as he scooted his chair back, leaned down to retrieve his tunic, and jerked it over his head. "It couldn't wait for a few more hours?"

"No. With everything that's been going on lately, I'd almost forgotten what day it is." The anniversary of her brother's death. Her stomach clenched in dread. She had to get in touch with her parents.

"What day is it?"

She winced, reluctant to talk about it, but he'd been revealing about his past, so the least she could do was return the favor. "Nine years ago today, my older brother was killed. He was on the way home from a football game his freshman year of college. His team won after he ran in the final touchdown." She passed information about the Earthan game to him through their link. A bittersweet smile curved her lips, remembering the excited sound of her brother's voice when he called them on his cell phone to tell them about his touchdown afterward. God, she missed him. She shook her head and sighed. "A man fell asleep behind the wheel and collided with Craig's car. They both died."

And then it was all over. A bright future wiped out in a single moment. Had he suffered? Alone on the side of road in the middle of the night. She swallowed, pushing away the questions she'd never know the answer to. "He was a great brother, an amazing person. Valedictorian, full scholarship to the local university, athletic."

"I'm sorry, Jana." Kyber's voice softened with sympathy.

"Me, too." She cleared her throat, staring down at the desk. The imager blinked, letting her know that a connection had been made on the other end. "Display call."

"Jana?" Her mother's face appeared. It was pinched with worry, the way it had been every time they'd spoken since Jana had last seen them.

"Hi, Mom. How are you? How's Dad?" The Sueni technology interfaced with the camera on her mother's laptop, so they could see each other when they spoke. At first, she'd thought it would comfort them to *see* her and know she was safe on the *Vishra*. Now, she knew she needed to have a conversation that wouldn't be a comfort to them.

Her parents had never recovered from Craig's death, and Jana had done everything she could to fill in the gap. She'd found a job she liked, that made her happy, because they wanted so badly for her to be *happy*. Being a flight attendant was great for the travel and interesting people, but she also knew it would let her escape their worry and expectation for days and weeks at a time.

After Craig died, she was *always* aware that she was all they had left. They'd smothered her in their overprotective attempts to ensure that nothing bad would happen to her. This last year had to have been a nightmare for them.

Her mother sighed. "I'm fine. Dad's good. He'll be in to talk in a minute. When are you coming home?"

The conversation was the same one they'd had every single time they spoke. Until today, she'd been grateful for the routine; it meant she could give the same answers, the same false smiles and promises, and then disconnect and bury herself back in her fanatical dedication to saving Kyber.

She met her mother's gaze. "I'm not coming home, Mom. I hadn't lived there for years before I bonded with Kyber, and I'm not going to live there now just to make you feel better about my safety. I'm not going to live on Earth ever again."

Her mother blinked at the blunt speaking, so unlike the prevarication she had to have grown used to. "General Arthur called to tell us that . . . that *Kith* man had escaped and that we might be in danger now." Her mouth twisted. "Please come back down here, baby."

"I know Kyber escaped the *illegal imprisonment and torture* General Arthur put him through. I helped save him." She felt Kyber twitch behind her, but he was out of view of the imager, so her mother couldn't see him.

Her father sat down next to her mother, his lined and worn face coming into view. He looked just like an older, more serious version of Craig, and the reminder made her heart clench. "How do we know for sure that's true? When we've seen you in these calls, you haven't looked or sounded good, pumpkin."

"Look." She made her tone matter-of-fact. "I know you want everything to be okay with me, but it's not okay, and I'm not going to pretend anymore." God, it felt good to say that, to admit it out loud. She loved her parents so much, and she did want everything to be all right, but there had to be room to admit when things *weren't* all right. "I know what Arthur told you, and it's a lie. When I went to Arthur and asked him to let Kyber go, he hurt me. He did horrible things to me. It wasn't Kyber or the Sueni who hurt me, it was Arthur."

"Honey, Arthur said they'd brainwashed you, that you're part of some cult or harem they recruit women for. We don't . . . we don't want to believe it, but all the things you've done lately have been crazy. You're not acting like the Jana we know." Her mom touched the screen, her gray eyes reflecting her worry and her desperation not to have to admit that Jana had had something horrible happen. It would take time, Jana knew, but that was their problem, not hers. She would be okay, truly, but not because she'd pretended it was so. Doing that had almost ended her life. If she had admitted to Kyber, to *anyone,* that things weren't okay, would she have had to go through so many months of mental torture?

Jana felt Kyber stiffen behind her, felt his concern for her pulse along their link. She pulled in a deep breath. "I'm not the Jana you knew, Mom. No one is forcing me to stay here, and everything I said is the truth. You're going to have to deal with that whether you want to or not. I did. Craig died and that wasn't okay, Arthur hurt me and that wasn't okay. Bad things happen, and I can't pretend they weren't *bad*. It takes time to heal, to be okay inside, but those things were and always will be *not okay*."

"I know." Her mother swallowed and looked aside, but Jana knew those two words were probably the hardest her mom had ever had to say. "I wish we could see you again. I miss you so much."

"I want to see you, too, Mom." She pressed her fingers flat to the desk. She took another deep breath, then another. "Mom, no matter what Arthur says, the Sueni are not here to take over the planet. In fact, I know for sure that Kyber's not going to stay here forever. When he leaves, I'm going with him."

A thought, a plan, formed in her mind. Turning, she held her hand out to Kyber. He took it without faltering, and that support warmed her. She smiled at him, pulled him into view of the imager, and perched on his lap. "Mom, Dad, this is Kyber."

Her parents paled, blindly reaching for each other. This was the monster Arthur had told them about. Jana's stomach turned as she remembered her hateful words to him. It was Arthur who was the monster, not Kyber, no matter what beast lurked beneath the Kith's surface. Her connection with him still vibrated with worry, his muscles were tense beneath her legs, but his voice was calm. "Mr. Townsend, Mrs. Townsend. It is a pleasure to meet you."

Her father's mouth opened and closed. Her mother's voice was no more than a squeak. "Hello."

Jana twined her fingers with Kyber's. "We'll be leaving Earth in the next week, and I've decided that we're taking you with us." She recognized the regal edge to her voice as Kyber's. How much of what she'd absorbed from him the day they'd bonded had helped her during the months they'd been apart? More than she'd understood until now. "This is not negotiable."

What do you think you're doing, Jana? The tension in Kyber's body doubled.

She prayed he wouldn't say anything to countermand her, that'd he'd go along with her until she could explain herself, and kept talking to her parents. "I know you'll want to meet Kyber in person, so we're coming to get you ourselves. Pack a bag, only the few things you can't live without, and be ready for us tomorrow night."

It would take time, but like her connection with Kyber, she wanted the chance to rebuild her love for her parents on healthier, more solid ground. They all had a lot to learn, but they could do it together. She wanted all the people she loved with her. She wanted that time to make things better. Not *perfect*, but better.

Her parents glanced at each other, their uncertainty obvious. Her father cleared his throat. "We . . . I don't know what to say."

"There's nothing to say." She reached out a hand to end the imager call. "I love you both, and we'll see you tomorrow."

Some emotion flickered in her father's face, but was gone before she could discern what it meant. "I love you, pumpkin."

Her mom swallowed and looked like she was going to tear up again. "I love you, baby. Be safe."

"I am." She ran her finger over the imager. "Good-bye."

Kyber's hand tightened around hers. "Are you going to tell me what that was all about?"

"Arthur wants to use the Sueni presence to start a war so he can stay in power." She scooted around in his lap to face him. "It's why he kidnapped you and hurt us both, right?"

"Right." His expression was closed, his gaze shadowed. The connection between them had narrowed to the point that nothing came through, and she couldn't tell what he was feeling or thinking. He didn't want her to know.

She swallowed and pushed on. "We've always known Arthur kept my parents under constant surveillance since you were kidnapped, and I'm sure that's increased since you escaped. He has to have bugged their house. He would have been listening. We've given Arthur an exact place and date when we'll both be on Earth, in a place that he thinks is secured."

"You're using us as bait to draw him out in the open." Kyber's eyebrows arched, a bitter smile kicking up one side of his mouth. "Knowing how he likes to handle this sort of thing himself once his victims are helpless."

"Right. He'll have plenty of men there already, so we'll be easy targets." She bit her lip, waiting to see what he would say.

His face remained that calm mask, telling her nothing as he stared at her. "This puts your parents at risk."

"They were at risk from the moment Arthur knew about them." And she'd been so wrapped up in her own shit, so busy pretending nothing was wrong, she hadn't done anything about that until now. She stomped down on the remorse, the self-doubt, the recrimination. She couldn't change the past, not with her brother, with Kyber, with Arthur, or with her parents. She could only move forward from here and make the best decisions she knew how to make. That was one of her more recent breakthroughs. "I don't know for sure that Arthur will show up, but we have to get my parents out of there anyway, so why not see if we can kill two birds with one stone?"

Kyber snorted. "Arthur will be there. I have no doubts. He enjoys toying with his prey too much to miss the opportunity."

She squeezed his hand, trepidation and determination twisting tight within her. "Then let's end this, once and for all."

Kyber tested his connection with Jana for the hundredth time. She still slept, dreaming in their bed, so he turned his attention to the gathering in front of him. He stood just inside the entrance to a wide hangar bay watching a dozen Guardians load explosives and other weapons into two shuttles. Bren and Farid consulted with each other over a small imager in Farid's hand. There'd been cloud cover over most of the Midwestern United States all day, obscuring views of the Townsend home from even the *Vishra*'s powerful imagers. They had no way of knowing what Arthur had prepared for them down there, but a delay in mission would only give him more time to plot and put the Townsends in more danger.

Six pilots slipped past Kyber to ready their fighter wings for takeoff. He'd wanted this mission to be small, but well armed. Too large an expedition, and he worried that Arthur would simply kill Jana's parents and call the whole thing a loss. Their involvement complicated things, but they'd had no better opportunity to get close to Arthur since Kyber had escaped. He was too well guarded, constantly on the move lest Kyber come after him. A grin quirked Kyber's lips. The man was evil, but he wasn't stupid. The feline within Kyber purred in anticipation of the challenge, the hunt for a difficult quarry.

It would all be over soon, one way or another. Kyber would be dead, or Arthur would.

Or both.

He turned at the sound of Tylara's voice in the corridor outside the hangar. She and Johar stood toe-to-toe, and she folded her arms over her breasts. Her expression was calm, remote even, but her eyes gave her away. The midnight irises glowed almost white with the speed of the sparks boiling to the surface. "Of course, you have to do your duty. I didn't say I didn't understand, I said I didn't like it."

"Yes, Admiral, I understand. You're not upset or scared, you just *don't like it*." Johar snarled in her face, hackles rising even in his human form.

Though he was more than certain Tylara could handle whatever situation might arise, Kyber folded his arms over his chest and propped his shoulder against the doorjamb nonetheless. "Is something amiss?"

"Yes, sire." Johar spoke first, cutting off Tylara's negative headshake. "Tylara is begging to be spanked for her lack of faith in her One."

A delicate flush raced up the woman's cheek, her anger rippled out in waves, but so did her self-doubt . . . and her desire. She was not worried or frightened by the man's threat to spank her. In fact, she seemed titillated by the prospect. Kyber hiked up an eyebrow. It was things like this that usually kept him from delving too deeply into his people's thoughts. Just because he could didn't mean he should, or even that he wanted to know what went on in the minds of the people around him.

A flush raced up her cheeks. "You almost died down there once."

"I'm not dead, but I have lost enough people that I loved to know that pushing away the things that mean the most to me is no way to live." He caught her chin in his hand, forcing her to look at him and only him. "Just as you have, I've witnessed firsthand how badly things can go in a One bond, but I have also seen how it can make you better, stronger. I want that, Tylara. I want that with you. *My One.*"

Her voice was softer than Kyber had ever heard it. "I love you, too. You know I do."

"Perhaps. You also think I will walk away from you because it isn't easy being bonded to a woman with more psychic power than I have. And you don't trust me to keep control of the animal within me. You expect me to dissolve into madness like my younger brother did. You expect me to turn on you the way his twin turned on *his* One." Johar ran his thumb over her lip, and she swayed toward him. "But I'm not my family. I am *Johar* Sajan and no other. And you, Tylara Belraj, are my One. I will have no other but you."

Her eyes closed, and her uncertainty rolled over Kyber in a wave. "What if I lose you? What if you don't come back?"

"Horrible things happen, my One, but they are no excuse not to live." He pulled her flush against him, slid his fingers into her dark hair, and kissed her hard. Kyber turned away to give them some privacy. "When I come back, whole and in one piece, we're going to bond, Tylara. No excuses, no more running."

Her laugh was almost a sob. "Come back to me whole and in one piece and I'll do whatever you want. Just . . . come back to me."

"I always have, I always will." Johar's voice reached Kyber's ears as he walked away.

He entered the hangar with his head down, double-checking the razer strapped to his hip. It was a Class Nine weapon, designed to kill. He glanced up to meet his cousin's gaze. Farid nodded, understanding of what was at stake this night in the older man's eyes.

Bren looked beyond Kyber toward the entrance. "Jana's not with you?"

The gathered Guardians paused, pinned their collective gazes on him, the same question in their eyes, and he tasted their relief that someone had asked. He fought a wince. "She won't be joining us. She's asleep."

The truth was she'd laid down for a nap and he'd sent her spiraling into deep slumber. He wasn't willing to bring her on this mission. He couldn't gamble with her life. Ever. She was too important to him. Her safety was too vital.

Johar walked in to join the Guardians, grunted, and jerked his chin at them. Tylara was nowhere in sight, and Kyber sensed that she had gone back to the command deck of the *Vishra*.

The Guardians hurried to finish belting their weapons on. They were a mix of Kith and Kin. Kyber had to assume Arthur would be deploying the same white noise machines that cancelled out Kith psychic ability.

Johar had been working with Sueni scientists to find a way to counteract the static. Simple earplugs had only minimal effect, the sensitivity of Kith hearing meant their ears needed to be completely blocked to remain unaffected. Machines that emitted wavelengths to nullify the white noise had the opposite effect on Kith—they became raving beasts. Johar had decided half-bestial soldiers were less of a liability than deafened soldiers or rabid animals. They would have to take their chances with the static, but Kyber found it bitterly ironic that all their advanced technology was being thwarted by a simple Earthan noisemaker.

"Kyber?"

He moved to stand beside his cousin. "Farid?"

The green-eyed man silently handed him a tiny comm. device to slip into his ear. Farid was coming along to handle Jana's parents. The diplomat would talk them into getting on the shuttle with them even though Jana hadn't come herself. Convincing people was the man's specialty, and he was more than welcome to it.

"Kyber!" Jana strode into the hangar bay, hastily securing a holster and razer to her waist. She wore the same dark gray tunic, blank pants, and boots that he wore. Beneath the tunic would be a thin undershirt of mesh armor that would protect her from Earthan bullets. She carried herself with the bone-deep confidence of someone who knew what she was doing, knew her place and her purpose. He scrubbed a hand down his face, dread wrenching at his insides. It was good to see her this way, he simply wished she'd chosen another time to be willful.

"Jana, I understand that you're upset—"

"Upset? *Upset?*" Her mouth dropped open and she pounded a fist against his chest. "Yes, I'm upset. I'm fucking pissed, Kyber. You left me in bed alone to go throw yourself into a dangerous situation for me."

"You did the same when you came to get me." He searched her face, but all he saw was unyielding fury. "I have to take care of this, Jana. I'll bring your parents back to you."

"No." She hit him again, then balled her fists in his tunic and shook him. "You don't leave me, Kyber. You don't leave me alone. Not *ever.*"

The breath whooshed out of his lungs as her desperation reached him. The beast within him writhed in agony at its mate's fear. But the man couldn't surrender on this matter. She was too important.

"Your Majesties." Johar stepped forward, his gaze flicking back and forth between them. "We should go."

She dropped her hands from Kyber's shirt and poked a finger in the Guardians' direction. "Don't think any of you are off the hook for letting him try to leave without me. Every last one of you is on my shit list."

A rumble of protestation came from the Guardians, each of the battle-hardened warriors scrambling to get back in her good graces. Kyber's lips twitched. Apparently, he wasn't the only one wrapped around her little finger.

She swung around to level a glare at him. "What are you smiling for? You're at the *very top* of my shit list."

"You are not coming. You've already tried to sacrifice yourself for me once. I don't want someone else to die for me. My life isn't more important than anyone else's."

Johar's voice reflected disbelief. "You're the *emperor*."

Kyber turned to face him. "And what have I done to earn that title? It doesn't make me better than anyone else. A life is a life. Mine is no more valuable than yours. I have to end this with Arthur. If I could do this alone, I would."

"But that's why it's *your* destiny." Farid shoved a hand through his blond hair. "That is exactly the kind of man I want as my emperor. Someone who puts his people before himself, who would die to protect them. You were born to rule for a reason, cousin."

A muscle in the Guardian captain's jaw ticked; he twitched his long braids over his shoulder. "You forget Arthur murdered my father and thousands of others who were on the *Anshar*. I want him dead as much as you do. I'm with you, Your Majesty. To the end."

"And I," said Farid. The words were echoed from every person there. Even Bren. Kyber closed his eyes, bowing to them to show his gratitude.

When he opened his eyes, it was to see both compassion and anger flashing across his One's face. "Jana—"

She sliced her hand through the air, cutting him off. Her gaze darted to the gathered people. "All of you get in the shuttles, please. We'll *both* join you in a moment."

The tone was that of command, of an empress, and the Guardians moved to obey without question. He arched his eyebrows. "You can't come."

Folding her arms across her breasts, she lifted her chin. "You're not leaving me here."

He mirrored her pose, crossing his arms. "I'll have you thrown in a holding cell if I have to and barricaded in by a legion of Guardians."

"If you want my parents to go anywhere with you willingly, you'll need me there. Farid's charm isn't going to cut it, no matter what you think." She shrugged, her tone conveying nonchalance while the little emotion that trickled through their connection told an entirely different tale. "Sure, you could knock them out, but it'll go a lot better and easier if they're cooperating."

"No." He couldn't even consider it. The thought of her within a thousand miles of Arthur or his men was untenable.

Shadows gathered in her gray eyes, hurt reflecting there. "You don't trust me. You think I'm weak enough to be as easy a target as he imagines."

"What?" Shock rocketed through him. He reached for her, but she stumbled back. "Don't you understand? What if something happens? What if Arthur hurts you again, or kills you? I can't risk it."

Her mouth worked for a moment and she pushed a hand through her short auburn locks. "What if something happens to *you*? What if Arthur hurts *you* again, or kills *you*? The Sueni need you to lead them. It's your destiny, remember? I just got you back, Kyber. I just learned to live again. I'm not going to stand around and watch something happen to you. That would be seriously *not okay* with me. This was *my* idea and these are *my* parents. I'm coming with you."

"No."

"Yes."

"*No.*"

Her lips trembled, and she shook her head. "I can be of use here, Kyber. I *can* help. I want us to have the chance to bond again. I want us to break down these damn walls, but it won't happen if you really don't believe in me."

"I believe in you." He laughed, and salty moisture stung his eyes. If she only knew how badly he wanted that bond with her, but even without the barricades, he couldn't consider re-forging their link when he might still die. If something were to happen to him, she would feel every moment of it. He couldn't do that to her. He couldn't put her in a position where she might die *or* where she might be willing to kill herself. As she'd said, she'd only just learned to live again. And he wanted her to *live*, even if it couldn't be with him. "Jana, I can't do it. I can't lose you."

"Neither can I." She cupped his face in her small, warm hands. "We're in this together, Kyber. We finish this *together*. Don't make me beg."

He choked, closing his eyes as his chest tightened to the point he couldn't breathe. "By Anun, you know how to cut the deepest."

Slipping her fingers into his hair, she pulled him down so his forehead rested against hers. "I learned from you."

"That's not comforting."

Her soft breath brushed his lips when she spoke. "I want us to have a future together, but neither of us can move on until we finish what we started."

As much as he hated to admit it, she was right. He chuckled, the noise little more than a rasp of air. "I cannot believe I'm agreeing to this."

"I can." Tightening her hands in his hair, she took his mouth in a hungry, desperate kiss. Then she broke away with a gasp. "Oh, crap."

"What?" He jerked back to look at her. "What's wrong?"

"I forgot my mesh armor." She latched on to his hand and dragged him toward the door to an armory storage room. "Come with me."

"Afraid I'll leave you while you're changing?" He grinned, allowing himself the pleasure of watching her backside sway as she walked. It might be the last time he got to enjoy it. He squelched the thought.

She shot a look over her shoulder. "You said you'd let me come, and I believe you." A wicked little grin curved her lips. "I just thought you might want to watch me take my shirt off."

A shout of laughter exploded from him as she pulled him through the storage room's door and shut it behind them. He couldn't believe that in a time like this, the woman had gotten him to laugh. She constantly amazed him and usually confounded him. He wouldn't have it any other way.

Dropping his hand to rifle through a storage locker, she came up with a small shirt of mesh armor. It was made of the same dark metal as everything else from Suen. She tossed it on the end of a long table in the middle of the room, unstrapped her gun belt, and set it down as well. Her nimble fingers flicked open the fastenings on her tunic, and before he even knew what he was doing, his hands were unhooking his own holster. Her top hit the table at the same time his razer did, and they shared a look of understanding.

It was possible neither of them would survive the coming confrontation. This might be the last time they had together, and they were going to take it. A grin kicked up the corner of his mouth, and he stepped farther down the table, away from their gear. "Well, they won't leave without us both, will they?"

"There are a few perks to this whole royalty thing." She followed him, her fingers going to the placket on his pants. One hand opened his trousers, the other stroked him through the fabric. His fingers dipped into her bra, stroking her nipples until they were hard little points. Each sweep across them made her shiver, made her eyes burn to molten silver.

She tilted her head back and offered him her mouth. He took it, shoved his tongue between her lips, and savored the way she moaned into his mouth. Her scent intoxicated, her flavor bursting over his taste buds until there was nothing but her.

He gritted his teeth as she brought him to full, aching erection in mere moments. She slipped inside his pants, pulling his cock free. His hips rocked as she pumped his dick hard between her fingers. Fire rocketed through him, and his hands fisted in the short strands of her hair. Her eagerness, her frantic need shot through their link and made him groan. He broke the kiss and pulled her head back to suck and bite his way down her neck.

"Oh, God, we have to hurry or they'll send someone to look for us." The sweet smell of her wetness intensified each time he nipped her throat, and the feline was wild for her, the man even more so. Bracketing her hips in his hands, he spun her around to face the table.

"Hold on to the other side," he growled.

She bent forward and stretched to grasp the far edge of the table, her body already undulating in a carnal rhythm that made desperation fist in his belly. He had to have her, one last time, had to have this one memory to hold on to. Reaching around her, he opened her pants and jerked them down around her thighs.

His fingers plunged between her thighs and into her hot, welcoming sex. She cried out, and her pleasure at having any part of him inside her billowed through their connection, spurring him on. He wanted her hard and fast, wanted the reassurance of his body joined with hers. He needed it, her. Now.

He dipped forward and bit the soft globe of her ass. She jerked and squealed, and when he straightened, he saw her knuckles had whitened on the table ledge. "Hurry, Kyber. I can't wait."

"Neither can I." And he proved it, plunging his cock hilt-deep into her slick pussy. Her back bowed as she pushed against him, her hips working him as he worked her. His claws dug into her waist as he held her for his thrusts. He could hear how wet she was as their skin slapped together, *smell* how wet she was, how needy. As needy as he was. His stomach spanked against her ass, and he drove them ruthlessly, pumping inside her until their breathing was ragged and sweat beaded on every inch of bare skin. Anun, he was going to come, she got to him that fast. But he was taking her with him into the madness, the rush of ecstasy sweeping from him to her made her sob. He moved one hand around to flick a single claw over her hard clit, and she jolted beneath him.

"Oh, God. Kyber, Kyber, yes! Just like *oooh.*" He heard her nails rake against the table, her hips heaving upward as she took him as deep inside her as she could and came hard. Her inner muscles squeezed him so tight he groaned, wondering if a man could die of such intense pleasure. Her ecstasy came spiraling through their connection, slammed into him, and shoved him hard and fast into his own orgasm.

His cum burst into her, and he filled her, plunging deep and loving the rough friction. She whimpered and came for him again, her walls closing around him in rhythmic pulses that matched the satisfaction echoing in their minds. He threw his head back, clenched his jaw to keep a wild roar in, and hissed between his fangs as his orgasm dragged everything out of him.

Wrapping his arms around her, he pulled her back against

him and buried his nose in her soft hair. He held her tight and prayed harder than he ever had in his life that she made it through this. He didn't bother with pleas for himself. All his hopes and dreams for the future rested in this slim woman's hands. Without her, there was nothing.

He loved her more now than he had ever imagined possible.

6

Arthur was there, Kyber could smell him.

The ships had started taking heavy fire before they were any-where near the ground. The fighter wings had their hands full dealing with the planes and helicopters Arthur had waiting for them. The shuttle jolted and spun midair as the pilot dodged missiles. More than one of the Guardians had turned green at the constant roll of the aircraft. Jana's fingers were white-knuckled where she gripped her seat's harness.

His heart hammered in his chest, and he asked himself for the millionth time how he'd been talked into bringing his One along on this trip. She should be safe aboard the *Vishra*, not landing in the middle of a battlefield. They'd gotten no more than a single raised eyebrow from Johar on why it had taken them so long to climb aboard the shuttle, but no doubt even a Kin could scent the sex on them. He gazed at Jana now, saw her jaw was clenched tight, her lips set in a stubborn line.

A concussive boom just outside the shuttle made his sensi-tive ears pop. He hissed as alarms blared in the small interior.

The pilot yelled from the cockpit, "Everyone hold tight! We're landing, but it's going to be a rough drop."

As long as we hit the ground in one piece, I'll be happy. Kyber made his mental voice sotto voce. The Guardians around him chuckled, grateful for the release in tension.

"Arthur's evacuated the town, so there are no civilians here." Bren's voice came through their ear comms., broadcasting from the second shuttle. "But some of those guys in uniform are working with us to defeat Arthur, so do your best not to kill anyone that doesn't try to kill you first."

Jana reached up and cued her comm. "My parents?"

"They're still here." Bren hesitated for a long moment as though bracing to give bad news. "He's keeping them as bait."

Assuming he was keeping them alive at all. No one said those words, but they all finished the thought themselves. Kyber pulled out his razer, flipping the setting to full charge. A silent Johar calmly pulled out an enormous razer rifle and charged it. The static was enough to raise the hairs on the back of Kyber's arms. Every other Guardian followed their lead, and the shuttle was soon filled with the sound of loading weapons.

He worked hard to steady his breath, to rein in the eager feline that wanted to hunt and kill its enemies. Soon, he promised himself and the beast. Glancing over, he saw that Jana had her weapon drawn as well. She met his gaze, terror and rage roiling like dark clouds in her eyes. He nodded, wanting to assure her he understood, but there was no time to talk now. They would have to save that for later.

If there was a later.

The shuttle jolted sideways, throwing everyone against their harnesses, and metal squealed as they bounced over rocky ground, but they were down. The door hissed as it opened, and everyone rose to ready themselves for the attack they knew was coming. Anticipation roared in Kyber's veins and his hand tightened on his razer.

Johar nodded to two Guardians, who slipped from the shuttle, silent as spirits. Two more Guardians took up positions on either side of Jana, and Kyber recognized them as Natheem and Dhalesh. The Kinsmen smiled grimly. Johar swung in beside Kyber. The remaining Guardians would ensure the safety of the shuttle. It did them no good to accomplish their mission if they had no way to leave once it was done.

As soon as they hit the open air, Kyber's psychic powers went dead. Arthur had obviously refined his white noise makers. Where before, Kyber had only been numbed, now it was as if the ability had been completely cut away. The beast rose greedily to the surface, always wanting to break free. He could smell the stench of Arthur. He didn't need the psychic side to know the man lay in wait, a serpent in the grass.

"This way." He pointed his razer to the left of the shuttle.

Jana's hand touched his back. "That's the way to my parents' house. Two blocks up, three to the left."

He nodded to indicate he'd heard her, and let Johar lead the way. Kyber's cat's eyes adjusted to the night, and he could see every detail clearly. His senses went on alert, taking in everything. The rattle of a bush from the breeze, the distant thunder of fighter wings that vibrated through his body, and streaks of orange flames and blue lasers trailed across in the sky as each side fired at the other. He wished his men well.

They'd gone no more than three of the five blocks they needed to go before they were engaged by enemies. Chaos unleashed around them as each side opened fire.

Blue lasers from the Sueni weapons lit the dark streets of the quiet little town. Men screamed, Kyber smelled death. Jana's slim body tucked in behind him as they crouched against a brick building. She aimed and squeezed the trigger of her razer, her shoulders rocking back each time a laser burst from the muzzle.

Natheem went down, a bullet ripping through his throat. He was gone before he hit the ground, his warm blood spraying over Kyber's face and chest. Fury pumped through him at the loss of one of his men, but there was no time to grieve. He wanted to tuck the emotion away, lock it tight within him, but the beast wouldn't allow it. It had control, and it fed on the full brunt of fury.

"Natheem!" Dhalesh choked, utter shock on his face.

Johar grabbed the man, hauling him away from the body. "He's gone, Dhalesh. We have to leave him or we all die. *Run!*"

They did, Johar dragging Dhalesh behind him. The humans were in hot pursuit, firing into the night. Kyber latched his free hand around Jana's wrist, needing to keep her near, to reassure himself as much as he could that she was unharmed. Sweat slid down his face, burning his eyes as he turned every few steps to fire.

Johar ran backward beside them. He pulled a small explosive from his belt and flicked his finger over the charge. Drawing back his arm, he released a leonine roar that could chill the blood and launched it at the humans. Kyber drew Jana against his chest to shield her as the device detonated. The ground beneath them shook with the explosion; dirt, rocks, and the sticky, sickening remains of bodies showered down on them.

She looked dazed when they stood but shook herself and pointed toward a tall wooden pole with a metal cone mounted near the top. "They're pumping the white noise through the town's tornado warning system. It's controlled down at city hall, which is about as far from where we need to go as possible, so I don't think we can stop it." Her finger redirected their attention to a corridor between two buildings. "But we can cut through that alleyway to my parents' place. Do you still smell Arthur that way?"

Lifting his nose to the air, he tried to filter through the stink of smoke and blood for the general's scent. He was near, but the wind made it difficult to pinpoint now. "I'm not sure. We'll go to the house and see if anyone is there. We have to check."

"Just go straight." He could feel the fine trembling in her muscles, the fear that shook through her, but also the courage that kept her chin up, that worked to conquer the trepidation. "It'll leave us vulnerable if we get caged in, but it's the fastest way. The alley ends a half a block from their house."

Dhalesh knelt beside them, and he glanced up. "We'll have to risk it. We're outnumbered, if not outgunned. Let's not lose anyone else to the general's men."

The Kin's face was hard with rage, both hands gripping the ends of large razers. Kyber nodded in return, in complete agreement. His Guardians were, by definition, the best at what they did and the hardest to kill. Another person who'd given up their life for him. He gritted his teeth and vowed Natheem's sacrifice would not be in vain.

"Let's go." Kyber jerked his chin at Johar, who moved out without a word. Kyber could feel the other man's silent fury, which was even more dangerous than when Johar yelled.

The strong emotions emanating from the people around him made Kyber's hackles rise, and he gave up trying to check the feline within, allowing himself to embrace this side without the guilt at his loss in control. He was both man and beast, he always would be, and he'd finally learned to accept it.

He was not a monster.

He was here to kill the monster who'd hurt so many, including him.

They ghosted across the narrow Earthan street and down the cracked, uneven cement path that was the alley. His nostrils flared, trying to catch familiar scents. They hadn't heard from the second shuttle yet, the comm. device quiet in his ear. They could simply be in a place where it was unsafe to speak aloud, the static hum that squealed through the town making it impossible to mentally speak with his cousin or the other Guardians. He tried not to let it make him uneasy, but the stillness of the night sent disquiet skittering down his spine.

Nothing moved as they crept down the long, endless alley, fenced in by the high walls. The four of them kept their weapons and gazes moving before them, behind them, above them to the rooftops. It went against his feral nature to be thus caged, and his claws and fangs elongated to their full, deadly length. The white noise reverberated through his mind, reminding him too much of his time as Arthur's prisoner. Cold sweat streaked down his temples, his heartbeat accelerating to a full gallop.

"We're here," Jana's voice breathed in his comm.

He could see the house, surrounded as it was by distinctive military vehicles. Smoke swirled up from a tank in the middle of the road, burnt out by the razer cannons on the Sueni fighter wings. A fierce, predatory smile stretched his mouth, his fangs scoring his lower lip.

Dhalesh spoke in a near-soundless whisper, "Soldiers."

Tension ripped through the group as a small coterie of Earthan warriors slipped onto the street between them and the house. Kyber hissed a string of Sueni curses that made the Kin grin back at him. Dhalesh lead them from building to building, moving along their side of the street as the soldiers began moving toward the Townsend house. A blue flash of light came from one of the windows, a razer being fired, and Kyber smiled. Someone had made it from the second shuttle. Whoever was in the house had wicked aim, and Kyber smelled both Bren and Farid nearby.

Thanks to Anun, they had survived.

"Let's give them a hand, shall we?" Johar's grin matched his and the Kith shot forward, superhuman speed making him barely discernable in the dark.

Jana sprinted after him, the Kin Guardian and Kyber just behind her. Gunfire lit the sky, and Johar disappeared behind the house with an inhuman battle scream. Dhalesh darted after his captain, passing Jana.

Then Kyber had no time to think of anything else except keeping Jana and himself alive. Four soldiers came at them, one hitting Kyber in the chest with a bullet. He stumbled, groaning as the metal hit his armor. He choked as he watched another soldier knock Jana's razer from her hand. She slammed her foot into the man's groin, and Kyber fought a reflexive wince. Righting himself, he turned on the soldier who'd shot him and fired his razer to hit him in the face, and the flesh and bone crumpled. Kyber was already on the other two before their comrade tumbled to the grass, slamming his razer into one's nose.

He hissed, slashing the other across the face, the feline reveling in the scent of an enemy's blood spilled. Both humans staggered before diving on him, and he went down with a roar. One drove his fist into Kyber's ribs, and the breath wheezed out of his lungs again, but he retaliated by stabbing his claws into the man's neck. He gurgled, drowning in his own blood. The other soldier struck Kyber's mouth, making his vision swim. Coppery blood coated his tongue, both his and the soldier's, when his fang caught on the man's fist and tore the flesh.

A high shriek of terror and pain split the air before the soldier slumped on top of Kyber. Dead. He shoved the body off him to see Jana with both her razer and his clutched in her hands. A bruise already darkened her jaw, but she looked unharmed otherwise. He grinned. "Nice shot."

"Thanks for taking three of the four." She gave him a small smile and tossed his weapon to him.

His hand shot out to catch it, the feline reflexes unerring. Pushing himself to his feet, he flipped his tangled hair over his shoulder. "It seems to have worked out well for us. Let's see who's in the house."

"Someone from the second shuttle, if they survived this little run-in with Arthur's soldiers." She mounted the steps, checked the door, found it locked, and jogged back down to flip over an odd little sculpture of a tiny, fat man with a pointed hat. Jana flicked him a grin, showing him a small metal object. "Mom always keeps the spare key under the garden gnome."

He shook his head and said nothing. There were no words to express how strange that practice was to him. Instead, he held his aching ribs and followed his One up the steps and through the front door. His muscles shook from the adrenaline humming through him and from the fight with the human soldiers. He kept his gun up and his senses focused on any movement in the house. There were people here. More than one. None of them Arthur. A few bodies scattered around the living room, no doubt courtesy of Bren and Farid. Whisper-soft footsteps landed on the ceiling overhead, others came from the room next to them. He touched Jana's shoulder, pressed his finger to his lips to indicate silence, and moved toward the doorway.

His heart rate sped, rushing in his ears, and he smelled Jana's fear on the air. She settled next to him on the wall, her gun at the ready. Her species were not natural predators like his, and yet she'd never faltered. He'd never been prouder of her.

Whipping around the corner of the door, his razer trained on three human soldiers standing at a kitchen counter before they'd even lifted their weapons. Two dove for their guns, and Kyber's razer cut them down where they stood. The third soldier lifted his hands and began to speak, but a feline scream from outside had him spinning for an open door. Johar came leaping into the room, landing on a table in the middle of the room. His fangs were bared, crimson splattering his skin and clothing, his blue eyes feral and his braids swinging loose around his shoulders. He snarled, shoving his face into the human soldier's.

The boy looked like he was going to wet himself, but he squeaked out. "I'm working with Sargeant Major Preston."

"He's not lying. He's one of mine." Bren's voice sounded from the room behind them. She stepped into the light, and Kyber saw how her face was streaked with dirt and blood. The skin beneath the grime was deathly pale, and one of her ears was caked with dried blood.

"I have another one here, or so he claims." Dhalesh had his twin razers pressed to an Earthan's back, propelling him through the same door as Johar.

Bren nodded to them. "Yeah, he's with us, too."

Dhalesh pointed his weapon away from the human, who relaxed a bit and let a breath ease from his lungs. "Good to see you, Bren."

"You, too, Zielinski." She jerked her chin at the younger human. "The two of you should get out of here before anyone sees you with us."

"Yep. Good luck to you all. We're gone." Zielinski grabbed the kid and suited action to words.

Jana looked around at the remaining people in the kitchen. "Everybody hanging in there?"

The Kin Guardian grinned. "It was mostly just cleaning up behind the wild man."

Johar purred, his tongue sliding down a long fang as he climbed down off the table.

After staring down at the two dead bodies in the room, Bren

glanced over at Jana. "Farid has your parents hiding out in the detached garage. He's keeping them calm the way only Farid can."

Jana's breath whooshed out, her relief a palpable force in the room. Johar stepped forward. "My Guardians?"

A tiny headshake was Bren's response. "The shuttle landed just fine, but we didn't even get the doors open before we were under attack. The pilot's dead, the shuttle's blown. We sent two of the wounded to your shuttle, and Farid and I came here with another Kin Guardian. We got caught in a firefight; the Kin didn't make it. Farid lost his ear comm. somewhere along the way, but is okay otherwise. Or he was a few minutes ago. I-I can't sense him through our bond with the white noise going." Her voice was flat, desolate. She shook herself and touched her bloodied ear. "We found the Townsends, but a bullet destroyed my comm. so we couldn't call for help. Talk about a serious goatfuck."

Johar barked out a laugh, the Kin behind him coughing into his fist. Kyber clapped his hand over the Earthan woman's shoulder, knowing how each death—Earthan and Sueni—tore at her, despite any jokes. "You did well. Thank you."

Her eyes went remote the way only a warrior's could. "We'll get through this. Let's finish the mission."

Jana hurried to the door Johar had come through, stepping past the Kin Guardian. "The garage is this way."

Dhalesh held her back, planting a hand on her stomach. "Allow me to go first, Empress."

Nodding, she moved aside to let him by. Everyone else fell into line behind them, Kyber bringing up the rear. Bren walked smoothly, and he sensed no injury besides the one to her ear. The comm. seemed to have taken the brunt of the bullet's damage, which was a good thing.

The side door to the garage stood ajar and Bren broke into a run, the scent of her fear leaving a rancid trail behind her.

Something was wrong.

His heart slammed against his ribs. He could smell his cousin drawing closer with each step, but that meant his body was near, not that life still flowed through that body. He loped behind Bren, easily keeping stride with the smaller human.

"Mom? Dad?" Jana called at the same time Bren yelled, "Farid?"

"I put them in the storm cellar under the garage." Farid staggered around the side of the building, one sleeve ripped off his shirt, his fangs bloodied as if he'd bitten someone. He slid his razer back into the holster at his hip.

Bren raced forward and he caught her against his chest. She bunched her hands in his tunic, searching his face. "Are you all right?"

Kyber could see how his cousin's fingers shook when they brushed back a loose lock of Bren's dark hair. "I am unharmed, my One."

She nodded, took a deep breath, and released his shirt as she let the air sigh out of her lungs. "Show us where you stowed the Townsends."

"In here. Don't stand out in the open." Jana disappeared into the building, and Kyber heard things thumping and crashing around. Subtle. Very subtle. His lips twitched.

The comm. in his ear buzzed with life. "Captain Sajan, we have two injured Guardians from the second shuttle here."

"We have the Arjuns. No other survivors." Johar's voice rang clearly in Kyber's ear as the other man walked into the garage. The rest of their team followed, and Dhalesh stood guard by the door.

There was a long pause over the comm. before the Guardian at the shuttle responded. "Understood, sir."

Johar sneezed in the musty gloom of the garage, and it took a moment for Kyber's eyes to adjust. A heavy door stood open, with stairs leading downward, and Jana drew an older couple up the steps and out toward them. Her gaze sought him out in the darkness, so he moved to her side and cupped her jaw in his palm, brushing a smudge of dirt from her cheek.

She glanced back at the older couple. "Mom, Dad, this is Kyber. Kyber, my parents."

The man held out his hand, and Kyber took it. Regrets swam in Mr. Townsend's eyes. "General Arthur came with men. We heard them talking about . . . how he'd hurt our daughter. How he was going to make you watch this time."

"There won't be a 'this time.' I swear it." He shook the man's hand hard and let go. "Arthur will be dealt with, but we need to get you and your wife back to my ship."

"We may have a problem with that." Dhalesh spoke quietly from the door. Kyber's sensitive ears heard the hum of engines over the squeal of white noise.

They moved to the windows. Bren groaned. "Okay, this just went from goatfuck to total clusterfuck."

"They know we're here or at least that we were not long ago," Kyber said.

Vehicles bearing far more soldiers than they could deal with pulled to a stop in front of the house. It was only a matter of time before they came to check the outer buildings. He watched Jana's hand lift to press her ear comm. "This is the empress. I need air support. I'd like you to blow as many of the houses on my parents' street as you can. They should be empty, so it won't kill anyone who might be working for us, but we need to give them something to think about besides finding us. So rain as much fire down on them as possible."

Her mother gasped in horror, and her father held her tight.

He nodded to Kyber, his jaw set in the same stubborn line Jana so often wore. Kyber almost smiled.

Then it came to him. Arthur's scent. He was close. He did smile, then. Anticipation of what was to come made him purr. "I've scented Arthur. Bren, Johar, and I will hunt him."

Jana's head bobbed in a quick nod. "Mom, Dad, come with me. *Now.*"

Farid checked the charge on his weapon, glanced up at Bren, and reeled her in with one hand for a hard, hungry kiss. Their bond almost shimmered in the air with the devotion pulsing between them. Kyber felt a stab of ugly jealousy, wishing that he and Jana shared such an open bond. He wanted that so badly he could taste it. The only way it would happen was if they both got through this, if he defeated Arthur, if he protected them all.

No more of his people should die for this expedition he'd brought them to the back end of space for. He would not, could not, fail them.

It ended tonight.

The image of her childhood home—her whole neighborhood—exploding into flames would be burned into Jana's mind forever. The remains of dead bodies that they'd left *inside* the house littering the once-pristine yard, helping her mother step over a severed, charred limb. The scent of roasting meat that she knew was human flesh.

Her stomach turned, but she pushed on.

It reminded her far too much of the day Kyber was taken. The smoke, the blood, the sizzle of razer fire. It was worse that the battle had taken place in a field not far from here. This little Midwestern town had been a warzone before because of their quarrel with Arthur.

Dhalesh moved out in front of them, Farid guarding the

rear. Jana held her razer steady, watchful of any approaching soldiers. Her mother clung to her other hand. "Jana, I want to tell you how sorry I am that I—that *we*—didn't believe in you."

Jana nodded, though she doubted her mother could see it in the dark, and kept moving. "It's okay, Mom. Don't worry about it."

"I'm so sorry I thought you'd been brainwashed and sucked into some kind of alien sex cult." Dhalesh shot an incredulous glance back at that, and Jana fought the wild urge to giggle. Her mother stumbled a bit, and Jana turned to catch her as her father reached forward to do the same. Her mother continued in a furtive whisper, "We were so worried that we'd lose you, too, we pushed you away. I'm sorry we didn't believe in you. That's *our* fault, not yours. I'm sorry we ever made you feel you couldn't tell us the truth when things went wrong. Thank you for coming to get us, for giving us a second chance. We're glad to be a part of your life, and we'll apologize to your Kyber, too. We'll do better, we promise. You don't have to pretend to be happy and perfect all the time. We can handle the truth."

Tears welled in Jana's eyes and she blinked fast to clear her vision. Her heart clenched hard and robbed her of breath. This was *exactly* what she'd always wished one of her parents would say to her, but the timing sucked. "Mom, seriously. I want to have this conversation, I really do, but not here and not now."

Her mother blinked back tears, too, but her voice was level and calm. "I know, but just in case something happens tonight, I don't want any of us to have regrets."

Jana pulled her in for a tight, one-armed hug. As nice as it was to have her parents understand that they'd hurt her, she knew they'd had their own grief to work through. They were human, just like her. They made mistakes and had problems and weren't perfect, just like her, but they could get better.

They could take the good as well as the bad, and that was what made everything all right. She didn't *want* to be perfect, she liked herself just as she was. It was a revelation a long time in coming, breaking through another of those walls in her mind, but better late than never. She smiled and breathed in the familiar scent of her mother's hair. "I love you, Mom. We're going to get through this, and we can finish this discussion on board the ship."

"Okay." Her mom squeezed her back, and her dad wrapped his arms around both of them, kissing the tops of their heads. "We love you, too, baby."

Farid spoke softly from behind them, "Your Majesty, we need to move."

They broke apart with an embarrassed laugh. Her dad patted her shoulder. "It's going to take some getting used to with people calling you 'Your Majesty.'"

"Don't worry about it." She shrugged and turned to tow her mom after their Kin Guardian. "You're my family. You still call me Jana."

She kept her gaze moving, watched for an attack, felt the ground rock beneath her as their fighter wings fired their razer cannons on something in the distance. An explosion lit the night sky, making the air around her vibrate. Farid snarled, and she winced in sympathy. The bombardment of noise wouldn't be good for the half-feline Kith. The white noise that made a low hum throughout the town made *her* temples throb, so she didn't want to imagine what it did to Farid.

She swallowed, trying to shove down her anxiety over what had happened to Kyber, where he was, what he was doing. The connection between them trailed to nothing, a deep void that scared her. It was worse than when he'd been kidnapped by Arthur. Then, the longer he was in the noise, the less she was able to sense him until he'd severed their One link entirely.

Whatever they were using now had been amped up, because she'd lost all mental contact with him the moment they'd left the shuttle.

It shook her more than she'd like to admit.

"We've got company coming." Farid's voice jerked her out of her worry about Kyber and brought her back to the here and now. They took cover in some bushes beside the road, but it wouldn't block a bullet. They were too exposed. Shit.

She adjusted her grip on her razer, tried to regulate her breathing and the way her heart had begun to race. Her hands only shook a little. "Protect my parents. They don't know how to fight."

Soldiers were on them in moments, bullets flying. Several went down in the charge, falling under the sizzling onslaught of razer fire. Farid shouted something else, some warning, but she didn't catch it. She was too busy keeping herself planted between her parents and danger. Her mother screamed once, but other than that, her parents remained silent and stayed out of the way of those with weapons and the knowledge to use them.

Three soldiers went down before her razer before two more crashed through the bushes, driving her into a wide, grassy yard. Farid took her place in front of her parents, and she watched her father slug a man in the face. She almost grinned but snapped her focus back to the soldiers before her. They had their guns trained on her.

One barked at her, "Put your gun down and surrender."

Yeah, right. She didn't bother with a verbal response, just shot him in the thigh and sprinted across the lawn toward a small house. Bullets send dirt flying into her face, and she leaped for the cover of the wooden porch, twisting midair to fire at the second soldier. She hit her mark, and he screamed and went down.

Another man grabbed her arm from behind and smashed

her hand into the porch railing. Her razer went tumbling under the deck and she felt his gun press under her ear. Slamming her head back into his face, she latched on to his forearm and pulled his pistol over her shoulder until she could bite down on his wrist. He shouted, dropping the gun. She kicked behind her, her boot heel making solid contact with his shin. Squirming free of his hold, she thrust the butt of her hand under his chin and snapped his head back. He stumbled away, into the front yard again, and she went after him. He pulled a huge, wicked knife from his utility belt. She swallowed and kept her gaze on the gleam of the blade in what little moonlight was revealed by scattered clouds.

He swiped at her, and she jumped out of his way. Their little dance took them in wide circles on the grass. Her muscles shook with strain, her breath racing in little pants. He lunged forward, slicing into her tunic, obviously expecting to hit skin. His eyes widened as his knife glanced off the mesh armor under her tunic.

"Technology rocks." She jabbed her fingertips into his throat, crushing it. He hit the ground and she had to brace her hands on her knees for a moment. She was so tired, yet so much adrenaline hummed through her that she felt like her whole body was vibrating.

"Jana." The low, gritty voice sent ice flowing through her veins.

She spun around, and there he was. Arthur. His craggy features, silver hair, and deep brown eyes might have been warm and friendly on any other man, but she'd seen the evil behind the mask.

Terror so huge it threatened to strangle her bloomed in her chest. She wanted to scream, to cry, to run, but it was far too late for that. So, instead of doing any of those things, she settled

312 / Crystal Jordan

into the fighting stance Bren had drilled into her and waited for him to make his move.

His gaze tracked her, anticipation heating his gaze as he looked her over thoroughly. "You're even prettier with your hair short, Jana."

It was all she could do not to heave her guts up. She arched an eyebrow. "I'll be sure to pass your compliments on to my husband. He's been dying to hear from you again."

He chuckled, and the sound scraped over her nerves like broken glass. They circled each other, each watchful for an opening. "Oh, we'll catch up later. Don't worry."

"I won't." She forced herself to smirk, but sweat chilled on her skin and her teeth chattered a bit. She could smell her own fear.

Apparently, he'd had enough waiting because he charged her. She sidestepped and kicked his legs out from under him. The man was built like a bull, and went down hard. Rolling, he caught her ankle and jerked her off her feet. The breath exploded from her lungs as she crashed over onto her back.

And there it was, her worst nightmare revisited. Arthur on top of her, her helpless beneath him. Weak. But unlike the last time, she didn't lie there and take it. If he was going to hurt her, she was going to hurt him back. She'd go down fighting, kicking and screaming instead of sobbing and begging. A fierce smile curved her lips while she pointed her fingers and drove the tips under his armored vest and into his side. He flinched away from the hard contact, and she took advantage, heaving him off her. She whipped her arm around, slamming her fist in his face. The crunch of bone and cartilage sickened her as his nose gave way.

He coughed and snorted up blood, lashing out with his foot to catch her in the hip. Pain rocketed through her, made black spots swim in her eyes. He rolled, straddling her waist. He slapped her hard across the face, and she felt her lip split. Blood coated her tongue, and her ears rang, but she couldn't give up, couldn't stop now.

His hands closed around her throat and she knew she was going to die. Just when she'd regained the will to live. Panic held her tight in its grip. Her vision darkened around the edges. Oh, God. She couldn't breathe.

She couldn't *breathe.*

Twisting under him, she punched and clawed at him. Anything to break his grip. She bucked hard, lifting them both off the ground. Then her hand shot out and caught him in the balls. She grabbed him in a death grip, wrenching at his privates until the breath whistled from his throat like a teakettle. The harder he squeezed her throat, the harder her fist crushed his gonads. She might die, but she was taking the part of him she hated most with her.

A deep roar ripped through the sound of Arthur's squealing, changed the expression on his face to pure horror in the blink of an eye. The hairs on the back of her neck rose in response, and her muscles tensed even further. She barely saw the blur of Kyber's movement before his black-and-white-striped body hurtled its enormous bulk through the air and tumbled Arthur away from her.

She gagged for air, her throat burning, and she rolled into a fetal position on her side. Forcing her eyes to stay open, she saw Johar and Bren race up behind Kyber, handling the remaining soldiers who tried to shoot at the emperor. Farid and the Kin Guardian helped her shaken, but unharmed, parents to their feet. They all watched the feline Kyber slice into Arthur's torso, ripping open the bulletproof jacket. Then the flesh parted under those deadly talons and fangs, and there was more blood coming from one body than she'd ever imagined possible. The general's screams echoed down the street, all the more terrifying for their helplessness. Bones broke under the weight of Kyber's massive paws. He snapped his jaw around Arthur's neck, shaking the general's body like a ragdoll. The shrieks cut off, and the silence made her shiver.

He continued to drag his prey around by the neck long after it was dead, shaking the carcass crushed between his curved fangs.

"Kyber," she whispered, but no actual sound came from her bruised and swollen throat. She coughed, and agony screamed through every inch of her. Stumbling to her feet, she swayed for a moment before she got her balance. Her father reached out to steady her, but she held up her hand to stop him.

Limping over to Kyber, she set her hand on his shoulder. Even at his most monstrously feral, at his most enraged, at his least controlled, she trusted him not to hurt her, not to turn on her. And that, finally, was the answer she'd been waiting for. This deep, unquestioning faith in him. She tangled her fingers in his silky fur and tugged. Her voice was barely more than a hoarse croak, but she knew he'd hear her. "Kyber, stop. Drop him."

His hackles raised and he growled low in his throat, but he leaned ever so slightly into her touch. She stroked her fingers down his neck, crooning reassurances to him. "It's all right, my One. It's over. Put his body down. It's over. He can't hurt us anymore."

He gave one last vicious shake before he flung Arthur's corpse far from them. Tears of relief streaked down her cheeks and she collapsed to her knees beside him. She smiled when he turned to her and buried his muzzle in her chest, a shudder wracking his body. It was over. It was finally, *finally* over.

Whatever happened to them, whatever they did to each other, she knew they'd never damage each other the way they had again. They had survived the worst. Arthur was a nightmare they could put behind them.

Staying with Kyber was one thing, but she was ready for the whole bond whenever he was. Even with the white noise blaring, she knew the wall on her side of their connection crumbled to nothing. She trusted herself to make it through whatever came at them and trusted *Kyber* with her life, her heart, her soul.

She loved him, she always had, she always would. The truth she had known the first time her eyes had met his hit her full-force. It was staggering in its simplicity. Kyber belonged to her, and she belonged to him.

The rest they would conquer. *Together.*

7

Kyber didn't know how long he'd slept, but it was deep, peaceful, dreamless slumber. He awoke in his bed, naked and wrapped around his equally naked mate. Jana's feminine scent made him hum in the back of his throat, and he buried his nose in the crook of her neck. The sheer feline lassitude that lulled his body into boneless relaxation beckoned once more, and he closed his eyes.

When he came to alertness again, it was to see Jana's beautiful face bathed in starlight from the skylight in their quarters.

He propped himself on one elbow, content to watch her sleep. Her chest rose and fell in the rhythm of deep slumber, and their link told him that she dreamed of him and the last time they had loved. His cock came to rigid attention at the erotic images flowing through her mind. A smile that was entirely smug crossed his face. Was there anything sweeter than knowing your woman had been well-satisfied and would likely be so again as soon as she awakened? He couldn't think of anything that could please him more at the moment.

Except, of course, renewing the bond with his One.

But there was time for that. Relief, profound and deep, wound its way through him. He hadn't earned any second chances, but destiny had blessed him more than he could ever have guessed, certainly more than he would have supposed when he'd been on his knees in chains. That was the past, and it would remain there. He had his One in his arms, his enemy lay dead by his hand, and he had *time*. Time to win her again, time to heal from all that he had suffered, time to help his people grieve for those they had lost.

"Mmm." Jana stretched her arms above her head, pointed her toes and arched her back, her body bowing off the gelpad. Her gray eyes opened and a grin curved her lips when she looked up at him.

He smiled at her, stroked back the dark flames of her hair, and dipped forward to kiss her. She hummed again, her palms lifting to cup his face. Their lips clung for a long moment before he let her up for air and grinned down at her. "Hello, my One. Did you sleep well?"

"I did." Tears misted her eyes, and a smile trembled at the corners of her mouth. "You make a wonderful body pillow."

"A profession the prophets never envisioned for me, I'm sure." He tried to keep his tone teasing and light, but the sight of moisture welling in her eyes made his chest tighten. He brushed his thumb over her cheekbone. "Something has upset you. Tell me and I'll make it right."

"You already did." She ran her fingers up his arm.

He shook his head. "I don't understand."

"You saved me." Her nails dragged gently over his shoulder, raising goose bumps on his skin and hardening his dick even further. "You made everything as right as it can be."

"I told you that you weren't allowed to die until I said so." He dropped his forehead to hers. "Nothing has happened to change that, my empress."

"Yes, Your Majesty." A grin flashed over her face. Her hand

stroked through his hair, and he leaned into her caresses. Her gaze searched his face and her smile faded. "Thank you. I don't know if I ever told you that. I'm glad you stopped me from killing myself, I'm glad you took me with you to Earth, and I'm glad you saved me from Arthur."

"I wish I had saved you from him the first time, that he had never had a chance to touch you." He bowed his head, allowing himself to feel the regret of all the things he hadn't managed to do, accepting the parts of this horror that had been his doing, and then set it aside. He couldn't erase the past, couldn't bring back those who had needlessly died, but he could learn from his mistakes and vow to embrace all of himself—man and beast—embrace his future, his destiny, and never to repeat those errors again. He owed it to all of them, and to his father who had sacrificed his life for him so long ago, to be the best emperor he could be, the best mate to his One, the best *man* he could be.

"Shh." She ran her palms down his chest, her fingertip circled his nipple. "There's no room for sorrow and regrets between us. There's only tomorrow and all the days after that to strengthen our bond."

"Yes. I want that, too." He nodded, meeting her beautiful eyes. More kindness and understanding shone in them than he could ever earn. Gratitude gripped him tight.

Lust followed swiftly on its heels as she curled her leg over his hip. He could be half-dead and he'd still react to her. He wouldn't have it any other way. The scent of her moisture reached him, and he dipped the head of his cock into her passage, rubbing himself over her slick lips. She was drenched for him already, and he groaned. He sank into her, his cock stretching her channel until he was hilt-deep inside of her pussy. "Jana."

Her eyes flared wide, her breath catching. She arched herself into him until her breasts pressed to his chest. "Kyber."

"Jana." This time his voice was little more than a satisfied purr. Her passion pumped through their connection, and he clenched his teeth, his fangs clacking together. *I crave you, my One.*

"Me, too." Her eyes grew damp again, but she tightened her leg around his waist.

He went utterly still, fearing he'd hurt her. Sucking in a breath, he tried to regain control of his rampaging desire. The beast struggled against the restraint. "And that's why there are tears in your eyes?"

"No. Yes." She gave a soft, breathy laugh. "I like that you called me your One. Not long ago, I never could have imagined you calling me that again. I want to be your One in every way."

He stared at her in stunned silence for long moments. When he spoke, it was slowly and carefully. He didn't want to make any assumptions that would scare her into withdrawal. They had already come so far in so short a time. "You mean . . . that you want to open our bond again? Fully?"

Her chin dipped in a nod. "Yes."

Uncertainty assailed him. He knew what he wanted, what he was willing to endure to have back what he had taken for granted the day he'd met her. Anything. For her? Anything. Except losing her again. He had to be sure. "You realize that we'll do other things to hurt each other, don't you? That I might make more mistakes that bring you pain?"

"Kyber, you're not perfect, I know that. I don't want someone who's perfect because God knows *I'm* not. And that's just fine by me. I don't need some fairy tale. *This* is better than that." She squeezed her inner walls around him, and he hissed. She grinned. "We both made mistakes and we'll probably make a lot more, but the kind of man I want to spend my life with is one who'll set things right when he finds out he's done something wrong. You've done that every time. You're who I want, mistakes and all."

"We are so alike, you were right about that." He brushed his lips over hers. "We will do the wrong thing sometimes. But we can learn from those mistakes as well. We can grow together, love together, live together. That's what Ones do. That's what I want for us, even though horrible things can and will happen again."

A tear streaked down her cheek, and her hands rose to clutch his shoulders, rocking herself against him. "You said . . . you said *love* together."

"Yes, I love you. I've always loved you, even when I hated that I couldn't escape that love. Never doubt that. *I love you.*" He brushed the tear away, lifted his hips with her gentle movements, and held tight to his sanity as the feel of her stimulated every one of his senses. His psychic gifts were irresistibly drawn to her, his feral nature demanding its mate be reclaimed.

"I love you, too." Her breath hitched on a little sob, but she kept writhing against him. "Bond with me again. Give me all of it. I want you. I love you."

He felt the last of his resistance, the final barrier in his mind, give way at her words. Anun, but he loved her. A hiss exploded between his clenched teeth. "Are you sure?"

She chuckled. "That's what I just said, wasn't it? Do you need me to draw you a map?"

Slipping out of her pussy, he eased back in, a single centimeter at a time to draw out the satisfaction for both of them. "No, this is territory I know well. My One."

"It'd be even better if you moved a little faster." She sighed, pleasure, both hot and sweet, in the sound. "And maybe . . . a little deeper."

"I think that can be arranged." His hand moved over her thigh, her back, every inch of her supple skin he could reach. Heat erupted deep inside him, and he had to concentrate on not coming every time he buried his cock inside her wetness.

She laughed, but the sound ended in a soft gasp as he rolled his hips, changing the angle of his penetration to make it even more perfect. "Good."

"Yes, it is." Her walls closed around him and he groaned, his muscles straining as he flexed himself deep inside her, purring low in his belly so she would feel the vibrations against her clit. She cried out, and he grinned, giving her a taste of the power within him. Digging deep into her mind, he plunged into the areas that would bring her to orgasm swiftly.

She thrashed in his embrace, her thoughts scattering into incoherent begging and pleading for surcease. He sank his cock and his mind into her, and she screamed, her ecstasy coalescing as her inner muscles fisted tight around him.

He groaned. "I can feel ... how good it is for you. How much you like this. I forgot—" He shuddered, thrusting a little harder without her having to ask.

The connection snapped tight between them, and she opened herself to him completely. The link told him how she liked to be touched, where, and when. His passion fed hers and soon her body had loosened, molding itself to his, heating until he thought her dampness would drive him to feral madness. The need cycled back and forth, a hot ebb and flow between them that built until it was as much pain as pleasure.

"Oh, my God." Her fingers curled over his shoulders, digging into the muscles there. He watched purple sparks flash in her eyes as his power filled her. "Kyber?"

"Yes?" He groaned, pushing himself deeper into her. He couldn't get enough of her. He never would, but he could try. Every day for the rest of his life. He purred, grinding himself against her hard clit.

A whimper slipped from her. "Tell me."

"I love you." He didn't hesitate, giving her everything, all of him.

Her breathing hitched every time his slammed deep inside

her, her pleasure becoming his pleasure. "I might . . . need to hear that every day."

"Then I'll tell you every day." Rolling her beneath him, he pressed her thighs flat to gelpad and thrust hard. Anun, but she felt good. Perfect. Sleek and hot and so tight he thought he would die, but it was too good to stop.

"Maybe more than once a day." Her slim legs wrapped around his flanks, her feet pushing down on the backs of his thighs to sink him even deeper inside her with each plunge.

"If that's what you need." He dipped his head, slanted his mouth over hers, and kissed her. "Since we are so well matched, I think it might be fair to say I need to hear it, too."

Her nails dug into his back, and she arched until she could gasp in his ear. "Every day, more than once."

"Yes," he growled, and even he didn't know if it was in agreement or because he could feel orgasm roaring through him. The beast clawed for freedom, and he let it loose.

He sank his fangs into her neck hard enough to leave a mark. She screamed, her wetness soaking his cock as she dampened even further. She raked her nails down his back, giving him the wildness he craved. "Love me, Kyber."

Her pussy flexed around his shaft, and he groaned in help-less response. "I do. I will. Always."

She clung to him, her desperate need echoing his, and her low cries told him she was as close to orgasm as he was. She laughed, but it erupted as a sob. "Always sounds just long enough to me."

Pulling back for the briefest moment, he grinned down at her. "Good, because it's all I'm willing to give you."

"Kyber," she breathed. There was no need to ask for what she wanted; he knew. Driving his cock into her at just the right angle and just the right speed, hitting her in just the right spot to make her scream, opening the connection between them wider with each thrust, he shoved them both over the sheer drop into orgasm. She bit his shoulder hard, her pussy milking the length of his cock over and over again until he felt like he was going to explode out of his skull.

Fire shot through him, the heat and passion they generated together all he would ever truly need. He rammed his dick deep, their skin slapping together, their breath mingling as their consciousnesses did the same. He came hard, spilling his cum inside her, a deep roar echoing in their room as beast and man claimed their mate. Forever. His thoughts stroked over hers, tangling and untangling until neither of them knew where his awareness ended and hers began. It was exactly as it should be with them, as it was destined to be.

They were One.